the Bishop's Girl

REBECCA BURNS

ODYSSEY
BOOKS

Published by Odyssey Books in 2016

Copyright © Rebecca Burns 2016

www.odysseybooks.com.au

A Cataloguing-in-Publication entry is available from the National Library of Australia

ISBN: 978-1-922200-64-8 (pbk)
ISBN: 978-1-922200-65-6 (ebook)

Cover design by Elijah Toten

For Claire and Tracy

And for this book's first readers – Abi, Eryn, and Sarah

To all, with love

Prologue

The old woman who kept the priest's house had told them that he was away at Amiens, seeing to those still recovering, so the men who stole into his churchyard worked quickly but without fear of discovery. The younger ones and those who still had all their limbs were given shovels and set about digging, while the strangers, not of the area, circled the walls of the churchyard, round and round, walking the line that separated the holy land from the rest of the town. But not many townsfolk came this way; the drizzle had been persistent and women kept their children inside.

Down the hill, away from the church, the men could hear the rush of the river that cut through the town, the water moaning and sighing as it swelled and breached its banks. The fields of potatoes and turnips from which, before the war, the town had drawn its livelihood, had become muddy quagmires in recent days, treacherous to those forced to cross from one end of the town to the other. The men had trudged through gelatinous grime on their way to the church, shovels and picks over their shoulders. Some of the locals who had fought and held the lines around Arras or east towards Ypres had grimaced as they'd pushed through it. They remembered the mud.

'*Ce que nous creusons pour*?' a boy asked, probably no more than fourteen. His wet hair was plastered over a misshapen skull and he gripped a pick. He stood in the churchyard, frowning down at the opening grave. A man nearby looked up.

'You want to know what you are digging for?' The man had large, wobbly jowls and, as he stepped closer to the boy holding the pick, pulled at his great coat. The boy-not-quite-a-man caught a glimpse of a white dog collar. 'Yes, I speak a little French.'

'Pardon?' The boy held up his hand, sensing he had transgressed. He made to slam the pick down in the mud again when the man spoke.

'Not what. Who. We're here to take someone home, to England.'

Another boy, about a year older, also shovelling the glutinous, slippery earth from the grave, muttered a translation. The boy with the pick mumbled again, brave with youth. '*Qui, alors? Qui pourrait être si important?*'

'Who could be so important?' The man wearing the dog collar spoke with a slow drawl. He looked into the grave. 'He was a bishop. Not a normal kind of bishop. He didn't have a cathedral. His church was the poor.' The man blinked once, twice and rain bounced from his lashes. 'He needs to be taken home.'

The boy with the pick and questions opened his mouth as though he were about to say something else, but his companion jerked an elbow into his side and the boy thought better of it. He brought the pick round, the end breaking apart a chunk of wet earth.

A bell tolled in the clock tower looming over them. The sound reverberated around the dirty, cracked stone. Twelve times, noon. In an hour a handful of villagers would leave the dry comfort of their homes and make their way to the church for prayers. Someone barked that they should work quickly, speed it up. More shovels, more boys to dig. Even the strangers helped.

'Not long, we're almost there,' said the man in the dog collar, and his fat face shook.

And then the boy, the one who had asked the questions, snagged the end of his pick on something. Cloth. He pulled back, curious. They had all expected their spades and shovels to break through to a wooden coffin, not this. Someone else jumped down into the grave, mud sloshing up the sides.

It was the man with the dog collar. His trousers and boots were soaked, but he dropped to his knees, uncaring, beside the cloth. He clawed at it, smearing aside more mud.

'Give me a knife, someone.' A short, stubbed blade was passed down. Those above the hole stared intently. They watched as the man wiped back mud, knife between his teeth. The cloth was slowly exposed. It was apparent from the length and shape that it was a bolt of canvas wrapped around a body. The wood of the bishop's coffin could be seen beneath.

'*Ce que je vois?*' the boy with the pick whispered, and the man in the grave echoed his words back, in English. 'Yes, what am I seeing?'

He used the knife. The canvas bag was split open and the hands of boys around the grave fluttered from shoulder to shoulder, making the sign of a cross. And then a gasp from someone as dirty white fabric was exposed beneath the mud-clarted canvas. An apron over a dress. Brown boots. And then, as the cloth was split in two, long, black hair tumbled forth, still attached to grey bones, now wet in the midday rain.

∾

The call of the crows was long and keening, and spoke of wrongdoing. Despite being sure in their purpose, the men looked up from the grave to peer at the birds circling above. Black, feathers as black as the coats the men wore to stave off the April chill; the crows gathered in tree-tops and on the stone edges of the church and watched as the body was pulled from the earth.

The youngsters had been sent away with a few francs in their pockets and an admonishment to tell no one about their work here this day. Of course, the older men knew that the youngsters' immature tongues would not keep still for long, especially after some of the boys had fainted. Drama like that had to be shared. Word would get out, back to the priest, and his rage at the desecration of his churchyard would be towering and hot. They had to work quickly, then, to collect the bishop and take him home. And do something with the body they had found with him.

None of them had had such a shock before. The American who spoke a little French, he of the fat, wobbling face and the slow, elongated accent, had felt gore rise in his throat as black hair spilled from the bag. A woman! How could a woman be buried with the bishop? When they set the body on the side of the grave, those who dared touch it looked for an item to identify her, but there was nothing. No locket, no photograph, no letter. The clothes were functional and worn, but this was not a whore or beggar who had come to be buried with the bishop through sheer chance.

Some of the group stood over her while the bishop's coffin was extracted. They closed the canvas about her again, their touch as brief as necessary, and stood in silent guard. A horse and cart had been commandeered from somewhere, and the bishop's coffin was tugged to the surface and then reburied on the cart under hay and farm goods. Now to close the grave again, in the lashing rain. And tend to the woman.

'We should put her back here,' someone muttered, possibly the man with the shaking cheeks. So the canvas bag was lifted carefully and returned to the mud. A few hands reached for shovels, to bury her again when there was a shout—'Wait!'—and this was definitely the fat man. He jumped down into the grave again and, with an instruction that they should look away, he took a bone from the woman's left hand. He wrapped it in his handkerchief and stowed it in his pocket.

And then the grave was filled, quickly. Shovels and picks were thrown into the dray and the men departed, walking briskly in the unforgiving rain, collars turned up, eyes set firmly in front.

Behind, a crow called accusingly.

Part 1

Jedthorpe

It was twelve-thirty and Marie was late. Jess stood against the cool marble of the reception wall, looking out into the street. Overlarge and imposing, the Shacklock Library leant heavily into the High Street, casting long shadows over the neighbouring coffee shops and expensive boutiques that had sprung up around Jedthorpe town centre with defiant ease in the past year. Cars and lorries drummed by, and the Shacklock's glass frontage shook. It was common knowledge that the library had been designed and built with the generous donation of an American church back in 1920s; maybe the money had gone to the architect's head, Jess had often thought. The library's ornately carved façade did not match the sober grey buildings nearby and was starkly out of place. And, for all the money thrown its way, the Shacklock Library was still cold. Freezing air blasted into the reception every time the door opened. Jess pulled her coat closer and shivered.

November had rushed upon her unexpectedly; it felt only yesterday that she was coercing her daughter into a pose in her new school uniform, ready for a photo, Megan's crooked smile betraying both embarrassment and pride. The girl had objected and wouldn't let Jess walk her to the bus stop for that first morning at the academy. 'I'm a big girl now, Mum!'

'You're not tagging along with me,' James had said in a new, low voice, and Jess had felt like weeping. First her son, then her daughter, growing up when she wasn't looking.

Jess checked her watch again. Just like Marie to be late. Jess glanced up and down the street again. She'd give her friend five more minutes and then try her mobile.

But there she was, appearing suddenly in front of Jess in the reception, all smiles. 'Sorry, sorry!' Marie, tanned and smelling of holiday, leant in for a kiss, smearing her mouth along Jess's cheek. Jess reached up to wipe the lipstick away, taking in her friend's newly darkened hair.

'Just had it done! That's why I'm late—new stylist, simply *had* to find out his life story.' Marie laughed and patted her hair mockingly, like their mothers used to do. 'The sun bleached it. Too close to grey, and that wouldn't do for Marie. Shall we go? I'm starving.'

And she looped her arm through Jess's and barrelled them both into the street. Jess, teeth chattering, wishing she had brought her scarf, scurried to keep up. 'I thought we could try Leonardo's again, further up the High Street,' she jabbered. 'They do a lunchtime special and the service is quick.'

'Fine, fine.' But Marie wasn't listening. 'I have Pilates at three, so would need to be done by then.'

Jess opened the door to Leonardo's with a tight smile. 'It's midday, Marie. I don't have three-hour lunch breaks.'

She followed her friend towards a booth, Marie's backside rolling from side to side like two squashed peaches. Marie wore an expensive pair of trousers. New shoes, too. Jess could see the labels on her heels. Not for the first time she wondered if Marie left them on deliberately.

They ordered quickly, Jess with one eye on the time. If the mains came without delay, she would have enough time to walk down the alley beside the restaurant and smoke a surreptitious cigarette before heading back to the library. She tapped her fingers on the table.

Marie leant back in her seat, spreading herself into the booth. Around them, office workers who had driven in from the business park ate pasta and ravioli, a daring few drinking wine. Waiters in stained white shirts and black aprons darted between the tables.

Marie nodded over towards a table of four men, uncorking a bottle of red. 'We should do that one time.'

Jess snapped a breadstick. 'A boozy lunch? Sure. When the Prof is off for the afternoon.'

'Is he still a bumbling arse?' Marie flashed a shiny grin.

Jess shrugged. Professor Waller, head of the research group at the Shacklock Library, was not a subject she liked to discuss in her free time. Today was lecture day for the students from Jedthorpe College who came over weekly, and she'd already been forced to photocopy his notes twice after he'd misplaced them in the disaster of his office. 'He has his moments.'

'Can't you quit? Tell him to stick his job?'

Oh, we're early into that one, Jess thought. 'No, Marie. I can't quit.'

'You could, you know.' Marie smiled up at the waiter bearing down on them with heaped plates and patted her place mat. 'Alec could support you.'

'Like Barrie does you?' Jess accepted her salad and looked for the Parmesan, averting her gaze.

Marie laughed. 'Oh, Jessie. I worked for that settlement. I'm going to enjoy it.'

Jess ate silently. She listened to Marie talk, about the holiday, the new kitchen, the divorce lawyer who kept phoning her even though it had been *years* since she'd employed his services, the mechanic who kept giving her a discount and wanted to give her something more … Marie went on and on. Jess's attention wandered, and she thought about the time she'd first met her friend. Back in college, on the first day when they matriculated. As mature students they stood out, wearing trouser suits instead of jeans and trainers. Jess had been seething—she'd debated for hours that morning over what to wear. She wanted to fit in, to be a real student like everyone else, and she'd got it totally wrong.

Marie, ballsy, brassy, with a loud mouth and a laugh like a hyena, had marched right up to Jess as they waited in line to matriculate, introduced herself, and then steered her towards the Student Union. The friendship had been sealed over several bottles of cheap red wine and even cheaper cigarettes. Jess had staggered home in the early hours of the morning, crashing into her bedroom and landing on top of an appalled Alec. Marie had been a friend ever since.

'So has Alec taken you on holiday? It's been at least six months since I saw you. He must have.' Marie leant over and helped herself to a piece of Jess's chicken.

'Nope. And don't pretend you're surprised.' Jess focused on the door and the rain now pattering the glass.

'He might surprise you, one of these days.'

'Marie, that would be the mother of all surprises.' Jess finally looked at her friend. 'If I left out the brochures, with a hotel circled and a number next to the phone, he still wouldn't get the hint.'

Marie shook her head. 'Oh, Jessie. If ever a man needed a kick up the backside, it's Alec. Closely followed by the bumbling professor.'

Rebecca Burns

Jess nodded. 'I know. I've been blessed.' But then she felt guilty. 'Alec does his best. He's a good dad.'

'Being a good dad is not the same as being a good husband.'

That was Marie, divorced for years and delighted with herself. In the fifteen years since her husband's affair, she had travelled, lost three stones ('Still got my bum, though!' and she'd slap her large rump), and she'd found herself all manner of lovers. The latest had been a yoga instructor. 'He bent me into positions I didn't think were possible,' she'd told Jess over the summer as they ate sandwiches in the park.

And, despite her shock and loss of appetite, Jess had laughed and felt jealous. She had listened to Marie chatter on, nodding in the right places and smiling when appropriate.

'Do you know what I fancy?' Marie was saying now. 'A nice, sweet, glass of wine!'

'I can't, Marie. I wish I could, but I've got some papers to find for the Prof.' Jess wiped her hands together, anticipating the dusty manuscripts she would handle later. 'He's got a new idea eating away at him again.'

'About the Cuckoo?'

At that, Jess chuckled. It was impossible not to, with Marie's face pursed into a mischievous pout. 'The Cuckoo'—the secret name they gave to Professor Waller's prized project.

For the past thirty years, almost all of Professor Waller's career, he had been obsessed with identifying a set of skeletal remains. They had been placed on top of Bishop Shacklock's coffin and were discovered when the bishop was exhumed from his grave in France and re-interred in Jedthorpe. That had been at the end of 1919, after the war had ended and the bishop's American supporters were finally able to cross the pitted French farmlands to reach the bishop's resting place. No one knew who the person was buried with the bishop; so far, the professor had found no record to reveal or indicate a name.

'We simply have no idea who this person is,' the professor had explained to Jess six years earlier, when she was first employed at the library and about to embark on one of Waller's many quests to put a name to the bones. 'They were wrapped in a canvas bag, very much like the ones used to bury soldiers during the Great War. It was quite a shock to his supporters when they came to exhume the bishop, I can tell you.'

'Is it a man or woman?' Jess had asked, her naivety a cruel mistress. Professor Waller had then given her a lengthy overview of the scientific tests the library had commissioned on the finger bone brought back with the bishop, and how the governing board had tasked him with finding out who the person was, back when he was a young researcher.

'A woman,' he'd said at the end, by which point Jess had a slight headache. 'A young woman who lived at the same time as His Grace. DNA tests indicate a close familial relationship, possibly a daughter. But, as far as we know, Bishop Shacklock had no children. And there's no hint in the archive as to whom she might be. We can only speculate.'

Except, Jess was to think many times in the years that followed, and with increasing bitterness, the Prof did not merely *speculate*. He *interrogated*. He devised new and outlandish ideas about the identity of this woman—'the Cuckoo' as Jess eventually referred to her in conversations with Marie—and the skeleton became a block to Jess's own research. It became a running joke in the library. For every year of funding the board found to cover Jess's salary, about half would be used by Professor Waller on sending her on a wild foray into the manuscripts. It had happened before, to male researchers in the past.

'But they all got fed up and told him to stuff it, that's the difference,' Marie said once.

'I can't.'

'You bloody can. You're too accommodating, that's your problem, Jessie.'

And Marie was probably right, Jess thought, sitting in the Italian restaurant, longing for one of the cigarettes that Alec still didn't know she smoked. *I should have told Waller to stuff it a long time ago.* But it was too late. So instead she smiled at Marie. 'He's always coming up with new theories. Though there's a sense of urgency now, given he's nearing retirement. I think he wants to go out with a bang.'

Marie cocked her fingers into a gun and pretended to fire into her temple. 'Boom boom.'

Jess laughed again, harder this time. She did love seeing Marie.

Marie sat back and crossed her arms, appreciatively. 'You're looking thin, babe.'

'Been playing badminton.' Jess shuddered. 'Christ, when did I become so middle-class? If my mother could hear me now.' She looked down at her thighs, shapely beneath her skirt. It had paid off, all those hurried dashes to the leisure centre.

'But you need a holiday.'

Jess snorted. 'I told you, Alec isn't likely to—'

'So go without him!' Marie waved her hand impatiently. 'Hell, go with me, if you like.'

'Ah, Marie, I love you, but a week with you would see me either an alcoholic or a murderer.' The words were out before she could stop them and Jess gasped. And then both women laughed again. Around them, diners turned their heads.

'I am going to London tomorrow, though,' Jess said as the waiter came to clear away their plates.

'With Alec?'

'No. For the Prof. He's paying my expenses this time, mind.'

'Your nameless lady?'

'Yep. On the hunt again. I'll be at the British Library for most of the day. Looking through endless papers for a hint of who that woman might be. I'll stop overnight. Alec should manage the kids.' Jess said this last hopefully. Alec had been unsure when she'd asked him. She'd had to write a list of the clubs he'd have to take the children to, and she'd stuck them to the fridge, alongside a bundle of takeaway menus.

Marie put her elbows on the table, thoughtful. 'You could do with a night out, though. Why don't you book a show?'

Jess cringed. 'I hate them, remember? Musicals—no thank you. I've no patience for all that wailing and gurning.'

'Me neither. Well, I could ask Hayden to take you out.'

'Hayden?'

Marie grinned. 'Your turn to remember. Hayden, my little lamb. My little treasure.'

Jess remembered. 'Your boy? How old is he now? Twenty-one? Twenty-three?' She thought of a teenage boy, pink and spotty, picking Marie up from an evening at the Student's Union, learner plates on the car.

Marie whispered. 'He's twenty-eight.'

'No!' And Jess was shocked. She sat back in her seat, suddenly very depressed. 'Twenty-bloody-eight?'

Marie covered her mouth. 'I know. Isn't it awful? If his girlfriend has her way, he'll be making me a grandma soon.'

'Oh Marie ...'

'Don't say it. I can't bear it. He works at Waterloo.'

Jess signalled for the bill. 'I wouldn't want to impose.'

'It's fine! I'll text him later and give him your number.' Marie rummaged in her bag for her purse. 'I'm getting this. No, bugger off, I am. I'll get him to arrange something. The girlfriend might come along. I haven't met her, never do. Wonder why?'

They drifted towards the door, Jess moving faster than Marie, thinking of the cigarette. There was still time. She gazed at the office workers dotting the street, shoulders hunched into the hammering rain, water dripping from their noses as though they were old men full of cold. It was not an attractive sight, but Jess wanted to be one of them. She hoped the walk back to the library would blow away the smell of the cigarette. She hugged Marie goodbye, and they parted. Jess waved goodbye as her friend's taxi sped away and then she found her place in the alley of smokers.

✑

Although she had never tried it out, Jess often suspected that Professor Waller would not notice if she didn't return one day after lunch. For all his demands of her, he was particularly useless when it came to office management and the whereabouts of his staff. One researcher had left to have a baby, and he had realised she'd left only when she brought her newborn in to see the team.

But there were occasions where the professor was scarily on the ball. His ability to demolish a journal paper was legendary. So Jess had not yet been able to summon the courage up to openly push the boundaries. Instead she made sure she was back at her desk on time, available, even when she longed to tell her boss where to stick his bag of bones.

The library was a high-domed construction. Bishop Anthony Shacklock, although never rich in his lifetime, had a few loyal and generous benefactors; after his death in 1917, some American followers, either not familiar or not caring about Shacklock's reputation as a trouble-maker back at the York diocese, set up a fund with the intention of locating the bishop's grave in France and bringing him home to Jedthorpe, to his parish, where they hoped to erect a permanent memorial at the church where the bishop preached. However, the money rolled in; a lecture tour to America, undertaken by the bishop ten years or so before he died, had seen his popularity rocket amongst the hardy, hard-working miners around Maryland. His preaching of love for the common man and a rejection of class distinction chimed well with the Maryland settlers who had fought for their livelihoods. The Shacklock Library's foundation stone was laid in 1919 and the building was completed in 1922. Many wounded soldiers from Jedthorpe had worked on the building, a fact Jess was sure would have pleased the bishop.

During her time at the library, Jess discovered that in the first years it was open, the library soon became a gathering point for radicals—union men and agitators in the north-east—much to the displeasure of the York diocese, thirty miles away. Later, in the Second World War, the library became a retreat for wounded and disabled clergymen serving in the forces. It became a place of recovery and healing. The nineteen-eighties saw the library come under the control of York University and become a depository for papers relating to Shacklock or the Synod at large. There was no shortage of researchers interested in Shacklock, many from Maryland who, with others, made the trip to Jedthorpe to wander the stacks and write papers in the reading room. Jess's first employment after qualifying as an archivist had been at the library. She had now been there for six years, moving from one project to another, depending on the funding. Each time she thought she had escaped Professor Waller, he stated a need for her help. The other academics were unable to stand up to him; he had been there too long. And he was unlikely to ever be fired, as he once confided to Jess.

Jess had not intended on working at the Shacklock Library. She knew all about it, of course, having taken the archivist course at York University, where research into Shacklock's work and legacy was well established. But her tuition fees had been high and the job advert had been attractive—a new archivist was required to help put the Shacklock papers into some order. Jedthorpe was only thirty miles from her home in York so, with Alec's encouragement, Jess had applied. She had been unsure which direction she had wanted to go in her career anyway and thought a place at the library would give her time to decide.

She read up on Shacklock before the interview, appreciating for the first time just what a thorn he had been in the side of the Synod.

Agitator for political reform, supporter of a minimum wage for the vulnerable masses dangling off the edges of society, proponent of birth control. It seemed if there was a cause controversial enough to send a blade into the heart of the establishment, Bishop Shacklock was happy to wield the knife. Packed off on a lecture tour of the United States in 1907 by an exasperated archbishop, Shacklock had returned in triumph and with a new following.

Jess had to admit that, at the beginning, she had been fascinated by Shacklock, and a little in awe of him. Such reverence had ebbed away, however, the longer she worked for Professor Waller.

Today the professor was waiting for her beside her desk, rocking on his heels. He wore his usual, ill-fitting tweed coat and bright blue trousers. The trousers were so garish that Jess had initially thought they were part of a workman's uniform, adapted for the office. That was six years ago; he had not worn anything else in the whole time she had worked at the library. Professor Waller had his own unique style, Jess once said to Marie.

'Jessica, good, I need you this afternoon,' the professor said as Jess laid her bag on the desk.

'Just the words any woman wants to hear,' she murmured. 'Oh? Nothing. What do you need me for?'

Waller cleared his throat. He had something significant to impart and liked to clear aside the remnants of conversation before making his announcements. 'You may, ah, have noticed I have been a little distant recently.'

Jess brought her hand slowly to her cheek, forcing her teeth against the soft flesh inside. It would not do to laugh. She could taste cigarettes on her tongue. 'Have you?'

The professor hooked his fingers onto his belt and looked at the ground. 'Yes, indeed. Well, I think I've cracked it.'

'It?'

'Our mysterious lady! I've been looking through the Synod papers you brought me yesterday. Good piece of work there, by the way. I think the indexing was a little haphazard, so you did well to find them.'

Jess rubbed her thumb and fingers together. The skin around her nails was pink and sore. She had spent hours rummaging through brown boxes, handling musty papers that had been stored in no particular order while on the hunt for papers relating to the bishop. She had no idea why and suspected Waller had even forgotten why he had asked her. There had been a mountain of documents to go through: since the 1980s, the amount of Synod papers deposited at the Shacklock Library had increased, to the extent that the building now held all the papers relating to the church in the Jedthorpe area.

'You're welcome.'

The professor continued. 'There was a reference, one that I must have missed. I think you've found me that archive before, and I hadn't noticed the relevance. Or, maybe I had, but I was following another line, possibly.'

Jess closed her eyes briefly and leant against the desk. She could hear the tap, tap, tap, of someone on a keyboard, no doubt writing up their latest discovery, making their mark in the academic world. As I should be doing, she thought.

'Well, by the by, I think there's something.' Waller's face was animated now. His unkempt white beard bobbed up and down as he bounced his head in excitement. That was his way, nodding towards a conclusion. He suddenly produced a bundle of papers from a pocket and started poking at them. 'You're going to the British Library tomorrow, yes? Forget whatever it was I asked you to look for—I can't remember what it was, now. Instead, I want you to look at Shacklock's correspondence for 1899. All of it. You see, the Synod papers you found yesterday refer to a strange anomaly in his history.'

'Do they?' Jess shifted her weight from foot to foot. The tapper on the computer slapped a finger on a key with surprising force, the snapping sound resounding in the reading room's high ceiling.

'Yes!' Professor Waller's head bounced on his neck. 'Look—look at this reference! If you remember, Bishop Shacklock was supposed to be in Malta for much of 1899. A posting the archbishop had arranged for him, no doubt to get him out of the way. But the Synod papers refer to a letter, sent by Shacklock that year, from *Greece*. Greece! Not Malta! Here, there's a note in the itinerary of papers for that year. I've never noticed it before, what with their indexing being in such confusion. Maybe a job for you later. But Greece!' The professor beamed.

Jess ignored the hint about the Synod papers' indexing and tipped her head to the side to feign interest. 'Really? How unusual. How far is Greece from Malta?'

'What? Oh, I don't know. Five hundred miles or so? Not outwith the realm of possibility for him to hop on a boat across the Ionian Sea. But why?' The professor ran his fingers through his beard, creating a scrubbed, scratchy sound that Jess had never failed to hate. She looked at him now, heaviness coming into her shoulders at the thought of what was ahead.

It could not be avoided. 'How much correspondence is there for 1899? How many letters by the bishop does the British Library have?' she asked and prepared herself for the answer.

'For 1899—about a hundred letters, I should think. Maybe more. You know the bishop. Quite the letter writer!' Professor Waller had the grace to look sheepish. 'If I had the time, I'd go myself. And, of course, it would be much easier if the powers-that-be running this library put their backs into it and finally purchased all of Shacklock's papers. It's a nightmare, what with some papers here and some down in London.' He placed his hands awkwardly on her shoulders. 'Dig around. Find out what Shacklock was writing, and where from. Why did he go to Greece, of all places?'

'It sounds thrilling.' From somewhere amongst the bowed heads over the desks, Jess heard a snigger. She threw a wave of hate to whoever it was.

'Glad you're on board.' The professor released her and rubbed his hands together. 'I'll look forward to your report on Monday. Nothing too detailed. Just a couple of pages.'

'I do need to see my kids, you know,' Jess said. Her weekend stretched out into a long session of rifling through old papers. She could imagine Alec's face when she returned home after two days, when she told him she'd be unable to clear up the destruction of her unsupervised house due to the pressing demands of her boss.

'Just a couple of pages!' And the professor was away, waving his hand over his shoulder, heading towards the stacks.

Jess stared resentfully at his disappearing back. 'What an arse,' she muttered, louder than intended. The anonymous snigger amongst the desks turned into a full-throated guffaw.

~ 2 ~

James had left his football boots behind the front door again, and Jess stumbled over them when she came home, catching her foot painfully against the radiator in the hallway. She hissed and rubbed her ankle, leaning against the wall. The train home to York from Jedthorpe had been packed, commuters pressed against each other. One man had stood the whole way with his elbow jammed by Jess's ear, reading something on his phone. She had tutted, repeatedly, but he had ignored her.

What she wanted now she had arrived home, more than anything, was a glass of wine, a cigarette and a hot bath. Preferably all at once, with some London Grammar on the stereo borrowed from Megan's room. What Jess heard, though, from the hallway, was the harsh sound of the PlayStation turned up to full volume in the living room, and Megan moving around upstairs, thumping out dance steps to a Katy Perry track.

It felt good to kick James's boots to the end of the hall. Then Jess grimly turned the handle to the living room. James was slumped on the sofa, still in school uniform, mouthing something silently at the television screen, holding a games console in his hand and directing his soldiers to shoot at what appeared to Jess to be unarmed civilians. He didn't look up as his mother entered the room.

'Hello, James,' Jess said. Nothing. She clenched her fists and resisted an urge to kick him like his boots. Instead she ruffled his hair, rougher than necessary, and went into the kitchen.

Alec was over the stove, wooden spoon in hand, a car manual beside him. He looked round as Jess entered the room. He held his body tensely, warily. The debris of last night's argument hung off him like a heavy coat. He moved his lips before speaking. 'All right, Jay?'

'Hi.' Jess put her bag down on the kitchen table and heaved off her coat. She sniffed dramatically. *Let's not fight again, I'm too goddamn tired.* 'Something smells good.'

'Cheesy pasta.' Alec licked his fingers, relief crossing his face. 'Good day?'

A simple question, but suddenly Jess felt like crying. The argument last night had been about the lack of such simple questions. About Alec's habit of coming home from work, prising off his shoes and turning on the television, without muttering a word. Sometimes he barely spoke until bed. 'You don't engage!' Jess had thrown at him, out of the blue, catching him by surprise. Professor Waller had been particularly annoying at the library yesterday, pulling Jess from one fruitless excursion into the manuscripts, and sending her on another. Her own research areas were a distant memory. The presence of women in the early church—they would have to remain undiscovered, while Jess had become, she considered, like many of those women she longed to research: subject to the whim of a man in a position of authority. Jess came home in a rage. Marie was not around, there was no one else to talk to. And Alec was too interested in the football to do more than grunt at her.

'I had a crap day, actually,' Jess said. But she had a smile on her face. She walked over to Alec and gave him a hug. *Thanks for asking.* 'Did James do his homework?'

'I said he could have half an hour on the PlayStation first. What?' Alec caught Jess's tight look. 'It saves on the arguments later.'

'He's fifteen. He should do as he's bloody told. And I banned him from it until the weekend.' Jess opened the fridge. An open bottle of Jacob's Creek stood, temptingly, in the milk tray, but she resisted. She reached for the orange juice.

James looked up as she walked back into the living room. 'You at badminton tonight?'

Jess sighed as she plumped down onto a chair. 'No.'

'Can you take me to Aaron's then?'

Jess snorted. 'Not a chance. I'm whacked.' She closed her eyes, ignoring her son's huffs and pouts. Upstairs the music stopped and Megan came tripping down, jumping into the living room with the energy of a pre-teen.

'Hi!' Megan slipped over the arm of the chair and onto Jess's lap. She kissed her mother and Jess leant down, inhaling the scent of her girl's hair. Megan beamed. 'I got homework today!'

'Big deal,' James muttered, fingers pressing frantically on the console.

'*James.*' Jess shifted around in her seat, adjusting Megan's weight. The girl was getting heavy. 'What's the homework?'

'Science!' Nothing Megan said was muted. She shouted everything. 'We've been desalivating seawater.'

Jess stifled a giggle. 'Do you mean desalinating?'

'Oh yes!' Megan laughed. 'I need to write it up. Mr Sanders said I was very good at experiments, but I'm not very good at recording everything. He said I need to focus. But I didn't understand, Mum. I don't need glasses, do I?'

Jess did laugh at this. Even James grunted, but quickly followed it up with a 'You're a moron, Megan.'

They ate around the kitchen table for once. Alec's efforts continued, and he loaded the dishwasher without asking after they'd finished. He threw half-smiles at Jess as he moved awkwardly about the kitchen, opening the wrong cupboards, wiping the surfaces with a cloth meant for the floor. But Jess loved him for it, grateful for his efforts. Later, when the kids went up to bed, he perched on the side of the bath as Jess took a soak.

'What a day.' Jess handed Alec the shampoo bottle. 'Do you mind?'

'Do you still have to go to London tomorrow?' Alec loosened her hair.

'Yep.' Jess relaxed and tipped her head back. 'That's nice. The Prof has an idea about the Cuckoo.'

'Another one?'

'He wants me to trawl through a load of letters this time. I'll probably be there all day.'

'Haven't you done that before?'

'Too many to count.' Jess sighed and tilted her head from side to side so Alec could rub the shampoo into lather. 'No doubt this will be another wild goose chase. But I thought I'd try to do a bit of shopping on Sunday morning. You know, get something out of it for a change. Covent Garden maybe.'

'Christmas presents? Why not? You could pick Megan up a chess set. She's been on about getting a new one now's she's joined the school club.' Alec finished with the shampoo and leant over for a cup to rinse it away. Jess caught him, his hands full of suds, and pulled them down to her breasts.

Alec froze for a second. And then he laughed nervously. 'Jay …'

'Won't you miss me?' she asked, hating the pleading in her voice.

'You're going to pull me in.' Alec eased his hands away, slowly, but firmly.

Jess sat up. Alec's hands were soapy and wet to the wrists. She stared at them, unable to look her husband in the face. How long had it been? A couple of months, at least. That night after the Preston's summer barbeque. They'd both had a lot of punch. 'So your efforts will extend to the kitchen but not to me.'

'What?' Alec stood up. 'I'm tired, that's all. And don't say things like that.'

'Why not? It's true, isn't it?'

'You always do this. You say I don't try, that I'm distant. So I try, but it's never enough.'

'It's been nearly two months!'

'Who's keeping score?' Alec's voice rose.

'Oh, forget it.' Jess passed a hand over her face. 'I'm tired, too.'

Although she couldn't see, she knew Alec was standing with his hands on his hips, looking around, as though an answer would spring to him from the bathroom cabinet or the tiles. They were silent for a long moment. The anger that animated Jess a second earlier evaporated. In its place she felt sadness, only. She wasn't surprised when Alec mumbled, 'I think I might crash out early, if it's all right with you. Megan's gym class is at eight tomorrow morning.'

'That's fine.' Jess pulled her knees up. She tucked her chin on the top, cold creeping down her skin.

And then the phone rang, releasing them both. Alec jumped, and tumbled down the stairs, a little too quickly. He walked slowly back up and handed Jess the phone. 'It's Marie. I've told her you're in the bath.'

Jess took it. 'Hi Marie,' she sighed, as Alec disappeared. 'Yes, I'm in the bath.'

'Good for you, darling. Hope you've got a glass of wine with you.' Marie's expansive voice was made no smaller by the telephone line.

'Later.'

'Well, I'm calling to say I've made contact with Hayden. He says he's free tomorrow afternoon and most of the evening, if you want to meet up.'

'Oh, Marie, I don't know.' Jess dredged the memory of Hayden from the mental boxes marked 'unimportant clutter' and 'people I won't see again'. She recalled a tall, spotty young man, with a feeble attempt at stubble splattered across a square jaw, and angular bones sticking through his clothes.

'Why not?' Marie took a gulp of something. 'It would be good for you. What else will you do by yourself in London after a day poking around in dusty papers? Go back to your hotel room and order room service?'

'The Prof hasn't booked me into anywhere quite so grand as to provide room service.'

'Not even a Holiday Inn, for God's sake?'

Jess had to laugh. Marie, for all her ease in the Students' Union bar, was a snob. 'Not quite. But somewhere in Kings Cross, near the library.'

'All the more reason for you to meet Hayden. He's different, you know, from how you remember him. Talkative now. Not that skinny rake anymore. Plays a bit of football with the lads on a Sunday morning, so he won't keep you up late.' Marie needled. 'Go on, Jessie. He's a gentleman. Alec won't mind.'

Jess thought of Alec's stricken face when she caught his hands and made him touch her. She closed her eyes. 'Go on, then.'

'Lovely. I'll tell him to say you'll give him a ring when you've finished. And don't spend all day in that bloody library, Jessie. You spend too long surrounded by books as it is. I'll text you his number later.'

And Marie hung up, turning up the jazz music in the background before disconnecting. Jess imagined a mechanic sitting on Marie's sofa, brandy in hand, naked and wearing a smile. She had to grin, too. And then she ducked her head under water, washing away the last of Alec's suds.

∽

The train from York to St Pancras was empty the following morning, so Jess was able to sit at a table and plug in her laptop. She chose a window seat in a quiet carriage and waited an age for the computer to load up, thinking again that she should ask the professor to fund an upgrade. She was hungry. Alec had slept with his back to her all night, far away on the edge of the mattress and, as always after an argument, Jess could not sleep. She'd rolled from side to side all night and then, as dawn broke, had fallen into a brittle doze. She'd slept through the alarm. By the time she had showered and packed a bag, the taxi was waiting and there was no time to eat. The train was quiet enough for her to risk a trip to the buffet car and leave the laptop to wake up.

It took just over three hours for the train to pull into London, during which time Jess had finished the latest report she had been working on for Professor Waller. The hunt for the correct Synod papers she had given the Prof the day before had taken most of the week, and experience had taught her to always write up her findings, even if Waller indicated he was uninterested. Once, soon after she'd started working at the library, Jess had ditched a pile of notes he had asked her to make when reading through a year of the bishop's correspondence. She had taken them to him at the end of a long day, her eyes stinging from hours of staring at the bishop's spidery handwriting. Professor Waller had glanced at them cursorily and then tossed them aside. 'Was wrong about that line of inquiry, Jessica. I think Shacklock ministered at the workhouse for only a week or so, and he doesn't mention meeting a woman there. No time for a brief fling. The mother of our mysterious lady isn't to be found here.' Jess, infuriated at having spent so long on yet another search for the Cuckoo, walked back to her desk and dropped her notes in the bin. A month later the professor asked her to go back over the same papers again and Jess, remembering her discarded notes and the bishop's tiny handwriting, fled to the bathroom and screamed into a roll of paper towels.

The hotel was a couple of streets away from the British Library. A white-fronted building that had seen better days, it was situated in a small crescent, not far removed from the roar of traffic. Jess had stayed there before on another of the professor's errands and the receptionist looked familiar when she checked in. She was given the keys to a room with a large double bed taking up most of the space. A small cupboard comprised the bathroom. She scuffed her legs between the bed and the wall as she struggled towards the dresser to dump her suitcase. But the room was clean and close to the library. Pocketing the complimentary biscuits to eat on the way, she swung her laptop bag over her shoulder and left.

The British Library was quiet, though Jess knew it would fill up later, full of tourists visiting the exhibitions, or weekend researchers, making a mad dash to London to stock up on notes. She showed the security guard her reader's card, which would give her access to the reading rooms, and opened her bag for inspection. Then she walked down to the locker room, scrabbling around in her purse for a pound coin. Once her bag was stashed, she tucked the laptop under her arm, along with a notepad and some pencils, and went up to the Manuscript Reading Room.

Although it was a Saturday, already half of the desks were taken. Set in lines of six or seven, researchers sat at green-topped tables, some frowning over papers, others chewing on pencils. The room was high-ceilinged with low-hanging, shaded lights and reference books lining the walls. It was also cold. Jess crossed her arms and rubbed her jumper, pleased she had remembered to wear an extra layer.

Luckily Jess had had time to pre-order the papers she wanted to see. On previous occasions the professor had rung her mobile while she was in the Reading Room, earning the hissed admonishments of those at the reception desk, and he'd demanded that she check out another batch of Bishop Shacklock's manuscripts. It could take up to two hours from the papers to be fetched up from the archive; time Jess spent in clench-fisted, mutinous fury, thinking of her own unwritten research papers that might easily benefit from two hours' worth of attention.

Today, though, the papers were waiting for her at the collection desk. They came in a box file with the collection's reference number printed on the top. Jess opened the box at the desk and checked through the inventory, casting her eye down the list of contents. Letters by the bishop to church colleagues, to members of parliament, and many others. Jess closed the box again with a sinking feeling in the pit of her stomach and found an unoccupied desk.

The bishop's letters from 1899 were written on a variety of types of paper, demonstrating Shacklock's readiness to turn anything into writing material. Some were written on clean, white sheets, some were jotted on scraps of yellow paper, which looked similar to the flysheets contained in books or prayer manuals. But the documents were all covered in Bishop Shacklock's unique writing. Six years of working through his papers had helped Jess to decipher his spiky hand, for which she never failed to be thankful. The bishop had an odd, crooked writing style; no two letters were the same. Some fell forwards where Jess expected them to lean back, others floated above the line when they should be below. Shacklock crossed words out where there seemed to be no need and, once he had filled each side, turned the sheets of paper diagonally and wrote across his already captured scrawl. In the beginning, Jess regularly fought the impulse to tear a paper to shreds, enraged by the futile task of picking out a word or a sentence here and there that she could identify. But, gradually, she became familiar with the bishop's writing, to the extent that his personality seeped through, rising to the surface like air bubbles. Jess was able to draw out the line of his thoughts and rearrange his tumbled script into decipherable sentences.

And she appreciated his humour. Shacklock had a wicked turn of phrase and, when writing privately and not for the archbishop or diocese, he could be quite biting. An unfortunate reverend at a church local to the bishop's mission in Jedthorpe, who had a protruding pair of ears, was referred to as 'that piddling Baptismal cup'; a politician who recurred in Shacklock's letters due to his opposition to the bishop's proposal of a food kitchen specifically for street urchins was known as 'the egg-sucker'. For all her resentment at the time she was required to spend reading through the mountains of the bishop's material, Jess could not help but like him.

There were eighteen pages of letters written in January 1899. Jess sighed. She was sure there were papers at the library back in Jedthorpe that no one had seen since the day they were written. The bishop and all the clergymen he consorted with were prolific in their correspondence and record keeping. The bishop had written thousands of letters over his life, half of which resided at the Shacklock Library in Jedthorpe, the rest stored in the vast archives of the British Library. Professor Waller wanted her to look at the bishop's correspondence for the whole of 1899 and the eighteen pages that Jess held were from the first week of January only. It was going to be a long day.

By lunchtime Jess had reached March 1899, and the bishop had just arrived in Malta. He may have physically been some distance from his diocese, but his ambitions for Jedthorpe's poor were undiminished. He wrote letters home to his sister, to the archbishop, to elders in his ministry, to politicians. Shacklock enquired after the latest discussions in parliament, which might affect those under the care of his mission; he pressed for more assistance from politicians in feeding the families of miners, killed in local collieries.

Jess knew that many researchers were drawn to the bishop, mainly because of his endeavours for the city's poor. After his trip to Maryland in 1907 he garnered even more supporters, some of whom retrieved his body from France at the end of the First World War. Yet for all the work that had been done on the bishop already, Jess could not help but feel that she was staring into a milky pond: she could see no link between these ordinary, humdrum letters and the woman's skeleton that had been buried with the bishop in the small, distant French town. The bishop's letters from Malta made no mention of a relationship, or meeting someone. Jess rubbed a hand across sore eyes and pushed the papers away. It was gone noon, and she was hungry. Time for a break.

The library cafe had a limited choice so Jess picked an overpriced egg sandwich and a coffee. She made sure she kept the receipt, ready to hand over with an expenses form to the professor on Monday. He would barely look at it, Jess knew, and the thought did cross her mind to slip out to a restaurant around Kings Cross—maybe even the new hotel at St Pancras—and order an expensive lunch. If Marie had been with her, it may have been a different story. But, alone, with the bishop's letters waiting on her desk, Jess ate quickly in the British Library café.

After, she retrieved her bag from the lockers and called home from the foyer, leaning against the escalators. Her voice flowed upwards into the wide space between floors. 'Meg? It's Mum.'

'Hi Mum! James is still in bed.'

Jess imagined her daughter bouncing in the kitchen, phone tucked beside her ear, still wearing her gym kit. Megan's face would be pink and shiny, eyes darting from window to table, to window, to Alec. The girl couldn't keep still.

'Did Dad wake him up?'

'He shouted up the stairs for *ages* but James wouldn't budge. He was still there when we came back from gym and he's still there now! When I went in to see him, he *swore*.'

Jess pinched the bridge of her nose. 'James has been told not to do that.'

'I know.' Meg swapped the phone to her other ear, breathlessly. 'Dad said he was going to ban him from the PlayStation if he didn't get up soon.'

'I did that already. Your dad will have to think of something else. Is he there?'

'Yep. Love you, Mum. Bye!' Meg passed the phone to her father.

'Hi.' Alec's voice. He sounded cautious and tired. 'Get there all right, then?'

Jess closed her eyes. *Why is it so hard to talk to you these days?* 'Yes. Train was on time for once.'

'Good.'

The two hundred miles or so between home and London seemed to double in their shared silence. 'I've got a lot to do for the Prof today.'

'Well. I won't keep you. James is refusing to get up. Says he doesn't have homework and there's nothing he wants to get up for.'

'Maybe a girl is at the root of it.' Jess didn't think so, but it was something to say.

'I doubt it. He doesn't shower enough.'

Unexpectedly, they both laughed. Jess held her phone tightly. *Please, let it be okay between us.* 'I'll miss you tonight.'

Alec coughed and Jess couldn't be sure if he was pleased or not. Instead he asked, 'Going out? What about a show?'

'I hate them, remember? No, I think I'll just have an early night and watch television in bed.'

'Sounds good. Well, bye, Jay. See you tomorrow.'

'Bye.'

Alec hung up softly. Jess held her phone in front of her face again, fingertips white from her grip. She was not surprised to feel tears ticking her nose, and swallowed awkwardly. The memory of the night before, clinging to the edge of a cold bed with Alec so close but so far out of reach, stung afresh. She rubbed her face.

Then the phone rang again. Jess, startled, almost fumbled and dropped it. In the split second before seeing the number flash up on her screen, she wondered if it were Alec again, phoning back to talk properly, to say they needed to work on things. That theirs was a marriage worth saving. But it was not Alec, and a number she did not recognise throbbed on the handset.

'Hello?'

'Is that Jessica? Jess?'

'Jess, yes. Who is this?'

'It's Hayden. Mum—Marie—gave me your number. I think she tex-ted you my number, too, but I haven't heard from you, so I thought I'd call. Am I disturbing you?'

Jess walked to the end of the escalator and found a seat against the glass rails cordoning the floor, looking out over the library reception area below. 'Hi Hayden. It's good of you to call. Been a long time.' She struggled to remember him, frowning as she tried to catch a glimpse through the shutters of memory. All she could recall was a young man, hampered by acne, waiting by his car as they stumbled from the student bar, apparently horrified at his mother's—and her own—drunkenness.

Hayden appeared to have the same memory, for he suddenly laughed. 'I haven't seen you since that last time I picked you up from the Student's Union, after your exams. Mum called to say you'd missed the night bus home again.'

Jess could remember more now, and the threat of earlier tears was replaced with the heat of embarrassment. She and Marie had gone straight from their last exam to the bar, pushing aside the younger stu-dents, ordering wine while the others around them ordered bottles of alcopops and cider. 'Oh, God. We were plastered.'

Hayden chuckled harder. 'Mum particularly. But she wasn't the one threatening to flash me unless I found her some cigarettes.'

'Oh. Oh, *God*,' Jess said again, and this time she did blush. 'Let's not talk about that. I'm all mature now.'

'Boring. Mum said you might need showing around town tonight?'

The foyer clock pinged around to two o'clock and Jess thought of the papers waiting for her on the desk. On the train down, she had idly entertained the idea of going to the cinema, if there was anything worth watching. If not, a long, hot shower, and unmolested control of the television remote had appealed. She'd forgotten about Hayden and Marie's offer. 'Well, I wouldn't want to make you change any plans. Not if you were going out already.'

'No plans.'

'Oh. Well, then.' Jess looked over the glass banister down to the ground floor, where a couple lingered outside the library shop. An exhi-bition about *Alice in Wonderland* was being held in the section open to the public. Jess wondered if she should pick something up for the kids. She imagined James's face and discounted the idea.

'So we'll arrange to meet? What time do you think you'll be finished?' Hayden again.

'Probably never. Am on a wild goose chase.'

'Ah, the nameless lady?' Hayden laughed. 'Mum told me about her.'

'I've been trying to identify this damn woman for the past six years.' Jess thought back to the many, many times the professor had appeared at her desk, scribbled piece of paper in hand, no apology for disturbing her work again, only a request that she disappear into the stacks for an hour to retrieve an obsolete file or archive.

'Any closer to finding out who she was?' Hayden sounded interested.

Jess paused. Alec hardly ever asked her about her work, even in the early days, when there was still enough heat in their marriage for him to pretend to take an interest. 'It's deathly boring, Hayden.'

'So you no longer flash men in return for cigarettes and you have a boring job.' Hayden sounded as though he were smiling. 'I would say you need a good night out.'

Jess laughed. 'I would say that's fair. Well, there's a pile of stuff to get through and I'll never get it all done today. I might as well finish early. I can always come back tomorrow. They are opening the reading rooms on Sundays at the moment. I should be grateful.' This last was said glumly, the prospect of an uninterrupted wander around Covent Garden receding into a tiny dot.

'If I were you, I'd tell my boss to stick it. I'm all for working the hours during the week but weekends? No. They're for me.'

'You sound like your mum.'

'She does make sense now and then. So … how about we meet in town, say about sevenish? Outside Leicester Square tube? The Charing Cross Road exit?'

Jess watched the couple outside the gift shop embrace and then wander outside, slowly, hand-in-hand. She sighed. 'Sure. Sounds good.'

'Excellent. You like Chinese food? We can walk up to China Town from there. There are some okay restaurants.'

'That would be great. But, ah, Hayden, it's been a while and I don't think …'

'I can't remember what you look like either. So here's the plan. I'll be carrying a *Times* under my arm. Left arm. You can carry a *Telegraph*.'

Jess suppressed a laugh. 'Very le Carré.'

'So, see you at seven?'

'Looking forward to it.' And, as Jess disconnected the call softly and held the phone to her chest, she realised she actually was.

Jess decided to allow herself time to shower and change before meeting Hayden, so returned to her desk in the manuscript reading room with the intention of finishing up around five o'clock. As she sat down, she noticed that a kind administrator had placed the latest bundle of Shacklock papers on the desk, this time covering April and May 1899. There were over fifty pages, all densely packed with the bishop's handwriting. The unexpected, good feeling prompted by Hayden's call disappeared. Jess sat down heavily, stomach aching from the over-chilled egg sandwich and with frustration. The old desire to grab the manuscripts with both hands and rip them into tiny pieces returned. *Well, that would be one way of quitting my job.*

But instead, Jess took her laptop out of her bag again and plugged it in. She found her report, opened it up and started squinting through the letters.

The first letters from April were very much like those from the preceding months. The bishop had settled into Maltese life, boarding with a family in a suburb just outside Valletta where he worked in a small Catholic church. The bishop had been keen to foster relations between the Catholic and Protestant churches and his visit to Malta appeared to be a step in this direction. In a letter to the elders of his own church back in Jedthorpe, he described the Catholic congregation in Malta. Many of them were elderly. There was no hint of meeting anyone or the beginnings of a romantic relationship. In another letter, this time to the Synod in Jedthorpe, Shacklock described a visiting dignitary from Spain and how the streets around Valletta became festooned with banners and ribbons.

Jess dutifully recorded a description of the contents of each letter, picking out key phrases that seemed important—though, of course, she could only guess. What she might consider important was quite different from the professor. In the early days he had chided her for her emphasis on the role of religious women in the bishop's life. 'Too focused on your own interests, Jessica, my dear,' he had said, quite unable to see the irony. Jess had bitten her lip and walked away, taking grim satisfaction in flicking Waller the finger behind his back.

She reached May 1899. It was now half-past three. Jess sat back, rifling through the pages, and decided she would finish after this lot. She would either come back in the morning, depending on how she felt, or would make the trip down from York again sometime during the week. She would not waste another weekend over it. She was done. She was not going to be at the professor's beck and call. Hayden's gentle, unexpected rebuke—that he would not give up his time so easily—sat with her. He was right. Of course he was right.

Jess turned to the May letters. The first, written again by the bishop, was to his sister. Unusually, it did not have an address in the top right hand corner, signalling from where the bishop sent it, and the date scrawled across the top had not been written in his hand. Possibly his sister's? Jess leant over, the muscles between her shoulder blades aching, and read on. The letter began quickly, without any precursory attempts at pleasantries.

'*You must remember Josiah Underwood? Josiah was at Stephens Theology College with me in York, so very long ago. He left without completing even a year—you will recall the scandal. Constance was at the heart of his leaving. His father was beside himself, his son giving up everything to marry a woman he had known only for six months. I received a letter from Josiah today. Somehow he heard I was in Malta, probably through the church. He lives in Piraeus, Greece, with Constance and their family. He's a doctor now, and wants me to visit. For one of the first times in my life, Mabel, I do not know what to do. He was my dearest friend at Stephens. And for all the scandal, he and Constance have stayed married. She must make him happy.*'

Jess sat back. The fingers of her left hand, used to trace the bishop's words, tingled. So maybe the bishop had gone to Greece after all. And to think that, all morning, hunched over the papers in the Manuscript Reading Room, squinting at the bishop's mundane reports from his Maltese visit, Jess had thought the professor was mistaken. True, the Synod papers she had found in Jedthorpe *did* refer to a letter that the bishop apparently sent to the Synod council from Greece, and it had been sheer luck that she came across it. The Jedthorpe Synod papers were notoriously complex and poorly categorised. Many researchers had attempted to pull them into some kind of order, but the archive was vast. So many clergymen, from Britain and overseas, corresponded with Synod members; their letters as well as the replies were, as far as possible, collected together. Letters cross-referenced other letters. Minutes of council meetings referred to correspondence received a year before, sometimes earlier. In addition, the archive had been moved to Doncaster during the Second World War and some of it had been lost in the bombing. Jess knew it would take a huge amount of money to shape the papers into a searchable database, probably in the millions. Money the big research bodies did not have. She had found the reference to the bishop's Greek letter only by chance, when going through a report of July 1899. The actual letter the bishop was supposed to have written from Greece, when he was supposed to be in Malta, was nowhere to be found.

And here was another letter by the bishop himself, written to his sister, referring to an old friend who lived in Greece. A friend who had had left the church under a cloud, to marry, no less. Jess wondered how Waller had missed it—had he not read all the bishop's letters? Maybe he dismissed them because they were written to his sister and were some-how more ... *domestic*. Jess thought of Waller's dismissal of research into women of the church, no matter what their role or connection—all save the mysterious woman buried with the bishop.

Jess did some calculations in her head. It was unlikely that Constance Underwood would be the mother of the young woman found in Shacklock's grave. The bishop was forty-five in 1899; Josiah and Constance Underwood would have been around the same age— meaning Constance was probably too old to have more children. Jess rubbed her temples. What of Josiah and Constance Underwood's chil-dren? Shacklock mentioned that they had a family. Did they have a daughter? Could she be a candidate for being the mother of the woman buried with the bishop?

Jess snorted, the sound low but carrying in the quiet reading room. The professor would implode, had she finally cracked it. He would have a heart attack. Maybe he'd stretch his bloody blue trousers to breaking point with an almighty erection, said a wicked voice inside, sounding suspiciously like Marie, and Jess did burst into laughter at that point. A man at a desk opposite looked up from his own work, quizzically. Jess raised her hand, nodding an apology.

The bishop's letter to Mabel, his sister, did not go on for much longer. There were a few enquiries about elderly acquaintances in failing health and references to the Maltese heat again, and then the bishop signed off. Jess hurriedly turned to the rest of the papers for May.

Nothing. Just more reports on his mission, more descriptions of his hosts and the food, more literary portraits of the eccentric congregation visiting the Maltese church. Jess read quickly, scanning through the twenty or so pages she had left. But there was no sign. The identity of the woman in Shacklock's grave was, as ever, elusive.

The clock on her laptop told her it was time to finish but, for the first time in a long time, Jess felt unwilling to stop. It was rare for the bishop to have a hold over her anymore, but this discovery was something unexpected. She wondered if this was what it was like for Professor Waller, to experience a kind of biting feeling, like a midge one had to scratch. There had to be something in what she had discovered. The bishop's trip to Greece must have happened. *If I was a copper, I'd say the circumstantial evidence all points the same way.* Jess slowly saved her work and shut the laptop down. She would be back tomorrow. She called at the desk on the way out and ordered the rest of the bishop's letters for 1899, not quite able to believe what she was doing.

A shower and a change took longer than Jess anticipated and she had to hurry for the tube. Although the hotel room was small and basically equipped, the shower was powerful; with hot water to stand under and proper, adult, scented gel only for her, Jess lingered under the spray. She'd switched on the six o'clock news when she got to the room—the bulletin had just begun when she entered the bathroom, and the programme was ending when she finally stepped out. The bedroom was full of steam, seeping under the bathroom door. Jess had to wipe the mirror over the tiny dressing table several times to apply makeup.

Jess didn't have to wait long to get the tube into town, though it was full. A group of Australians crowded around Jess as she stood in the aisle, talking between themselves about pubs in Fulham and Putney. A couple jostled into her good naturedly, tanned, enthusiastic, inviting her along. Secretly pleased and relieved she didn't look completely out of place, Jess grinned and wished them a good night as she stepped onto the platform at Leicester Square.

There were four exits to Leicester Square and Jess worried for a moment that she'd chosen the wrong one. She looked at her watch—just after seven. She had a suspicion that Hayden would be the type of man to be on time … and he was. Standing in the street just outside the station, *Times* under his left arm. Seeing the paper, Jess suddenly realised she'd forgotten to pick up a *Telegraph*.

'George Smiley, I presume?' she said as she walked up to him. She felt coy. *What if it's not him and just some random bloke? He'll think I'm a right nutter.*

But it was Hayden. He stood up straight and smiled. 'Jess? Or is it Jessica? Jessie? Which do you prefer?'

He was taller than she remembered, a good three inches above her, and his hair was different. She recalled a young man with a buzz cut, almost down to his scalp. Now his black hair was worn long, past his ears, and he was clean-shaven. No hint of late-teen stubble across his face. He wore a brown coat and, under that, a blue shirt—practically the same colour as the professor's trousers, Jess noted, and she laughed.

Hayden raised an eyebrow. He had a wide smile. 'She laughs. We've just met and she laughs at me. And how do I know if it's really you? What were you supposed to bring, so I know you're not an imposter?'

'I don't know if I should tell you.' Jess played along. 'You could be a double agent, trying to entrap me.'

'Entrap? That sounds interesting. Doesn't that have to involve a room that charges by the hour and intriguingly placed audio equipment?'

'Well, the night is young.'

Hayden's eyebrows had almost disappeared into his hair and it was his time to laugh, loudly. When he did so, he raised his face upwards, hooting for everyone to hear.

'Shall we start again?' Jess said, her face pink. 'I'm Jess. I was supposed to bring a *Telegraph*.'

'Hayden.' He held out his hand. 'Hungry?'

'Starving,' Jess said, shaking the extended hand, and then following him into the throng of people milling on the streets.

Hayden led them away from the busy square, up a street with a cinema on the corner, towards the three or four streets making up China Town. The evening was cold, but the place was packed. Tourists and locals walked together, some wandering, some going about their business briskly. A group of elderly Chinese practiced Tai Chi, watched by a small crowd. Someone was playing on drums. Restaurants and cafes offering dim sum jostled for position. Hayden talked, pointing out good places to eat as they passed through an archway shaped like a dragon. Jess listened, inhaling the sour, vinegary scents, peering at patrons bent over bowls of noodles or handling pancakes. Hayden nodded towards the butcher's shop, ducks and chickens strung up in the window, heads still attached, ringed with red flesh. Jess pulled a face, but looked, nonetheless. She wondered what Megan would make of it all.

After a while, Hayden steered them into a doorway just off Gerrard Street and up some stairs. The staircase opened out into a large room, crammed with tables. To the right of the entrance stood a hot buffet. Hayden, who was obviously a regular, raised a hand to a waiter, pointed to a table near the window at the other side of the room, and within minutes they were seated. Their table looked out onto the street below, and Jess craned her neck to watch the crowds, meandering through their Saturday night.

'I don't know what kind of Chinese food you like, so I thought a buffet would be a good idea,' Hayden was saying, not at all apologetic. 'It's not fancy, but the food's good. I come here at least once a month.'

Jess shook her head. She had been impressed by the ease and confidence with which Hayden settled them in the restaurant. Their table must have been one of the most popular in the room, with its excellent position by the window. 'It's fine. Anywhere is fine, actually. I'm famished.'

'The library cafe not up to much? Wine or beer?'

A waiter stood beside the table, holding a black felt-tip pen. Jess looked at it, puzzled. He had no notepad. 'Wine for me.'

'Bottle of house red, please—unless you prefer white? All right, red, then. And two for the buffet, please.' Hayden gave the order and then sat back. The waiter said something in return, leant forward and, with the black pen, wrote out the prices on the tablecloth.

Jess stared, only then realising that the tablecloth was made of paper. Hayden grinned. 'Like I said, nothing fancy.'

They were silent for a few moments before the wine came, watching the street below. Jess nodded quietly to herself, favourably. It was smart of Hayden to find a busy place, with a good spot to people-watch. It was easy to fill the gaps in conversation by pretending to be interested in those around them. And the waiter obviously knew him, for the response to Hayden's requests was quick. Only a few moments after giving their order, a bottle of wine was placed unceremoniously on the table, along with two glasses and two white porcelain plates, still steaming from the dishwasher. Hayden poured, glancing up at Jess. A slight indentation on the bridge of his nose hinted that he ordinarily wore glasses.

It seemed appropriate to clink glasses and then Jess, hungry and still nervous, took a huge gulp. The wine was cheap but light, and she sat back, trying to relax. Hayden stood up and walked over to the buffet, returning with a plate of starters. 'Bit of everything okay?'

They talked as they ate. Jess considered him over a piece of prawn toast. 'I don't think you look much like your mum.' It was true. Hayden was slim where Marie was big; his chin single and pointy whereas Marie had several. He was pale, too, and did not have Marie's hearty ruddiness.

Hayden shook his head. 'More like my dad.'

'I never met him.'

'They divorced when I was about thirteen. He went back to Wales soon after.'

'I didn't know he was Welsh.' Jess thought of James and Megan, how they might cope if she and Alec couldn't stop the cracks appearing. 'It can't have been easy to cope with. Your parents splitting up, I mean.'

Hayden shrugged and dropped a chicken wing back onto the plate. 'You adapt. Have to. Plenty of other kids do it. I figured I could either get on with things or become one of those navel-gazing teenagers spending all my time in my room.'

'I've got a son like that.'

'Mum said. James, is it?'

'He's fifteen.'

Hayden picked up another wing. 'Not an easy age. All those hormones.'

Jess took another drink of wine, a sip this time. 'He used to fight to be on my lap. Now I'm lucky if he notices when I walk in the door.'

'I used to ignore Mum. She'd give me a crack. I had red ears for most of my teens.'

Jess laughed. 'Marie used to scare the younger students witless.'

Hayden cocked his head. 'You'll have to tell me more.'

'And give away my best friend's secrets? Not likely.'

Hayden winked. 'What did you say earlier? The night is young.'

By the time they had finished their starters, the bottle of wine had almost gone. As Hayden poured out the last into Jess's glass, she was alarmed to realise that she'd had most of it. Hayden had drunk a couple of glasses, maybe. He ordered a second bottle and Jess resolved to slow down. She had barely eaten all day.

Hayden was right: the food was good. They shared duck, aubergines cooked with chillies, chicken and cashew nuts, and bowls of sticky, egg fried rice. Around them, diners talked, cutlery clinked on plates, people shouted for the waiter's attention. Cars hooted in the streets nearby, tourists in rickshaws peddled up and down Wardour Street. Jess warmed into the evening. Hayden was funny and interesting. He had a habit of staring right at her when she spoke, never looking down at his plate, or around the room, or out the window. He nodded at the right moments. He smiled.

Jess sat back in her seat, suddenly full, and suddenly aware that she felt at ease for the first time in a long time. She grinned at Hayden.

'What?' he asked. He stretched out his arms, also full.

'It's just that I'm having a good time.'

'You didn't expect to?'

'It's not that. Well, maybe.' Jess circled her hands on the paper table-cloth, now damp from spillages. 'Your mum was quite insistent that we meet up. I wasn't so sure.'

'Why not?'

'Well, I don't know you, I was wary of interfering with any of your plans. And, to be honest, a night of telly in bed sounded appealing.' Jess was aware of how that made her sound. 'I'm not that old, really.'

Hayden leant forward. 'Jess, I'm afraid you sound like an old fart.'

At that, Jess nearly tipped backwards in her seat, laughing at the ceiling. She knew the wine had something to do with it, but Hayden's serious face … it took an age for her to calm down, and when she did, he was watching her, bemused.

'I'm sorry,' she said. 'Long, boring day. I'm glad we met up.'

'Me too.' Hayden held out his glass for them to clink again. After they drank, he started patting his pockets. 'My turn to apologise. I'm going to nip out for a smoke. You're welcome to join me, unless …?'

Jess stood up, taking a few notes from her purse. She waved Hayden's protests away. 'I'll pay for dinner if you can spare me a fag or two. No, haven't managed to quit. Can I pinch one?'

They smoked in the street, Jess glancing surreptitiously from side to side, as though Alec or the professor might suddenly loom around the corner. The night had grown cold. Jess pulled on the cigarette for warmth. Hayden stood beside her, his own coat open. His jeans were tan in colour, held up by a thick, dark brown belt. He blew smoke into the sky. The top button of his shirt was open, pale skin visible.

'I'm glad Mum suggested we meet up,' he said.

'Me too.' And Jess meant it. 'What would you be doing otherwise, if you weren't entertaining your mum's friends?'

Hayden made a face. 'Nothing much. Probably down the pub. I live in Fulham. It's always lively down there at the weekend.'

Jess, remembering the Australians on the tube, nodded. 'What do you do?' she asked suddenly. 'I've just realised I haven't asked about your job at all. Marie said you worked at Waterloo?'

'I'm a data analyst,' Hayden said. 'Yes, it's as dull as it sounds. But it pays well, and I'm good at it. I work for a small company. I'm not one of those arses, up at the crack of dawn, home at midnight, raking the money in but never able to spend it. I spend what I make, sometimes a bit too quickly.'

'I'm afraid I'm one of those arses who *is* up at the crack of dawn. Spend what I make, too, but I'm a control freak—I like to account for every penny.' Jess thought of the housekeeping, the bills paid on time, the standing orders leaving her account every month.

'Funny.' Hayden looked at her. 'You don't strike me as a control freak.'

'No,' Jess agreed. 'Only at home.'

'I suppose with a family you have to be. I'm not there yet. Not even close.'

'Oh?' *Didn't Marie say something about a girlfriend?* 'I thought there was someone.'

Hayden threw his cigarette stub on the ground. 'Was. Look, it's only nine o'clock. I can get you back to the tube if you like, but maybe we could go for a drink somewhere. I'm having a good time. Are you?'

Jess considered, trying to remember the last time she'd been asked that. 'I am, actually. Yes, a drink would be great.'

'Fulham okay? I promise to get you back to Kings Cross.'

'Sure.' Jess threw her cigarette out into the street, just as Hayden had done. 'Why not?'

~ 4 ~

Hayden offered his arm as they walked back towards the tube station, and Jess took it, wobbly from the cigarette and the wine. She leant into him, glad of his warmth. Around them, the crowds had increased, and those who were out were louder than before. As they rounded the corner to the tube, a group of men crashed into them, in good humour, but Jess nearly stumbled. One of the men stopped to help her, checking she was not hurt.

'I'm all right,' she said, waving him away. 'Thanks for stopping, though. More manners than your dickhead friend who barged into me.'

The man pulled a face and seemed about to say something, when Hayden took Jess's arm and said loudly, deliberately, 'Well said, Jess.' He was much taller than the man who had stopped to help, and stood in a certain way as if to indicate that it would be wise not to look for trouble. The hapless reveller held up his hands and backed away, hurrying up the street to catch up with his friends.

'You really all right?' Hayden asked, dropping his hand slowly down Jess's arm to her elbow.

'I'm fine.' Jess moved gently away, pulling her arm from Hayden's grasp and back to her side. Her ankle stung. The same ankle she'd bashed on the radiator the day before, tripping over James's shoes. She wondered if she should phone home again. Better not. *Alec will know I've had a drink.*

They caught the tube to South Kensington and then on to Fulham Broadway. They could hear the boom of the pubs from the station; exiting onto Fulham Road, Hayden steered them past the Broadway Arms, just livening up, and onto a neighbouring street, lined with quieter bars. The noise of the Broadway followed them, shouts and thumps of music.

'This okay?' he asked, opening the door to a bar. The inside was lined with dark wood and it was not too crowded. Mellow dance music slid out into the night air, along with a rush of air, scented with liquor and perfume. Jess nodded, liking the music already, and followed him in.

The bar was small and most of the seats were taken. There was a couch available, just opposite the bar. No table. Jess sat down while Hayden went to the bar. She felt hot and removed her coat. Around them, couples swayed and talked to the music. It wasn't too loud; Jess could hear Hayden talk to the barman, laughing conversationally. She watched as he pushed a hand through his thick hair, hooking a thumb in his back pocket. His coat was ruffled up. He appeared comfortable, at ease in this place. Jess cleared her throat, remembering the unhurried way he had seen off the stranger in the street, the one who seemed on the edge of arguing with her. She tried to remember how old Marie had said he was. Not too young, not cocky. But young enough to still be brave, she thought.

Hayden came back with two shot glasses. 'Southern Comfort okay?' He handed her one. 'I didn't fancy more wine.'

'Me neither.' Jess took a sip. Her chest burned a little from the cheap wine at the restaurant. 'Ah. You've got a good memory. Marie and I used to drink this in the student's union after we'd finished with the wine.'

'I know,' and Hayden grinned.

'Don't worry, I won't flash you again.'

'Pity.' Hayden stuck out his bottom lip. Jess gave a yelp of laughter and moved up on the sofa, making room so they could squash in together.

'This a regular place for you, then?' A new track came over the stereo, one she had not heard before. Jess tapped her foot.

'Sometimes. I tend to end the night here. It's a good place to relax before heading home. And they have a late bar.'

'How late?'

'Two in the morning.' Hayden raised his glass. 'Fancy it?'

Jess snorted. 'I haven't done that since—since—'

'The last time you were out with my mum?' Hayden drained his glass and rolled it in his hands. 'Since she left Dad, she's been quite the party animal.'

'Understandable. Letting her hair down, and all that.' Jess thought of her own role in that party time. The 'Handling Manuscripts' course at the university had lasted for three years, and at least once a month, Jess had met Marie in the student's bar, leading to her getting home late and stinking of cigarettes.

'But for fifteen years? Party's got to stop some time.'

Hayden did not look at her when he said this, lips flattening out into a thin line. Jess watched. She suddenly felt guilty. Her memories of the nights out with Marie were sketchy, usually drunken, and always fun. Hayden's tight expression indicated that he had different memories of such times. Jess looked down at the glass in his hand, and had a strong urge to take it from him, and link her fingers with his.

'Look, Marie's my friend and I don't want to betray her confidence. But I can't imagine it was much fun for you to be on taxi duty for two plastered women, one of them your mother—and to do it more than once. For what it's worth, I'm sorry.'

Hayden looked at her for a long moment, his face set and unchanging. Jess wondered if she had upset him, if she had said something that really should have been said by his mother. But then Hayden smiled.

'I didn't mind.'

'You don't need—'

'No, honestly. I thought it was quite cool. That's not to say that I wasn't grateful for the fact that Mum was hitting the student bars after I'd graduated. It would have been mortifying to see a boy in Doc Martins draped around my mother.'

Jess held up a hand. 'That never happened.'

Hayden laughed. 'I respect you standing up for your friend. But you didn't go out with her every weekend.'

'Oh Lord.' Jess covered her face. 'I'm going to be sick.'

Hayden looked at her in alarm for a second and then realised she was joking. He nudged her in the ribs. 'You know what she's like. There's always some bloke hanging around.'

Jess waved a hand. 'I don't want to hear it. Ugh, no thanks.' She smiled and then took a drink. 'You know, you aren't that dissimilar to her. Not in that way, I mean. But in others.'

Hayden looked surprised. 'I thought you said we don't look alike.'

'Not that. Just ... other things. You both seem to know what you like. And she doesn't suffer fools gladly. I get the impression you're like that.'

Hayden grinned, showing all his teeth this time. 'I'd say that's true.'

'All the same, it can't have been easy for you. Dealing with your parents' divorce, and then your mum and her inappropriate friends rolling in at all hours.'

Hayden broke in. 'It wasn't all bad.'

Their legs nudged each other companionably, and then Hayden eased off his own coat. He left his left arm along the back of the sofa, behind Jess's head. She could smell aftershave—something sporty, not at all like Alec's preference for wood spice—and another scent beneath that; husky, warm. Jess bowed her head over her glass, searching for the smell of Southern Comfort.

'Did you find what you were looking for?' Hayden asked suddenly.

'At the library? I think so. The professor might be on to something after all.'

'Really?'

'Possibly. I'll need to go back there tomorrow, or arrange to come back in the week.'

'What did you find then?' Hayden stood up and took Jess's now empty glass. 'No, wait a sec. Tell me in a minute.'

He walked to the bar again and was back quickly with another two drinks. They chinked glasses before Hayden edged onto the sofa, arm again behind her. His fingertips brushed Jess's shoulder, and she arched away, just a little.

'Tell me,' Hayden said. 'What could possibly send you back to a library on a Sunday morning?'

Jess laughed. 'It is as boring as it sounds. Well, maybe not. You know Professor Waller—my boss—has been trying to identify the body of this woman buried with the bishop for most of his career?'

Hayden nodded. 'Mum said.'

'He's been working on it for years. It's driven him crazy.' Jess thought back to the many times the professor had been consumed with an idea, how his desk became a wasteland of papers and scraps of notes, how he missed lectures and meetings if he felt close to naming the woman buried with the bishop. 'I've lost so much time on it. Six years. You know, I wasn't employed to work for the Prof, but he commandeered me.'

'Can't you tell him you want to move somewhere else? Another project?'

The simplicity of Hayden's suggestion and the truth it contained made Jess smile. 'I could. I should. But it's too late now. I need to find out who this woman was as well. I'm not hooked, not like the Prof. But—'

'You have to justify why you've allowed the last six years to be given over to someone else,' Hayden finished. He raised his eyebrows. 'Yes?'

'Yes.' It was true. Jess took a sip of the Southern Comfort. She considered Hayden's direct approach, how it cut through the fog of why she had allowed Professor Waller to dominate her research time and pull her away from other interests. Hayden spoke the truth. The only way to explain away, to rationalise—to *excuse*—the last six years would be to name the woman buried with Shacklock. The woman's bones had hooked into Jess just as much as the skeleton had a hold over the professor.

'I may have found something,' Jess went on. 'Just a reference to an area we've not looked at before. The bishop may have taken a trip that we didn't know about.'

Hayden nodded. 'Somewhere new? A place he hadn't been before?'

'Yes. Greece, I think. He was supposed to be in Malta.'

'So he's off the map, then?'

Jess nodded. 'No one seems to know he was there. And the woman who was buried with him, she was young. Possibly in her late teens or early twenties, and Shacklock died in 1917.'

'And he travelled to Greece—when?'

'1899.' And an idea that had been at the periphery for the last few hours, since leaving the library, took shape.

Hayden cupped his drink. 'Meaning the bishop may have met a woman on this mysterious trip and—'

'—had a child in Greece and the woman buried with him is his daughter.' Jess sat back. 'We know from DNA tests that the woman is most likely to be the bishop's daughter. But we can't find any evidence as to who she is. Or who her mother was. Shacklock's movements have been plotted, all accounted for, and there's been no hint of a relationship.'

'You can't know where someone is every second of the time.' Hayden turned a little in his seat, thigh pressing against Jess. She looked down at their legs, so close together, and suddenly thought of Alec. She'd told him she would be in the hotel room tonight, watching a film and having an early night. He had no idea she was in a bar, in Fulham, with a man, teetering on drunkenness.

'Sometimes it's better that way,' Hayden continued. Then he took the glass from Jess's hand and set it down on the floor beside them, along with his own. 'Better to not know where everyone is, all the time. Opens life up to other possibilities, doesn't it?' His hand moved from brushing Jess's shoulder to the nape of her neck. His fingers were cool from the glass.

Jess sat up, knowing she should remove his hand, that she should stand up and thank him for the evening and then leave. But she did not want to, that was the truth of it. Instead she turned full on, knees parting, Hayden's own knee filling the gap between her own.

'You know, I didn't need you to buy a newspaper and carry it under your arm like a relic of the Cold War,' he was saying. 'I could remember exactly what you looked like.'

∾

He had promised to get her back to Kings Cross before the last tube, and Hayden did not let Jess down; only he did not wave goodbye at the entrance to Fulham Broadway tube station or even outside her hotel near the British Library. Instead he accompanied Jess right up to the hotel reception desk where she had left her key, right up to the lift, right up to her bedroom door, and then inside.

Jess switched on the lights as they came in and looked around. She could see her face in the mirror; white from the cold, but eyes shiny, cheeks pink. Startled and something else. *Switched on*. Hayden came up behind her and held her round the waist.

Jess turned, and his hands slipped inside her coat, resting lightly on her T-shirt. She started to say something, but gave up, and kissed him again.

In the bar, they had kissed quickly, almost furtively. Jess had wondered if her mouth had been pulled into a round circle of surprise—she had kissed no one like that, apart from Alec, for twenty years. Hayden's mouth was different to her husband's; his lips were fuller, wider. He was clean-shaven and, as he dropped his mouth to her neck, Jess felt only smooth skin against hers. Alec was always stubbly. In the old days, he used to leave the flesh around her breasts and thighs mottled and sore.

In the tiny hotel room, her calves pressed against the bed, Hayden and Jess kissed slowly. His hands drifted from her waist to her arms, and then into Jess's hair. And then down again, under her T-shirt, inside her bra.

I haven't had too much to drink to be able to stop this, Jess thought once, wildly, as they threw aside the clothes and towels left on the bed from earlier. But again, the truth was she did not want to stop. She did not want Hayden to stop. She sighed softly as he pulled down her jeans and kissed her stomach, forgetting about the stretch marks, the lines that spoke of her children.

He asked, once, when they were naked and shiny with sweat, if she was sure. Jess replied by pulling him into her, deeper than they both expected. Hayden's eyes were closed as he moved above, and when they could hold back no longer, they were not so drunk that they were unable to say each other's names, over and over.

∽

Noise from Euston Road leading down to St Pancras and Kings Cross filtered into the room, even at that time of the morning. Cars and buses thundered by, a noisy gabble of drinkers screeched and shouted their way towards the tube. Jess lay on her side, Hayden curled behind her, both on top of the quilt despite the cold. Hayden's arm was slipped beneath her head; Jess pressed her face against his upper arm, the salt of his sweat on her lips. He murmured and cupped her close.

'What did you say?'

Hayden's voice was muffled, mouth in her hair. He sounded tired. 'I said there's a night club nearby. It will get even noisier later when it's throwing out time.'

Their legs were plaited together, Jess moving her feet down Hayden's shins. His chest was smooth, but hair started just below his navel. She turned and placed her face on his chest. His eyes were closed, and he yawned.

'Did we wear each other out?' Jess asked softly and touched his face.

Hayden's eyes opened, briefly. 'A little. Too much wine as well.' Then a thought seemed to cross his mind and he sat up, leaning on an elbow. 'Do you want me to leave?'

'What? No!' And Jess was up, too, easing along the headboard. 'Unless you want to?'

Hayden traced a finger down her ribcage, her flesh whitening in the cool air. 'I think that's unlikely. I am tired though. Not how your standard hot stud would behave, I know, but ...'

'Me too.' Jess pulled up the quilt. 'I'm cold.'

'Oh, I can do something about that.' Hayden ducked under the covers with her. And, although he had said he was tired, it was not long before the quilt became twisted again and kicked to the floor.

⁓

She was not sure how long the phone had been ringing before the sharp, tinny noise finally registered. Jess threw out an arm to the bedside table, scrabbling for the handset. Her eyes felt glued together and a dry, sour taste filled her mouth. She groaned.

Home flashed up on the phone. Groaning again, Jess flipped the handset and answered. 'Hi.'

'Morning!' It was Megan. The girl's high-pitched squeal reverberated around Jess's head and she grimaced.

'Hi baby. What time is it?'

'Almost eight o'clock! No one else is up yet. Dad's still in bed, so I thought I'd make him some toast and take it up.'

Jess heard plates being moved around. She imagined her daughter bouncing around the kitchen, smearing butter everywhere, toast crumbs ground into the rug beneath the dining table. 'That's kind of you.'

'I can't remember what he likes on it, though.' Megan sounded breathless, and she now appeared to be opening and closing cupboards. 'Marmite? Jam? Or is it peanut butter?'

'Just jam.'

'Okay, there's some raspberry here. That will do. When are you coming home?'

Jess pinched the bridge of her nose. Outside a lorry started to screech, signalling it was about to reverse.

'Mum?'

'Oh, later on. This afternoon, probably.'

'Aw.' Megan was licking her lips. 'Be back in time for *Dr Who*, though, won't you?'

'Of course.' Next to her, Hayden stirred.

'What was that?' A door opened in their kitchen and Megan squealed again. 'Dad! I was going to surprise you!'

Jess sat up quickly. Hayden's arm lay heavily across her thighs and she swung her legs over the side of the bed. Hayden sighed and pulled the duvet over his shoulders.

Jess walked into the tiny bathroom and shut the door. Down the phone she could hear Alec's low voice and the exchange of toast. Then he came on the line.

'Morning.'

'Hi.' Jess gripped the phone tightly. Her stomach began to hurt. 'How was your night?'

'All right.' Alec yawned. 'Finally prised James from his bed at four yesterday afternoon, only for him to be up all night watching the TV. So what are your plans?'

Hayden coughed in the room behind the closed bathroom door and Jess turned, bending over the phone and holding it close to her body. She tried to keep her voice calm.

'I need to head over to the library later. Still more to do.'

'Will you get a chance to go shopping?'

'Maybe.' Jess felt a pinch of tears. She'd forgotten about the plan to take some time for herself and Christmas presents. So much had been forgotten in the last twelve hours.

'Well, I could do with you back here, to be honest.' Alec was chewing Megan's toast. 'James is driving me round the twist, and Megan wants to go to Chloe's.'

'That's not a problem, is it?'

'I don't know where Chloe lives.'

Jess closed her eyes. 'Near the leisure centre. Megan knows where. Get Chloe's mum to text Megan the address.'

'If you're home, it makes it easier.'

A flare of anger now ignited in Jess's chest. She thought of all the times she had raced around with the kids at the weekend, dashing from sports class to friends, to home. If the Minstermen were playing at home, Alec disappeared off at noon, leaving her to it, only returning at teatime. 'It's not difficult. When do you ever have to look after the kids at the weekend, Alec?'

'What?' Alec cleared his throat. 'All the time! Last week I took James to Aaron's.'

'You dropped him off, and then Aaron's mum brought him home on Sunday afternoon. It's hardly the sort of running around that I do.'

'Oh yes, I'm getting above myself. I shouldn't try to compare myself to you.' The sarcasm in Alec's voice was unmistakable. There was a clatter as he put his plate down on the kitchen counter.

'Don't take that tone with me.' But Jess knew she was biting at a barb that wasn't really there. And that her frustration was not solely with Alec.

'Go shopping, Jess. Treat yourself. We'll see you when you get home.'

'Fine.' And Jess said this last just as Alec hung up. She stared at the phone, shivering, her insides twisted. *Why shouldn't I have some time to myself? I get little help at home as it is. I deserve a treat now and then.*

And then Hayden coughed again, and the momentary anger Jess felt evaporated. It was replaced with a heavier feeling, a sense of unsettlement. She leant against the shower cubicle, a ticker tape of thought going round and round in her mind. *What a mistake. What a dreadful mistake I've made.* And then the thought was replaced with another: *Alec must never know. It would destroy us. Imagine how I would feel if it were him …*

Tears came then and, blindly, Jess reached out for the shower. Hot water blasted out, the room quickly filling with steam. She stepped under the water.

She did not hear the tap at the bathroom door but suddenly Hayden was beside her. He peeled back the sliding shower cubicle door and smiled sheepishly. His hair stood up in thick tufts. 'Morning.'

Jess wiped her face, hoping Hayden would think the water in her eyes was from the shower. She smiled back, just a little, conscious of her body.

Hayden stepped in behind her, dipping his head under the water. 'Headache?' He placed his hands on her shoulders.

'A bit.' Jess reached for the shower gel, turning away from him slightly. A small gap came between them, but there was not much room to move in the tiny space.

Hayden's eyes narrowed, and he held out his hand for the gel. 'You all right?'

'Yes.'

'No, you're not.'

'That was my husband on the phone.'

'Ah.' Hayden scrubbed the gel into his hair and then rinsed. 'Awkward.'

'You could say.' Jess looked down at their suds, mixing together, sliding down the plughole.

'Jess, I don't think you … no, this is impossible. Wait.' Hayden reached behind Jess's head and switched off the shower. He rattled the door open and grabbed towels for them both. 'I can't talk to you properly in here.'

They dried themselves and then perched on the edge of the bed. Jess held her towel primly around her body and, she knew, a little redundantly. *It's not like he hasn't seen it all.* But she could not let go of the towel. It was wrapped around her firmly, as snug as the elastic hold of the phone call from home.

'When Mum suggested we meet up, I remembered who you were instantly,' Hayden said. He sat naked and comfortable next to her, hair long and wild, towel in his hands. 'I used to look forward to the phone calls from Mum, asking me to pick you both up.'

'You did?' Jess shook her head, marvelling that she had barely remembered what Hayden looked like. *What different memories we have of that time,* she thought. *We see our past in a variety of ways.* And then she also thought of Marie, her insides cringing. *Marie would hate me if she knew.*

'So I was curious to see you again.' Hayden rubbed the towel over his hair. 'But it doesn't have to be more than a one night thing, if that's what you'd like.'

Jess sighed, insides pulled by both relief and annoyance. 'It sounds as though you've said that before.' She knew the instant she spoke that she was not being fair.

Hayden shrugged easily. 'Maybe. The same could be said of you. But I do like you. And I want to spend some time with you. I know, I know, your time is precious.' He held up his hands. 'I'd just like to see you again. Take you out. We had a good time, didn't we?'

And Jess had to nod. She could not remember the last time she had

laughed and drank like last night, and there was all the other stuff …
she bowed her head. Her back still ached from the pressure of Hayden
above her, from the rolling from side to side. Her thighs, too; Hayden
had not been the only one to take control, to guard the pace.

'It's up to you,' Hayden was saying. 'If you want to see me again, that's
great. If not—' That relaxed throw of his shoulders again. 'It was fun.
And I'm not one for idle talk.'

Jess looked at the sharp cut of his shoulder blades and the ropey, taut
shape of his arms. She imagined he had had plenty of women. Bound
to. But, at this moment, he was there with *her*. And his words; he wasn't
offering to fit her in, somewhere, when it suited him. Instead he was
there if—when—*she* wanted.

He should leave, Jess knew. Hayden should leave and she should
dress and go to the library and then catch an early train home. She
should pretend this had never happened.

Except, when her towel slipped, and Hayden eased it away, Jess did
not object. When he dropped to his knees, hands parting her thighs,
she lay back, arching towards the ceiling for him.

~ 5 ~

As Jess hurried from the train on Monday morning, she knew the professor would be waiting by her desk, and she was not wrong. Professor Waller was drumming his spidery fingers on the green, cushioned back of her chair, his impatience a tattoo of noise. Jess saw the bright blue of his trousers from the moment she stepped into the reading room; she had to pause, breathe deeply, and try to not think of Hayden. She set up a murmuring chant inside. *Do not let Waller annoy you. Do not let Waller annoy you.*

It had been a fraught Monday morning. Jess had arrived home late on the Sunday evening, just as the music to *Dr Who* had begun. Megan was sitting anxiously in the chair by the lounge window, peering through the curtains every few minutes, squinting into the streetlights and heavy rain as she looked for her mother. When Jess finally walked through the front door, the girl yelped and pulled her down onto the seat beside her.

'I thought you were going to miss it!' Megan clung to Jess, oblivious to her mother's damp coat.

James was sprawled along the sofa, Nintendo DS in hand, having been banned from the PlayStation. He cocked his head in a greeting and then returned to his game. A noise of plates being loaded into the dishwasher signalled Alec's place in the house, and his displeasure at Jess's late return.

Jess had nearly fallen asleep watching the television with Megan. A hangover lingered stubbornly at her temples, pressing against the thin skin in a rebuke. Hayden had finally left her hotel room at noon earlier that day, giving Jess only a couple of hours at the library. Jess had showered again before checking out. She had looked down at her body, tender in places, marvelling at the betrayal carried in its soft form. Her arms, wrapped for so long around Alec, wrapped around her children, had been thrown around another man, just moments ago. Her ankles, thankfully still thin despite the hefty weight of James and Megan, had locked with the ankles of another, heels stretching out on the sheets, toes pointing upwards. Jess stood for a long time under the hot water, mind shuttling around the glass doors, bleary with guilt and—yes—excitement.

There had been nothing else to find in the bishop's letters for 1899. Jess had forced herself to read through his correspondence, her head throbbing, and had to stop twice and stand outside the library to smoke a cigarette. Apart from the one cryptic letter to his sister, the bishop had not mentioned a trip to Greece, or referred to Josiah and Constance Underwood again. In fact his letters seemed strangely detached and not as detailed as before. He didn't refer to the church in Malta, or the parishioners. Rather, he commented on political matters and world events, and none of the letters were addressed. The envelopes also seemed to have been lost. Jess had sat back in her seat, tapping a pencil against her teeth, both wondering and trying not to let her mind wander. *I bet he feels this way*, and she meant the professor. There was something in letter, the note written by Anthony to Mabel, the bishop to his sister. It had hooked her. For the first time in a long time, Jess felt drawn in to the bishop's story, and to the nameless bag of bones found with his body.

The professor padded up and down beside Jess's desk, waiting for her to battle through the Monday commuters and reach the Shacklock Library. He cleared his throat as she came closer.

'Well?'

'Morning, Professor. Let me put my things down first?' Jess eased her sodden bag off her shoulder. The rain had been thick and unrelenting all night, and all morning. Jess moved awkwardly. Her feet were soaked, too. She wondered if it would be the done thing to remove her boots and socks and put them on the radiator in the staff room.

'What did you find? Have you the report?' Waller's face was pink with impatience.

'Well, I've done half of it—'

'Half! That's not good enough.'

'I worked hard on it—'

'I needed you to read through the whole papers for 1899. Otherwise it would have been a wasted journey.' The professor held out his hand for the print out of Jess's report. It was four pages long, the first three detailing the months of January to May. The last page outlined the bishop's letter to his sister, and Jess's speculative thoughts about what it might mean.

Taking off her wet coat, Jess watched the professor closely. It was not like her to comment on her findings. She was known in the library as the type of researcher whose skills lay in transcribing, rooting out missing manuscripts, tracking down texts referred to in obscure foot-notes, but presenting her findings only. Jess had finished the report on the train home, meaning to tidy it up again when she got back to home. But she had been too tired and had printed it out in a hurry that morn-ing. The comments and suggestions she made about the relevance of the bishop's odd letter were raw and unrefined. Probably riddled with spelling mistakes, too, she thought.

The professor was silent, reading through the document. One hand strayed absently to pluck at his beard. He pursed his mouth up as he reached the end, an image of thoughtfulness. 'You make an interesting case.'

Jess finally sat down. She had not realised till then just how tightly knotted her stomach had been. It had felt increasingly important, as the train sped home yesterday, for her findings in the British Library to mean something. She was not sure why it was so important. She had been on countless excursions to the library before, on another hunt for a name for the mysterious woman to whom her boss was so in thrall. This visit had been so different. She could not allow herself to think of Hayden right now, especially with Professor Waller staring at her so intently.

'I did read all the letters for that year,' Jess said eventually. 'There's nothing else. But, I don't know, I just think there's something.'

The professor nodded. 'It certainly poses a question. If Shacklock did go to Greece to see his friend Underwood—and this letter to his sister and the reference in the Synod papers suggest he did—well, he kept it secret, didn't he? Why? Could he have met someone over there?'

'A woman? And had a child? That's what I wondered.' Jess rubbed her wet feet together in an attempt to keep warm. 'The woman buried with him was in her late teens, wasn't she? The bishop was forty-five in

1899. He could easily have had a child with someone he met in Greece and the skeleton in his grave could be his daughter. The dates all fit.'

Professor Waller drew up an empty chair next to Jess. His face was animated now and Jess recognised the old familiar look, the light of interest that had creased the skin around his eyes so many times before. 'Jessica, what do we know about the Underwoods? These people that Bishop Shacklock refers to in his letter to his sister?' He turned and snapped his fingers towards another researcher sitting nearby. 'Butterfield—get me a *Life*.'

Jess tried not to smile at that but the double meaning to the professor's request would have been lost on him anyway. *The Life of Bishop Shacklock* was Professor Waller's baby. A detailed chronology of the bishop's life, it had been the professor's pet project almost as long as he had been searching for a name for the bones buried with the churchman. It charted the bishop's beginnings, his rise through the ministry, and recorded his many, many confrontations with those powerful in politics and in the Synod as he established a haven for the poor out in Jedthorpe. Half of *The Life* contained appendices, listing the bishop's friends and acquaintances, and giving an overview of their lives as well. Jess had had reason to look through the book frequently and privately thought it was an unwieldy, excruciatingly detailed work. She had yet to tell the professor that the book might have been better received and gone to a second print run had he slimmed it down. There was no need for the mountains of facts, and highways and byways cluttering its pages. No one needed to know who Shacklock's wet nurse and school teachers were, unless they were of relevance to his life and work. The professor, however, obsessed as he was, could not leave a scant detail unexposed or unaddressed. It was as though he wanted to capture the very essence of the bishop within the pages of his book.

Butterfield, a stocky man in his mid-thirties, who looked as though he would be more comfortable on a rugby field, appeared at the professor's shoulder with a copy of the book. He handed it over wordlessly, making it clear—to Jess, at least—that he did not appreciate the intrusion into his work. Jess rolled her eyes at him, a signal of solidarity.

Professor Waller thumbed the pages, slow in his purpose. He found the section on the Underwoods and sat back in his chair, reading aloud.

'*Josiah Underwood, 1852-1915. Early friend of Bishop Shacklock's,*

*fellow student at the Stephens Theology College. Third son of William
Underwood, resident of Threadstone Hall, Woking. Shacklock was known
to accompany Josiah on visits back to the hall during breaks between
semesters. Underwood and Shacklock were members of the Stephens
Theology College cross-country team: Shacklock is credited with saving
Josiah from near collapse on one race; he carried him for the better part
of a mile to safety when Underwood became ill and was unable to complete the course. Accounts of their contemporaries at Stephens refer to
them as great friends; however, their relationship deteriorated dramatically when Underwood met Constance Fowler (1851-1900), daughter of a
Woking baker. Underwood dropped out of the theology college and married Constance, to his family's and Shacklock's disapproval. Josiah and
Constance Underwood settled in Greece where Underwood worked as a
doctor. He does not appear to have had any contact with Shacklock after
leaving Stephens College in 1874.'*

The professor exhaled and looked up at Jess. 'Well, now. What you
have found seems to suggest that the Bishop and Underwood did have
contact after all.'

Jess nodded slowly. 'It looks that way.'

The professor placed the *Life* deliberately on the desk. He pushed the
fingertips of each hand close together, making the frame of a steeple.
Watching, Jess remembered Megan once attempting to play the child-
ish game of making a church from her own, fat toddler hands. 'Here's
the church, here's the steeple! Open the doors, and there's the people!'
Her podgy, undexterous fingers never quite managed it.

'What I can't believe is that we've not wondered about the Underwoods
and the Greek connection before,' the professor was saying.

*Maybe because you couldn't be bothered to read Shacklock's letters to
his sister.* Out loud, though, Jess said something else. 'Maybe you did,
back in the day.' She nodded towards the book on her desk. 'Maybe you
saw the reference to the Underwoods in Shacklock's letter to his sister,
but without evidence proving—or at least suggesting—that the bishop
went to Greece, you would have dismissed it. The letters from 1899
all point to him staying in Malta. Without that reference in the Synod
papers that I found last week, we would have carried on thinking that,
too, whatever his letter to his sister said. It was purely by chance that I
found the Synod paper, referencing a letter from Greece.'

Butterfield, sitting at an odd angle at his desk behind the professor, coughed loudly.

Professor Waller did not appear to have heard him. He was still tapping his fingertips together, mouth resting softly on them. 'We have an opening here. Something new to interrogate.' He suddenly dropped his hands to his knees and leant forward. 'Do you know, Jessica, how long I've been trying to find out who this woman is? Thirty years!'

'Yes.'

'And I'm nearly out of time. I'm due to retire in the summer. I can't stress how important it is that I finally give this woman an identity. It would be my crowning achievement.'

Butterfield set off another volley of coughs, almost bent double over his desk. The professor flicked him an annoyed look and then turned back to speak to Jess.

'So I want your full attention on this, Jessica. For the next six months. Set aside all the other bits and pieces you've been working on.'

'My research is more than bits and pieces.'

'Yes, yes. But when compared to this ...' Waller held out his hands expansively. 'And I will need you to take more trips to the British Library.'

Jess gritted her teeth and bit back the anger swelling within. She thought of her own research and all the papers she wanted to write, floating away from her like leaves on a river.

'I need full commitment,' Waller pressed. 'Where are the Underwood papers stored? Threadstone Hall? Butterfield?'

Butterfield, making a show of not listening but obviously taking in every word, agreed. 'Yes, but there's a good compendium to the papers here, in this library. I, ah, worked on the Underwood family for my doctorate.'

'Fine, whatever.' The professor swivelled back to face Jess. 'Talk to Butterfield. Read through what you can here. Clear all other research off your desk for the foreseeable future. I would like a report by the end of the day.'

'About the Underwoods?'

'Yes. And what they did in Greece. Who their friends were. Who was in their circle. Get a list of names, Jessica. Women the bishop may have met.'

'Right.' Jess idly wondered when would be the appropriate point to slap Waller around the face. An ache started to throb at her temple and she felt as though she were on the edge of a precipice. On one side lay Waller and the bag of bones; on the other lay her own interests and work. 'I have to take my daughter to a dentist appointment at eleven. I told you last week.'

The professor stood up, snapping his head left and right, looking around the library. Jess knew his mind had moved on already, to another part of the puzzle. 'Can't she go by herself?'

Jess shook her head and felt the headache start to pinch. 'She's eleven. Not really.'

The professor sighed and then Jess finally felt the anger connect to the rest of her body. She stood up as well, her head almost at the professor's shoulder. She could see egg yolk on his jacket collar and frayed cotton on his neckline. This man needs a good kick up the arse, she thought, not for the first time. The image of hectic weekends crowded her mind; jostling reports and hours in front of the computer with gym classes and football matches. And for the next six months! She crossed her arms.

'You know, you haven't asked if I'm able to give up my weekends. You haven't asked if I mind being away from my family or putting my own work on hold to do this for you.' Her voice trembled more than she liked, but it held in the quiet room.

The professor was looking in the distance, towards the end of the stacks. Jess couldn't tell if he was deliberately ignoring her or just 'throwing a deaf one', as Alec said about James. Her fury deepened.

'Are you listening? You sit here and tell me how you want all this commitment, and you can't even do me the courtesy of looking at me!'

The professor did look round at her then and the shock was clear in his face. 'I ... of course ... look, I understand about your family—'

'Do you? Well, good.' And then Jess felt redundant and a little foolish. She glanced over the professor's shoulder, to Butterfield's desk, where the researcher was sitting silently, listening. 'That's good,' she repeated flatly. She dropped her arms to her side. The professor watched her closely, uncertainty and then relief crossing his brow in waves. Sensing that the moment was over, he nodded curtly, and stalked off to the other end of the library.

Butterfield, from his desk, offered a slow handclap. Jess bit her lip and then grabbed her bag. She rummaged around for the pack of cigarettes and, to Butterfield's continued rhythmic patter, headed for the door. But not before she stopped to flick the younger man the middle finger.

∽

Butterfield was bent over his work when Jess returned. She had stood outside the library for a time, smoking, for once not caring who saw her. Her hand shook around the cigarette, body rippling with the sensation that a monumental decision would have to be made. For the past six years she had repressed her own anger at Waller, deflecting it with muttered comments and bitching sessions with Marie. But still Jess had done the work, finding papers for Waller, writing reports, pushing aside her work and research. Her papers on early women in the church went half-written, locked away in drawers or languishing on her laptop. She continued to ask herself why she did it, why she allowed Waller to control her time at the library. He rarely showed gratitude and there was no prospect of progression.

But the truth was that Jess felt fortunate to have the job at the Shacklock; there were students on her course who had been forced to give up their plans to work in an archive and find employment elsewhere. Even Marie had tried to find a position for a brief while. Jess knew some of her old classmates looked at her enviously. She also came from stock not long out of the mines and mills; periods of unemployment were not uncommon when she was growing up and, as a child, she became used to wearing clothes until they became threadbare. It was not a time Jess thought of often but she carried forward a horror of the same difficulties facing her own children. If she were to quit the library, they would manage on Alec's wage, but the treats, the PlayStation, the gym classes would go.

Jess finished the cigarette, thinking hard. A new option had emerged in recent days, providing a glimmer of hope: Waller would retire soon. Jess crushed the cigarette end under her heel, staring down at the wet pavement, rainbows of oil forming on the shiny surface. She only had to stick it out for another six months. She wiped her damp face and walked back inside.

From the exaggerated way with which he traced the words on an open book, Jess knew Butterfield was aware of her presence. She walked up to his desk and stood beside it. 'It's Billy, isn't it?'

The researcher pushed the book away slowly and looked up. His face was as round as his body was squat, shirt straining across his chest. He carried the memory of a fitter man in his frame. 'Unfortunately it is. I had careless parents. Billy Butterfield. Not William. You can imagine what it was like at school.'

'Right.' Jess moved back to her own desk and pulled her chair over. 'Do you mind me interrupting? You said something about a book on the Underwoods.'

'Yes. *The Underwoods of Threadstone Hall*. It's my thesis. There was enough interest in the Underwoods at the time for the University Press to publish it.' Butterfield threw his pen down. 'For all it did me.'

Jess smiled in wry agreement. 'Understood. So I don't want to keep you from your work. No need for Waller's obsession to affect anyone else. But if you could help me, I'd be grateful.'

'I wondered if you'd ever speak up to him.' Butterfield considered her with narrow eyes. His eyelashes were pale, almost blonde, and faint acne brushed his cheeks. 'All this time he's had you running around like a mad hare, and you've never once told him where to stick it. I would have done, a long time ago.'

'Are you the sniggerer?' Jess suddenly recalled Friday afternoon, after she'd come back from lunch with Marie. Someone had laughed after the professor had tasked her with the trip to London.

Butterfield beamed. 'That's me. I've been praying for the day when you'd actually say out loud what you mutter. You nearly did today.'

Jess sighed. Somewhere in the library the professor was barking at another researcher. She wanted this moment over with as quickly as possible. 'The Underwoods?'

'Right.' Butterfield turned back to his notes and flicked through his pad. 'Quite a family. Influential in so many areas. Josiah was a doctor. Try pages seventy-one to seventy-three. That section deals with Josiah's time in Greece.'

Jess raised her eyebrows. 'You have an accurate memory.'

Butterfield stared at her. 'I spent three years of my life on that family.'

Jess stood up, thanked the researcher, and pushed her chair back to her own desk. As she did, so she wondered what it must be like to be Billy, to research a subject exhaustively and then move on, leaving that project behind. She hurried her step into the stacks, thinking forward to the summer after Waller had retired, when there was a faint glimmer of hope that she would be able to do the same.

As with most documents and texts in the Shacklock Library, the book was not in the place it should be, but Jess found it fairly quickly on a shelf nearby. *The Underwoods of Threadstone Hall* was a slim volume and, as she flicked through the pages, she realised with relief that there were no appendices, unlike Waller's mammoth *Life of Bishop Shacklock*. The Underwood's story was instead contained neatly within the two hundred pages or so. Jess took it back to her desk, made herself a coffee and sat with it, turning the pages.

By the time Jess had to stop and go and meet Megan, she had a list of five names, of female patients and friends that Josiah Underwood had been in contact with during his time in Greece. The book referred to other Underwood family members and the section on Josiah's generation was brief. It revealed he had made a home with Constance in Piraeus, Greece, in 1875, the year after they married, and they returned to England after the death of Josiah's father in 1900. They had one son, Edward. Jess jotted the name down as well, for future reference.

Megan's trip to the dentist was over quickly, being only to check the growth of teeth in her cramped little mouth. Jess made another appointment for three months' time and then dropped her daughter back at school. She was back at the Shacklock Library just after lunch. She glared at Professor Waller's hunched shoulders, bent over papers in his office, and ate a sandwich at her desk.

Butterfield was sighing over his work when Jess pulled up her chair again and presented him with her list. 'Here. Women who Josiah Underwood knew in Greece, who might have met the Bishop. I got them from your book. Nicely written, by the way. Not too fussy or overly academic.'

If she intended flattery, her words had a positive effect. Butterfield smiled and seemed to shed a layer. He lay down his pen on the desk carefully this time and looked over Jess's note.

'Ah. I'm afraid that isn't much of a list. Three of them were invalids and would have been unable to bear a child. The other two were elderly.'

'Oh.' Jess felt deflated. She imagined another light along the path towards identifying the woman's skeleton being snuffed out. 'What do you suggest now? Should I go to the Underwood's family home at Threadstone Hall? Look at the archive there?'

Butterfield answered slowly. 'I think so. Seems the most sensible thing to do. If anything, you could read Josiah's letters from 1899. He kept in touch with his brother after leaving England. Josiah doesn't mention the bishop in his letters to his brother, I'm almost positive, but there might be something in them. Something cryptic—remember, we've always thought that Josiah and Shacklock never spoke again after Underwood left the theology college. Josiah can't have referred to him openly in his correspondence. I would have noticed it when I did my doctorate. Professor Waller would have known.'

'It must have been a secret meeting then, between Shacklock and Underwood?'

'If they did meet at all.' Butterfield paused. 'You know, it wasn't just luck that made you find that Synod reference to Shacklock's letter supposedly sent from Greece. I heard you putting yourself down in front of the professor. It wasn't luck—you're like a terrier in the archive.'

'Is that a compliment?'

'It is.' Butterfield raised his eyebrows. 'Unusual? Don't reduce what you do. Don't make it small, especially in front of Waller. He doesn't value you enough as it is.'

Jess looked at Butterfield curiously. *What's with his sudden interest?* The memory of Hayden's touch and his firm direction in the bar on Saturday night flitted back into her mind's eye. His interest had shocked her, too. She stood up abruptly.

'Threadstone Hall, then. Must be worth a visit. Where is it?'

'Woking. About an hour from central London. You could be there and back in a day.'

'Thanks.' Jess began to walk away, fighting to make some order of the collision of her thoughts. It had been too difficult to think of Hayden on Sunday night—it had been noisy at home, and Alec was too visceral, too angry. She had been exhausted, as well, and fell asleep quickly. The train that morning had been surprisingly quiet, and she had tried to doze. And Waller had infuriated her, providing another, welcome distraction. Jess had embraced the feelings of anger he prompted, returning to them again and again as she took Megan to the dentist, burying herself in academic frustration when Hayden's memory threatened a return. He was too difficult, too unguarded, too *loose* to think about.

'Wait. Can I ask you something?' Butterfield again. His question pulled Jess back to his desk, and he motioned to her chair again. 'Please? I'll make us a cuppa.'

And Butterfield was up and off, trotting over to the small kitchen where researchers stored their lunches and milk. An urn of hot water stood in the corner and Butterfield was soon back, two mugs of watery tea in hand.

Jess accepted hers and took a sip. 'What do you want to know?'

'About these bones. The ones that have driven our dear professor crackers for the last thirty years.'

'You don't know anything about the Cuckoo?'

Butterfield smiled. 'Only that she was found on top of the bishop's coffin in France when he was exhumed.'

'That's right. Wrapped in canvas. Heavy duty kind of cloth, like you'd expect the army to use. Or so the record says. The canvas has been lost.'

'It seems very strange for a woman to be buried like that. When did the bishop die? 1917? Before the war ended, anyway.'

Jess blinked her agreement over the mug of tea. '1917. The bishop was well travelled, but spent the last year of his life working in a hospital for recovering soldiers in a little French town called Villers-des-Champs east of Amiens. Most of that area was decimated in the war. It was a stroke of luck that Villers was far enough away from the fighting and the cemetery the bishop was in was untouched.'

'Otherwise you would have never have known another person had been buried with him.'

'Quite.' Jess said this sourly, thinking of both the unsavoury image of the destruction of a cemetery, and the possibility of never being involved in the long hunt for the woman's identity.

'So have you looked at an army connection? Given the canvas the woman was wrapped in?'

'Yep.' Jess placed her mug on Butterfield's desk and prepared herself to give the long list of archives she had exhausted in an effort to give the woman a name. 'The woman must have been buried between 1917 and 1919—either at the same time as the bishop's death or soon after, and before he was exhumed. There were no female soldiers during that time, of course, though there were nurses in a hospital at Villers, working as part of the Voluntary Aid Detachment. Some local women worked there, too.'

'Could the woman have been a nurse?'

'Possible, but there's nothing in the archive. The nurses were all registered with the VAD authorities before they left for France and they all returned. Waller had me recheck the records, though he'd looked there, years ago. And we don't think the woman was a local woman, either, from Villers. Researchers over the last thirty years have been out to Villers to check the parish records for any a suggestion that the woman was a villager. Nothing. Everyone accounted for, as far as possible. We simply do not know who this woman is, and how on Earth she ended up being buried with the bishop.'

Butterfield was shaking his head, but his eyes were gleaming. Jess could see he had been hooked. His hands had become still, the tips of his fingers pink around the hot cup. Jess had to begrudgingly accept that it was not difficult for young, green researchers to become swallowed up by the mystery.

'So where is the woman now?' Butterfield was asking. 'What happened to her?'

'Well, it was quite a shock for Shacklock's supporters, as you can imagine.' Jess remembered the letters she'd read, describing the find. 'They'd travelled from Maryland to retrieve him—without the knowledge of the Jedthorpe Synod but with the support of Shacklock's congregation. A rector led the group and paid a gang of young boys from the town to help with the dig. Several of those present when the grave was opened recorded later that they fainted.'

'I should think so,' Butterfield said dryly.

'The woman was reburied quickly, in the churchyard at Villers-des-Champs. The rector had the foresight to remove a finger bone. It was taken back to Jedthorpe as proof of what they'd discovered.'

Butterfield sighed.

'I know.' Jess paused. 'It's wrong, isn't it? To disturb this poor woman and then take a part of her body, like a trophy. But that's what they did. And the professor was able to order some tests in the eighties, to determine her age at death.'

'She was young?'

'Late teens or early twenties. Until the tests revealed the familial link, there was all kind of speculation as to who she was. Lover, friend, one of those crazies who followed churchmen from place to place. Then DNA tests on the bones revealed she was most likely his child. They'd compared her DNA with the bishop's, from hairs on his hairbrush, you see. But we're no closer to finding out who she was, or her name and her story.'

'She must have been buried there in secret.'

Jess picked her mug back up and drank again. 'Definitely. And that makes me think she was buried during the war, and that she died soon after the bishop, or even at the same time. It's possible that the villagers might not have noticed a grave had been disturbed—they'd have had other concerns, after all. Their menfolk away at war, for one. I can't imagine it would have been difficult to take a body up to the cemetery, in the middle of the night, without anyone seeing.'

'So no local records, nothing in the bishop's papers, nothing in any other archives. I can see why the professor has spent so long on it.' Butterfield turned back to his laptop. 'It could be anyone.'

Jess finished her drink and stood up slowly. Despite the tea, she was cold again. 'It could indeed. Right, I'm going to look at train timetables down to Woking. And work out what I'm going to say to my husband. I've only just got back from London.'

Butterfield also stood and gathered the mugs together. 'If you find anything, let me know. I haven't been to Threadstone for a few years, but I can find my way around.'

'Sure.' Jess pushed her chair back to her desk. The last thing she felt like doing was dragging another researcher with her, disturbing some-one else's work. But Butterfield seemed interested and, Jess told herself, he might help. It might even speed up the research and free her from Waller a little earlier.

~ 6 ~

The train home was back to its normal crush, and Jess had to squeeze alongside other commuters on the journey from Jedthorpe to the outskirts of York where she lived. There were many stops along the way and Jess was jostled against men in suits and women in sharply tailored jackets. Some smiled benignly as the train lurched from side to side; others tutted and clicked their tongues as passenger knocked into passenger. Jess stared at the emergency alarm, trying to block out the uncomfortable squash and the cold blast of air funnelling down the carriage every time the doors opened. She tried to focus elsewhere, reining her mind away from Hayden, forcing herself to think of the nameless bones found on the bishop's coffin. As a suited man's thick thigh crammed against her side, Jess wondered again if the woman's final resting place was of her choosing. She had been lain on top of a man, presumably for all eternity, and maybe that was not what she had wanted.

A feeling close to sympathy for the woman was beginning to creep alongside these thoughts when suddenly Jess's phone went in her pocket. A text message, vibrating. She fumbled for it.

It was from Hayden. *Hope you got home safe and sound. I had a great time. If ever you are in London again, let me know. Mum would never forgive me if I don't take you out again.*

Jess read it three times and then put the phone back in her pocket. It was an innocuous text and, Jess suspected, deliberately so. If Alec were to see it, he would think nothing. *Hayden mentions his mother, for goodness sake!* It was rather clever of him.

But he'd got in touch. A smile formed and Jess could not help it. For the first time since leaving the hotel on Sunday morning, she allowed herself to think back to the weekend. They had not moved far from the bed but, given the smallness of the room, it was not so odd. After their shower, after their legs had tangled again beneath the sheets, Hayden had made coffee. The complimentary packets of instant powder were stale, but that did not matter. They sat next to each other, bare arms pressed together, hair still wet from the shower, leaving damp patches on the headboard. She couldn't remember much of what they had talked about. Hayden had mentioned the football match he was missing; he had laughed and said staying in the hotel with Jess was a much better option. Gallant, unadventurous words, which felt appropriate. The audacity of their coupling was enough for Jess. On that morning, she could not have coped with exciting conversation as well. They had talked a little about bars, restaurants, the cinema. Alec, James, Megan, Marie, the nameless, faceless ex-girlfriend—they did not exist in that Kings Cross hotel room. Jess felt like a different person. After they had finished their coffee, she had taken Hayden's cup from his hand, thrown back the sheets, sat astride him and placed his hands on her breasts. He had responded and Jess's memory of Alec's taut face in the bathroom at home, just two nights ago, when she had done the same to him, drifted away.

Crammed into the train, her smile was impossible to contain and a tall man wearing a brown duffel coat looked down at Jess. He had smiled back bemused and cocked his head. *Share the joke*, his eyes said. But Jess turned away, hot and pink, waiting for the train to stop.

James was making tea when she arrived home. Jess put down her bag on the sofa and listened to the crash of plates and saucepans. 'What's this?'

Alec, sitting with the television remote in hand, face tired, explained. 'Christmas party. Over-sixteens only, but Aaron's brother has said he can get them both tickets.'

'Ah,' said Jess, understanding. She moved carefully into the room, feet wet again. 'Feathering the nest so we'll say yes?'

'Something like that.' Alec moved up the sofa, making room. 'Megan will he home later. Chess practice.'

'Good day?' Jess spoke cautiously. She could see no signs of anger in her husband. The lines that had creased his forehead last night had disappeared and now he looked at her directly when she spoke.

'Usual. You?'

Jess sat down next to him. She could smell the wood spice aftershave Megan had given him for his birthday. His collar was open. She rolled her palms together, wondering how to frame her news. 'I've got to go to Woking tomorrow. Not overnight, but I'll be home late.'

Alec turned away from the television to face her. 'You have to?'

'Yes. Waller, he needs me to go.'

'But it has to be you? No one else can go?' Alec cleared his throat, his skin moving up and down. He had been running his hands through his hair and, in the light of the streetlamps blazing through the open curtains, he seemed to have more grey. The glare of a passing car picked out the check on the curtains, making the white whiter and the black blacker.

'It has to be me, I'm afraid. The professor wants me to go to an archive in Woking where they've got some papers. The Cuckoo again.'

'Again,' Alec repeated. 'You realise you've only just got back from London?'

'I realise, of course I do.' Jess was irritated. Alec was speaking slowly, as he did when annoyed. Over the years it had begun to grate on her nerves. 'As I said, I won't be stopping overnight.'

'But you'll be back late.'

'Right.'

Alec suddenly blew out a noisy gust of air. 'Fine. I can't be bothered to fight about it.' He looked down at the remote and flicked the channel over. Jess waited, wanting to move, but not sure to where. She finally reached out for her husband's hand. The skin was rough and his nails were brutally short. Alec had always bitten his nails. When they first got together, he let Jess paint her 'Stop and Grow' polish on them in an attempt to kick the habit. Jess touched Alec's fingertips, turning his hand over in hers. 'I can do a casserole and leave it in the fridge for tomorrow night.'

'We'll manage.' Alec squeezed Jess's hand briefly before dropping it and repositioning on the sofa. He had released her, that much was clear. The gap between them on the sofa, between Alec's thin legs and narrow hips and Jess's smaller frame, seemed to widen with chintzy indifference. Jess had felt it more and more in recent weeks; a tipping away from her, the way a book falls apart from the others on a shelf.

After a few minutes of silence, Jess got up and walked into the kitchen to find her son frowning over a bubbling saucepan of beans. 'Making dinner?'

James grunted. 'Beans on toast. Should I save Megan some?'

Jess thought of Megan's face upon being presented with a plate of cold beans and toast. 'Don't worry. I'll make her something when she comes in. Thanks for doing this though. Want me to butter the toast?'

She moved to a pile of bread, some barely brown, others blackened, and started buttering. Next to her James stirred, scraping a metal spoon over the bottom of the non-stick pan. Jess resisted the urge to tell him to stop.

'Mum?'

'Yes?'

James opened and closed his mouth, hunting for the right words. He did not have the patience to pick the right moment, to make the right play. Jess knew what he was about to say. 'There's this party, right, and Aaron's brother can get tickets. Over-sixteens, but I look sixteen, don't I? Anyway—'

'James, let's talk later, shall we? After you've done your homework. I'll put these on the table.' Jess walked away with the toast, ignoring James's tuts. She felt guilty, however, for cutting him off. She knew she had only done so because of how Alec had been earlier. She had done so to redress the balance.

They ate in silence, made more apparent by Megan's absence. Marie texted during tea and Jess, forgetting her rule of no phones at the table, read it. *Hayden said he saw you and you had dinner. Hope it brightened up the weekend! Am away next week—meet on Thursday for coffee?*

Jess laid the phone down on the table again. Her appetite had disappeared, and she put her knife and fork on the side of the plate. She took cover in Alec's sympathetic look, who was himself forcing down the burnt beans and chewy toast. James was pushing his own meal around his plate.

'Need a lift to Aaron's tonight?' Jess asked. James's glum expression had not gone unnoticed, and an idea was forming in her mind.

'Yeah, could do.' James became animated again and shovelled in a forkful of beans. Jess watched her son reassess his chances of going to the party.

James took a bag of homework with him and, leaving Alec to load the dishwasher, tea towel draped over his shoulder, Jess led James out to the car. Parked on the driveway since Alec came home, it was already covered with frost. Jess rummaged around in the glove compartment for a scraper and then gave up, using a credit card instead.

James gave her a quick kiss outside Aaron's house. Although only mid-November, Aaron's mother had the Christmas decorations up. Jess shuddered. She had tried not to think about Christmas, with the torment of finding the right present for her children and her mother.

It was almost freezing, but Jess drove the car around to a side street, not far from Aaron's house and parked up. She got out and lit a cigarette, the smoke indistinguishable from the clouds of warm air leaving her body. As the cigarette burned, she extracted her phone and looked through her contacts.

She found his number. Pressed the screen and waited.

'Hello?'

'Hayden? It's Jess.'

A sigh, but not unhappy. 'I wondered if you'd call. Is it awkward for you?'

'Not especially.' Jess shivered in the cold, trying to keep the chatter out of her voice. Someone in a house opposite drew the curtains together in an upstairs room. 'I've just dropped my son off at his friend's house.'

'Did you get home okay yesterday?'

'Fine. Bit late though, by the time I left the library.'

'You didn't get as much time there as you'd hoped, did you? Should I apologise?'

Jess blew out a gust of smoke. She knew that he was joking, but she did not feel like laughing. 'No. Never.'

There was a pause. It was an oddly emphatic word to choose—*never*. It was the rougher, harsher opposite of 'forever', which was, of course, a word to join lovers or those *in* love. *'Never' sets us, Hayden and I, at a different angle*, Jess thought. 'Never' was a word that pointed to a back-to-front kind of union. Something permanent was framed, paradoxically, in a kind of denial.

And then Hayden spoke, his voice equally serious. 'Good.' Music played in the background. 'When are you coming down here again?'

Not *do you have any plans to come down here?* Jess noted. The openness of Hayden's want for her was thrilling. 'Actually ... tomorrow.'

'Tomorrow!' And then Hayden did laugh. His was a forceful, shouting kind of hoot. 'Tomorrow?'

'I've got to go to Woking. To Threadstone Hall. Do you know it?'

'No. More research?'

'Yes. There's a train that gets into Woking at nine-thirty tomorrow morning. The hall is about a mile away from the station.'

'What time do you have to be back?'

'Tomorrow night. I've said I'll be back late.'

An unspoken understanding passed between them and Jess waited. She suddenly felt foolish, wondering what on Earth she was doing. A married mother of forty-one, standing in the cold street smoking a furtive cigarette, talking on the phone to her lover. Her younger lover. *Who am I kidding? Not my lover. Just my one-night-stand.* And Jess both feared and hoped that was true. She knew what her mother would make of it all. *She'd say I need to be sectioned.* As for Alec, she could not bear to think of him. Instead she felt embarrassed for him, married to a woman prepared to make a spectacle of herself. If Megan ever behaved like I have, Jess thought, I would die of shame.

'It's probably not a good idea,' she started to say, wanting now to back away. But then Hayden interrupted her.

'No, it could work. You'd need to research in the morning, right?'

'Yes. At least until one o'clock.'

'I have a meeting until two. I could meet you at three.'

'You don't need to check with anyone at work? You can just leave?'

Hayden paused and when he spoke again, Jess heard the smile in his voice. 'I don't need to check. What time is your train home?'

'There's one at seven. It's get me back to York at about half-past ten.'

'Is that too late?'

Now is the time, a voice screamed inside. Now is the time to say yes, too late, too much, and end the call. *I could just hang up on him.* But Jess could not. Instead she nodded into the phone and took another drag on the cigarette. 'It's not too late.'

'Good. Tomorrow, then. Meet you at Woking station?'

'Yes. Tomorrow.'

And Jess pressed the call-end button on her phone before she could change her mind. She stared at the screen. Hayden's number didn't have a face next to it, unlike the others in her contact list. She wondered what he'd say if she asked for a photograph.

The cigarette had burned down to her fingers, and she finally noticed.

She threw it out into the road, already shiny with ice, and remembered how she and Hayden had smoked outside the Chinese restaurant on Saturday night. She watched as the red light of the fag bounced once, then twice, and came to rest against the opposite pavement. It had dropped another couple of degrees and Jess shivered. But her hands felt sweaty and her coat hung about her shoulders like a suffocating blanket.

'What the hell am I doing?' she asked out loud. Her words hung smokily in the air, offering no response. Eventually she got back into the car and drove home.

✑

The taxi driver was right: it took just over ten minutes to drive from Woking station to Threadstone Hall. Jess was in the car at nine-thirty and, by quarter to the hour, the taxi was pulling up outside a smallish brown building on a busy street. Jess peered through the window. A square building stared back at her; the winter sun bounced off the windows on the second floor, seeming to blink down at the car.

'Is this it?' Jess asked the driver doubtfully.

'Yep. Threadstone Hall.'

'I expected it to be bigger.' Jess had imagined a house sitting at the end of a long, poplar-lined drive, with a landscaped garden and turrets at the rear. The tired little building set back only a few yards from Woking High Street was a disappointment.

'Six-fifty,' the driver said, pressing buttons on his meter.

Jess paid up, collected a receipt, and opened the car door. She looked up at the building. Four windows on the first floor, split in half by a wide front door. Four windows above. A pair of arched skylights suggested the attic had also been used by the Underwood family. The brickwork was pale brown and, at some point, had been covered with plaster. Jess was reminded of the pictures her children drew of houses when they were little—wobbly but compact. Unadventurous.

There were three steps leading up to the hall's green front door. Jess rang the bell and an elderly, dainty woman wearing glasses answered.

'Mrs Morris?' the woman asked. 'Professor Waller's assistant?'

'That's me.' Jess stepped inside where it was only slightly warmer.

She looked up and could see why it was so cold. Whereas the building looked nondescript from outside, the inside was ornate and imposing. There was no ceiling to the entrance hall; instead it stretched right up to the roof of the building, where another skylight, this one not visible from the street, threw down a sallow kind of hue. Jess squinted; the window appeared to be engraved with images of wood nymphs and goblins. Similar figures decorated four archways leading off from the hall, two on each side.

'I'm Barbara Newman, the curator. We don't get many researchers now. Only the occasional school trip.' The woman was well wrapped up, wearing a red gilet over a blue jumper, and a wool skirt with thick tights beneath. She extended a hand to a room on the right, through one of the archways just off the entrance hall. 'That's the reading room. It's warmer in there; I've moved a heater in.'

'That's very kind.' Jess rubbed her cold nose. Her bag was over her shoulder and she tried to remember if she had stuffed a cardigan alongside her notepad and pens.

The reading room was dark. A single desk stood against a narrow window opposite the door and a heater blasted out hot dry air on the floor nearby. The rest of the room was lined with books. Jess looked around, estimating that there must be at least a couple of thousand volumes crammed onto shelves. Most were the ruddy or gold coloured tomes she was used to seeing in country houses; there were a few recent publications on an end shelf.

'Researchers who have published work on the Underwoods send us copies,' Barbara Newman explained, noticing Jess's gaze. 'There was a flurry of interest in the eighties when the Pre-Raphaelites came back into fashion but, as I say, we don't get many researchers nowadays.'

Jess dropped her bag on the desk. 'I'm sorry, the Underwoods is not my area. The Underwoods were connected to the Pre-Raphaelites?'

'Not in a positive way. Old William Underwood who built this house was a fierce critic of the group. He wrote to the newspapers of the day, condemning their paintings as blasphemous. William also corresponded with Charles Dickens about the same issue—both took issue with Rossetti and Millais. The Underwood-Dickens link has interested researchers over the years.'

Jess thought of the carvings of sprites and goblins in the hallway. 'But what about those figures out there?' She motioned to the door. 'They seem to be part of the world of magic; it doesn't chime with someone concerned with blasphemy.'

Barbara nodded, smiling. Her teeth were mottled and filmy. 'If you mean the decorations around the archways and the skylight, you're right. They were a later addition. William was a tyrant in his family and not popular. When he died, one of his sons had them added. A sort of snub to his father, you could say.'

'I'm here to find out about one of William's sons.'

'There were three of them. Which one?'

'Josiah.'

'The youngest. William never forgave him when he gave up the church and married a baker's daughter.' Barbara moved over to the bookshelves, to the section where the newer books were kept. She ran her fingers along their spines and then pulled out a slim paperback. 'Here, take a look. There's an article in here about William Underwood and his criticism of the Pre-Raphaelite group, too. It might give you an idea of the flavour of the man.'

'Thank you.' Jess put the book down next to her bag carefully. 'I don't have much time today, and what I really need to do is to see what you have in your papers about Josiah's movements in 1899.'

'Aren't you here all day? We don't close until six.'

Jess hesitated. 'I have to leave by two-thirty. So, you see, if you have anything by Josiah around that time, I would appreciate it.'

Barbara considered, and then held up her hand in a silent request for Jess to wait. She left the room and Jess heard her open another door somewhere. After a few minutes she returned, holding a cardboard box containing a bundle of papers tied with a grubby white ribbon.

'One of the researchers from Jedthorpe helped to catalogue the Underwood papers a few years back. You may know him—Billy Butterfield? Unfortunate name. Anyway, he made it remarkably easy to find things. These are all the letters received by Josiah's brother, Charles, in 1899. He was the only one living at home with his father at that time. William died in 1900 and when he did, Charles added the carvings you saw outside. Josiah didn't write to his father, of course, but he did keep in touch with his brother. You may find some letters by Josiah in this lot.'

Barbara put the box down on the table and Jess peered inside. There were about fifty pages, all with different styles of handwriting.

'Thank you. I'll take a look.'

Barbara nodded and made as though about to leave. She paused, however, and came closer to the desk. 'You said that the Underwoods aren't your area. What are you looking for, then?'

Ah, where to start, Jess thought. 'Josiah Underwood was friends with someone I've been researching for a long time. Bishop Anthony Shacklock. I'm trying to find out if Josiah and Shacklock met up when Josiah was in Greece.'

'Josiah was there from 1875 till 1900. A long time. He returned to England after his father, died. Josiah brought his family to live here.'

'Is that so?'

'The whole family came back, even Josiah's grown-up son and daughter-in-law. It must have been strange for the younger Underwoods to come to a wet, cold place like this. Of course, they weren't children then, but still. Josiah's son and the son's wife had been born in Greece, I believe. I don't think Edward ever saw England as a child, though the daughter-in-law spent her school holidays in London.'

A thought tried to form in Jess's mind but, weak and milky in the fog, it would not come. 'Why was William so against Josiah marrying Constance Fowler?' she asked instead. 'She was the baker's daughter you mentioned, right? Surely he could have married her and completed his studies.'

Barbara laughed. 'Oh, you really should read more about the Underwoods. Constance had a child when she met Josiah. Illegitimate. She never said who the father was, but the baby was six months when they married. Old William nearly imploded.'

Jess's eyes widened and, again, an unformed thought appeared briefly and then disappeared. She wrestled with it impatiently, trying to give it shape. 'Did Josiah take the child on as his own?'

'He would have done, but the child died soon after they married. A girl. They were getting ready to leave for Greece when she caught measles.'

'Oh, how sad.'

Barbara shrugged. 'They were different times. And Constance and Josiah had a son, Edward, in Greece, so that must have been a comfort.

Well, I'll leave you to it, Mrs Morris. There's a bathroom just off the hall and my office is at the top of the first flight of stairs. Let me know if you need anything.'

Jess thanked her and eased her coat off. With the door shut, the room warmed up, just slightly. She pulled out her notepad and pens, and then her phone.

There were two texts. The first from Alec, asking if she wanted him to leave her out a plate of dinner and to say the car was due in the garage that weekend. Jess texted back to say she would get something to eat and that she'd remember about the car, wondering if she should end the message with a kiss. She did not. The second text was from Hayden.

Meeting cancelled. I can see you earlier if you are free.

Jess's stomach did a slow flip, and she pressed her fingertips down hard onto the phone's screen. She hadn't eaten that morning; the alarm had gone at five and she had walked to the station for the train down to Woking. Each morning she barked at her kids about breakfast, badgering them to eat, but today she was unable to follow her own advice. Now she had heartburn.

She looked at the box of papers again. Realistically it would take a whole day to read through them properly and make notes. Of course, the professor wanted a report again, but the laptop had become so slow that Jess had resorted to handwritten records. Even if she skimmed through half of the box, she would not read everything by noon.

She texted back. *Tempting but no. I have a lot to do. Meet at 3 as planned?*

The reply came within seconds. *No probs. See you then. Will have a* Times *under my arm.*

Jess snorted at that, the sound raspy and sharp in the room. Despite the heater, the room was still uncomfortably cool. Jess checked her watch and resolved to work for an hour, before asking Barbara Newman for a cup of tea.

The first letters of 1899 received by Charles Underwood, Josiah's brother, were from casual acquaintances of his, confirming arrangements to meet when they were in London. January of that year appeared to be a busy social time for the middle Underwood brother; he met with school friends, colleagues at the Skinner's Guild in the City, cousins down from Scotland. Jess quickly read through those, training her eye to look for a mention of Josiah's name, of which there was nothing.

After she had read through the January letters, Jess took the whole bundle out of the box. Impatience gnawed at her. She longed to be away from this room, from this desk and the yellowing manuscripts. She knew why she felt like that, of course, and pulled out her phone again to read Hayden's texts. It was half past ten. Four hours until she could leave for the station.

She put the phone away, forcing order upon her shuttling thoughts. She tried to remember the date the bishop had sent his letter to his sister, when he had mentioned receiving a letter from Josiah. She was almost sure the bishop had sent it in May of 1899, and he had been in Malta for a couple of months by then. Maybe Josiah heard his old friend was just across the water soon after he arrived, Jess wondered. Maybe Josiah wrote about it to his brother, though he must have referred to it cryptically—Professor Waller would have known about the reference, otherwise.

So Jess shuffled through the papers and found Charles Underwood's letters for March 1899. Again, there were notes from colleagues and friends, even a jeweller discussing a brooch he had ordered for his wife's birthday. And then, at the end of the month, Charles received a letter from Josiah. Jess read Josiah's writing quickly, pen in hand, ready to transcribe the letter onto her notepad.

'*... move onto another matter. I have heard that our old Corinthian is across the water, only a few hundred miles or so. This is the closest he has been for twenty-five years. I think I will write to him. Constance is still troubled by her back, but delights in our new daughter-in-law ...*'

Jess sat very still. Our old Corinthian? Did Josiah mean his old friend, Anthony Shacklock? She tried to remember the stories from Sunday School, all those years ago. Why Corinthian?

She stood up suddenly and scanned the bookshelves. There had to be a bible in this room, particularly given William Shacklock's religious fervour. She was right and found a copy, the paper binding crumbling in her hands as she held it.

Jess sat down again and turned to *1 Corinthians*. The only thing she could remember about the book from the Bible was its reference to men with long hair. *Did the bishop have long hair? He hardly seems the type.* Jess flicked through the pages. Then she found a reference that gave her pause.

Know ye not that they which run in a race run all, but one receiveth the prize? So run, that ye may obtain. And every man that striveth for the mastery is temperate in all things. Now they do it to obtain a corruptible crown; but we are incorruptible. I therefore so run, not as uncertainly; so fight I, not as one that beateth the air. But I keep under my body, and bring it into subjection: lest that by any means, when I have preached to others, I myself should be a castaway.

Jess read the verse again, her interest rising. She remembered the description of Josiah Underwood in Professor Waller's *Life of Bishop Shacklock*. Both Josiah and Shacklock had been cross-country runners during their time at the seminary. The bishop had even rescued Josiah during one race, when his friend had become ill. Jess also recalled how the pair had become estranged following Josiah's marriage to Constance Fowler. She wondered if Josiah described Shacklock, his old friend, as a Corinthian because of the biblical reference to self-restraint and control, the 'keeping under my body'. Shacklock had a habit of attaching monikers to people he came into contact with; maybe Josiah did the same thing?

Jess wrote furiously on her pad. The Corinthian mentioned so cryptically and fleetingly in Josiah's letter home to his brother Charles may well have been Shacklock. Jess wrote 'Corinthian=Shacklock?' three times, underscoring it purposefully.

It was easy to become animated now and Jess turned hurriedly to the papers, hunting for more of Josiah's letters. Now she knew his handwriting, it would be easy to spot his correspondence in the mass of papers.

She found another letter by Josiah in the bundle of papers received by Charles Underwood in June. She scanned it hurriedly, skimming past his references to the social scene in Greece and political developments. She found what she was looking for at the end of the letter.

'*... Our Corinthian arrives this week. I cannot quite believe it, but he is coming. Constance has been in bed for the past four days but resolves to get up and meet him. How we shall receive each other, I do not know, but we will surely find the words. And tell me of Father and his latest outrage? I read that a painting had been exhibited in the National, one to which he would surely object ...*'

Jess copied down the passage from Josiah's letter, her heart pounding.

She had a sense of catching a glimpse of something hidden in a corridor of mirrors. She flicked through the rest of the papers, looking closely.

There were two more letters from Josiah, one sent in August and the last sent in October. The first letter was a lengthy record of Josiah's thoughts about his father's reaction, were he to travel home to attend a memorial service for an aunt who had just died. As Jess read it, she could see that Josiah Underwood was obviously tormented; the yearning to come home was fervently expressed, but tempered by concern for Constance who continued to be unwell, and a wariness of how William might react upon seeing his son again after many years apart. The letter ended with a decision: Josiah would not travel to the service but would send a telegram, expressing his sorrow at his aunt's passing. He asked that Charles read it out during the service, acknowledging that even that might bring the rage of their father down upon his brother.

Although the August letter did not refer to the bishop, Jess read it all, welcoming the picture and sense it provided of Josiah. The letter was muted in tone compared to the previous ones Jess had read, and she started to feel a wave of sympathy for the man, detached and removed from his family simply because of the woman he married. She wondered why Bishop Shacklock had abandoned Josiah as well. William Underwood seemed a resolute, intransigent man and, if Barbara Newman was correct, he had been a bully and dominating presence in his sons' lives. But that was not the case for the bishop. Jess doodled on her pad. Although the bishop irritated her with his short-tempered, occasionally misinformed foray into local politics, he was an amusing correspondent. And Jess could not fail to see that he championed the dispossessed and vulnerable; many times he angered the Synod by going into the homes of his congregation, helping them clean, cooking their meals, tending to the sick. Shacklock did not hold with keeping the clergy distant from those to whom they preached. But why would a man as liberal and people-loving as the bishop turn against his friend simply for marrying, even if she did have an illegitimate child? Jess could not straighten out the quandary in her mind.

She checked her watch and saw it was almost eleven-thirty. She pulled out the last of Josiah's letters for 1899 and decided to read it before seeking out Barbara Newman.

The tone of this letter was different again. After spending six years

of reading the bishop's correspondence, Jess had become adept at deter-
mining the mood of the writer. In this last letter of 1899, written in the
October, Josiah Underwood had been furious. The letter was short and
compact, nothing like the meandering stream of thoughts penned when
he was trying to decide whether to travel home for his aunt's memorial.

'*I can barely believe what has happed. Allegra has left our house
without warning. She simply got up one morning, took one of our mules
and disappeared back to her father. There is no explanation, no reason.
Edward is devastated though, of course, he tries not to show it. Coming
so swiftly after the sudden departure of our Corinthian, called back to
Malta, it is a grievous blow. Constance has rarely left her bed and does
nothing but weep. I would try to get some sense from the girl but I am
afraid for what I might say. In all my years, I have never known the like.
Our old friend, Mrs Isobel Greene, has tried to talk to Allegra but has
been unsuccessful. Allegra simply refuses to explain her actions. If it were
in my power, I would send the girl home, to your house, where your excellent wife could reason with her. But I do not wield that sort of authority.
Her father is the major and idolises her. I understand he took her in without question. Thank goodness her own mother is not alive to witness this
disgrace. Perhaps, too, it is a good thing that our Corinthian has left. I can
imagine his words at such a family drama.*'

The letter ended curtly and Josiah had signed his name with an
extra flourish. Jess read the letter again, marvelling at the sudden turn
of events. A huge domestic upheaval had occurred. She transcribed
the letter onto her notepad, trying to work out who the characters in
the saga were. Barbara Newman had said that Edward was Josiah's son.
Could Allegra be the daughter-in-law?

The quickest way to work out the relevance of the letter and plot
the players on the Underwood family map she held in her mind was
to speak to Barbara Newman. Gathering up her notepad and pens, Jess
left the reading room, closing the door behind her in a vain attempt to
keep in the heat.

Barbara Newman had said her office was at the top of the stairs and
Jess found it easily. It was little more than a store cupboard, and Barbara
sat behind an oversized desk with the door open. Files and piles of paper
lined the walls and, balanced on top of these were several pot plants.
The effect was that the room felt even smaller, but not uncomfortably

so. And the room was warm. A coffee maker was balanced on one end of the desk.

Barbara looked up from her computer. 'Getting on all right?'

'Yes thanks.' Jess nodded to a chair. 'May I? I have some questions you might be able to help me with.'

Barbara waved her hand and turned back to her screen. 'Just give me a minute to finish this booking. Coffee's hot if you want one.'

Jess took a clean mug gratefully and helped herself. She looked around; a wall calendar covered the wall behind the desk though there weren't many dates filled in. Barbara mumbled to herself as she tapped away.

'Just grateful for any booking we can get,' she said, seeing Jess's curiosity. 'We used to have three or four school parties a week. And researchers fighting for space downstairs. Now the funding's been slashed, and we're lucky if we see a school or a researcher in a month.'

'I'm sorry.'

'Yes, it's a bugger. But it gives me time to catalogue and fill in endless applications for money.' Barbara pushed her glasses up and finally turned to face Jess properly. 'What can I help you with?'

Jess set her notepad down on the desk. 'I've found a letter from Josiah to his brother Charles. It was sent in October 1899. Let me read it to you.' Jess recited the letter she had transcribed downstairs. Barbara nodded slowly as she spoke.

'What do you want to know?'

'Well, who is Josiah talking about? The Corinthian, I've a suspicion about. But who is the Allegra who left the Underwood home so abruptly? I haven't studied the family, so I don't know who fits where.'

Barbara turned swiftly behind her and plucked a sheet of paper from the printer. She cleared a space in front of her and then jotted down names, adding lines between them. 'I don't know about the Corinthian, but here's a basic family tree. Josiah and Constance—parents. They had a son, Edward. Edward married Allegra Lucan, daughter of a major in the British army. They had one child, a girl.'

'So Allegra left Edward?'

Barbara shook her head. 'If she did, it must have only been briefly. They had their daughter just after a year of marriage, though I can't remember her name.'

Jess looked at the hastily drawn map and the letter on her notepad. 'The tone of Josiah's letter was one of anger.'

'Possibly. From what I recall, Allegra was twenty when she married Edward and was considered quite a catch. Josiah had to work hard to encourage the match. Allegra was an only child; her mother had died in childbirth. Her father was a retired army major, and he treated his daughter like a princess.'

'Didn't you say they all returned to England, though? Did Allegra come with them?'

'Yes. The marriage must have been back on by then. They all accompanied Josiah back to London, and Edward and Allegra's child was born shortly after. The whole lot of them settled here, for a time, at Threadstone Hall and Josiah opened up a private practice nearby. I believe that Edward and Allegra separated again, though, when their daughter was only a few years of age. Constance had also died by then; she was not strong.'

'Did Constance die in England or in Greece?'

'In Greece. Early 1900.'

'I see.' But Jess didn't really. She had thought she was onto something, picking up on Underwood's cryptic references to the bishop in his letters home. Again a thought tried to form at the edges of her mind, but would not press through. 'I think I should look at the letters from 1900, if I can. Anything you may have by Josiah. He must have talked to Charles about his plans to return to England. Maybe he mentioned the bishop as well.'

'It's certainly worth a look.' Barbara eased her chair back and tentatively edged her way around the desk. 'With all the spare time I have, you'd think I'd relocate to a bigger office.'

Jess offered a small smile and also stood up. It was not possible for Barbara to get past her while seated, so she went out onto the landing. Her watch told her it was midday. She wondered if Hayden was getting lunch.

'Is there a cafe round here?' she asked. 'I thought I could grab a sandwich while you're getting the papers.'

'Go out the main door and turn left. There's a Spar at the end of the road. Will you be long?'

'Ten minutes.'

'That's fine. I won't be any longer than that, but I'm going down into the basement and won't hear if you ring the doorbell to get back in.'

'Understood.' Jess followed Barbara down the stairs and back into the reading room. She collected her coat and bag and, checking her phone again, walked out into the damp November air.

There was not much of a selection in the shop just round the corner from Threadstone Hall, but by the time Jess stood in front of the fridge surveying the cellophane wrapped sausage rolls and soggy sandwiches she was starving. She took seconds to pick up a ham sandwich and a bottle of water and paid, silent whereas the assistant was chatty.

Jess stood in the street. Before she ate she needed a cigarette, so she moved some distance from the shop and leant against the railings to an office block. A few feet away a group of office workers stood together, smoking in the cold. She shared a rueful smile, the type smokers gave each other when forced by their habit from a warm room, and rummaged around in her handbag for a lighter.

In a few hours she would meet Hayden and she thought about the fact that she had taken a longer shower than normal that morning, and conditioned her hair, even though it didn't need it. Drawing on her cigarette, Jess realised just how easily Hayden had made a dent in her routine. He had even influenced the pattern of her family life: on Tuesday nights, Alec cooked a curry—a routine formed from the days when Jess was on her university course and would get home late after class. Today she had texted her husband to say she would arrange her own dinner, and for him not to save anything. *Is that cheating too?* Jess asked herself. *To let someone else, who has no right at all, to shape what my family does? Is it just as bad as what I've already done? What I think I still might do?*

She thought of her children. They would be fine without her for one evening, too. Both were old enough to come in from school on their own and fix a snack before Alec got home. But Jess still found herself shifting her feet uncomfortably on the street at the thought of James and Megan. She wondered what type of person she was becoming, acting in such a wilful way that might damage her family. She breathed deeply on her cigarette and took a slow walk back to the hall.

Barbara Newman was just coming up from the basement when Jess rang the doorbell. Barbara held another cardboard box of papers, lighter this time. She handed it over to Jess.

'That's everything Charles received in 1899. I don't expect there will be many letters from Josiah; he had moved back to London in 1900, remember. No reason for him to write to his brother when they were living together.'

'Thank you.' Jess peered into the box as she walked back to the reading room. Barbara was right; not as many manuscripts as before. It shouldn't take long to look through them all. She set them down on the table, eased off her coat and held her hands over the heater for a moment, before sitting down to work.

She found the first letter from Josiah almost immediately. Dated 16 January 1900, the letter briefly imparted the news that Constance had died.

'*My heartbeat,*' Josiah wrote, '*stopped at four o'clock this morning. We had some warning of what was ahead, and we were able to be with her when the time came. Edward is bereft, as am I. Allegra has been a great help, keeping visitors at bay and sending notices to the newspapers. We expect to bury Constance tomorrow. Perhaps, if Father is able to receive such news, you might tell him.*'

Jess copied out the letter, unable—as ever—to detach herself completely from the sadness of the archive. She had never been able to shrug off the emotion transmitted by such documents, despite the distance of many years. Sometimes she had come across references to the death of infants or young people in the bishop's papers; despite knowing this was an unfortunate reality for those times, Jess always grabbed her children when she arrived home on such days, squeezing out a tight reminder that her reality was so different. She transcribed Josiah's letter ruefully, noting his request that Charles inform their father of Constance's death; indeed, the death of the person who had become such an obstacle between father and son. Perhaps Josiah's reference to William being 'able to receive such news' suggests that William was also ill, Jess thought. He did die later that year, as Barbara Newman had said.

In fact, the next letter by Josiah, received by Charles in March 1900, discussed William's death. The old man appeared to have died from complications of gout; Josiah had been unable to contain his rather sardonic amusement at such a turn of events. Jess smiled as she read Josiah's words: *'that a man who preached abstinence in all areas of life was unable to restrain himself—was in fact* glutinous—*it is the definition of irony'*. The letter quickly moved onto Josiah's plans to return to London with his remaining family, Edward and Allegra, who was now almost eight months' pregnant. They were all to stay at Threadstone Hall with Josiah's brother. There was a discussion about the rooms they should take and Josiah's thoughts about opening up a surgery in the area.

The bishop was not mentioned again. Nor did his name appear in Josiah's last letter of 1900, sent just before the Underwoods sailed for England at the end of March. In his brief note, Josiah provided the name of their ship, when they were to arrive at Southampton, and the arrangements he had made for their possessions to follow on.

Jess sat back, deflated. Again, nothing. Again the bishop had slipped from view, and she had had such a strong sense of being on the edge of a discovery of some sort. But a lingering sense remained that the Underwoods and Shacklock were strongly connected. Jess could not explain why and was a little afraid that her feelings of certainty would bleed away if she interrogated them too much, but she felt positive that the identity of the unnamed woman buried with the bishop was contained somewhere in the web of Underwood relations. Professor Waller referred to this type of hunch as 'a sniff'. 'I've got a sniff of something in the Synod papers,' he had said recently, and sent Jess on a mission into the archive. Today, Jess felt as though she had 'a sniff' as well; the difference between her and the professor was that, unlike Waller, she had no idea where to go next.

She checked her phone. It had only taken half an hour to look through the letters of 1900 and there were still a couple of hours to go before meeting Hayden at the station. Jess knew if she did not keep herself busy between now and then, there was a strong chance she would back out of the meeting. If she did not bury herself in a box of papers or a textbook, Jess would text Hayden, cancel the whole thing, and get on an early train back home. Back to Alec. And the truth was, if she allowed herself a moment to admit it, was that Jess did not want to cancel. She wanted to see Hayden again; those hours in the hotel room at the weekend had lingered at the edges of her mind, even though she had done her best to avoid thinking about them. But, stubbornly, they took on a shadow form and hovered in the background, just as the figure of the bishop lingered, hung around, adding shade to her thoughts.

Jess collected the papers together again and put them back in the box. She thought briefly about asking Barbara Newman for the letters of 1901, but did not want to disturb her again. In truth, she did not expect the papers to tell her much, especially as Josiah and Charles lived together after April 1900 and had no need to correspond as in the past. So, instead, Jess moved over to the bookshelf where the recent publications were stored. She was not sure what she was looking for, but the sense that the Underwoods held the key to the mystery of the bag of bones buried with the bishop persisted. She picked up a couple of books, flicking through them in search of anything of relevance, and then found a slim volume of essays about the Underwood women.

Jess sat down again and looked at the contents page, feelings of surprise and embarrassment building. She had had no idea that the Underwood family were so well connected, despite the past six years researching the bishop's life. Josiah and Charles's father, William, was one of seven Underwood children, many of whom had made their way in some prestigious field or another. One brother had been a scientist; another became an MP. William himself corresponded with men of import and status, mostly about ecumenical matters. The book Jess held was a series of essays about the women in the family. William's younger sister became a pioneering nurse. A niece became a suffragette, much to the disapproval of her uncle. Then, unexpectedly, Jess found a short essay about Allegra, Josiah's daughter-in-law. She had been a Greek national born to English parents, and owned a theatre in Earls Court. Jess read on, intrigued, not sure where this fitted in but sure it had some kind of relevance.

The essay revealed that Allegra's father came from a long line of army officers. His brother had been part of the Household Cavalry and, as a child, Allegra sometimes stayed with her cousin in Hampstead. Allegra's own father had been commissioned into the army and had settled in Greece where his daughter was born. After her own marriage and the birth of her daughter, Allegra left Edward and sank her small inheritance—left to her by her father—into the purchase of a theatre. There was a photograph of her at the end of the essay—slim, delicate featured but with a fierce dimple in her chin, hair pinned into a bun.

Jess read the brief essay again and made a few notes. The feeling that a revelation was just within grasp nagged at her. She turned her writing pad over to a clean page and sketched out the few details of which she was certain.

1. Shacklock visits Josiah in June 1899. Leaves some time before October 1899.

2. Josiah's wife dies in January 1900. William Underwood dies in March 1900. Josiah and his family return to England April 1900.

Jess stared down at her jottings. There was more, she was sure, just beyond her reach. She carried on writing.

3. Edward Underwood marries Allegra, sometime before May 1899. Marriage in crisis October 1899.

And there it was. The link. Bishop Shacklock had left Greece just as Edward and Allegra's marriage floundered. By the time Allegra came to London in March 1900 she was, according to Josiah's letter to his brother, eight months' pregnant. She must have conceived in the summer of 1899.

Jess held her breath. Was Allegra the woman? Was she the mother of Shacklock's daughter, who would later come to be buried with the bishop? It was certainly possible, Jess allowed herself to admit. Josiah's letters made it very clear that the bishop had visited Greece, without the knowledge of the Synod who thought he spent that whole year in Malta; maybe he had an affair with Josiah's daughter-in-law, damaging her marriage.

A thrill ripped through Jess. She already knew that the bishop would have been in his late forties at the time the woman buried with him had been born. Allegra would have been around twenty, given the information from Barbara Newman. Quite an age difference, but still … Jess wrote out a sentence carefully. *Allegra and the bishop may have had an affair=child. Josiah didn't know? No hint in his letters. Did Edward Underwood know about the affair? Did he take the child on as his own anyway? Did the bishop know Allegra was pregnant before he left Greece?*

Jess imagined the professor's face when she presented her report. She hesitated, though, to pick up her mobile and phone the library. There was nothing concrete, no hard proof. No letters in the archive regarding Allegra and revealing details of a clandestine relationship, even assuming she would divulge such a scandal in a letter.

Jess tapped her pen on the paper, working out her next move to find supporting evidence. It was difficult to think clearly, her head swam. So much balanced on so little, her ideas were a house of cards. Jess thought hard. There must be some way to prove all of this, there must be something, somewhere, to add meat to the bones.

And then her phone beeped with a text message. Marie, again, asking again to arrange coffee the following week. *Don't pretend to be busy—I can smuggle you out for a latte. I won't even mention that you didn't get back to me yesterday. It's quite all right. Not really hurt.*

Jess looked at the message, uncomfortable. It wasn't like her to ignore a text from Marie, and she knew she could only pretend to forget or be too busy for so long. If she didn't reply, there was a danger that Marie would phone. Jess picked up the phone hurriedly. If Marie called that afternoon when she was with Hayden, it would be excruciating.

Sorry, have been busy. Lots of research for your favourite Prof. Coffee sounds good. Am free most of this week, if we meet for an hour or so. J xx

It was a light, ordinary text, the sort that Marie was quite used to. Except Jess's insides felt twisted and torn as she tapped it out. In just over an hour she would be packing up her work and heading to the train station to meet Marie's son and, after that, well, Jess could only guess.

She stood up quickly, a need to keep busy enveloping her. Except there was nothing more to read on the shelves, other than journal articles about the eminent menfolk of the Underwood family, and Jess could not bring herself to read those. Her resentment towards the Bishop and Professor and their dominating presence existed only just below the surface at the best of times.

So, instead, she pulled on her coat, packed away her notepad and pens and walked up the stairs to Barbara Newman's office. Barbara was screwing up her face at the computer screen.

'Everything all right?' she asked, looking up. 'Need anything?'

'I think I'm going to head off,' Jess said and wondered if her voice sounded as apologetic as she felt. 'I've found what I was looking for.'

'Good. If you do need to come back, you'd be welcome.'

'Thanks.' Jess waved a goodbye and then turned back down the stairs, leaving Barbara to mutter at her screen and poke the keyboard with a heavy hand. Jess let herself out, into the now drizzling rain. She thought she could remember the way to the station. She started to walk in that direction.

✑

Hayden had said his train would get in around three and Jess arrived a few minutes before. She had time to buy more cigarettes and visit the ladies, where she stared at herself in the mirror for a long moment, waiting for another person to slide out of her skin and confront her. *I'm Bad Jess*, she imagined this second self would say. *I'm the person you are becoming. I bet Alec wouldn't recognise you.*

Except, of course, that didn't happen, and Jess was nudged to one side by an impatient, harassed commuter waiting to use the sink. She apologised and then found her way back to the platform.

The 15.02 from Waterloo pulled in a minute later; men in suits and women trailing suitcases tumbled from the doors. There was much jostling. Jess stood back, against the wall, no desire to be amongst all those busy, harried people, with their desperate urge to get their business done and then return to the excitement of London life. She watched them mill past, trying to pick out a face.

And there he was, stepping down from the open doors. Hayden carried his coat over his arm and in the other held a briefcase. He wore a suit over a pale blue shirt, but no tie. He was one of the last off the train and the platform was clearing. Slowly, smiling, he walked over to Jess.

'Hi.'

'Hi.'

On the walk to the station Jess was not sure how this first meeting would go; would they embrace? Kiss? Would they look at each other, embarrassed, the cold glare of the station lights illuminating their folly?

None of those things happened. Instead, Hayden moved closer and, swinging his briefcase from one arm to the other, reached over and took Jess's hand. His fingers were warm against her cold skin. He squeezed gently. 'Let's go somewhere we can get a coffee. Somewhere dry.'

There was a cafe just outside the station, facing into the busy, throbbing street. They walked through the main doors and Hayden, hand moving up to the small of Jess's back, guided them in. The windows were steamy with condensation and the room was gloomy; the winter afternoon had drawn in and the cafe staff had yet to switch the lights on. Hayden and Jess sat at an empty table by the window, looking out at the commuters and taxis. Around them people sat alone, reading papers, tapping on phones, stirring mugs.

Jess undid her coat and eased it off, aware of her wet feet and damp hair. She had been foolish to walk all the way to the station, especially as she did not have an umbrella. However, she had felt propelled to do it. The idea of taking a taxi to the station felt somehow wrong. She'd tried to wring out the reason it had felt like such a bad thing as she walked; the closest she got to any kind of answer was that taking a taxi seemed far too certain, far too determined. Take a taxi to meet the man with whom she cheated on her husband just two days ago? Hurry towards him again? Jess had looked at her feet as she walked the street towards the station, knowing she was heading towards Hayden anyway, whether walking or riding in a car. Yet it rested easier to think she was drifting that way rather than hurtling along at thirty miles an hour.

Her socks were soaking now. Yet again her boots had leaked. She shuffled uncomfortably as Hayden ordered two coffees from the waitress. He turned back to face her, nodding towards the wet hair plastered against the sides of her face.

'Did you walk?'

'Yes. It wasn't too bad when I set off.'

The coffees came and Jess took a sip, teeth grinding against the bitter heat. Her hands circled the mug gratefully, and she stared down at the Formica table. She had no idea what to say.

And then Hayden's hand came snaking across the shiny surface and purposely pulled Jess's fingers from her mug. He entwined his hand with his. 'Relax,' he said. 'I don't know a single person in this room. Do you?'

Jess shook her head. 'Of course not. It's not that.'

'You can't believe you're here?'

'Yes.'

Hayden gave a brief smile. 'Well, I'm glad you are. I had a premonition on the train that you'd bail. Stand me up.'

'That's the thing.' Jess squeezed Hayden's fingers and then withdrew her hand. 'I wouldn't have done that—and *that's* what I can't believe. I walked here—didn't want to take a taxi. I had a mental block about it or something. But I knew I'd meet you. It ultimately didn't matter how I got here. Just that I was going to be here, regardless.'

Hayden sat back, his face still and unreadable.

Jess heard herself speak. 'I mean, I've been married for sixteen years. I have two kids. A mortgage. I've never done anything like … the weekend.'

'And yet here you are.'

'Here I am.'

A silence for a moment and then Hayden spoke. 'I'll tell you what I remember from all those years ago. When you and Mum used to meet up once a month and go out drinking.'

'You make us sound like hardened boozers.' Jess gave a small laugh and picked up her mug.

'I remember your tattoo.'

The mug paused against Jess's lips. 'On my back?'

'You were in our hallway putting your shoes on before going out. I must have been about twenty-two, twenty-three. I was coming down the stairs, and you and Mum were deciding where to go. Your jumper came up as you bent over to fasten your boot straps.'

'Oh.'

'I can't remember what you were wearing, other than it probably being long and baggy. You like your woollens, don't you? But I saw that black lettering on your back. Is it Chinese?'

'Mandarin. It means traveller. I got it when I was eighteen. A friend and I had all these plans to see the world. Not very original.'

'Maybe not. But it surprised me.' Hayden stretched out his legs under the table, his calves pressing against Jess. 'Here was my mum's friend with her long tops and jeans, hair always tied up—your hair was longer then, wasn't it?—and you had a *tattoo*. I mean, it was obvious you liked going out with my mum. You weren't a fuddy-duddy or anything like that but you seemed … sensible. You know what I mean? I knew these nights out with Mum were just one-offs for you; ways to relax and have a blast now and then. The following day I knew you'd be up, looking after your kids, making sure there was cereal in the house, remembering to wash their clothes, not bringing home random men.'

Jess stared silently.

Hayden shrugged. 'Your tattoo stuck in my mind, that's all.'

And then Jess's hand unconsciously drifted behind her, to touch the skin of her back over her clothes. Weeks could go by without her thinking about it. It had long ceased to be a discussion point or something she kept hidden from her mother. It had been there before she met Alec. He rarely mentioned it either; she could remember that the anaesthetist had made a brief comment when inserting the blessed epidural when she had James, and *that* had been the most it had been spoken about in nearly twenty years. 'You really remember my tattoo?'

Hayden nodded. 'It's what I remembered most about you. And I'd very much like to see it again.'

Their hands closed upon each other again and Jess held tightly. Pressure was building in her chest. She remembered the excitement she had felt as a teenager when she and her friend visited a tattoo parlour in the city, remembering the sense of pride that she had done something unexpected and permanent. She looked up at Hayden, clean shaven, thick hair falling by his ears. A light was switched on somewhere in the cafe against the growing gloom and the room was thrown into stark relief. The plastic tables and cheap porcelain mugs gleamed. Outside the rain came down harder. Inside, Hayden got up out of his seat and moved Jess's bag. He sat beside her, hands slipping inside her coat, fingers on her naked back.

'You know there's a contradiction to what we're doing, don't you?' Jess said softly after a few moments.

'What do you mean?'

'Well, here's you, saying you were struck by the fact I had a tattoo when I come across as so *sensible.*' Jess shuddered. 'Horrible word. And yet what I'm doing now isn't sensible. You talked about my being the type of mum who makes sure her kids have breakfast, that kind of thing—you talk about it as though you wish it had been your experience. But here I am, with *you*. Doing something that could destroy all of that ... *steadiness*. Destroy it for my family, I mean.'

Hayden blinked. 'I can't explain why both sides of you are so attractive. But they are.'

Of course, there was nowhere to go, and they were hardly likely to sneak into a private corner—if such a thing existed in the busy cafe or the station nearby—so they ordered more coffee and sat close together at the table. But the intimacy of those hours together, Jess thought on the train home later that night, was deeper than the rolling tumult of their time in the hotel. The hotel had been about shock and discovery, and transgression. The hours in the cafe were quieter but no less urgent. Hayden's hand had grown warm against the naked flesh of Jess's back; he traced a circle around and around, over her tattoo, moving slowly and purposefully, the heat of his touch travelling down her spine until it seemed to pin Jess to her seat. Hayden rested his other hand on her knee, reaching for his mug occasionally, only to return to the sharp bones that moved and flexed beneath his touch. She allowed him to touch her, having no fear that he would go too far, that he would embarrass them in the dingy cafe. She allowed it because there had been a shift within. Caution was now replaced by intent. On the long journey home later that night, Jess considered that the change had been swift, but perhaps not unexpected. She thought she had been moving in that direction for some time, sometimes drifting, sometimes determined. In the cafe she leant against Hayden with her whole weight, pressing into his body, leg to leg, ankle to ankle. She wanted to stretch the length of her against the length of him.

After two more mugs of coffee and some curious stares from the girl behind the counter, unused to travellers staying so long at a station with a regular service, Jess suggested they move elsewhere. 'I'm hungry, anyway,' she said, and disentangled herself reluctantly to put on her coat. 'There's bound to be an overpriced restaurant along the high street.'

They found a small Balti house a short distance away. Jess hesitated in the restaurant doorway, thinking of Alec cooking at home, but Hayden eased her inside. They sat side by side again, unlike the few other diners who sat across from each other at small, wobbly tables. The waiter served their meals and suggested wine. When it came, it was thick and strong. Hayden drained the first glass and exhaled noisily.

'Is it that bad?' Jess asked, indicating towards the bottle.

'No, it's fine. I was thinking about tomorrow. Got lots of paperwork. I fired someone today.'

'You did?' Jess put down her fork and wiped her fingers on a napkin. 'I didn't realise that was part of your job. I thought you were a data analyst or something.'

'I am.' Hayden refilled his glass. 'I have a team working for me. One of the guys hadn't been pulling his weight. Not for a long time.'

'Was it difficult? Firing him?'

Hayden shook his head. 'Not especially. It means a bit of work for me though. He'd been given warnings, performance reviews. We have to produce these reports, every few days, for our clients. They want to know where to invest. Long-term investments; they're not in for a killing. We work for charities and pension funds, mainly. So we have to consider all kind of things, not just the market. Foreign politics, the media.'

'And this guy you fired, he wasn't producing the goods?'

'No he wasn't. Not because he wasn't capable. The reverse, actually. He was very good at looking ahead and planning for the unexpected. The problem was he was taking too long. A report that should have taken a day or so to write took a whole week. Sometimes longer.'

'Oh.' Jess thought of her own work, the hours spent poring over yellow papers and letters that had long since ceased to be relevant, all to find a clue, a kernel of information that might just point to a name for the ever-present bag of bones.

'Can't do it in our game,' Hayden went on. 'We're required to read, consider, and conclude. Bang-bang-bang.' Hayden knocked his knuckles on the table. 'Just like that.'

'Churning it out?'

'Churning it out,' Hayden agreed. 'It's no good dragging your feet, like this chap was doing.'

'Maybe he was worried he'd get it wrong. The analysis. Lose someone's money.'

Hayden shrugged and took a piece of Naan bread. 'So what? That's business. We don't lose money, by the way. We're good at what we do. We'll be better now the procrastinator is out the door. Are you warm?'

Jess's cheeks were pink but, even though they had chosen a table next to the radiator, it was not the heat making her flush. She thought about what she had discovered that day at Threadstone Hall. She knew there were more steps to take, more questions to ask, but could not see far enough ahead to work out what they were. She wondered what Hayden would make of it all, of the slow pace of her discoveries. He wouldn't like it, she suspected. 'Sometimes, it can take time to draw conclusions. From data, I mean.'

Hayden raised his eyebrows but said nothing.

Jess sighed. 'Take what I'm doing. You know about this skeleton, don't you? Six years I've been trying to find out who she is. My Prof has been trying for thirty.'

'Your work is different ...' Hayden began, but Jess shook her head.

'Maybe not. For example, even if I do find out, how certain can I be?'

'DNA?'

'That's been done, and it's only given us part of the answer.' Jess looked at the rain, relentlessly pounding the window. She wondered if Alec had thought to close the conservatory window above the tumble drier. But then she pulled herself back, to the table and conversation. *Maybe that's my problem too*, she mused, wearily. *Too distracted.*

Hayden had waved his hand and was requesting water. 'Finished?' He nodded towards their plates.

Jess nodded and let the waiter take the remains of the meal away. She drummed her fingers on the table, needing to say something but unsure of how to start.

Hayden drained his glass and brought out a packet of cigarettes from his pocket. 'There's a smoker's canopy outside, at the back. We won't get wet.'

They gathered outside, close to each other. Spices and the smell of fried food wafted over the shining rooftops. They were in a small garden; a couple of wheelie bins and black bin liners were crammed at the far end. The windows of a block of flats next door winked down at them, feeling close enough to touch. In one, a woman took off a blouse, standing boldly under the light bulb. A man came behind her and passed her a dressing gown. An elderly man crossed behind another window, a plastic microwave meal tray in hand.

Hayden slipped his hand down and laced his fingers with Jess's. Agitated, Jess drew on her cigarette quickly and Hayden watched her. 'What is it?' he asked.

There was a line of tension in his voice and Jess suddenly knew what had brought the wariness to his tone. She smiled, released his hand, and touched his face. 'I'm not getting cold feet,' she said. 'Well, I am—and soaked ones thanks to these bloody boots—but not *that* kind.'

'What then?'

Jess finished her cigarette and lit another. 'I think I've found something. About the bag of bones.'

'Go on.'

Jess relayed her discovery, about Allegra Underwood and the possibility she had had an affair with the bishop, resulting in the child who would grow to be a woman and be buried with Shacklock. 'It's speculation,' she said. 'But it's closer than I've ever been before. Closer than the professor has ever been.'

'Sounds like it.' Hayden leant against the wall of the Balti house. 'So what's the problem?'

Jess hesitated. 'I'm not sure. But the longer I've been working on this stuff, the more I resent handing it all over to the Prof.'

Hayden nodded. 'I can understand that.'

'I mean, it's *my* work. *My* time that's given up, *my* research that's abandoned to embark upon another wild goose chase. All so Waller can go out on a bang. He's retiring next summer.'

'So don't tell him.' Hayden had his hands in his pockets and looked at her, clear-eyed. 'Don't tell him a thing.'

Jess shook her head. 'He's going to want to know what I've found.'

'Say there's nothing. And then keep digging and write it all up yourself.' Hayden removed his hands from his pockets and held them out, palms up. Drops of rain fell onto his skin. 'Why should you give it all to him? Would he give you any credit when he makes his big announcement?'

'Probably not. I'd be lucky if he put my name on the paper as a researcher. Certainly not a joint author.' Jess kicked at a sodden mat at the restaurant's back door. She could imagine it; Waller standing at the front of the Shacklock Library's lecture room, packed with students and scholars. Thumbs hooked into his awful blue trousers, bobbing his head frantically as he surged towards his conclusion. *I am delighted to reveal the name of the woman buried with the bishop; a name that has eluded scholars for years that only came to light after a long period of painstaking and dedicated research ...* If he asked Jess to send out invites to the event, she'd be tempted to drop them in the bin.

'If you've done the hard work, you should get the credit.' Hayden spoke simply, but his voice was steady.

Jess sighed. 'I have to go.'

The rain outside was coming down in sheets and the gutters on the street had overflowed. When they left the restaurant and headed back towards the station, they had to jump onto the pavement, avoiding the splash of waste water and the rush of cars.

Hayden saw Jess back onto the train. There were a few minutes before the 19.07 back to York and his own train to Waterloo. They kissed on the platform beside the open door, hearing the automatic hiss and swish as the doors slid shut. Later Jess remembered the sound as a rebuke, a mechanical disapproval of her deeds. But, at Woking station, in that moment, she did not care. Their coats were undone, and they held each other tightly, shirt against blouse.

'Soon,' Hayden murmured against her ear. 'We'll go to Fulham.'

He meant his flat. Jess said nothing, but nodded. She waved goodbye as the train pulled out of the station, fighting to keep her balance as the carriage jerked. She was shaken from side to side until she eventually reached out for a seat to steady herself. The train sped her back to York, but she knew it was taking a different Jess north, and that a thing unsaid had been left behind with the son of her friend.

~ 8 ~

Jess arrived at the Shacklock Library early the following day and straight-away pulled up a chair next to Billy Butterfield's desk. She placed a copy of Allegra's photograph that she had found online and printed before leaving the house in front of the surprised researcher.

'I take it you found something at Threadstone Hall?' Billy asked. He was wearing a new rugby shirt and appeared to have cut himself shav-ing; there was a pink smudge on the neckline.

Jess nodded. 'Is Waller in yet?'

'No. But he will be, any moment.'

'Meet me in the stacks in five minutes.'

Jess picked up Allegra's photograph and hurried away to the long lines of book shelves behind the island of researchers' desks, not need-ing to look behind her to see Billy's astonished expression. She walked to the end of the section on church history and waited.

After a few minutes Billy appeared. 'What's going on?'

'Have you ever heard of Allegra Lucan?'

'Sure. She married Josiah Shacklock's son. Edward.'

'Did you read the papers at Threadstone Hall about their marital problems?'

Billy nodded. 'But it can't have been serious. Allegra came back to England with the family in 1900. She had a daughter with Edward.'

Jess's voice dropped to a whisper. 'I think I've found evidence that the bishop visited the Underwood family in Greece, in 1899. He kept it from the Jedthorpe Synod. He stayed in Greece until October 1899. Allegra separated from Edward soon after. And she was pregnant.'

Butterfield's mouth fell open, and he instinctively looked behind him. A researcher passed by the top of the aisle; apart from that, they were alone. Waller had still not appeared. 'You think Shacklock was the father, not Edward?'

Jess shrugged but could not keep the smile from her face. 'It's possible. I need to find out more about Allegra.'

'And you aren't going to tell Waller?'

'Not yet.' Jess watched Butterfield closely. He clasped his hands together under his chin, a surprisingly childlike expression of glee.

'Allegra was involved in the theatre,' he said. 'She owned a theatre in Earl's Court. There's probably a mountain of correspondence relating to her somewhere.'

'That's where I need your help. Don't worry,' and Jess held up a hand, 'I'm not about to ask you to wade through it with me. But we might not have to. Someone is bound to have written a thesis on Edwardian theatre. Maybe a couple of people. They might have researched Allegra— after all, a woman owning a theatre would not have been usual at that time. Could you find out?'

Billy ran a hand through his hair. 'I may know someone, but I don't know if she's stayed in academia. There was a girl a couple of years above me, when I did the PhD. I think she researched actresses at the turn of the century. I could find out what she knows of Allegra. But we don't need to spend too much time on it.'

'No?' Jess shifted her weight from foot to foot, glancing up and down the stack. Waller would be here soon; it was almost eight-thirty.

'You think Allegra Lucan was the mother, yes? Well, skip past her straight to the daughter. Billy tapped his hand on a shelf. 'You just need to know the name of her child.'

Jess had thought of this. 'Of course, it *is* the daughter we want to put a name to. But even if we know the name and the identity, then what? After all this time, all these years put into finding out who this woman is, we need more—what we need is the *story*.'

'You're sounding like Waller.'

'He's right sometimes. If this woman found buried with Shacklock is Allegra's daughter—his daughter, too—how did she get there? She must have found out he was her father. Did Allegra tell her? Did Edward know? What about the bishop himself? Maybe he had no idea this woman was his daughter. Maybe she never met him and only discovered who he was after he died. But how did she end up being buried with him?'

Butterfield stroked his chin.

'You see?' Jess opened her hands expansively. 'We need to know the story. Finding out the identity of the set of bones buried with the bishop is just one part of a big jigsaw.'

Butterfield started to smile. 'I think she's hooked you.'

Jess grinned, knowing there was truth in his words. 'So can you find out what's been written about Allegra already? We might be able to order up your friend's thesis. And while you speak to her, I'll have a dig around online to find out the name of Allegra's daughter.'

'I was working on something else, you know.' But Butterfield said this last half-heartedly. He was already swaying, eager to be off.

'As interesting as this?'

Butterfield did not reply. Instead he turned and walked back up the aisle, waving a hand over his shoulder.

By the time Waller arrived, Jess was bent over her laptop and did not notice him enter the building. When she did see him, it was as he brushed past her desk on the way to his office. She looked after him, curiously. He had not stopped to see what she had discovered at Threadstone Hall, which surprised her greatly.

Instead he had sat down at his desk and was looking at a document. He looked defeated and unusually weary. He was wearing yesterday's shirt, which was not so strange; this one, though, had gravy stains down the front, in addition to the dried egg, that he had evidently not noticed.

Jess watched him for a few moments and then turned back to her computer. She had found a birth record online relating to Allegra Lucan and Edward Underwood.

It was there. Allegra Underwood had given birth to a daughter in April 1900. Violet.

By noon, Butterfield and Jess were ready to reconvene. The library had mostly emptied out, save for a few PhD students working through a pile of box files at the opposite end of the research area. Waller had gone for lunch; Billy and Jess had the place practically to themselves. Billy spoke up from his desk.

'I'm about to email something to you. Give it a minute.'

Jess waited, clicking the refresh button on her inbox. 'Got it.'

Butterfield scooted over to her desk on his chair. 'There's quite a large file attached.'

Jess opened the attachment and sat back while it loaded. 'What is it?'

'My friend's thesis. She was one of those organised types who always backed up her work. After she got her doctorate, she paid for storage space online. She stuck her thesis there, along with other bits and bobs.'

Jess was impressed. 'You should do that.'

'And you.'

'I don't have a doctorate.'

'Oh.' Billy seemed to be embarrassed. 'I just assumed.'

'I trained as an archivist.'

'Right.'

'Can I still think of myself as an academic?' Jess asked. She was teasing, but only mildly so.

Butterfield blushed. 'Of course, if you want to. Well, Maggie's thesis. She didn't stay in academia but she said she used parts of her research for the odd paper, here and there.' Butterfield pointed at the screen. 'Your laptop's slow, isn't it? Scroll down to chapter four. There's a brief section on Allegra Underwood.'

Jess scanned it quickly. Maggie, Butterfield's friend, wrote in clear, undramatic prose, capturing the facts of her subject and their period without embellishment. It appeared that Allegra had bought a theatre in 1905, soon after the death of her father. On Colbert Mews, near to the Earls Court tube station, the theatre offered steady work to a small band of actors and actresses. The enterprise was reasonably successful, and Allegra capitalised on the difference between her cosy theatre, with room for an audience of about a hundred or so, and the huge, nearby monolith that was the Olympia. Then, at the end of 1917, the theatre abruptly closed. 'It was a mystery,' Maggie, Butterfield's friend, had written. Jess said the words out loud, tracing her finger across the screen. ' "Money was always tight and Allegra made certain personal sacrifices to ensure her actors were paid. But they continued to work throughout the war, even booking productions some months in advance. Allegra Underwood's decision to close a successful theatre came as a shock to many." '

Jess turned to Butterfield. 'That's odd.'

'Isn't it? I spoke to Maggie this morning, and she said it was her one

frustration that she had been unable to come up with a convincing the-
ory as to why Allegra would close down her business without warning.'

'Do you think it's relevant to our search? To Allegra's daughter?'

Butterfield shrugged. 'Possibly. The daughter would have been seventeen in 1917.'

'That's the first question, then,' Jess said and reached for her notepad.
'We need to make notes about this. One: the Synod papers I found in
this library referred to a letter written by the bishop, sent from Greece in
1899. The bishop should have been in Malta that year. Two: Shacklock
writes to his sister in April 1899 saying he had been invited to Greece
by his old friend, Josiah Underwood. The letter to his sister is at the
British Library.'

'You haven't told me what you found at Threadstone Hall to make
you think Shacklock actually went to Greece.' Butterfield looked around
briefly as he spoke and shifted nervously on his chair, as though Waller
might hear him.

Jess paused. 'Josiah doesn't state it explicitly. He doesn't even say
the bishop's name in his letters. Instead he talks about his friend, the
"Corinthian".'

'I remember,' Butterfield said slowly. 'But what made you think he
meant the bishop?'

'Josiah and Shacklock were cross-country runners in their youth,
weren't they? When they were at Stephens Theology College. There was
something in Waller's *Life of Bishop Shacklock* that referred to a race;
Shacklock helped Josiah to the finish line when he became ill during
a cross-country run. There's a section in *Corinthians* that talks about
running. And I think Josiah shared Shacklock's habit of giving people
nicknames.'

Butterfield sat quietly, tapping his lips. Jess went on.

'Yes, I know it's weak. But go with me. Shacklock—the Corinthian—
visited Josiah in the summer of 1899. I think while he was there he
met Allegra, Josiah's daughter-in-law. They had an affair and Allegra
became pregnant.'

'Did you find a name for the child?'

'Yes.' Jess turned back to her laptop, clicking away from Maggie's thesis and back to the genealogical site. 'Ready? Violet. Violet Underwood,
born in April 1900.'

'You really think she's our woman?'

Jess blew out a noisy gust of air, suddenly anxious. She had been so certain up to this point but, in relaying her discoveries to Billy, she saw how tenuous they were. Certainties melted like frost under the fingertips and the more she thought about it, the more anxious she felt. But she had to have faith, she told herself. It was the best lead she'd ever had.

'I think there's a strong possibility that Violet Underwood is really Violet Shacklock, and she was buried in the bishop's grave.'

'Do the dates match? Does the family history confirm when Violet died?'

'That's another curious thing.' Jess moved her cursor over the screen. 'I can't find any further records for Violet. No marriage or death records. No records to say she had a child. Sometime after 1917 she disappeared from the archive.'

Butterfield contemplated. 'Or died a great distance from home and no one knew. Now, I'm not saying that body in Shacklock's grave is her, but … yes. There's a chance.'

'I need more to be able to prove this. Who might Allegra have confided in once she became pregnant?' Jess looked at her notes. 'I can't believe she kept it to herself. Josiah's letter said that she left Edward for a brief time in October 1899 and went home to her father. Maybe she had just discovered she was pregnant and didn't know what to do. Who were her friends? Wouldn't they have rallied round?'

'Probably. But would she have confided in them?'

Jess thought of Hayden. And Marie. If Hayden were not Marie's son, she suspected she would have confided in her friend, that she had started an affair. As gossipy as Marie could be, Jess knew she could keep a secret. She suddenly felt a strong longing for her friend.

Butterfield was speaking. 'You've got to remember that in that area of Greece, the British ex-pats were a close and closed group. They all knew each other. Gossip was rife.'

'You think Allegra might not have trusted her friends?'

Butterfield shook his head slowly. 'Not over there. But she might have written about it to others. Relatives?'

Jess remembered something and pulled out a bundle of papers from her bag. She flipped through the pages looking for the brief jottings she had made the day before about Allegra, drawn from the article she found at Threadstone House. 'Here—Allegra's father had a brother who was in the Household Cavalry. She sometimes spent the school holidays with his daughter—her cousin—in Hampstead.'

'It's a start. If you can trace her cousin, you can see if they left any documents.'

'More archives.' Jess looked at the printout of Allegra's face, imagining her picture becoming drowned in a sea of papers.

Butterfield smiled ruefully. 'It's what we do, I'm afraid. And you have a better idea of where you're going with this than ever before.' He shuffled forward on his seat. 'What are you going to tell Waller?'

'Nothing. Yet.'

'If you're going to Hampstead, you'll have to tell him something.'

'If I go. I might find something online. Or there might be nothing. If Allegra did write about the bishop in letters to her cousins, she might have asked that the letters be destroyed.'

'You won't know until you do some digging.'

Jess sat thinking. The image of bending over boxes of yellowing papers and sitting in cold, damp rooms wearied her. She thought of Hayden's co-worker, fired for procrastination. Would more leafing through manuscripts lead her closer to her target or further away?

She suddenly leant forward, towards her computer screen. The genealogical website was still there, adverts flashing silently in the corner. It did not take long to trace Allegra's cousin through the census records. The daughter of Allegra's father's brother appeared in the 1881 census. 'There,' she said triumphantly. 'Allegra's cousin was Emily Lucan. Information found all for the cost of a subscription. Which the library thoughtfully buys every year.'

'Now what?' Butterfield asked, eyebrows raised.

'Looks as though Emily lived until 1942. Let's look at the last available census—that's 1911—and see where Emily was.' Jess clicked on a few icons on her screen and within minutes had downloaded a blue and white form, covered with neat handwriting. Butterfield crowded forward to look.

'There. Emily Lucan. Spinster. She was forty-seven in 1917.' Butterfield looked at Jess's notes about Allegra. 'Makes Emily's date of birth somewhere around 1870.'

'Nine years older than Allegra, who was born in 1879. Just the right type of person for the motherless Allegra to turn to.' Jess looked at the address on the census. 'Hampstead. Emily was still living in the family home in 1917.'

'Any family papers she had would have either been destroyed after her death or ...'

'... passed to other family members. Or a given to a local library?' Jess opened up a search engine and tapped in a search for libraries in the area. 'West Hampstead Library is close by. I'm going to phone.'

She picked up her mobile and walked away. Butterfield watched her stroll about among the stacks, her voice carrying in the high ceiling. Waller was nowhere to be seen, but Butterfield could sense that time was ticking on. The lunch hour was almost over.

After a while, Jess returned, her face thoughtful. 'Stroke of luck,' she said. 'Emily died in 1942, yes? The librarian I've just spoken to said that the building was partially destroyed in 1941 in a fire bomb.'

'It's unlikely that private papers would have been deposited before a person's death. We're lucky that Emily lasted until 1942—if her papers had reached the Hampstead library the year before they may have gone up in flames.'

Jess put her phone back on the desk. 'Correct. The librarian is going to check if they hold anything.'

They both fell silent, contemplating. Jess felt a little dizzy. The years of patient, plodding research seemed to have rushed towards a cliff edge and the speed of today's discoveries made her feel breathless. She wasn't sure if she liked the feeling; as hated as they were, there had been some security in the box files and folders of old, musty parchment.

'Do you think you'll have to go there?' Butterfield asked.

'West Hampstead? Maybe. Depends what they have.' Simultaneously, Alec and Hayden's faces crowded into Jess's mind. How far was Hampstead from Fulham? And what would Alec have to say if she told him she had to disappear again? Jess could guess.

At that moment, just as she was thinking of Alec's response to the prospect of her going to London again, Jess's mobile rang. She jumped and then grabbed it from the desk, the tinny, disco sound reverberating shamelessly around the high vaulted ceiling. Butterfield shook his head, mockingly pointing to a sign on a nearby wall that informed the library users that mobiles were to be kept on silent at all times.

Jess connected the call quickly, noting a split second before she answered that it was Alec ringing. Her stomach did an odd roll, the kind she had not experienced when thinking about Alec for many years. Almost twenty years of companionship had dulled the excitement of receiving a call from him. Last night, when she got home, conscious of the smell of the Balti house on her clothes and Hayden's aftershave on her neck, Alec had already been in bed. He didn't stir when she came into their bedroom and took a shower in the ensuite, not even when she left the bathroom door open, steaming up the place in a way he usually hated. But Jess knew he wasn't asleep. He was totally silent, for a start, which he never was. Usually he twitched or grunted or, if he'd had a beer on a Friday night, he snored. But last night he was as rigid and mute as a statue. They'd slept back to back, not touching. *It's been like that too often recently*, Jess thought.

'Hello?'

'Jay? I need to speak to you.' On the phone, Alec was brisk.

Jess held the mobile tightly. *What does he want to speak about?* She was afraid to ask. She thought of her clothes and her bag, brought home with her last night. There was nothing of Hayden's in there. No telephone number on a scrap of paper, no card of a hotel she had no business staying in. But still she could not ask. 'Where are you?'

'Downstairs. In the reception.'

'Of the library?' Jess frowned, trying to remember the last time Alec had ever come to her place of work. She couldn't think of one single occasion. 'Why aren't you at work?'

'Took an early lunch break. Are you coming down?'

'I'll be there in a minute.' Jess hung up. She turned to face Butterfield, who was staring over at the stacks holding all the library's manuscripts. He'd obviously been listening but tried to act as though he hadn't. 'That was my husband,' Jess said. 'Something must have happened. He's here. I need to go and speak to him.'

'Oh, all right then. I'll make a start on reading up about Allegra.' Butterfield swung his chair back to his own desk. 'Will you be long?'

'I have no idea,' Jess muttered and picked up her bag.

Alec was leaning awkwardly against the vacant reception desk when Jess got down there. She saw him from a distance of about fifty metres; thin, hair grey at the temples, shoulders stooped. Jess slowed her step.

It is an odd experience, she thought, *watching my partner—the man I've been with for twenty years, the father of my children—when he doesn't know I can see him. Is this the real Alec here in this reception? Tired and washed out? Or will the real Alec spring out when I appear?* Jess came to a complete stop and ducked behind a display cabinet. She was glad there was no one else around to see her act in such a way, just as she was relieved—for a change—that the soles of her boots were soft and did not betray her as she neared her husband. She watched as he stared down at his own shoes, flexing his toes. He did not look up at the ornate, high ceiling; his body was closed in upon himself.

Then Jess stepped out from behind the display cabinet, hating herself for spying on him. She pressed her feet down heavily on the marbled floor, so Alec would hear the sound and know she was approaching.

'Hi,' she said, rounding the reception desk. She leant up and kissed him on the cheek. He hadn't shaved properly, and he held himself back, not moving forward to embrace her.

Jess pretended not to notice. 'Do you know, I think this is the only time you've ever been to the Shacklock!' She kept her voice light.

'Probably.' But again, Alec did not look at his surroundings. He was wearing a tie Jess had not seen before and he crossed his arms across his chest. The fabric of his Super Dry coat made a scuffing sound. 'Is there somewhere we can talk?'

Jess nodded, feeling sick, feeling her heart bursting in her chest. She led Alec over to a small anteroom off the reception area that was mainly used for meetings. Her palms were wet when she grasped the door handle.

Alec followed her, and she shut the door, closing them in. Immediately the air between them seemed to change; they were confined, closed in together, filling a space so unlike the wide openness of the foyer. Jess spoke, noting how different her voice sounded now that the door to the small room was closed. 'What is it? You look very serious.'

'I am.' And Alec reached into the pocket of his suit jacket, worn under the Super Dry. He took out a small packet and placed it on the table.

It was a box of condoms. Jess gasped and for a horrible, split second, thought that Alec had found out about Hayden. Her breath caught in her throat. *Where had Alec found them?* Jess shook her head, a tiny, imperceptible movement. She hadn't taken any to London—of course she hadn't. Hayden had them with him at the hotel. Probably he carried them with him all the time. Or maybe he had picked them up in the bar in Fulham before they'd left. She hadn't asked. Jess squinted down, trying to make out the brand, knowing it was pointless as she didn't know what kind Hayden had used.

'Shocked?' Alec was watching her. His face was pale though his eyes were red and bloodshot. 'I couldn't believe it.'

Jess reached out for the back of a chair and held it tightly, her hands trembling. She still didn't know what she was dealing with. *Did I have any in my bag? What if some fell in there, off the bed at the hotel?* She breathed out noisily, releasing the air that boiled in her throat. 'Where did you find them?'

'In James's sock drawer. I found them yesterday.'

Jess tried to control the pounding in her temples without Alec noticing. He knew her so well; he would know the difference between shock at his discovery and shock of a different kind. She cleared her throat. 'Wow.'

'Wow, indeed.' Alec stared down at the packet, looking glum.

'Are you sure they're his?' The throbbing in her head had eased a little and Jess tried to think. Alec didn't know about Hayden. She wasn't dealing with the breakdown of her marriage. And, the second she had that thought, a hot feeling of guilt settled in her stomach, more troublesome than the threatened migraine. *James is fifteen and I'm focusing upon whether I've gotten away with sleeping with another man, rather than worrying about what my son is up to.* Self-disgust was new and Jess didn't like the way it plucked at her insides.

'Of course they're his,' Alec was saying. 'They're not ours and they're hardly likely to be Megan's, are they?'

'No, I mean—maybe they belong to a friend. Maybe James is just keeping them for him.' But even as she said it Jess knew how unlikely it was.

Alec watched her. 'They belong to James. Our fifteen-year-old son.'

The words fell between them, padded, loaded in the closed room. Jess felt the weight of them press against her. *James, when did all this happen?* She thought of the sensitive and gentle boy he had been. Always the first to share his achievements at school—the credits for reading or maths, the selection for the football team. Always the first to cry if a game got too rough and an older boy hurt him in a tackle. But always the first to be comforted and made to feel better by a hug from his mum. Now Jess was lucky if he hugged her on her birthday and his sensitivity had been replaced by a cruel and defensive mocking tone.

Still, Jess knew that some girls were attracted to that kind of teenage swagger. Obviously very attracted.

Jess touched the packet. The condoms weren't the top market brand but a lesser kind. Straightforward, unfussy condoms. Not the ribbed, flavoured kind, Jess thought, and a laugh bubbled from somewhere. *If he'd bought Trojan Lover Extra Ribbed Extra Minty, I think I would gasp myself into hysterics.*

'What's funny?' Alec asked. He didn't see anything amusing; his mouth was pursed and tight.

Jess picked up the condoms and turned it over in her hand. 'Nothing. No, it's not funny. I mean, James is under the age of consent. If he's having sex with someone, there could be serious trouble. But there is one good thing. At least we know he's being sensible and taking precautions.'

Alec shook his head slowly, little snorts of air now audible. 'You must be joking.'

'No, I'm not,' Jess considered. 'It explains his moods. All the sloping off to his room and sleeping late. We thought it was down to teenage angst, but maybe not. Maybe there's a girl at the root of it.'

'He isn't old enough for any of this.'

Jess held up her hand. 'No, he isn't. Look, I'm not happy about it either.' She placed the condoms back on the table and wiped her hand down her skirt. The brief wave of amusement had disappeared and what was left was an anxiety for that tender little boy of old, who clung to her at toddler-group or shied away from her friends when they came to visit. She hoped a girl wouldn't hurt him and break that heart of his, still soft under spiky layers. She remembered her own mother, years ago, trying to keep her from boys who would ultimately hurt her. *If you were a different person, Mum, I'd want to talk to you about this.*

'I'm going to have it out with him,' Alec said. He looked weary but had a determined kind of air that Jess recognised.

'No, don't.' She said it quickly, feeling certain it was a wrong move. 'Jay—'

'Look, if you confront him, he's going to think you've been snooping in his stuff and he'll never trust you again. Do you think giving him a bollocking will stop him from having sex with someone, if he is at all? Maybe he hasn't yet—maybe he got them in Sex Ed at school.' Jess pushed her hair back from her face. 'Maybe he bought them for a dare from a chemist. You know what boys are like, especially if they're with their mates. But if you have a go at him, he'll just clam up and we'll never know what he's doing.'

Alec's mouth was open slightly. 'I can't believe you're saying this. I thought you—more than me—would be livid.'

'I'm not happy about it,' Jess said quietly.

Alec bounced his head from side to side, whiskers scratching his collar. Jess thought of Professor Waller and the way he rubbed his beard with his stubby fingers, and how much she hated it. 'There's something very wrong about keeping secrets,' Alec said. A pained look came into his eyes. 'We've always told the kids that, haven't we? To talk to us. Tell us what they're worried about.'

'James is hardly likely to share something like this.'

'Why not? Especially something like this, I should say. He should tell us if he's met someone.'

'Should he?' Jess turned to look out of the small window at the far end of the room, the only natural light. It threw a small yellow square onto the table, leaving the rest of the room in shadow. The room had fluorescent strip lights, but she did not want to switch them on. The glare was too harsh and sometimes the bulb flickered in a horrible, nauseating way.

'I'm going to talk to him.' Alec's voice was firm. 'I can't bear the thought of something as serious as this going on and us saying nothing.'

Jess said nothing. Outside the rain came again, and she thought of the night before when she said goodbye to Hayden at the train station. The rain had lashed down then, washing along the street, surging through the gutter and turning the pavements into puddle-soaked obstacle courses. Jess's feet had been drenched by the time the train came in; as soon as her carriage had slipped away from Hayden at the platform, she had stripped off her boots and socks and hung them over the small, heated blower under the table. It had actually been quite pleasant, to sit with bare toes nudged against the heater, despite the odd glances of late-night travellers. There was something thrilling about removing a layer unexpectedly and letting the air wind its way around her body. The memory of Hayden's hands around her waist lingered, the skin on her back glowing from the press of his fingers on her tattoo. He had held onto her until the last minute, until the guard blew his whistle and she had to go.

'I'm going,' Alec said, breaking into her thoughts. 'I want to eat before getting back to the warehouse.'

Jess turned her gaze from the window to her husband, taking in the sag of his shoulders and the lines under his eyes. He looked worn out. She pushed the thought of Hayden away, bottling up the spiralling guilt in her chest. 'Where are you going?'

'Just the sandwich place on the corner.'

'I'll come with you.'

Alec held up his hand. *No.* 'I'm meeting someone from the suppliers.'

'Oh.'

'See you tonight, though. What time will you be back?'

'Usual.' Jess thought of Waller and the library down in Hampstead. *Hayden.* 'It's getting a bit hectic, though. Waller's retiring in the summer, at the end of the academic year. He really wants to identify this woman by then.'

'You mean he wants *you* to identify her and then wade in at the end.'

Please, don't, Jess thought. *I had this conversation just over twelve hours ago with a very different man.* 'I'm going to be very busy. Might have to go to London more regularly.'

She expected Alec to say something, to object. His reaction earlier that week had been one of frustration. She braced herself, not sure of what she would say in return, not sure if she could bring herself to push for it.

But, instead, Alec gave a tired shrug. 'You do what you need to do.'

'You sure?' Jess looked at him uncertainly.

'It's not a problem.' Alec sighed. 'Look, I'm going now. I'll see you at home.'

He moved away, opening the door before Jess could get round to him, to kiss him goodbye. Instead he waved over his shoulder and was gone, striding into the reception.

~ 9 ~

Jess stood in the doorway of the small meeting room of the Shacklock Library, watching her husband walk away. Alec didn't look behind him, though she willed him to, sending out a small part of herself to him as he marched towards the exit. But within seconds he was gone, and she was left alone.

She leant against the door and a heavy feeling of sadness sank low into her stomach. She felt Alec—and James—spiral away from her. *When did you become so old?* Jess thought, but she wasn't sure if she meant her husband or her son, or even herself. *When did you stop speaking to me?*

A blast of cold air rattled through the reception as someone walked through the automatic doors. Jess checked—it wasn't Waller. If he saw her hanging around the reception, he'd ask questions—nothing she couldn't handle, but Jess didn't relish the thought of an interrogation.

She retreated back into the meeting room. Again she felt the walls hug her, ease against her. She was taken by a strong urge to linger here, in this room. It felt like a little bubble, disconnected from her complicated life beyond the library's front door and the research still to be undertaken inside. She wondered how long she could stay without her absence being noticed.

Slowly, Jess pulled her phone from her pocket. She dialled a number and waited.

'Hello?'

'Hayden? It's me.'

'Wait a minute.' There was a sound of fingers hitting a keyboard and a chair being pushed back on a carpet. Jess closed her eyes and imaged Hayden in a high-rise in the city, pale light streaming in at the windows, rows of screens flickering around him. He spoke again. 'I can talk now. You all right?'

'Yes. Just wanted to say hello.'

She heard the smile in his voice. 'That's nice. Hello. Get home without any bother last night?'

'Fine. Train was on time for a change. Bit tired, that's all.'

'Well, I can't claim any responsibility for that. This time, anyway.' There was a pause into which Jess said nothing. 'What's wrong?'

Jess sat down at the table where, moments before, she had faced her husband. 'Alec came to the library to see me today.'

'Oh?' Cautious.

'He'd found condoms in our teenage son's bedroom.'

'Oh.' An explosion of air, Hayden obviously relieved. 'Remind me how old your son is?'

'Fifteen.'

'Bit young. But, you know, at least …'

'He's taking precautions. That's what I said.'

'So what is it? Alec didn't agree?'

Jess remembered her husband's face as she tried to make that argument. 'He didn't. We'll have to work it out.'

'You will.' Hayden waited.

'It's just—when did I get old enough to have a son who is having sex?'

Hayden laughed. 'Is that it? You're worried you're getting old?'

'A bit. James doesn't seem old enough to have spots, let alone girlfriends. But he has. And what does that make me?'

'Yeah, you're knocking on now. He'll be making you a grandma soon.'

'Don't, Hayden.' Jess gritted her teeth. She remembered Marie's words in the restaurant just last week. *That Hayden had met someone who might make Marie a grandma.* Jess wondered again what had happened to the girlfriend. 'I had a moment of panic when Alec showed me the packet. I thought they were yours for a second, but I had no idea what type you'd used.'

There was a noise in the background and Jess heard Hayden move along a corridor, his shoes clicking on the floor. 'Not the actions of a woman who's past it, is it?' he said. 'Meeting a younger man, spending a night with him.' Hayden's voice was low and filled Jess's ear. 'You're lucky there was a machine in the pub toilets. Or else what would we have done?'

'I'm sure we would have thought of something.'

Hayden gave a shout of laughter. 'I'm sure we would. Sensible, daring, cautious, risk-taking Jess. Are you always so contradictory? Yes, we would have filled the time.'

The image of Alec walking away from her faded from Jess's mind. 'I might have to come to Hampstead soon. Is it far from Fulham?'

'No, not far. When?'

'I'll let you know.'

'Send me a text. I'm out the next couple of nights but should be clear by the weekend. Look, I've got to go. Don't worry about your lad, Jess. It sounds as though he's just like you—careful, but likes his fun.'

And with that, Hayden hung up. Jess heard another voice in the background just before the call was disconnected, asking about a report. She looked at her mobile, watching as Hayden's number faded away and the screen saver came on. She had the sense he thought he had sorted things for her, that he had punched right through to the heart of the problem and resolved it. Her worries should now be wiped away. And of course, they weren't. Suddenly, the urge to phone Marie came upon Jess with crushing force. She was just the friend to understand about James, to take her side against Alec, to listen to her worries, to back up her belief that she should give her son the distance to make his own decisions, despite his age.

But she couldn't phone Marie so soon after speaking to Hayden. The need to call her friend was matched by a deep, guilt-filled sadness.

Butterfield was on the phone by the time Jess got back to the desk—the portable office phone usually kept in Waller's office. He held up a hand as she approached. 'Yes. I understand. No, we are used to it. I'll let her know, thank you. Bye.'

'The librarian at Hampstead?'

Butterfield disconnected the call, nodding. 'Yes. She had couldn't reach you so phoned here direct. She's had a look through Emily Lucan's papers. She found some letters by Allegra.'

'Did she say what they contained?'

'Of course not.' Butterfield trotted back to Waller's empty office and returned the phone. 'That's your job. But they were dated from 1899.'

Jess pulled up her chair and sat down heavily. She felt as though she had been spun around, whisked from one shock to the next. The events of the morning swilled around in her mind and she drew her fingers into an arch, index fingers nudging her brow.

'Jessica?'

She looked up to find Butterfield staring quizzically down at her. She smoothed her fingers down her eyebrows and shook her head. 'Nothing. Just something going on at home. Right. Allegra. Hampstead.'

'The letters were dated from 1899,' Butterfield repeated. 'If Allegra was going to confide in anyone about a possible affair with Bishop Shacklock, it might have been her cousin.'

'Lots of ifs and maybes,' Jess said. On top of the dizziness she felt weary.

'But it's a better lead than you've ever had,' he pressed. He dragged his own chair next to her and sat down. He frowned, lines appearing in his meaty forehead. 'What's happened? You were all fired up earlier.'

'My kids.' Jess exhaled noisily. 'No, you're right. It is a good lead. Well worth checking out.'

'Definitely. Look, you'll be going to Hampstead, right?'

'Yes. Do they open on Saturday?'

'Check online.' Butterfield nodded to Jess's laptop. 'They're bound to. But, look ...'

'Yes, they're open all day,' Jess said, fingers tapping on her keyboard. She turned back to look at Billy Butterfield properly, with his pink, jowly face and the unapologetic, fierce acne. Not for the first time Jess felt sympathy towards him. She wondered if he'd ever had a girlfriend.

'I'd like in on this,' Butterfield said.

'What?'

'*This.* Giving a name to the bones. It would be spectacular—could kick start anyone's career. But it's more than that.'

'What?' Jess repeated, still taking in his words. *In on this? Is Billy like Waller, after everything, wanting to barge in at the last minute and take the credit?*

Butterfield glanced over his shoulder at the quiet library and the slowly ticking clock suspended from the ceiling at the far end of the room on iron chains. 'The thing is, I'd really like to stick it to Waller.'

'You would?'

'Yours isn't the only career he's scuppered.'

Jess sat back, saying nothing. Her head ached again.

'He never supports any of my funding applications or speaks up for me at departmental meetings,' Butterfield continued. 'I've made five applications for council funding to support my research in the three years I've been here. Waller has shot down every last one.'

'He has?'

'He isn't interested in anything unless it compliments his own work. I think the Underwoods are a fascinating family—so many influential people, so many leaders in their field. There are a dozen research papers crying out to be written about them. You must have glimpsed that when you were down at Threadstone Hall.'

Jess thought of the pixies and nymphs carved into the hallway, and the fire and brimstone severity of William, the Underwood patriarch. And she thought of the women in the family who broke away from William's dominance and forged their own careers, all at time when being female was an obstacle. 'Yes, I did.'

'Waller isn't interested in the slightest. He thinks the Underwoods are a sideshow, nowhere near as important as putting a name to that sad little collection of bones buried with Shacklock. That's all he thinks about. It's the one part of the bishop's life that he can't interrogate, dissect, and compress into that insufferable *The Life of Bishop Shacklock*, or whatever the hell it's called. Think Shacklock, think Waller—that's what he wants. Except people think of Shacklock and think about an unnamed woman buried with him.' Butterfield cleared his throat. 'I want to be part of the team that blows apart all Waller's ambitions. It would serve him right. You and me. We could be that team.'

Jess blinked, shocked to hear the thoughts she'd had many times over during the past six years being said so clearly, unequivocally, by another researcher. The image she had of Waller standing in front of a room full of people making his announcement about the woman buried with the bishop was replaced by a different image: one where she was behind the lectern, Waller somewhere in the background with his head in his hands as Jess read aloud her paper in which she presented incontrovertible evidence as to who the mysterious skeleton was. Finally she would be noticed. Finally she would be recognised and her name known in academic circles.

'I do understand that,' she said.

'So?'

'So—what?'

'Can we buddy up on this? You could tell Waller you might have a lead and need me to assist. He wouldn't bat an eyelid.'

'You want to come to Hampstead with me?'

Butterfield spread his hands. 'Why not?'

Why not, indeed? Jess allowed the thought to form in her mind why she had wanted to go this alone. *Hayden*. Hampstead, London, Fulham. An overnight stay. She remembered the night in the hotel and shivered.

But with that thought came an admonishment: *it's not even been a week. I barely remembered who Hayden was when I met Marie for lunch before the weekend. What is happening to me? Maybe taking Billy with me would give me the reality check I need—I couldn't get away with sneaking off to see Hayden if Billy is hanging around.*

So before she could talk herself round, Jess nodded. 'Sure. Let's do that.'

Butterfield beamed. 'Great. And whatever we find, I think we should write it up. You and me. Not Waller.'

Jess took a breath. 'We need to think about that carefully. It could blow up in our faces. That sort of thing—going behind your Prof's back—it doesn't sit well with those who make funding decisions.'

'Well, I'm not convinced. But when do you want to go down there?'

'Saturday?' The answer came quickly. Jess's heart beat fast, and the migraine throbbed at her temples. She could imagine Alec's face when she broke the news, especially after the events of today. And there was Hayden, creeping back into her thoughts, his voice in her ear.

Butterfield drummed his fingers on the table, obviously impatient. 'Saturday will have to do. We could travel down together, get a full day's work in, and then travel back.'

'I might stay over,' Jess said. 'Christmas shopping on Sunday.'

Butterfield—obviously oblivious to the approaching season—shrugged. 'Whatever. Do you want to book the tickets? After checking with Waller?'

'Yep.' *And after telling Alec*, Jess thought. *What a week.*

❦

Jess arrived home that night just as the shouting began. Megan was downstairs in the living room, wide-eyed, television on mute, while James yelled and hollered at his father upstairs.

'Mum?' Megan said as Jess came in and shrugged off her coat. The girl's voice was shaking. 'What's happened? Why is James so mad?'

Jess shook her head and sat down on the sofa, drawing Megan to her. She tucked her head into her hair, breathing in her daughter's sweet scent. Not for the first time she wished her children wouldn't grow up. In the room directly above, James's room, doors were slammed, and she heard Alec's voice.

'I wasn't snooping, James! I was putting your washing away, which, if you remember, is your job. If you tidied up after yourself I would never have found them.'

'Oh, it's my fault you like to go poking through my things!' James yelled, and followed it up with a choice expression that must have been doing the rounds at school.

Megan gasped and Jess had to smile into her hair. She doubted if Alec even knew what a 'ball-bag' was, but Megan had obviously heard it before.

'I can't believe he said that,' Megan breathed. She was quaking a little but, Jess suspected, was also a little thrilled.

Another shout and then the sound of a door being slammed. Alec marched down the stairs, his face grim and white. His fists were clenched, and he stopped in the living room doorway when he saw Jess.

'You caught some of the floorshow, then?' he asked.

'Just the last bit. He shouldn't have called you that.'

Alec shrugged. 'It sounded cool. I might remember to use it next time one of the lads drops a pallet at work.' He saw Megan's pinched face and leant over to stroke her face. 'Don't worry, chicken. Your brother needs to calm down and then apologise. He'd better do it quickly if he wants to join us for tea tonight.'

'Why don't you watch one of your programmes?' Jess said, handing Megan the television remote. 'Free, unfettered control of the telly while your brother sulks upstairs. Doesn't happen very often.'

Megan sniffed and turned back to the television. Jess eased off the sofa and followed Alec through to the kitchen. He peered into the cupboards.

'You decided to confront him?' she asked quietly.

'Yep. I told you, Jay, he's too young to be messing about like that.'

'Do you think it helped?'

Alec took out a packet of rice and turned to face his wife. 'You don't, obviously.'

'I just think we could drive him away if we go in too heavy. He'll clam up and never tell us anything.'

Alec bent down to the fridge and brought out a packet of minced beef. 'Sometimes, Jay, being a parent is about being tough. I don't want to be James's mate. I want to be his father.'

Jess reached for an onion from the vegetable rack and started to slice. She kept her eyes firmly on the chopping board and tried to quell the anger rising inside. 'I'm fully aware of what being a parent involves, Alec. Who was it who stayed at home with them until James went to secondary school? Who was the one who spent the seven years of his primary school being known as "James's Mummy" instead of Jess or Mrs Morris, remember? It drove me crazy.' She put down the knife and forced herself to become calm. 'I'm afraid that James won't talk to us if we tackle him head on.'

Alec sighed. He was stirring the mince in a frying pan and suddenly looked exhausted. 'You talk to him, if you want. For what good it will do.'

'Okay, I will.' Jess went to the sink and washed her hands. She touched Alec's arm briefly. 'If he calls me something better than a ball-bag, I'll let you know.'

James's door was closed and Jess heard the sound of gunfire and explosions as she climbed the stairs. He was obviously working out his anger by playing on his PlayStation.

Jess tapped on the door and opened it slightly. James was on his bed, staring at the television perched on the edge of his desk. His jaw was clenched, and he pressed the buttons on the console with force.

'Can I come in?' Jess edged round the door, careful to respect her son's space.

James shrugged and Jess took that as approval. She moved aside James's trainers cluttering the end of the bed and sat down. James shifted his position, peering over her shoulder at the screen.

'Quite an argument,' Jess started. She wasn't sure where to go with this or even what she wanted to say. Her son's feet nudged her leg, the distance between his ankles and toes almost as long as the distance between her wrist and elbow. James had thrown his socks on the floor and hair sprouted along the tops of his toes. Jess resisted the urge to touch it, to tease it down. He wouldn't like that.

James said nothing and instead thumbed the console viciously. A grenade was thrown over Jess's shoulder.

'I want to talk to you, James,' Jess persisted, keeping her voice low. 'Can you put that on pause please?'

James puffed out his cheeks and jabbed at something on the handset. He threw it aside.

'Thank you,' Jess said. 'Why did you shout at your dad?'

'He was looking through my stuff!' James flashed, animated. 'He has no right—this is my room.'

'And what did he find, James?'

James glared down at his fingernails, bitten to the quick. His hair was damp, and he looked hot.

'James, I understand this is your room. I never pester you about tidying it, do I? Only that you bring down your dirty cups and dishes.' Jess looked pointedly at a cold mug of tea on the desk. 'Your dad found the condoms while putting your washing away.'

'So he says,' James muttered.

Jess raised up her hand. 'Your dad doesn't snoop. We both respect your privacy. But this is a pretty big deal. You must see that.'

Silence from James. Static from the television droned in the closed room.

'We're just concerned.' Jess touched her son's leg. 'If you have a girlfriend, we'd like to know.'

'Why?' James flashed. 'Why does it matter?'

'Well … we'd want you to be careful.'

'If you found condoms, I obviously *am* being careful, aren't it?' James's voice was heavy with sarcasm.

'James.' Jess looked at him, wondering again where her tender boy had disappeared to.

'It's not fair!' James thumped the mattress, making Jess jump. 'I should be able to have a life without you two poking your nose in! It doesn't matter if I have a girlfriend. It's not like I'm married or anything, or cheating on someone. It would be a big deal if I was, but I'm not!'

Jess eased back, mouth dry. Her son trembled with rage. The skin around his jaw was flecked and dotted with shaving rash, and he had a couple of spots on his neck—but he looked more like Alec than ever. He glared at her with Alec's eyes, screwed up his mouth with Alec's lips. He was five years younger than Alec had been when Jess had met him.

The thought barrelled across Jess's mind with frightening force. She was looking at a younger version of her husband, that was all, and James's outrage was a glimpse of what Alec might feel.

What he might feel if he knew. If he ever finds out about Hayden. Jess licked her parched lips, feeling the heat in the room for the first time, wafting from the radiators in thick waves. *Madness. I've been mad all week. I could destroy this family.*

She took a breath and tried again, sensing she should rein back control of the situation. She shifted uncomfortably on the bed. 'James, it's a big deal because of your age. Fifteen is too young to be having sex.'

James jumped from the bed, knocking his trainers to the floor. He was still wearing his school uniform, and he towered above Jess. 'Who says I am? You're as bad as he is! If you must know, Aaron and I bought them after school one day. To see if we could. For a laugh.'

'Calm down.'

'Why don't you just fuck off and leave me alone?'

'That's enough!' Jess sprang to her feet, shock and anger rising. James was still taller; she came up to his chin. She pointed a finger in his face. 'Don't you dare speak to me like that.'

James kicked out at the trainers, bouncing them off the wardrobe. His fury was unchecked; sudden, rapid and brutal, the anger brought a sheen to his forehead. He started looking around for something else to throw.

'All right, all right.' Jess saw the time to back off. She moved towards the door. 'We'll talk about this later.' A tactical retreat was in order; she swept back the bedroom door and stepped onto the landing. As the door closed behind her, a book thudded against it.

Alec was at the bottom of the stairs, looking up. Megan peeped through the banisters from the hallway below.

'It went well, then?' Alec asked. He was not smiling and his tone was not sarcastic. Instead, his face was white and pinched.

Jess sighed and passed a shaking hand through her hair. She padded down the stairs. From James's room came the sound of the PlayStation again, turned up loud. It followed Jess as she rounded the bottom step and stood beside Alec.

'What's going on?' she asked. And then she shook her head. 'I need a drink.'

~ 10 ~

The rain had finally stopped the following morning but a crisp, bone-chilling cold greeted Jess as she stepped off the York train as it pulled into Jedthorpe Station. She pulled her scarf close to her neck and wrapped her coat about her. The streets on the way towards the library were slippery with ice and a couple of times she skidded, putting out a steadying hand to the shop walls lining the route.

Some sensible soul had turned up the heating in the foyer of the Shacklock Library and Jess gratefully lingered for a few moments, knowing the research room where her desk was would be cooler. It always was, and dry as well, to preserve the manuscripts lining the stacks.

She leant against a radiator for longer than was necessary. Her skin throbbed with heat but she did not move, enjoying the brief respite from being Jess the researcher, or Jess the run-around, always at Waller's beck and call. Instead, standing in the foyer, she was just another face threading through the building; she wondered if people brushing by might give her a cursory glance and decide she was on a field trip from Maryland, or was a mature student making the journey from York. The foyer offered a space where she could forgo a name, a role, or a duty.

It was only when the blare of the radiator became uncomfortably hot that Jess reluctantly pulled herself away and headed towards her desk. When she finally made it into the research room, Waller was already there, waiting for her. His tall frame was bowed over her desk, white hair smoothed down, glasses trembling on his nose. He touched a notepad, moved a book. He stood up as Jess approached, no sign of embarrassment that she had found him going through her work.

'Jessica, I hoped you'd be in soon.'

'Morning, Professor.' Jess undid her coat and took off her scarf. 'Do you need something?'

'An update. It suddenly occurred to me that I didn't ask you about what you'd found at Threadstone Hall. I would have asked in the afternoon but the meeting with the dean dragged on and you'd left by the time I got back here.'

'Threadstone Hall. Right, yes.' Jess tried to shake away the drama of the last few days. The trip down to Woking seemed a long way away. Last night she had tossed and turned, conscious of Alec's usual rigid form on his side of the bed. Jess looked around for Butterfield but he wasn't in yet. 'There may be something in the Threadstone archives. Some mention of other papers that reference the bishop. Down in Hampstead.'

Waller shifted on his heels slightly. 'Where in Hampstead?'

'At the West Hampstead Library. The Underwood papers mentioned a friend who knew the bishop.' Over her shoulder, Jess heard Billy Butterfield come in. His footsteps slowed as he got closer and saw her talking to the professor.

'Which friend? Who was it?' Waller's jaw wobbled with confusion.

Jess paused. She sensed she had stumbled towards the edge of drop, over which lay a kind of furtiveness she was not used to. *Well, this is the week for it.* She had left Alec early this morning without saying goodbye, not sure if he was awake or not. Megan was up, getting ready for school, but there was no movement from James's room. She'd laid out cereal for breakfast, wrapped sandwiches for their lunchboxes, and then set off. Alec's car was in the driveway, windscreen frosted, a white, unseeing eye in the frigid cold.

'Which friend?' Waller repeated, voice insistent. His shoes squealed.

'A clergyman.' And Jess toppled over the line. She had never lied to Waller before, despite everything. 'The Underwoods knew a vicar in Hampstead who had met Shacklock. It's a long shot, but there might be something there.'

Waller pursed his lips together, considering. His jaw moved slightly, as though he were chewing. 'I've never come across a friend of the bishop's in Hampstead.'

'It might not amount to much. I could go on Saturday.'

'Right, right.' Waller nodded.

'There's one other thing.' Jess resisted the urge to look over towards Butterfield. 'There might be quite a lot of stuff down there, at the library in Hampstead. I could do with some help. Billy has offered.'

'Butterfield?' Waller turned and stared openly at the researcher. Butterfield had the grace to pretend not to notice. Instead he sat down at his desk and rummaged around in his bag.

'Yes, Butterfield.'

Waller shook his head and, with a discretion that was unusual, motioned to Jess to follow him to his office. She did, with a sideways look at Billy.

Waller's office was a riot of strewn papers and bent textbooks. The chair behind his desk was empty, but the one in front—to be used by visitors who never came—was piled high with box files and manuscripts. Mugs perched precariously on the edge of bookshelves and the bin emitted a faint, unpleasant odour. Jess stood in front of the desk, unwilling to even attempt to clear a space on the groaning chair.

Waller flopped down on his chair and pushed his glasses up his nose. He cleared his throat. 'Are you sure you need Butterfield?'

'Yes. Two hands, and all.'

Waller flexed his own hands, cracking the knuckles before tapping the end of his nose delicately. 'Well. I'm not sure how much help he'd actually be. You might end up babysitting him.'

'I don't think so.'

'You realise he's never expressed an interest in identifying our mysterious lady?'

'That isn't a crime, Professor.' Jess spoke lightly, keeping her voice level. 'If anything, a bit of distance from the case might be a benefit.'

'How so?'

'Objectiveness. Clarity. We've been looking for a name for this woman for so long that our judgement and ability to find a clue might be impaired.'

Waller pushed his nose up slightly, his fingers prodding the fleshy end. Jess watched, repulsed. She hoped his fingers wouldn't slip inside and extract something as yellow and arcane as the manuscripts littering his floor.

'Maybe you're right,' Waller said eventually. 'Though I still have my reservations about Butterfield. I think he's wasted far too much time on the Underwood family. Every new research project he proposes or asks for funding for is somehow connected to them. He's obsessed.'

Jess forced herself to become still and silent, to swallow the snort of derision bubbling so perilously in her throat. She had been exposed many times to Waller's hypocrisy, his inability to see his own obsession. It was bad enough that it dominated him and had shaped his career for the past thirty years. It was worse that he imposed it upon the careers of researchers round him.

'I think, Professor,' Jess began carefully, 'that there is a great deal of work still to be done on the Underwood family. Billy was very helpful in giving me the background before I went down to Threadstone Hall, and I think he's right to be so interested in the family. They were involved in all kinds of movements and organisations in the mid to late nineteenth century.'

'Yes, yes.' Waller flapped his hand dismissively. 'I daresay there might be enough material down there to drag out a PhD or two. But that's beside the point and not relevant to our own work, which—I might add—is on a different level. If I can identify the woman buried with Shacklock, then it will have international repercussions.' An odd thing happened to his face. His head bobbed a little closer to the desk. 'So much of who I am as an academic is tied up with that bloody woman.'

Jess watched him carefully. It was rare to see behind the professor's brusque, single-minded exterior. But, she realised, he was right. His academic career had been staked on naming the woman buried with the bishop. She spoke again, cautiously. 'So Billy can come with me at the weekend?'

Waller shrugged and then nodded reluctantly. 'But I'm only willing to cover second-class train fare. You'll be there and back in a day?'

'Yes. Though I may stay over. Haven't decided. Christmas shopping.'

Waller grunted, and it was clear his mind had moved on, that he was barely listening. His attention was on a scrap of paper half-buried under a pile of books. He squinted down at it. Jess, as far as he was concerned, had left the room.

So Jess did leave, too used to Waller's behaviour to feel annoyed. She walked back to her own desk and Butterfield looked up from his chair. His eyebrows were raised.

'You can come with me to Hampstead,' Jess said and opened up her laptop. 'I'll have a look for train times just now.'

'He was all right about it?' Butterfield glanced towards Waller's office, the distaste apparent on his face. Jess could see he was torn between wanting to stick it to the professor who had stymied his career and resentment at being pulled into the very work Waller valued above all else.

'He wasn't exactly fine, but he's gone along with it.' Jess waited for the laptop to connect to the library's WiFi. 'Let's just make it worth our while when we're down there.'

'Absolutely.' Butterfield threw another look in Waller's direction, distaste replaced with hostility. 'Right, what day is today? Thursday? I'm going to spend today finding out what I can—if anything—about Allegra's cousin, Emily Lucan. I'll trawl through the newspapers online and see what there is. There might be an obituary for her and that's a good place to start.'

'Sounds like a plan.' But Jess was elsewhere. She was thinking that it was only Thursday. A couple of days left before the weekend, time for her to come to her senses and make the right decision. Time, in other words, to decide if she should text Hayden and meet up.

And then her phone rang again, the disco music rattling around the library. Jess scrabbled for it in her bag, conscious of the throat-clearing and grunts from Waller's office. Mobile phones were a particular hatred of his. Butterfield snickered to himself as Jess fumbled for the handset, tossing aside the contents of her bag.

She answered quickly, without checking the number first. Marie's fruity voice filled her ear. *Damn.*

'She answers! Finally, darling. Are you free for that coffee?'

So like Marie, straight in, no messing about or small talk. Jess— caught out that it was her friend—gaped. 'Hello Marie. I don't know, to be honest with you.'

'Look, I've got a massage at a place just round the corner this after-noon—yoga injury, I'll spare your blushes—and I thought you could treat me to a latte and a slice of carrot cake at Dempsey's. Three o'clock okay?'

I know what a rabbit must feel like, caught in a snare. But Jess did not have time to speak before Marie broke in again.

'It would just be a quick one, sweetheart. I know how the old Prof doesn't like you far away, but it would be good to see you. I'm away again next week.'

'Another holiday?'

'Tour of Italian vineyards. With a man from my supper club.'

'Supper club?' Jess closed her eyes briefly.

'Don't say it. I know how it sounds. But it is a great way of meeting people and the meals are fantastic.' There was a pause and the sound of a cashier passing an item across a till. 'I'm picking up some last minute outfits while I'm in town. So, three o'clock?'

Jess could think of nothing to say to dissuade her friend. It had always been that way. *Quick one in the Student's Union after the lecture? '80's Retro Night in the dance hall this weekend—I've got tickets, so just get Alec to have the kids.* Jess had little power—or inclination, if truth be told—to resist Marie. Just thinking about declining now made her feel guilty. She missed Marie. 'I guess. Quick one. Promise?'

'They're my speciality!' And Marie hung up, laughing gaily.

⁓

Marie was already seated at a table when Jess arrived at Dempsey's Coffee Shop, just after three o'clock that afternoon. Marie had ordered them both lattes and sat stirring her own, a pale brown fluffy drink in a fluted glass. She licked her spoon as Jess approached.

'Latte with only half a shot of espresso, just how you like it.' Marie beamed. Jess couldn't help but smile back and felt a rush of affection for her friend. Marie looked relaxed and slightly pink. She was wearing a low cut top, which appeared to be cashmere and, after putting her spoon down next to the glass, started to twirl a gold necklace.

'Thanks, Marie.' Jess took a grateful sip. The rain had come on again just as she had left the Shacklock Library, accompanied by a biting wind. Jess had walked quickly, ducking below shop awnings and avoiding the splashing puddles.

She had left Butterfield still skimming through online newspapers. The library had subscriptions to many databases and Butterfield had scrolled through the digitalised copies of the nationals and local papers. He had struck lucky with a small newspaper of limited circulation; the *Hampstead Echo* carried an obituary of Emily Lucan, Allegra's cousin who may have known about a relationship between Allegra and Bishop Shacklock. But the obituary revealed that Emily's funeral had been a quiet affair with only a handful of mourners. None of the Underwoods had attended. There was no further information in the bigger papers. Butterfield had persevered though. He'd switched his attention back to Allegra, knowing of her involvement in the theatre. By the time Jess left to meet Marie, he had read several articles about Victorian and Edwardian theatre and had filled pages of his writing pad with tiny, cramped notes.

'Did the eminent professor object to you leaving the factory?' Marie asked.

'He isn't around.' Jess broke a piece of biscotti in two and dunked it in her drink. 'He disappeared at lunchtime.' Waller hadn't come back to his office after leaving at noon and he hadn't said where he was going. He'd been doing this more and more recently. In the old days, he would always stop by Jess's desk and let her know what he was doing, or who he was meeting, and he usually gave her a task to complete before he returned. That hadn't happened today.

'See?' Marie pointed at Jess knowingly. 'That's what you should do. I keep telling you.'

'Yes, Marie. So, what's new?'

'Not much! Just getting ready for this trip. It's been a bit of a last-minute thing, but my companion is paying for most of it.'

'Your companion?' Jess raised an eyebrow. 'Is that what you call him?'

'What else?' Marie smirked. 'My plus-one?' She leant over the table, hissing. 'My fuck-buddy?'

Jess couldn't help but laugh, though too loud. The waiter, drying mugs at the counter, looked over. 'I hope you enjoy it, Marie.'

'I intend to. Sounds like you had fun with Hayden the other night.'

The piece of biscotti in Jess's mouth suddenly felt very dry. She crunched slowly and swallowed. 'You spoke to him?'

'Tuesday night. He'd just got back from meeting a friend for a curry. Phoned him to tell him about this trip of mine—not that he cares—and he said he'd enjoyed meeting up with you on Saturday.'

Jess kept her eyes on her drink. 'Yes, we had a nice time.'

'It was probably what you needed.' Marie nodded briskly. 'Letting your hair down and all that.'

Jess wondered if the heat creeping up her neck and spreading across her cheeks was visible. Perspiration gathered under her arms and in the middle of her back. She hoped Hayden hadn't told his mother where-abouts he'd met his mysterious friend for a curry on Tuesday night: if Marie were to discover Jess had also been in Woking, she would have made a quick connection.

'Did he say anything to you about a girlfriend?' Marie asked suddenly.

'No. Oh, I think he said he had been seeing someone, but it had ended.' Jess thought of their meal at the Chinese restaurant. The self-assured way Hayden had ordered their food. How they had smoked outside and the way he imposed himself on the man who had banged into Jess as they walked to the tube.

'Strange. I thought he liked this one.'

'Oh?'

Marie shrugged. 'What do I know? I never met her. Couldn't even tell you her name, but I think he'd been seeing her for a few months.'

'He didn't say.' Jess bent over her drink again. Hayden loomed large and powerfully in her mind and it was difficult to think clearly. There were too many ways to slip up or reveal herself.

'That boy hasn't had a girlfriend for longer than six months. Ever.' Marie spoke quietly, looking out at the steady rain. Her fingers strayed to the necklace again and deep creases appeared around her eyes.

'Is that so?'

'The longest he ever dated anyone was a girl when he was sixteen. I think he really fell for her but one day she forgot to meet him after football practice. That was it. Boom. Over.' Marie clapped her hands together for emphasis.

'Sounds tough.'

'Hayden's like that. You maybe didn't pick up on it at the weekend—he would have been on his best behaviour. But if he wants something, or someone, he goes for it. The moment a girl does anything to disappoint him, it's done with.' Marie sighed. 'Cut and dry. I wouldn't say he's impetuous, but he goes for what he wants when he wants it, and when he's over it, when he's had enough, he moves on. Doesn't look back. Listen to me—how can I judge? Like mother, like son, at least since Barrie.'

Jess stayed silent. She wasn't sure what she thought. Hayden had gone back to the hotel with her, and if his actions in the bar in Fulham were anything to go by—their closeness on the sofa opposite the bar, the way he took her drink and placed it on the table—well, yes, Jess considered, maybe she *had* met the Hayden that Marie described, that person who knew what he wanted. *But this isn't a man I like the sound of,* and Jess thought of her own softness and habit of procrastination. 'Has he always been like that?' she asked.

'He wasn't so bad when he was little, before the divorce.' Marie sighed. 'Age-old story. Parents separate, child develops issues. We did our best to prevent it but he probably shouldered some of the fall-out.'

'Did he overhear arguments, that type of thing?'

'Probably. Especially after Barrie had his little fling.' Marie drained her latte and picked up her spoon to scrape out the last of the foam. 'Hayden and I moved out, and he had to change schools. The house belonged to Barrie's mother, and she wasn't likely to let the woman who refused to forgive her philandering son stay there.'

Jess thought of Hayden's hand on her tattoo, the circle his fingers made around it. *What had he said about it? Something about liking that his mother's sensible friend had another side to her.*

'Anyway!' Forced brightness on Marie's part, but it was a part she knew well. She motioned to the waiter, and he brought over two pieces of cake. Marie watched him return to the counter. 'Enough of my woes. What's going on at Chez Morris?'

'Nothing much.' But Jess was glad of the change in conversation. 'Oh, Alec found condoms in James's room.'

Marie, fork halfway to her mouth, paused. Then she burst out laughing. 'Did Alec lose his shit? I bet he did.'

'Somewhat. He came to the library to talk to me about it.'

'Did he confront James? What did James say?' Marie snorted and held up a hand. 'Don't tell me, I can imagine.'

'Do you know what a ball-bag is? He told Alec he was one.'

Marie laughed again, head thrown back this time. Jess saw the shiny whiteness of her teeth and the blackness of old fillings.

'Oh Jessie, that's priceless. Good on James.' Marie giggled as she returned to her cake.

Jess smiled too, but subdued. 'It's serious, though.'

Marie pursed her mouth, so-so. 'What would be worse is if he comes home to say he's got some girl knocked up. It was the stuff of nightmares for me when Hayden was that age.'

'James is fifteen. Too young for that kind of thing. He told me he'd bought them when he was with his mate. Just messing around, he said. I don't know if I believe him. And I didn't agree with Alec confronting him, but he's right to be concerned.'

'Concerned, yes. But come on, Jessie. Kids are active earlier these days. Just look at the newspapers—always screaming on about under-age mothers and benefit scroungers. I'm not making a political comment,' to Jess's glare, 'but be thankful James at least won't become another statistic.'

Jess sighed. 'I said pretty much the same thing to Alec. He didn't take it well.'

Marie shrugged. 'What you gonna do? James will be out there, falling in love, getting drunk, whether you want him to or not. If he's protecting himself at this age, that's no bad thing.'

Jess smiled ruefully. Marie's reaction didn't surprise her at all and secretly she thought her friend was right. It felt affirming to hear her own thoughts being said out loud, and Jess could imagine Marie laying down the law to Alec, were they to meet up. They had only met a couple of times, over two uncomfortable dinners. Each time Marie had brought a different date and drank too much wine.

They finished their cakes slowly, watching the rain hammer the cafe window. Occasionally an office worker darted inside for a coffee and left again, hovering at the door for a moment, gathering courage before stepping out into the wind and water. Jess looked at her watch and thought of her own work, waiting for her back at the Shacklock. Reluctantly she pulled on her coat and reached for her purse.

'Time to go. I'll get this. When are you away?'

'Monday.' Marie hunted in her bag for her purse. 'Let me, Jessie.'

'Bugger off, you paid for lunch last time. Give me a hug, then.'

The women both stood and embraced. Jess squeezed Marie tighter than expected and, to her embarrassment, felt tears gather in her throat. Marie looked at her curiously.

'Is everything okay, Jessie? Something going on?'

'I'm just being daft, that's all.' Jess flapped Marie away. 'Tired, stressed, too much to do. Let's meet again when you get back.'

'Sure.'

They stood at the counter together while Jess paid and then hugged again before parting. Jess lingered for a second, watching her friend's plump form slip away towards town and the multi-storey car parks. She watched until she could no longer see Marie through the winding streets, feeling the chord between them stretch and become thinner. And then she pulled up her own collar and started on the brisk walk back to the library.

~ 11 ~

It was Friday night. Jess had arrived home from the library to find that Megan was at Chloe's house and James at Aaron's. She listened to Alec explain where the kids were, feeling slightly deflated. It had been a long week; she'd wanted to see them, especially James. He'd barely spoken to her since their row and Jess longed to hug him. Every time he grunted or sniffed in her direction she had analysed the sound—was that a friendlier grunt? Was he coming to terms with her concern?

Alec was standing in the kitchen holding a takeaway menu when Jess came in. His shoulders were round with fatigue and he looked as though he hadn't shaved for a few days.

'You look shattered,' Jess said, opening the fridge and taking out a bottle of wine.

Alec shrugged. 'No more than usual. Pour one for me.'

Jess emptied the bottle into two glasses and they wandered back through to the living room. James's school bag was hanging over one end of the sofa, half-open. Jess gathered the contents up and put it on the floor. She resisted the urge to look inside. 'Is he talking to you yet?'

'Nope.' Alec sat on the armchair opposite and took a deep drink.

'Me neither. It will take awhile.'

'He knows our feelings on the subject.' Alec's line of vision was fixed, at the stereo under the window, not at Jess. *Is he angry?* she wondered, heart heavy that she was no longer sure.

But it was Friday night, the kids were out, there was wine. Jess kicked off her shoes and sat back. Outside a neighbour trundled a wheelie bin back up their driveway. A car door slammed shut somewhere, a teenager yelled.

'Did you have a good day?' Jess asked.

'All right. Nothing earth shattering. Busby dropped a pallet of olive oil when loading it onto a lorry. Took ages to clean it up. Called him a ball-bag. I must thank James for passing that on. It was the highlight of my day.'

Jess leant back against the sofa cushions. 'Mine was Waller yelling at a researcher.'

Alec snorted. 'That old fart.'

Jess nodded sagely, agreeing. In truth, Waller's outburst had startled her. It had been weeks since he had last lost his temper—it used to be that he'd blow up every couple of days. The unfortunate PhD student who had taken too long to transcribe a document had quailed in the face of Waller's rage. She was only a first-year, too. Jess had turned round from her desk, as had everyone, to see what on Earth what was going on. The student was shaking and, after Waller had finished raging and stalked off to his office, the girl had sat down at her own desk on the verge of tears.

'Talk to her,' Butterfield had said to Jess, and Jess, knowing the rise and fall of Waller's temper better than anyone, had slipped over and crouched down beside the girl's chair.

'Don't take it personally,' Jess had whispered, though her heart ached to see the student dab her eyes. Jess handed the girl a tissue, pity boiling with anger. *He really is losing it, the old scrotum.* 'He's yelled at everyone in this library. Me, Billy. Ask anyone.'

The student had said nothing, only nodded. It was clear she wanted Jess to go, to leave her alone. She cast a quick glance behind her to Waller's office, obviously worried he would see her talking to Jess.

Jess had squeezed the girl's hand and stood up. 'He's a swine. But he'll forget this in a matter of minutes, don't worry.'

'I heard ...' The girl faltered. 'Is he leaving in the summer?' There was hope in her voice.

'Yes.' Jess smiled, pity now the strongest emotion. 'We'll no longer have to put up with his tantrums.'

She left the student frowning through her tears and walked back to her own desk. Butterfield was watching and leant over when Jess sat down.

'I can't wait to wipe the smile off that old bugger's face,' he hissed and jabbed a finger at his notes. 'Just wait until we can ram our findings right up his ...'

Jess had nodded, agreeing. *More* than agreeing. Now, sitting on her sofa at home, she nodded again, small movements, remembering. 'You're quite right, Alec. Waller is a …'

'Ball-bag,' Alec said solemnly. 'What do you want? Curry? We didn't have one this week as you were in Woking.' He passed over the menu.

Jess took it, tense, remembering the evening with Hayden in the Balti house. She felt hideously guilty that the usual Tuesday-night curry with Alec had been abandoned so easily. It was ridiculous to attach so much to a meal, she told herself in a half-hearted attempt to push the regret away, but it didn't work. Alec had begun the practice of cooking them a curry on a Tuesday night when Jess started on the archivist's course. It had been so much more than a simple task in the kitchen; it had signalled his support, his adapting to Jess's absence while she was at college.

And Jess realised two things almost simultaneously: first, she hadn't texted Hayden to confirm they would meet up. At the library, Jess had tapped out a message to Hayden on her phone, only to delete it. *Will be at Kings Cross at ten o'clock tomorrow.* He hadn't contacted her either. Each time her phone had pinged with a message she had checked, hurriedly, to see if it was him. She supposed he was keeping to his word, leaving it up to her to make contact.

And, second, she hadn't told Alec about her weekend plans, either. She stared down at the takeaway menu in her hands, not seeing. She had spent so long mulling over whether to meet up with Hayden that she had forgotten to tell her husband that she would be away. Jess traced a finger over the menu, trying to remember if the Minstermen were playing at home tomorrow. If Alec were forced to miss the football so he could run around after the kids, he'd be livid.

There was nothing for it but to speak up. Jess sighed and looked over at her husband. 'Alec, I'm so sorry. I have to go to London again tomorrow. Early morning. We're getting close to finding out who Waller's skeleton is.'

Alec sat, mute. He continued to gaze at the stereo.

'I'm sorry,' Jess repeated. 'It's been a last-minute thing but I should have told you. Is there a home game tomorrow?'

Alec finally looked at her. 'No.'

'What time are the kids due back? Will you get some time to yourself tomorrow morning?' Jess noted the hopeful tone to her voice and hated it. Alec sat so rigidly. Separated by only a few feet, he was like a rock in their living room; immovable, inanimate. The soft humour linking them together only a few minutes ago had disappeared.

'Are you stopping overnight?' Alec answered her question with one of his own.

'I don't know. Possibly, maybe. It depends what we find. The library might not be open on Sunday, so if you're not okay with it all, I could come home.'

'Would it matter if I said it wasn't?' Alec had transferred his gaze to his glass.

'Of course.' The words fell from Jess's lips but they sounded hollow. There was no conviction; they were separate, disconnected phrases only. What felt real was Hayden, hovering in the background. His flat at Fulham.

And even Alec didn't believe her. She could see it in his face but, when he finally looked, there was an edge to his stare that puzzled her; it did not contain the anger she expected. She would have understood if he had been unable to contain his frustration; that here she was, bailing out again for the weekend, and after all that had happened that week with James. *I should be at home, being the kind of mum he needs. What's wrong with me?* Now they were older, her children rarely made Jess cry, but she felt close to tears now.

Alec spoke, his voice odd and contorted. 'If you need to take a few days down there, go ahead. We'll be fine here for a while.'

'What?' Of all the things she expected, it was not this. 'You're angry. I knew you'd be angry.'

'I'm not angry.'

'*Take a few days*? Of course you're angry.' Jess tossed the takeaway menu aside, appetite vanishing. She wondered if this disinterest and distance was a new tactic, to make the point about his annoyance.

But, instead, weariness rather than anger seemed to fold around Alec, his limbs drawing in, closing him off. He held himself quietly on the sofa. 'I'm sorry.'

'You're sorry?' Jess stared at him. The direction of the evening had her bewildered; the moment of ease and humour, the tentative approach about her trip, and now this.

'I've been having an affair.'

She almost didn't hear him. Alec's voice was so low. So she asked him to repeat himself, even though she knew what he had said.

'I've been having an affair. It's finished, it's over.' Alec picked at something on his fingers.

Jess shook her head, over and over. The disbelief bounced her chin from side to side. *Did he really say affair?* 'What?'

'It lasted a couple of months. That's all.'

'What?'

Alec's pale blue eyes cut through the soft light of the living room. 'An *affair.*'

The breath came back into Jess's body in a rush. 'Who with?' She leant back on the sofa, part of her marvelling that shock could be experienced so physically.

'Laura Preston.'

At that Jess started to laugh. She couldn't help it. A hiccupping bray burst from her. 'Laura Preston?' Their friend, who lived a few streets away. They had been at the Preston's summer barbeque, like they always did. And then Jess's laughter stopped—that night had also been the last time she and Alec had made love. They'd staggered home with the kids, tipsy on homemade punch and too long in the sun, and had fallen into bed soon after James and Megan had hit the hay. Jess tried to remember; it had been over quickly, which was unusual for Alec, especially after a drink. She'd giggled then as well, nudging him, whispering he was like a teenager.

Alec remained silent, hands moving restlessly.

'When did it start?' Jess suddenly asked.

'Ah, in September. When the kids went back to school. James and Alice went on that residential, remember? Laura and I drove them up to Cumbria.'

Alice—Laura's daughter, a classmate of James's. Jess gaped. 'James… is Alice—'

'I spoke to Laura this week about it. James isn't seeing Alice.'

'Well, that's lucky, given you're boffing the mother.' Laura Preston? Jess struggled to believe it. Laura was their friend, but she was never out of a business suit and chain-smoked. Alec hated smoking. 'Did you stop off somewhere on the way home? A little lay-by for a leg-over?'

Alec flinched. 'Don't, Jay. It wasn't like that.'

'What was it like then?'

'If you must know we only slept together a couple of times. Never overnight.'

And, as had been the case every spare moment this week, there was Hayden, looming into view. The fury burning in Jess's chest subsided. The sarcasm on the tip of her tongue dissolved. She hung her head in her hands. The irony of feeling betrayed by Alec after what she had done this week overwhelmed her.

'I'm sorry.' Alec reached out and touched her knee. 'It was the most stupid thing I've ever done. I don't even know how it started. But you and I were distant from each other, we were both working so hard—'

'Don't.' Jess held up a finger, her head still bowed.

Alec edged forward on his seat, his knees popping. 'Most of the time Laura and I just talked. That's all. Talk—like you and I used to do.'

Jess raised her head slowly, face pink. 'It was just a couple of times?'

'Yes.'

'Where?'

'Jay ...'

'No, I want to know. Not overnight, so where? Not at your work, surely. I can imagine the lads' faces if you'd been caught in the warehouse. Where then? The car?'

'Once at her house. The other ...'

'Not here.' Jess closed her eyes briefly. 'Not in our house.'

Alec said nothing and into the silence Jess read his guilt. She pushed her hands outwards, as though she were trying to force the image away.

And then a deep-seated desire to move took over. She stood up, surprising Alec, who sat back in his armchair, head thrown back to look at her.

'Where are you going?'

But she did not answer. Instead, grateful she had only taken a sip of wine, Jess picked up her handbag and car keys, and left the house.

Once outside, the cold struck her and she regretted not grabbing a coat. But, despite the ice in the air and the white clouds spiralling from her mouth as she breathed, her skin felt clammy and her clothes itchy and uncomfortable. Shock warmed her. Alec's words flowed like a ticker tape, and every few seconds Jess snagged on them. *Laura Preston? In our house?*

Finally the cold seeped in. She had walked out the house but had no idea what to do next. She looked down at the car keys in her hand, bewildered, as if to say 'how did these get here?'

Then a light came on in the hallway, streaming across the driveway. Jess opened the car door quickly and started the engine. As she reversed onto the road, she saw Alec's figure lingering by the door. She wondered if he would come out, if he would try to make her stay. But the light in the hallway went off as Jess drove up the street.

With one hand on the steering wheel she fumbled inside her bag. An open packet of cigarettes was in there somewhere and she wanted one. Pausing for a brief second to consider what Alec would think if she lit up in his car, Jess flicked on the lighter anyway. *Too cold to wind a window down. He'll just have to suffer it.* She pulled on the cigarette, leaving it to droop from the corner of her mouth.

Even though she was now driving, Jess was no clearer about where she was headed. The engine made an odd rattling noise, and she remembered Alec saying the car was booked in at the garage that weekend. But she drove on. The streets were emptying, the last of the commuters making it home for the weekend. Some early revellers were heading for the various pubs dotted along the high street, women tottering in heels they would later resent. Jess drove slowly, careful of the late-night shoppers blundering out into the road. And then finally she was out of town, accelerating along country roads.

Her mother lived nearby but inwardly Jess scoffed at the idea of stopping by. Her mother would ask questions that demanded answers. Jess had formed the art of gritting her teeth and answering as best she could without actually giving anything away. Except, tonight, she didn't think she would be able to hold anything back. So Jess drove past the road leading towards her mother's house and carried on.

She drove for miles, out of the city, away from the lights. Finally she knew where to stop. The Jedthorpe Crags, thirty miles away from home. Jutting out in stark contrast to their flat, grassy surroundings, the Crags were sharp slabs of sandstone, some fifty feet high. No one was sure where they came from, so incongruous were they with the rest of the area. Jedthorpe lay in a low valley, a peaceful plateau some distance from the Pennine Dales Fringe separating the east of the country from the west. Yet the Crags were dramatic and unapologetic. They were favoured by rock-climbers, walkers and ramblers, keen to scramble their way to the top and look down at those below or out across the valley. Jess used to go out to the Crags as a child for Sunday picnics before her father died; later, when James and Megan were small, she and Alec continued the tradition. There was a parking area on a ridge near to the Crags and Jess turned her car in that direction.

There was just one car in the car park when Jess pulled in; walkers, finishing up. A couple in their fifties, Jess guessed. They looked at her curiously as she parked, muttering to each other while pulling off their walking boots and changing their socks. Jess gave a half wave in their direction. It was odd, she supposed, to be arriving at this time of night, while it was dark, and alone. *They must think I'm meeting someone—a clandestine rendezvous.* Jess smiled sadly. If only they knew.

The walkers got back into their car with one final suspicious glance in Jess's direction, and then they drove off. Jess sighed and lit another cigarette. She looked inside the packet. Half empty. She would have to swing by a shop or off-licence later.

She smoked while staring at the shadow of the Crags. The rocks were a deeper black than the sky above, a full, thick darkness held within their frame. In the daytime, birds nested in the nooks and cracks, but none could be seen or heard now. The Crags were separate and distinct in their solidity. Jess wondered what it would be like, to stand on the Crags at night; if she would become part of their shadow, swallowed up by the dark. Or if her body would be visible to others in the car park, a little glint of light in the velvet space.

Jess finished her cigarette and moved her handbag to reach the heater, turning it on full blast. Her mobile phone fell forward, the green battery light beeping steadily. She looked at it for a moment before picking it up.

It took seconds to tap out the text to Hayden. She had drafted and deleted it so many times that day and knew what she wanted to say. No fuss, no embellishment. *My train gets into Kings Cross Station at 10am tomorrow.* But Jess waited. She did not press send. Instead she stared at the message, the ten words or so, and allowed the questions to form.

When a week is weighed against two months, what's the difference?

Alec said he had been with Laura only twice—how many times did she have sex with Hayden in the hotel? Three? Or was it four? A ridiculous amount, anyway; a frequency that had not occurred since the first weeks when she and Alec got together.

The cold was weaving through the vents in the car despite the heater and Jess rubbed her feet together, cursing again that she had left her coat. The phone sat like a piece of shining flint in her palm. She could go one way or the other, on either side of the blade. She went one way. She pressed send, and the text was gone.

Then it was too cold, far too cold, even with all the heaters pointing in her direction. It was difficult to control the shiver in her legs as she drove away, and her hands trembled as she smoked another cigarette.

✑

Billy bought them both coffees as their train pulled out of York the following morning and, as the train sped south, he returned to the coffee kiosk and bought Jess another one. He'd said nothing about her crumpled clothes and lines under her eyes, although he must have wondered. After leaving the Crags car park, Jess had driven to a late night supermarket where she had eaten a stale sandwich, bought another packet of cigarettes, and a cheap sleeping bag. She had then gone back to the house and parked on the driveway where she had tried to sleep. The lights were all off when she arrived back home, the door pale in the streetlight. But she could not go inside. Instead she wrapped herself up in the sleeping bag on the back seat and spent a cramped, cold night. At around six o'clock in the morning Jess had let herself inside and retrieved her coat and work bag. She considered padding upstairs to their bedroom to pack an overnight case, but didn't want to risk waking Alec.

Hayden had texted back last night, while she was in the supermarket. *Flat 67, 400 Fulham Road. Come whenever you are ready.* It was short and direct. Jess had stirred her hot chocolate and sat in the café, rereading the text several times. The message was as seamless as silk; there was nothing in it to misunderstand or misinterpret. Under the fluorescent supermarket cafe lights, Jess allowed herself to ride along on the text's smooth surface, feeling herself drift closer to Hayden.

Butterfield had typed out his notes about Allegra Underwood and her involvement in Edwardian theatre and, as the train chugged through fields and small towns, Jess tried to read. It was impossible though; her eyes hurt, her shoulders ached. She was wearing yesterday's clothes and was sure Billy must have noticed. Again, though, he didn't mention it, and said nothing when Jess pushed the notes away and leant her head against the headrest.

As they neared London, she woke up. Tall, terraced houses with oddly shaped roof extensions sped by; green fences lined the track, broken occasionally by graffitied bridges and power stations. The conductor made a muffled announcement and other travellers gathered their belongings around them. Some pulled down weekend bags from the overhead compartments, others pulled out tube maps. Jess looked over, envious. A day in a library awaited her, not Oxford Street or a visit to a gallery. A headache throbbed at her temples and she felt sick from lack of sleep.

'I can't do this today, Billy,' she said as Butterfield stood up to retrieve his briefcase. He sat down again opposite her.

'What do you mean?'

'The library. I'm sorry. Something happened at home and I need to meet up with a friend.'

Billy blinked. 'I wondered. I mean, you look tired.'

'Can you go to Hampstead without me? I'll try to meet up with you later.'

Butterfield shrugged though his face pinked up. Anxiety or delight at the responsibility, Jess couldn't be sure. 'You've got my number?'

Jess took it and punched it into her phone, noting the battery was running low. 'I really am sorry. But I need to sleep and I'll probably crash at my friend's house.'

They parted at Kings Cross, Billy heading to Baker Street and the Jubilee line to Hampstead. Jess stood at the top of the stairs leading down towards the tube, leaning against the banister and allowing other commuters to rush past her. Her foot dipped and bounced on the top step, phone in her hand. The battery was now completely flat. If she was going to go to Fulham, she wouldn't be able to text in advance and let Hayden know. She would just have to turn up.

Someone banged in to her from behind and tutted as they hurried past. Jess stepped back, weary. The station announcer called out a platform change for the train heading back to York and a swathe of people suddenly changed direction, like swallows on the air. Jess watched them, feeling a pull towards the flock like a hook behind her belly button. Her muscles throbbed with the effort of resistance, her body pushing towards a different place. A moment, and then she set off down the stairs to the tube.

It took a few seconds to work out which line to catch and then Jess took the escalator to the Piccadilly line. She held the electric banister, exhaustion adding to her puzzlement as the handrail moved faster than the stairs. She felt herself pulled forward and had to jerk her hand back. The tube took her to South Kensington where she changed for Fulham, remembering making this journey with Hayden just a few days ago. She sat opposite an old woman circling programs in a television guide.

The Broadway Arms near Fulham station was closed as Jess walked out into the street, though there was movement inside. Somebody shouted; a crate of bottles was slammed on a hard surface somewhere. Jess turned left up the high street and walked on, almost to the Chelsea ground. Signposts around the stadium informed passers-by that the road would be closed in the next hour in advance of the home game. A couple of hamburger vans were setting up and the smell of frying onions wafted down the street.

Hayden's flat was in a block about three storeys high, right next to the football ground, set behind a small, fenced garden. Each level had a row of flats, glass-fronted, with narrow, iron balconies. A bike stood on one balcony; pot plants on another. The block seemed well maintained, free of the backpackers who bunked in the area. The gate to the garden was unlocked and Jess stepped through.

Hayden's flat was on the top floor. Jess walked up the clean stairs and along the landing. 65. 66. Finally, 67. A thin, red door beside a kitchen window. Jess could see a newspaper on the counter and a bottle of orange juice. A shadow moved in the background. Jess paused, and then knocked.

Hayden answered, dressed in a T-shirt, shorts, and running shoes. His hair was damp at the temples and he hadn't shaved. He was wiping his face on a towel and breathing heavily. His eyes widened when he saw it was Jess and he lowered the towel. 'You're earlier than I expected. I've just got in from a run.'

Jess nodded and walked in, without waiting to be invited. 'Where's your bed?'

A burst of laughter from Hayden. 'What?' He closed the door with a bang.

Jess dropped her bag on the floor, just in the entrance to the living room. A large, open-plan room with a staircase on the right wall and glass doors at the far end leading to a balcony. The television was on and a plate of toast sat on the coffee table. Jess pointed to the stairs.

'Upstairs? I need a shower and a sleep. And I need to charge my phone.'

Hayden followed her into the room. 'What's happened?' His T-shirt was damp and clung to his skin.

Jess bowed her head as she took the first step. 'I slept in the car last night.'

'Right.' And that appeared to be enough for Hayden. 'Bathroom is at the top of the stairs. Shower's running, actually. I was just about to get in. You'll find the bedroom to the right. Give me your phone and I'll charge it for you. I'm bound to have a cable that fits.'

The bathroom was small but clean and Jess undressed slowly. Deodorant and shaving foam cans were dotted around the sink and she stared at herself in the mirror. Her eyes were bloodshot, eyelids heavy. Her hair needed a wash. *I look like I've been camping*, and Jess remembered a holiday many years ago, when the kids were small. They'd taken them to the Lakes, hoping for sun, hoping for a good time. Instead, what they got was a washed out tent and tick bites. Jess didn't sleep properly for the three nights they were there. The thought of her children now brought a pinch to her nose, and Jess passed a shaking hand over her face. She wondered what Alec would tell them when they arrived home from their friends'.

Steam eventually clouded the mirror and Jess stepped under the water. She stood still for a long time, head throbbing from tiredness. The weariness of the past twelve hours swamped her, turning her mind milky with fatigue. She thought about what Hayden would say if she ran a bath, if he would mind.

From downstairs she heard the clink of dishes in the sink, providing a cue to finish up. She washed with Hayden's shower gel and dried herself on a thick, purple towel. And then she stumbled towards Hayden's unmade bed, wound herself in his duvet and fell asleep.

~ 12 ~

Jess was still under, still weighed down by sleep when Hayden lay down next to her. Her eyes fluttered open, hot and sticky. Hayden had also showered and changed his clothes, and was wearing a clean T-shirt and tracksuit bottoms. His head rested on the pillow.

'Better?' he asked softly.

Jess groaned and rolled onto her back. The curtains were closed—*were they closed when I came in?*—and the noise of the road and gathering football crowds outside was muffled by the thick glass windows. She rubbed her face. 'What time is it?'

'Two o'clock. You've had about four hours.'

'Not enough.'

'I made you coffee.' Hayden nodded to a pair of mugs on the bedside cabinet. 'I have juice but that always makes me feel sick if I've not slept. Sits like a blob in my stomach.'

'Coffee's fine, thanks.' Jess pulled herself up, making sure she dragged the duvet with her. She remembered she was naked and was not yet ready for Hayden to see her. That would take time.

'So you slept in your car?' Hayden leant across her to reach his own drink. 'Been a while since I've done that but it has been known.'

'It's not as exciting as it sounds, is it? My neck is killing me.'

'What happened? Were you out with Mum again?'

Jess thought of Marie's bewildered face in the coffee shop earlier that week, when she worried about her son. She couldn't remember the last time they'd been out on the town.

'Nothing like that. I'm angry at Alec. It's better if we don't talk about it.'

'Sure,' Hayden shrugged. 'Tell me when you want to.'

They finished their coffees in silence, listening to the cheers of the fans surging into the stadium, the clip-clop of mounted police, and the bray of vendors yelling out prices for replica shirts and programmes.

'Ever go to a game?' Jess asked.

'Once or twice. You can see half the pitch from the roof.'

'Of the flats?'

Hayden grinned. 'Only half, mind. You might see all the action, or none of it. Depends.'

'You aren't bothered by the noise outside? The disturbance?'

'It's a laugh, actually. I make sure I get my run in before they close the street and then I watch from the balcony. The crowd is always good-natured. Listen.' Hayden got up and opened a window. Chants and shouts threaded into the room, along with a cloud of biting cold. Jess shivered and pulled the duvet close.

Hayden got back onto the bed and edged underneath the duvet as well, bare feet touching hers. 'They're winding up to kick-off. They're deafening when the team comes out.'

Four days ago, Hayden's hands had been under her clothes, on her back, round her waist. Now, in Hayden's bed, Jess allowed her legs to tangle with his.

Then, as the street roared below, Jess thought of Alec and his trips to the York City ground. He'd had a season ticket for their home games since forever. He didn't go in for buying new replica shirts every year, preferring the faded old top he'd bought twenty years before but, every August, he took himself off to the ticket office and bought a season ticket for the following year. Once Alec had offered to buy one for James, but their son, more interested in computer games and hanging about with his mates, knocked him back.

Alec never went to away matches. Or did he? Jess tried to remember. Had he gone to any this season? *Or did he say he was going, but he met up with her instead?* Jess wondered, lips pursing together. It was possible. Maybe it wasn't just twice, with Laura Preston. Maybe it was still going on.

Hayden lay silent and still next to her. He seemed content to wait, though the events of the morning must have puzzled him. The smell of his sports deodorant was on the sheets.

And then Jess rolled onto her side, close against him. His T-shirt had come up and his skin was smooth and soft. Despite the cool of the room, he felt warm. She stretched out an arm and laid it over his chest, fingers tracing the line of his ribs, and then she moved downwards, sliding further into the bed. The duvet pressed back, she heard him sigh. His erection brushed her cheek and suddenly, clearly, she wanted him. His hands were in her hair. And then he was as naked as she, letting Jess, this new Jess, move above him.

Outside the crowd grew louder, cheering and bellowing, throbbing towards the gate and the start of the game.

⁂

The noise of Jess's phone disturbed them about an hour later. They lay on top of the duvet, skin cooling, damp gathering in dips and indentations. Hayden's eyes were closed though he wasn't asleep; his hand rested on Jess's breast.

'Do you have to get that?' he murmured, pressing his face against her shoulder.

Jess sat up. The phone's disco music wailed up the stairs, pulling on her insides. 'It might be my kids.' She picked up Hayden's top, lying on the floor. She tugged it on quickly and padded down the stairs. Outside the crowds had disappeared; they were watching the game in the stadium, yelling and roaring as one.

Jess got to the phone just before it rang off. She disconnected the charger and answered. 'Hello? Megan?'

'No, it's—it's Billy.'

Billy. The disappointment that it was not her child surprised Jess with its force. She walked slowly back up the stairs to where Hayden was sitting up, leaning against the headboard.

'Are you feeling better?' Butterfield talked quietly. Jess wondered if he was in the library, hidden in an aisle somewhere, breaking the rules by being on his phone. 'I thought I'd leave you for a bit. You looked shattered.'

Jess sat down on the edge of the bed. Her back and thighs ached. Hayden reached forward and cupped her round the waist. 'Yes, I went to my friend's flat. She let me crash for a while.' Jess felt Hayden's smile against her shoulder.

'Jessica, you've got to see this.' Butterfield's voice was serious. He panted a little. 'It's all here.'

'What?'

'Letters from Allegra to her cousin. She tells Emily everything. *Everything.* Where she met the bishop, when they started their affair, the baby. What happened in Greece, what happened when she came back to London ...'

'She talks about Shacklock? Mentions him by name?'

'First name. Anthony. That's why no one's linked the dots. None of Emily's family would have known which Anthony. *We do.*'

Jess turned to look at Hayden. He looked curious. She shook her head. 'I can't believe it, Billy.'

'Me neither. Look, if you're feeling better, get over here. The place is open till six and there are hundreds of letters.'

'As much as that?'

'It looks as though Allegra wrote to her cousin all her life. The letters are so detailed. There's a full record here.'

'Does she say if her daughter travelled to France?'

'I haven't got that far. There's so much to get through.'

Jess imagined Butterfield rubbing his forehead frantically. 'Did you say the place is open till six?'

'Yes. The manuscript librarian seems interested in what I'm doing; we might be able to persuade her to open up again tomorrow for a few hours.'

'Can you stay?' Jess glanced over her shoulder at Hayden.

'No. My wife is expecting me back.'

'Your ... oh.' Though she couldn't say exactly why, Jess felt crushed. So she really didn't know Billy at all: she'd had him pegged for so long as single. *Be honest, you thought he'd never had a girlfriend*, she admonished herself. *I guess that shows how little you can tell from someone's appearance. Or how rubbish I am at judging people.* It wasn't the first time that day Jess had had that thought and something deep within curled up into a ball.

'What about you? Can you stay overnight and go to the library tomorrow?' Butterfield moved the phone from ear to ear, the handset scuffing against fabric. 'At your friend's?'

Jess paused. She wasn't sure if Hayden could hear the other side of the conversation or not. 'Maybe. I'll see. I'll come over. Be about an hour or so.'

The call ended and Jess held the phone against her chest. Behind,

Hayden breathed steadily, chest rising and falling against her back. He waited patiently, ready to listen when she wanted to speak.

And when Jess did, the words felt so alien, so strange in her mouth that she couldn't believe them. She had wanted to say them for so long, mainly to be rid of Waller and his obsessive work. But Jess had also wanted to say those words because she also needed to know who this strange, mysterious woman was, who came to be buried so unceremoniously with the bishop. Waller had once shown Jess the nameless woman's finger bone, wrapped in brown paper and stored in a locked safe in his office. Parts of the bone had been cut away, no doubt for the DNA testing ordered some years before. Jess had stared at the sad, grey little piece lying lonely and dislocated in Waller's palm, simultaneously overwhelmed by a powerful feeling that such irreverence for a woman's body was wrong, and that there was not a damn thing she could do about it. The only way to put an end to the poking and prodding and testing was to find a name—the woman's name—and give her an identity. That way Waller would leave her alone and possibly allow the bone to go back to France, to be reunited with the rest of her.

Jess reached for Hayden's fingers and entwined her own. He squeezed gently, firmly. His fingers were long and smooth. Dark hair gathered at the wrists and Jess touched it.

'That was a colleague from the library in Jedthorpe. He travelled down with me today. The woman I told you about, who was buried with the bishop—we've found a name.'

'Really? Where is he now, your friend?'

'He's at Hampstead. There's a mountain of papers to get through but it's there.' Jess turned round to face Hayden. 'I can't believe it. Six years of work and we might just have found out who she was. I need to help him.'

Hayden released her. 'Are you coming back?'

Jess hesitated. 'Yes. I'll need to phone home. Talk to my kids, at least.'

Whether Hayden read more into this and wondered why she did not want to talk to her husband, he did not indicate. Instead he simply retrieved Jess's clothes from the bathroom and handed them over.

Jess finished dressing and went downstairs again to collect her bag. She found a comb inside and brushed her hair, realising she had nothing, absolutely nothing with her. No toiletries, no change of clothes.

Only a work bag with notepads, her laptop, pens. If she was going to stay another night, she would need to pick up some things.

Hayden followed her down the stairs, dressed in boxers. He paused at the bottom and watched Jess gather her things. 'Can you remember how to get to the tube?'

'Sure. It's not far.' Jess patted her pockets, an empty gesture that signalled her readiness to leave. The feeling of being set adrift, of being anchorless, was there again and threatened to overwhelm her. But then she looked at Hayden, leaning against the wooden banisters. With an effort she surged towards him, holding him round the waist, head thrown back so she could see him as he stood on the bottom stair. 'I'll be back later.'

Hayden's hand dropped into her hair and Jess remembered their time in his bed an hour before. He had wound his hands in her hair then, gasping and twitching as she pushed him on his back, her own head bowed over his body. 'Of course. I'll be here.'

'Can I ask you something?' Jess smiled, sheepish. 'I need a few things. Toothbrush. Deodorant. Do you mind?'

Hayden smiled back and locked his hands behind her neck, so that her head relaxed against his fingers. 'Of course I don't. As long as you promise to come back here to use them.'

'I promise.'

And then they let each other go reluctantly. Jess cast a look over her shoulder as she closed the door behind her; Hayden still stood at the bottom of the stairs, watching her go. The elastic connection between them hummed and warmed as it became stretched, and Jess had to force her feet onwards, down the stairs, towards the tube and Hampstead.

Part 2

Piraeus & Earls Court

~ 13 ~

June 1899

A man hung upside down from the foremast. His legs were curled around the horizontal slat of wood, a knife in his mouth. Dangling so precariously he seemed easy fodder for the stiff winds shuttling around Piraeus Port but, to those watching from the safety of the dock, his thighs must have been made of iron, for he stayed in place. The sailor's hands were busy, tugging at a rope, and occasionally his shouts filtered down to the small knot of people standing on the dock below. Some in the group marvelled at the man's courage, others at his foolishness. But all shared a smile when the man released the rope he was wrestling with and righted himself. He then skidded down the mast to the deck and busied himself with the trunks and packing boxes, the spoils of the merchant.

Allegra Underwood was in the gathering on the quayside. She had held her breath as the sailor did his work, only breathing again when his feet landed on the relative safety of the deck. He looked younger than she; Josiah had told her stories of men, boys coming to see him at his clinic, bones shattered from a fall from a mast, flesh pounded by the spillage of towers of crates or torn apart by a hook or whale spear. Her father-in-law didn't tell her these things to shock her, though sometimes Allegra had difficulty turning back to her reading or finishing her meal after hearing the latest story. She still listened, knowing it was Josiah's way of cleansing himself. His son, Edward, went to his gentlemen's club at the marina; Josiah talked.

A vendor selling kolatsio called out from a stall nearby, the smell of frying cheese and pastries drifting over. Josiah, standing at the front of the group, right on the edge of the wharf, turned round, distracted. Allegra saw his eyes were red and rimmed with tiredness. Constance had confided that he hadn't slept since the letter arrived. He'd taken to coming into Constance's room in the middle of the night to talk, even though his wife was sick. Sometimes, when Allegra arrived to help Constance up in the morning, she found Josiah asleep in an easy chair, cheek propped on an elbow.

Edward stood a small distance away, holding up his mother as the surf crashed about them. Constance had been difficult to rouse that morning but had insisted on coming down to the port. 'I need to see him, too,' she had said, and Allegra had eased her mother-in-law into her clothes, fastening her corsets as tight as she dared. Constance had mumbled a little as Allegra pulled the stitching together and tied her skirts. Curious as to whom this visitor was, the stranger who had dissolved her father-in-law into a tense, twitching ball of nerves, Allegra had listened to Constance's incoherent mutterings. After several weeks of it, she was none the wiser.

She'd tried to talk to Edward about the visitor. One morning, when he was particularly relaxed after a few hours at the baths, Allegra had approached him. But her husband knew nothing either, having never heard the stranger's name. He had flapped her away, turning back to his newspaper, a demitasse cup of thick, black coffee at his elbow.

Suddenly, a movement. Josiah was up on his tiptoes, straining. A ship crested the harbour wall, looming into view, dirty grey sails flapping, sailors on the bows waiting to throw out ropes and dock. A tall, imposing vessel, the merchant ship dwarfed the smaller punts and fishing boats bobbing in the blue of the Aegan Sea. Josiah shielded his eyes from the blazing sun and squinted; Allegra could see the cords on his neck stand out with the effort. Then her father-in-law turned back to the group.

'It's his ship. That's his.' His voice cracked at this last and he turned back to the water, back to the deep blue mirroring the cloudless sky.

Those working the port at Piraeus were old hands, and the ship docked quickly. Gangways were thrown down and sailors hopped down from the vessel, tugging trunks and boxes. Passengers disembarked slowly, some shakily. They moved as if in a dream. Allegra supposed it must be the strangeness of being on dry, steady land. She had felt like that sometimes when visiting London during the school holidays as a child; Emily, her cousin, always laughed to see Allegra take her first wobbly steps onto the pier at Southampton. Now, Allegra watched as women of all ages held onto outstretched hands and allowed themselves to be dragged onto the dock. Their skirts trembled with effort.

Josiah moved restlessly, shifting his weight from one foot to another. Behind him Constance sighed. And they waited.

Then a man wearing a black hat and a white shirt appeared on the gangway. He scanned those on the quayside, eyes coming to rest on Allegra and her little group. She saw a smile form at his lips, and he stepped forward. Josiah was breathing rapidly. Constance began to tremble and Allegra moved to her side, to help Edward support her.

The man walked forward, stepping with ease onto fixed land. He carried a small travel bag in one hand. With the other he reached out to Josiah. His broad, tanned face broke into a grin.

'Anthony?' Josiah whispered. 'Is that you, after all this time? My old Corinthian?'

The men grasped hands, bodies still apart, the stranger in the white shirt nodding his head. 'Yes, it's me, Josiah. It's me.'

And then suddenly the bag was down and the men embraced, arms clasped around each other, bobbing from side to side, laughing, crying. Allegra watched, tears in her own eyes, amazed as the man lifted Josiah clean off his feet, bending his back, whooping and crying out. Around them the disembarking passengers looked on curiously, wondering at what type of reunion this was. The men were like boys, wiping the tears from their eyes, breaking out into fits again, slapping each other on the back.

Then Josiah remembered his family, watching in silence. He passed a shaking hand across his face and ushered his friend closer. 'Anthony, this is my family. My son, Edward. His wife, Allegra. And you remember Constance. Everyone, my old friend. Bishop Anthony Shacklock.'

At her name, Constance edged closer. She pulled away from Edward and Allegra's hold and stood alone in front of the stranger. The two stared at each other, Shacklock's face becoming still and careful. He wiped his brow and held out his hand.

'Constance. It is good to see you again.'

'Anthony.' Constance nodded, before retreating stiffly to stand beside her son and Allegra again. Allegra slipped an arm around her mother-in-law; Constance's back, so troublesome in recent weeks, was taut and rigid. Allegra held her, feeling the older woman strain with the effort of containment. Allegra recognised the physicality of the moment, though why this was so today, when meeting an old friend, she couldn't understand.

And then the bishop was reaching for Edward's hand and shaking it, offering his greetings, nodding his head in a polite bow as he approached Allegra. She smiled back, seeing the strength of the man, seeing the knot of muscles on the tip of his shoulders. He had wide, wide blue eyes, creased by a thousand lines, and grey hair at his temples. He wasn't much taller than she, certainly shorter than Edward and his father.

Josiah had gathered himself and spread his arms outwards as though he were embracing his family. 'My old friend, shall I take you to my home? There is plenty of room. You must stay with us.'

Shacklock held out his hand in thanks, and Josiah led the group back to their cab, the driver and horse waiting patiently. And they were away, into the hills of Piraeus, winding away from the port, picking their way along dusty, rocky terrain to Josiah Underwood's home.

~ 14 ~

Constance was in the bath. The weather was baking outside, peeling paint from the wooden balustrades lining the veranda, turning washed bed sheets into stiff boards, and still Constance couldn't get warm. Allegra came each morning, rising early from her own bed, to tend to her mother-in-law. Today she slipped into Constance's room and ran a bath, letting brown water fill the iron frame, mixing in almond oil as the boiler banged and strained and funnelled. All the while Constance shivered under the feather duvet, moaning as her feet pressed the stone hot water bottle, now cold. When Allegra touched her on the shoulder, Constance swung her legs painfully round and stood up slowly. Allegra helped her to the bathroom and silently peeled Constance's damp clothing away. She had perfected the art of seeing only what she needed to see, and the sight of the older woman's sagging, tired flesh no longer shamed her.

Except this morning. Standing beside the bath, Constance gasped, held her stomach, and urinated on the floor. Both women stared as pink, foul liquid spilled between them. It puddled around their feet and spread like honey on the tiles.

Allegra felt tears pinch her nose and, not sure why, she dropped the bundle of Constance's clothes. The white nightdress soaked up the fluid, and she watched, repulsed, fascinated, as soft roses bloomed on the fabric. Constance shook. The older woman closed her eyes. She had a look about her of a woman vacating her flesh, willing herself somewhere else. Allegra, whose own mother had died at her birth, was unused to women. She touched her mother-in-law nervously.

'Into the bath, Constance,' she said quietly and, with careful hands, cupped her Constance's elbows and helped her into the bath. It was deep and wide, large enough to lie back in and float. Constance rested her head against the metal and let her hair slide away, swirling in the water like an opening flower.

Allegra kneeled down to wash her. Clouds of pink oozed from the tired, grey point between Constance's thighs and Allegra hitched in her breath, pushing it away with a cloth. Constance was looking up at the carved ceiling and hadn't appeared to have noticed that she had soiled herself again. Allegra said nothing. Constance might know that her body was changing, was failing her but she, Allegra, knew her *own* body. She knew the way her little toe on her right foot curled in, sometimes making wearing shoes uncomfortable. She knew that her breasts were too small and stomach too hollow and boyish. She knew her monthly cramps, how they slid across her stomach like a sharp blade, and Allegra also knew the feeling of weary hope that accompanied them. Edward refused to talk about it, the fact that they still hadn't made a baby. Instead he fled for the club at the marina whenever she brought it up.

'Did you say something, Constance?' Allegra sat back on her heels. The older woman's lips were moving, two pieces of white coral rubbing against each other. Her face had thinned in recent weeks. She coughed and spoke again.

'Don't mention this to Josiah.' Constance moved an arm, churning the water around her stomach.

'Constance ...'

'Especially now.'

'The bishop?'

Constance dipped further down in the bath and Allegra wondered for a moment if she would go under. Instead the water lapped around her mouth and she rose again. 'He has waited to see his friend for so long.'

Allegra stood up, cramp gathering in her ankles. 'Josiah would still want to know.'

'Later, then. They have so much to talk about.'

'Are they friends of old?' Though Allegra knew the answer to that. The physicality of their reunion, the way they hugged each other spoke of a shared boyhood. Josiah was not so free with Edward, his own son.

'They will talk for so long, but sometimes forgiveness comes easily.'

Constance sighed and her eyes closed. Her breath grew steady, and she dozed.

Allegra leant against the sink and said nothing. What there was to forgive, she could not guess.

After a while she helped Constance out of bath and into fresh clothes. It was clear her mother-in-law was now incontinent, though Allegra did not know if it was momentary or more permanent. She helped Constance into a dress and padded out her underwear with strips torn from old sheets.

'There now,' she said, feeling she had to say something. 'It will be like when you were younger, when the monthlies came.'

Constance looked away.

The bath emptied and Allegra washed the remnants of the old woman's water away. She cupped her hands and threw water onto the iron base, unwilling the touch the rose shadows that still lingered. Constance lay on the bed again, worn out. The effort of waking, bathing, dressing exhausted her. Allegra settled her in and put a blanket over her shoulders, even though the sun was rising and the grass outside the window was burned brown. 'Will you eat something?' she whispered, hand on Constance's shoulder. 'Some yogurt? Honey?'

Constance moaned, sleep approaching. She waved a hand towards the armchair and Allegra knew she wanted her to sit down. The old woman sometimes liked Allegra to stay in the room while she dozed. Bundling the dirty night clothes inside a laundry bag for later, Allegra sat down and watched her mother-in-law's chest rise and fall steadily.

Outside cicadas hummed in the brown grass and bee-eaters chirruped in the tree line away from the house. There were not many people about, save for the maids walking out occasionally to hang washing. It was too hot to sit on the veranda, too hot for visitors to linger. Josiah's house sat like a glittering ball on the edge of a rocky outcrop, high windows glinting out across the Piraeus bay.

Allegra jerked, suddenly aware she had also been drifting. She passed a hand over heavy eyes, rubbing the fatigue away. On the bed, Constance snored gently. Allegra thought again about waking her and making her eat, but the woman looked so peaceful, so free from pain that Allegra could not disturb her. She wondered how long she could keep the latest change in Constance's condition from Josiah. Even with his visitor, Bishop Shacklock, he would surely notice. Allegra glanced at the soiled clothes piled on the floor. Constance left her rooms rarely enough as it was; she would join the rest of the family less and less if the incontinence didn't resolve itself.

There was a voice out on the landing. Two voices, in fact. Allegra sat up, listening. Whoever it was talked quietly at first, then a laugh, then the conversation took up again, louder this time.

Allegra twisted in her chair towards the door, slightly ajar. Through the crack she could make out Josiah's tall, thin form and the stockier, powerful frame of the bishop.

'I can't believe you kept it!' Shacklock's full, low voice. He seemed to be squinting at something hanging on the wall. 'After all this time.'

'My time at the theology college wasn't all a bad memory.' Josiah's wry tone. He reached out; Allegra saw his tapered fingers touch something on the wall. 'Do you remember when the photographer came? Such an adventure.'

'We'd never seen a camera before. A right contraption.'

'It was. He had us stand still for so long.'

'Was it raining? I seem to remember it being very cold.'

Josiah sniffed. 'February, I think. Damp enough.'

Shacklock said something that Allegra didn't catch, and there was a snort of laughter from Josiah. 'That's quite right. He was a tyrant, that master. Remember when he had us write out a passage from Luke one hundred times because John Bryant was late for prayers?'

' "You also must be ready, for the Son of Man is coming at an hour you do not expect," ' said Shacklock solemnly, and Josiah laughed again.

'The mater's daughter came to visit him once, at Stephens. I met her. Showed her to her father's rooms. She was as quiet as a mouse.'

'No surprise with a father like that.'

'Yes, I suppose it is a common theme. Dominant father, dominant husband. She married George Dearing.'

Shacklock made a sound rather like a bark, or a yelp. Allegra jumped. She peeked again. The men stood close to each other on the landing, Shacklock shaking his head.

'Master Dearing was a bully and a thug,' he said. 'I meet so many men like him in my work. Men who rule their wives and children like little kings, breaking them down, controlling every aspect of their lives.'

'He may have changed,' Josiah said quietly. The floorboards on the landing creaked as he stepped back, away from the photograph on the wall.

'I doubt it. Men like him never do. Yes, the law has changed, apparently making it easier for women to get a divorce. But the reality is very different. I've seen women stay with men who beat them—and their children—because they are into the drink. And why do they stay with these men? Because they cannot afford to go to court.' The floorboards squealed again as Shacklock paced. 'Divorce is for the rich, you know. Poor women have little protection.'

'Easy, friend. You're beginning to sound like a suffragist.' Josiah sounded as though he was smiling, though Allegra couldn't see his face.

'Maybe I am.' Shacklock clapped his hand on his friend's shoulder. 'Maybe I am. But I'm thirsty. All this anger parches the throat.'

Both men laughed and moved away, their voices no longer filling the space outside Constance's room. Allegra had been concerned they would wake her, but her mother-in-law slept on, breathing easy and relaxed. Not even the men's laughter disturbed her.

Allegra waited until Josiah and Shacklock were down the stairs and in the kitchens. She could hear cupboards being opened, water splashing in the sink. The cook would have left after breakfast, setting out lunch in the cold box, and would return in time to prepare the evening meal. The men must have found lunch, for sounds of cutlery on plates and guilty giggles drifted upstairs. Allegra smiled, thinking again how like children they were when together. Such a difference in behaviour now, compared to the anger Shacklock expressed only a few moments ago. Allegra thought of his words again, how he knew women with violent husbands. She wondered how. A man of his standing would surely not mix with the lower classes. But then, maybe he did. Allegra thought of Shacklock's easy manner, the way he had pumped the servants' hands upon introduction—startling them and making Edward tut. Maybe Shacklock did go into the houses of his congregation and see for himself what it was like to be poor and a woman.

~ 15 ~

June 1899

In the afternoons, when the sun was hot and high, Josiah's household had the habit of retiring to the body of the house where it was coolest. Jugs of water were set on every table so family members and servants alike could drink, though the servants tried to complete their chores by two o'clock, escaping to their own rooms or down to the seafront where the breeze whipped along the pier and through the many taverns.

Edward slept for two hours each day and had made it clear that he disliked the sound of Allegra writing her letters or turning the pages of her book while he settled in their bed. In the first weeks of marriage she had tried to rest with him, thinking it was what good wives did—rest with their husbands. She even told herself it was romantic, especially when she was hopeful of a baby. Now she took her sheets of paper and books to the visitor's parlour, where no one ever came and she could scratch out letters to her cousin without being disturbed.

It had been a few days since Constance had started to soil herself. Allegra had fretted over her mother-in-law's condition, once almost telling Josiah. Instead, she waited until he was out walking with Shacklock one morning and sneaked into his study, looking through his medical textbooks for a diagnosis. It was impossible. Other than failing kidneys, Allegra didn't understand much more. The books were odd; there were drawings of body parts that repulsed her so much she had to keep flicking back and looking again, just to be sure. A drawing of what looked like a deformed goat, two sad, shrivelled sacks resting at the end of two horns. *The female reproduction system.* A soft bag of skin and a hairless protuberance. *Male genitals.* Allegra's father didn't own books like these. She had picked up what she knew about the body from Emily and other relatives. Sometimes she overheard the servants.

She continued to worry about Constance. Anxiety licked the inside of Allegra's stomach and refused to go away. She could not tell Edward, knowing he would be angry at her for keeping his mother's secret for the past few days. She also knew Edward would not be able to hide his dislike of female bodies and their functions; Allegra could imagine his shudder and pale face should she divulge the story of his mother's problem. Josiah could not be told, and there was no one else. Allegra's father lived a day's ride away, and—without a wife for twenty years, since Allegra's birth—he would struggle to hear this.

There was only Emily. Patient, cousin Emily, who sent letters from London with tales of reading groups, church outings, eligible Hampstead bachelors. The white little packets that arrived each month were like pearls in Allegra's hands; precious, smooth orbs of news from a distant world. Allegra stalked the quayside when the time came for another delivery, eyes scanning the horizon for the steamboat bringing the post. She spent over half of her allowance from Edward on the cost of sending letters to Emily, hiding that fact from her husband. But Emily was her only friend and she could not let her go.

She sat in the parlour that afternoon, glass of water on the table, writing. Outside the crickets grumbled, and the sun burned. It turned all non-native plants and shrubs into forlorn balls of twigs that crunched underfoot. Every year, Constance would order seeds from London and grow fragile shoots of daffodils, cowslips, primroses. And every year, sometimes only weeks after planting, the unfiltered Greek sunshine boiled the life from them.

Allegra paused and rubbed her wrist. She had written almost three pages to Emily, confiding in her about Constance, and Edward. It had only been three months since she and Edward had stood side by side in this very parlour, Allegra dressed in a white robe that had been her mother's, and made their vows to each other. The major, Allegra's father, had sobbed into his dress uniform, drawing amused glances from Josiah. There had been no woman friend to divulge the secrets of the wedding night, but Allegra had read. She knew her Shakespeare, and the major had never tried to censor the books she borrowed from the small collection of English books at the town hall. But, still, she thought it was her fault when Edward turned away, night after night, his body sealed to her.

She had written something of this to Emily and asked for advice, not sure what her spinster cousin could say. Emily had tried to respond, out of love for her cousin, though Allegra suspected it mortified her to do so. Mostly she counselled patience.

Allegra had picked up her pen again when there was a noise in the doorway and a man walked into the room. It was Shacklock. Allegra turned and stared. His face was red and his collar was undone. His hair was wet at the temples and unkempt, shirt different shades of white. Greyer at the armpit, brilliant and bleached at his chest. He was out of breath.

Shacklock nodded and, licking his lips, strode over to Allegra's table. She sat back in her chair, eyes wide, and watched as he reached for her glass of water and drowned it in two gulps. He panted and refilled the glass from a jug on a side table and emptied it again.

He sat down on a small stool beside her. He had the air, she noticed, of someone who didn't care where he was. The stool was fragile, more for display than use, but Shacklock sat upon it solidly enough, dusty feet planted unashamedly on the carpet. 'I beg your pardon. That was incredibly rude. But I have been walking up Aigaleo, and I foolishly didn't take enough water.'

Allegra was shocked. 'You went up Aigaleo? Just now, in the heat?'

'I did. But only in the foothills, really.'

'You do know such a thing is madness? It is not just a pretty hill; it is a mountain!'

Shacklock laughed and a bead of sweat tracked down his throat. 'I wouldn't go as far as that. But, anyway, I wasn't completely idiotic. I took a hat.'

'Why on Earth did you go up there? There aren't any temples or monuments, as far as I know.'

'There are villages.' Shacklock smiled. 'Not everyone comes to Greece for the history. I like to meet people as well.'

'The heat can kill you. You're lucky you didn't get lost.'

'I'm good at finding my way around. Writing a letter?'

Allegra turned back to the table and looked at the paper, covered in her small, cramped writing. She didn't waste an inch of space in her letters to Emily. She was less frugal when writing to her father, who lived further inland. A servant or one of their children usually took a letter to her father once a week, for some drachma, and Allegra sometimes included sketches of the gardens, or the port.

'I'm writing to my cousin. She lives in London.'

'Do you write often?'

'Every month.' Suddenly Allegra's cheeks burned. 'I know how that sounds. But I'm not rich. Emily is the only person I write to in England. I spend most of my allowance on it.'

Shacklock held up his hands. 'I wasn't thinking anything.'

But something had been pricked within and Allegra could not stop. 'I have no one else to talk to here, and sometimes a girl needs a friend. You maybe wouldn't understand that. But it's true.'

'I'm not judging you,' Shacklock said quietly.

Allegra was ashamed to feel tears. She had written Emily's name dozens, hundreds of times on a sheet of paper and folded it to make an envelope, creasing her ache for a friend within the pages. Sometimes it was enough just to send a letter and pass it into dirty hands of a worker on a steamboat. She could keep her longing at bay and walk back to Josiah's house, picking up a book from a seller to displace the grief. But there were days when the absence of a real person, a warm-bodied person who would sit and nod and smile and laugh, became overwhelming. Some days Allegra felt her loneliness in a physical sense; empty, heavy arms, smiles that would not come to her lips.

Allegra thought all of this as she sat under Shacklock's gaze. When she finally looked at him again, tears brimmed over. 'I'm sorry.'

Shacklock said nothing but poured water into her glass and passed it over. He wiped the rim with his sleeve and Allegra took it. She knew Edward would not approve and that he would see something unsanitary in drinking from another man's glass. She sipped.

'Do you have family?' she asked.

'A sister. We write occasionally, see each other once a year. I'm too busy for much more. The people I work with are my family.'

'Not other ministers, though? I heard Josiah say that you spend a lot of your time with the poor.'

'It's true.'

'There are many poor people in Greece.'

'Yes.'

'Not so many here, in Piraeus. It's the port, it makes men rich.'

'*Certain* men.'

'Yes.' Allegra paused, thinking of the vendors she saw in the city, wearing patched, faded clothes, sometimes standing for hours, hatless in the sapping heat. And the children, too, sitting quietly beside their parents as they worked, teeth brown and shoulders thin. 'Do you—back in Jedthorpe—do you help families where the mother has died?'

Shacklock looked curiously at her. 'Sometimes.' He left a tiny space before speaking again. 'Having a baby is dangerous and not all women survive. Or the child.'

'That's what happened to my mother.'

'Yes.'

'You knew that?'

'Josiah told me.' Shacklock had a habit, Allegra noticed, of clenching and unclenching his left hand; not an aggressive movement, more skittish. It surprised her to see Shacklock act so, twitching the way a rabbit might before it burst from an otherwise silent and still bush. He was doing it now. 'Is there something you wanted to ask me?'

'I don't think so, Your Grace.'

'Please, I am staying in your father-in-law's house, sharing your hospitality. You can call me Anthony.'

'I don't think that would be polite.'

'Why not? "What's in a name? That which we call a rose by any other name would smell as sweet."'

'"So Romeo would, were he not Romeo call'd, retain that dear perfection which he owes, without that title."' Allegra spoke quickly.

Shacklock's grin was wide. 'You know Shakespeare?'

'We used to act together. My father and I, just us.' Allegra thought of being a child, and her father, on his knees while she stood on a chair, he fighting back the giggles as they acted out the balcony scene from *Romeo and Juliet*. Always at night, always after the housekeeper had gone home, and they had the house to themselves.

'You acted with your father?'

Allegra blushed. 'At home. Not on the stage, or anything as wild as that! He knew I loved it.'

'"It is a wise father that knows his own child."'

'That's from the *Merchant of Venice*, isn't it?'

'Yes. Did you put on plays together?'

'Not really. We'd read a scene. Nothing beats going to the theatre for real. When I used to visit my cousin, Emily, we would always take a trip to the West End. We once saw *An Ideal Husband*, before all that business that put Wilde in the papers.'

'I liked his *The Importance of Being Earnest* better.'

Allegra looked at Shacklock curiously. 'I didn't expect you to know the theatre.'

Shacklock shrugged. 'We sometimes put on amateur productions in the parish in Jedthorpe. On Sundays, after service. It gives the congregation something to look forward to.' He puffed up on his chair. ' "I must to the barber's, monsieur; for methinks, I am marvellous hairy about the face: and I am such a tender ass, if my hair do but tickle me, I must scratch." ' He made a show of scratching at his face, rubbing the whiskers with short, stubby fingers.

Allegra cupped her hands over her mouth, giggling. '*Midsummer Night's Dream*? My father always loved to play Bottom.'

Shacklock's face was animated, red and cheery. He nodded encouragingly as she laughed.

'I can understand why your father would find the role appealing. It's wonderful to let go and act like children, isn't it? Makes the world seem a friendlier place.'

They smiled at each other for a long minute, before Allegra blushed, embarrassed. As though had noticed her high colour, Shacklock stood up and smoothed down his trousers. 'I'll leave you now. I could do with a cool bath and a sleep, if there's time before dinner.'

'There's time. We eat late here.'

'Well, till tonight, Allegra.'

And now the use of her first name didn't shock her. She hesitated, tasting her reply first. 'Goodbye. Anthony.'

Shacklock made a brief movement with his waist that may have been a bow, and he left the room, emptying it of energy. Yet Allegra herself did not feel alone because of his absence. Instead, she picked up her pen again and turned to her letter, a smile on her lips.

~ 16 ~

Josiah had given the servants a few days' warning to prepare for his grand plan and they made sure they were ready. The downstairs rooms were cleaned and dusted, windows were thrown open and shrugs and fabrics on the sofas were aired. The housekeeper made sure fresh flowers were placed in every room and the cook ordered lamb and a basket of barbounia, tasty red mullet, from a seller on the harbour. And, even though there were no plans for the guests to stay overnight, sheets were laundered and guest bedrooms made up. The washroom was never out of use; Allegra heard the maids humming and laughing as she approached with Constance's nightclothes, stained pink. She had paused in the doorway, stepping back so the girls wouldn't see her with the bundle and offer to clean them. She had to come back another time.

As Josiah's birthday approached, he became more animated. He crackled about the house, laughing long with Shacklock over breakfast, cutting short his afternoon naps. He and Shacklock walked together down to the harbour many times, Josiah returning with olive flat breads and coffee, boiling up a pot himself in the kitchen—much to the amusement of the cook—and pressing Allegra and Edward to drink a cup. In the evenings, he sat with Shacklock in the parlour, sharing cigars and whisky. Allegra heard them go to bed long after midnight on more than one occasion, their boots stumbling up the stairs, giggling and hiccupping like children. Edward lay stiffly next to her, and she wondered if he had heard them too. Once Edward had tried to sit up with them in the parlour, but the conversation became stilted, and he had returned to their rooms, gloomy and annoyed.

'They just want each other's company, not mine,' he said the following morning, and put on his hat before walking down to the marina, without a single glance back at Allegra.

As the days wound down to Josiah's birthday, Allegra tried to ask Edward what would be a suitable present for her father-in-law. 'Is it a significant birthday?' she asked one morning as Edward shaved in their bathroom and she brushed her hair.

'Isn't every birthday at his age significant?' Edward tapped his razor on the porcelain. 'A reminder that he's not dead yet?'

'That's not what I mean.'

'I don't know.'

'Perhaps we should get him a pocket watch. Oh, no, your uncle Charles sent him one last year. What about a new journal? For his notes?'

'Sounds fine.'

'Or maybe something more interesting. I saw a vendor down at the harbour selling wooden carvings. They were beautiful—boats, flowers, birds.'

Edward poked his head around the open bathroom door. 'I will not allow you to buy a present for my father from a street vendor.'

'Oh.' Allegra was deflated. 'Well, what then?'

Edward threw his razor into the sink with a clatter and grabbed at a towel. He wiped the foam from his face and strode into their room. 'I neither know nor care. You sort it out yourself.' The skin stretched over his thin, bare chest, shone with heat. 'He won't pay it the slightest attention because it won't be from him.'

'Who? *Shacklock?*'

'Since that man came here, my father has barely said two words to me.' Edward tossed the towel across the room towards their laundry basket. 'Has he even seen his patients recently? One of the men at the club told me his wife has been trying to get an appointment with him for over a week.'

'I don't know, Edward,' Allegra said quietly. She watched her husband stride around the room, arms swinging in agitation. His sudden burst of temper puzzled her; reserved, aloof Edward rarely allowed his displeasure or favour to be displayed so openly.

'Well, I'm getting tired of it now. How long has Shacklock been here? Two weeks? I doubt my father has even been to see my mother in that whole time.'

'Have *you*, Edward?' Allegra asked, keeping her voice level. 'She likes it when you take your meals in her room.'

'That's not the point.' But Edward stopped pacing. There were flecks of black around his jaw, where he had shaved unevenly. 'How is she, anyway?'

'Fine.' Allegra spoke quickly, hoping Edward would not pick up on the way her voice chattered. 'She's sitting up more now and eating well.' This part was true. Constance was moving around more easily and her appetite had returned. However, her body leaked still, pink water sliding onto her sheets and soaking the padding Allegra replaced every couple of hours between her legs.

'She'll join us for this dinner then?'

'I think so.' Constance had said as much, planning on getting up to be there for Josiah's celebration. She had taken care to rest in the last few days and had given an old gown to the maid to wash.

Edward pulled on a shirt and trousers. 'Get me my shoes, will you?'

Allegra stood up, hair lying loose on her shoulders. 'Are you going to your club again?'

'I'll be back at noon.'

'I thought we could spend some time together this morning.' Allegra moved slowly to the wardrobe and pulled out Edward's boots.

'We have. We had breakfast together.'

'Not like that.' Allegra's cheeks burned. 'Some proper time together.'

Edward stood up straight, hands on his waistband. He did not look at her. 'Oh, for goodness sake. There's plenty of time for that.'

'Is there, Edward?'

'We've only been married for three months!'

His voice was raised and Allegra held out her hand, shushing him. It made her skin itch to talk to him this way, but the desire for a baby was so strong. It seemed to lie with her like a shadow at times, adding grey to her days. When she saw the Greek babies in town, she had to turn away; she couldn't understand the talk of the mothers, gathering at the town square with their prams, but the way they held their bundles and dropped kisses onto smooth, sweet foreheads, cut Allegra in a way she had not thought possible. If one of Josiah's patients brought their baby to see him, she locked herself in her room.

She remembered how hopeful she had been when she married

Edward. An ideal of what it would be like to be a wife had blinded the days of preparation, when she sewed her dress and ordered the veil. There would be romance and passion. And babies. Three months with Edward had blunted those hopes, and the image of a young wife, breasts and belly heavy with a child, faded from view.

'Will you stay this morning, at least?' Allegra moved back into their room and gave Edward the towel. She touched his chest, briefly, straining to catch his eye. He was so much taller than she.

But Edward stepped back and put on his hat. 'I will be back for lunch. And, Allegra, I would appreciate it if you would stop bringing this subject up.' With that he was gone, striding down the stairs, leaving the door open behind him. He did not look back.

Stones in her mouth, tears too big to swallow, Allegra closed the door behind him and sat on her bed. Outside a bird chirruped cheerfully, the sound ripping through the quiet room.

∽

Josiah had invited two married couples to the birthday dinner. Richard Southwell and his Greek wife, Adelphe Constantios, arrived first, pulling up outside the house in a horse and trap. Josiah waited in the doorway for them, Constance leaning heavily on his arm. She was wearing an old dress: a deep blue velvet, gathered in a ruffle under her chin and pulled in at the waist. It hung from her thin frame and was loose across her back. Allegra had helped her dress and had offered to lend her something of her own, but Constance had refused. It had taken all her effort to be up at this time of the day, and she was determined to see the evening through in her own clothes.

Josiah made a show of shaking Richard's hand and bowing to Adelphe. He muttered something about being honoured they could attend, and Allegra, standing back beside Edward, noted the proprietorial way Southwell gripped Josiah's shoulder, fingers flared, pressing down into Josiah's blazer.

'My new wife, Adelphe,' Southwell said and propelled the woman into the house.

Allegra thought how similar the motion was to the maid's movements when serving a platter of meat at the table. But Adelphe moved smoothly, olive skin on display. Her dress was cut tight and low, no bustle gathered at the back but allowed to fall seamlessly to the floor. Grey but not austere, a piece of black lace skimmed the top of her breasts. Allegra fidgeted, conscious of her own clothes, thinking her pale pink dress a poor comparison. Standing beside her, arm held out stiffly for Allegra to hold, Edward looked down at her.

'She looks half his age,' he murmured. 'Her father was Southwell's gardener, I heard. Outrageous.'

Allegra watched as Adelphe greeted Constance in excellent English, Richard rocking on his heels beside, wide grin upon his face. Allegra offered a smile as Adelphe approached; she was unsure why, but she felt sympathetic towards the young woman. She held out her hand.

But Adelphe did not seem to need Allegra's sympathy. She greeted Allegra coolly, briefly, and passing over the words of welcome, reached for Edward's hand while Allegra was still talking.

The housekeeper was on hand to serve drinks and Edward, taking up the role of host, led the guests into the drawing room. Allegra hesitated, not sure if she should follow or not. Over her shoulder, Adelphe cast her a look, her beautiful head dipping like a swan.

Allegra was saved by the arrival of Josiah's final guests. A portly, elderly couple puffed their way up the hill to the front of the house, lumbering past the myrtle bushes and lemon trees. Allegra couldn't help but smile to see them. Frederick and Isobel Green were also friends of her father and she knew them well. Frederick's face was scorched and shiny in the evening sun. His bald, bare head gleamed. Isobel had fared no better; wet patches bloomed under the arms of her dark green dress and jacket.

'My friends, why do you do this to yourselves?' Josiah cried, tripping down the steps to meet them. He waved to the housekeeper who quickly brought out the tray of drinks. Josiah passed glasses over to the couple, who were breathing hard. 'Will you ever hire a cab?'

'You know us, Josiah,' Isobel said, her breath crackly in her throat. She drank deeply, the loose flesh at her neck wobbling. 'If we can walk, we will.'

'But dressed like this and in this heat?'

'It's only three miles!' Frederick took a handkerchief from his jacket pocket and wiped his face. Watching, Allegra longed to take it from him and wipe the top of his head as well.

Spying her looking at him, Frederick Green smiled and held out his arms. 'Allegra, sweet child. Come and let your old friend embrace you.'

Allegra walked over easily. Frederick had once served with her father and was a regular visitor to Major Lucan's house. He had given Allegra a puppy for her fifth birthday; she had been inconsolable when the dog had died after running out in front of a horse. She remembered these things as Frederick hugged her tightly. Being held so close made her think of her father and she sniffed.

'My turn now, dear.' Isobel returned her glass to the tray. She also held out her arms and Allegra allowed herself to be passed to her, though a little stiffly. She did not know Isobel as well as her husband, Frederick having married Isobel when Allegra was in her early teens. Isobel had trod roughly in the first days, bustling into the Lucan home with Frederick when they came visiting, attempting to smooth out the warm chaos of Allegra's home, tidying up the crumpled rugs and piles of books covering every surface. Allegra had objected and there had been a few uncomfortable scenes. Eventually though, the women came to an understanding and gradually Allegra saw Isobel as a woman who had come late to marriage, with no hope of motherhood, but with love to give. In the days since her own marriage, Allegra had thought of Isobel more and more.

Now, Isobel hugged Allegra to her solid breasts and released her, nodding down into Allegra's face. 'Married life must suit you.'

Embarrassed, Allegra moved away, back to Josiah and the house-keeper, who was still holding the glasses. If only Isobel knew; the nights spent lying beside her husband's rigid, cold form, the times he brushed her hands away when she tried to embrace him. Edward was as immoveable as marble. His flesh seemed to shrink under her touch.

But Allegra didn't want to tell Isobel any of these things. Instead, she hung back as the Greens were shown into the drawing room, where Edward made the introductions to Richard Southwell and his wife. Edward was good at pleasantries. A smoother, friendlier Edward seemed to enter his skin when he was beating the social engagement drum. He laughed at the right moments, muttered encouraging phrases to those unsure or unused to these kind of functions; he knew just the right time to bring another guest into the conversation. It was empty, facile work that Allegra typically hated—her father rarely had gatherings at their house and most of his guests were old army friends, who spoke kindly, but bluntly. Allegra had enjoyed their company and felt comfortable in their relaxed, informal conversations.

Edward was managing well and had already found something the Greens and Southwells could talk about together. Both merchants, Southwell and Green struck up a conversation about the latest ships to dock and the rising cost of olive oil. Allegra hovered in the doorway, listening to the boom of talk.

'Am I late?' A soft voice at her ear. She jumped and turned around, finding Anthony Shacklock standing close by, Josiah and Constance behind him. Shacklock's trousers and boots were dusty, his shirt damp.

'Been walking again?' Allegra asked.

Josiah approached and slapped his friend on the shoulder. 'You old devil, you're not dressed!'

Shacklock gave Josiah a little bow. 'I apologise. Yes, in answer to Mrs Underwood's question, I was out walking again. Further up Mount Aigaleo this time, to Kikrani, a little village a few miles into the foot-hills. It took longer to get back than I anticipated.'

Constance edged past Shacklock, Allegra and Josiah who formed a little knot in the doorway. 'You have time to wash and change,' she murmured. 'We don't sit down to dinner for another fifteen minutes.'

Shacklock looked at her oddly, and Allegra realised that this was almost the first time Constance had spoken to her husband's friend directly since his arrival. Constance had only made it to dinner with the family once during Shacklock's stay, and rarely ventured from her rooms. Shacklock had not been to see her, as far as Allegra knew. She watched as Shacklock and Constance stared openly at each other, and wondered over the connection between them. Then, Constance straightened up and patted her hands over her dress, masking the shak-iness that Allegra knew was there.

Shacklock clicked his tongue and moved quickly away, heading to the stairs to his room. The moment he had disappeared, Constance's shoulders hunched over again, and she sagged in her clothes. Allegra took her arm.

'You should sit down,' she said. Constance nodded and allowed Allegra to settle her on a hard-backed chair. She sat down nearby while Josiah joined Edward and his guests.

The household didn't ring a bell when dinner was ready, unlike other English homes in Piraeus. After twenty years in Greece, some of Josiah's English habits had slipped. He either didn't mind or didn't notice when the maids hung the rugs and bed sheets out of the villa's windows once a week in an attempt to air them and rid them of dust. Neither did he object to the late hour that meals were served, and the traditional mid-afternoon practice of taking a nap was tactfully respected, even enjoyed. After living alone with her father, save for a few maids and a cook who had conformed to the major's whims, Allegra had found the transition to Greek customs a little strange when she and Edward were first married. She soon adapted, however, and had particularly come to relish the brief, two-hour window in the afternoon when the house would fall silent.

A maid stood quietly to the side as Josiah spoke with Southwell and Green and, when there was a gap in the conversation, she tapped Josiah's arm. Dinner was ready. Adelphe, making limited talk with Isobel about the availability of fruit at the markets, tilted her beautiful head to the side, eyes sliding over the maid in a way that made Allegra think of the scorpions that occasionally ventured into the garden. Adelphe's pink mouth pursed up as Josiah thanked the maid and announced to the group that they should move to the dining room.

'In our house, we use a bell to announce such things,' Adelphe said quietly to Isobel Green. Allegra, helping Constance to stand, followed Adelphe into the dining room, her eyes sending little arrows of dislike to the haughty woman.

The table had been set for nine, with Josiah at the head and the remaining eight were arranged with four down each side. With unspoken regard for Constance's poor health, Josiah pulled out a chair for his wife to the right of his own, instead of at the opposite end of the table. Constance nodded her thanks and allowed Allegra to settle her in.

Just as the other guests were sitting down, Bishop Shacklock appeared. He was wearing a fresh shirt, open to the neck, and grey trousers with a high waist. He still wore his black boots, though they had been cleaned and, unlike the other men around the table, he went without a cravat and jacket. His face was still pink from the walk, though his hair was smoothed back and tidy. He held up his hand as the group made ready to rise again.

'Please. Again, apologies Josiah. Shall I sit there?' Shacklock pointed to an empty chair next to Frederick Green, opposite Allegra. At the head of the table, Josiah motioned to the seat.

'Friends, meet the unpunctual Bishop Anthony Shacklock, a friend of mine from many moons ago.' Josiah raised his wine glass in the bishop's direction. 'I've only been planning this birthday celebration for a week, and today he decides to go for a walk up Mount Aigaleo, as far as Kikrani.'

There were approving sounds from the Greens while Richard and Adelphe Southwell glared at Shacklock. Isobel leant across her husband, breasts scuffing the china. 'Mrs Isobel Green. We must talk about this hike of yours later—I'm intrigued as to how you managed it all in one day.'

Frederick Green grunted and said his own name. Shacklock bowed his head.

'And what must we call you?' Richard Southwell's cool voice. 'Your Grace? Your Honour?'

'I'm not a judge,' Shacklock said, smiling broadly. 'Anthony is fine, actually.'

Southwell's eyebrows met in a way that signalled his discomfort with such a request. 'Perhaps Bishop? I have not yet met a man of the cloth with whom I would think it appropriate to be on first name terms.'

'Maybe you'll change your opinion after tonight.' Shacklock took a glass of water, glancing at Allegra.

Southwell sniffed and motioned to his side. 'My wife, Adelphe Constantios. Can I ask, humour me and refer to her as Mrs Southwell?'

From his seat at the head of the table, Josiah cleared his throat. 'Excellent, introductions out of the way. I've asked the cook to prepare asparagus for the soup course.'

As if on cue, the maid pulled open a small cabinet at the back of the dining room, one that Allegra had barely noticed, and produced two plates of soup. She served them to Constance and Isobel Green and returned to the cabinet, producing two more. Allegra stared, watching the plates crowd the table as if by magic.

'So, Bishop, that walk up to Kikrani. Must be nearly twenty miles, all told.' Isobel dabbed her lips with a napkin. 'Did you take a mule?'

'A mule?' Shacklock sat back and muttered his thanks to the maid placing a plate in front of him. 'Why would I take a mule? I had no desire to ride any of the way.'

'For supplies, man,' Frederick Green answered. 'Fresh water, food. You would need to be well equipped for an excursion such as that.'

'Oh, I had a canteen with me. There were plenty of streams along the way.'

Adelphe raised her eyebrows and turned her head towards her husband. Allegra saw Richard Southwell tuck his bottom lip beneath his teeth in a disapproving gesture.

'And food?' Isobel persisted.

'The villagers were generous.'

At this, Richard made a hissing sound and raised his spoon to his mouth. Adelphe continued to look away, shoulders taut.

'Interesting,' Frederick said. 'I suppose they were grateful of a few drachmas?'

'Oh, they didn't take any,' Shacklock said cheerfully. 'They were happy to welcome me into their homes.'

There was a silence around the table as this sunk in. Allegra felt Edward's leg twitch next to her.

Finally, 'Excellent,' Josiah said from his position at the head of the table. 'The curate of the church at the port mentioned only last month that the heat keeps some families away from Sunday services. Too far to travel.'

'Is this likely to be a regular activity of yours?' Edward asked. He was sitting opposite Shacklock, with Allegra to his right and Adelphe to the left. His voice was tight. 'A ministry up in the hills?'

'Why not?' Shacklock answered casually. 'If there's a need.'

Richard Southwell clinked his spoon on the side of his plate, a sharp, high-pitched sound. 'Where do you minister normally? That is, where is your church?'

'In a little town called Jedthorpe, about thirty miles from York.'

'You are here for a while?'

'A few more weeks, maybe.' Shacklock cast Josiah a slow grin. 'I was sent to Malta by my superiors and have work there. A short hop across the Ionian Sea was too much to resist to see my old friend.'

'It has been a long time,' Josiah said. Although he had not drunk much, his face was flushed.

'Too long.' Shacklock raised his glass of water in his friend's direction.

'Did you know each other as boys?' Isobel Green looked curiously at both men, as though she were trying to see the child they once were in the faces of men they had become.

Shacklock laughed. 'Young men, more so.'

'We were at Stephens Theology College together,' Josiah added.

'I didn't know you trained for the church, Josiah,' Frederick Green said, his voice one of surprise. He looked at his wife. 'Did you?'

Isobel shrugged. Sitting beside her husband, Constance moved slightly on her seat, rising and falling like a bird on a wire.

'I felt it was my calling, once,' Josiah said. Allegra watched as his eyes became dreamy, far-away.

'But you became a doctor in Greece instead. To our benefit.' Richard Southwell doffed an imaginary cap. 'We wouldn't have it any other way, of course—but I'm curious as to the change.'

'Another time, perhaps.' Josiah took a piece of bread and held it in front of his mouth. 'When the wine has been flowing.'

Richard glanced up and down the table and then, smoothly courteous, tipped his head to the side to signal deference. Allegra was again reminded of a swan, just as she had been when watching Richard's wife indicate her disdain at the dinner arrangements. *Perhaps I should remember them as the Swans, not the Southwells*, she thought, a little giggle bubbling in her throat. She coughed and pressed her fingers to her lips. Edward looked down at her, frowning.

They moved onto the next course, the Greens turning the conversation back to walks around the area. As all at the party had visited some of the many relics and temples nearby, the talk flowed easily. Even Allegra added a comment here and there, describing a ruin near to her father's house, or agreeing with the consensus that the monuments and history of the hills around Piraeus added much to the cultural value of the area.

Only Shacklock stayed silent, eating slowly throughout. *He eats like he isn't interested in food*, Allegra thought, sneaking a look here and there when Shacklock's head was bent over his plate. After soup came the fish course, the barbounia ordered especially. The whole group commented on it, and how well the cook had prepared the dish, with a simple dressing of lemon juice, herbs and olive oil. Shacklock made sounds as though he were interested as the conversation wove about him, but then Allegra noticed him pick at the pink flesh of the fish and push the accompanying salad around the plate. It was the same when the lamb came, served with tomatoes, onions and garlic. Shacklock ate a sliver or two but left most of it. Only bread seemed to interest him, and he took three, four thick slices from the serving platter in the middle of the table. At one point, even though he could not have failed to have noticed Adelphe's eyes narrow, he poured olive oil onto the corner of his plate and dabbed his bread into it.

There was a break between the lamb and the cheese course, and the guests sat back in their chairs. Josiah had kept the dining room windows open and drapes thrown back, but it was still fearsomely hot. Edward touched his high collar, again and again, perspiration gathering at his temples. Frederick Green pulled at his blazer and even Richard Southwell waved his hand in front of his face. Shacklock, sitting comfortably in his white, open shirt, shook his head and smiled.

'Why don't you gentlemen remove your jackets?' he said. 'I'm sure the ladies won't object and it is too hot to sit and bake simply for the sake of ceremony.'

Adelphe coughed.

A look passed Southwell's face, as if he were pained. However, he did turn to Constance and ask, demurely, for permission to remove his coat.

'Of course,' Constance said, voice barely a whisper. She wriggled again in her chair. Allegra thought of the padding she had wound between the older woman's legs and around her thighs. There had been so much of it; surely it hadn't become damp already?

The men around the table took off their coats, sighing as hot air was released from their bodies. White rings stained the fabric of Edward's shirt and he grimaced, uncomfortable.

'Was it as hot as this in the hills today, Shacklock?' Frederick Green asked. 'It is usually cooler by the shore and the devil's heat itself in the country. Beg your pardon.' He coloured, fearing offence.

Shacklock raised his hand, knocking back any apology. 'It was very hot, it's true. Some of the villagers told me they had not been able to till the soil for the past few weeks. Too much like rock.'

'Always a problem,' Isobel said. 'I worry for the Hera temple nearby. So fragile—you just don't know what damage the sun can do to the stone.'

'It's been there for two thousand years, my dear; I daresay it will be safe enough.' Frederick dipped his head down into the fat of his neck.

'There are groups of people who do what they can to protect them,' Adelphe said. 'My father is part of an organisation that clears the temple of weeds. The vines grow quickly; they get into the rock and can split it.'

'Her father was my gardener, you know,' Southwell broke in, proudly. 'One of the best local men around. Of course, I always tell him the most accomplished thing he grew was his daughter.' He smiled broadly, not appearing to notice his wife's pinched mouth and how she looked away. Southwell continued. 'I give a donation, now and then, to old Costas's temple enterprise. For tools and equipment. They do a wonderful job protecting the history of the place.'

'I'm more concerned with the health of the children,' Shacklock said quietly. He looked up and down the table, uneaten food on every plate. 'The soil is unworkable. Crops cannot be grown, and I was told today that the olive harvest is in danger of failing.'

A silence fell and then Richard Southwell sniffed. 'Of course, as Christians we do not wish to see suffering. But it is the way of things here, as it must be back in Jedthorpe. There are poor everywhere.'

'Yes, indeed.' Shacklock turned to look at him fully. 'I see families in my parish who are quite destitute. Families where the babies are given away because there are already too many children to feed.'

Allegra saw Constance squeeze her eyes shut.

'A terrible situation.' Isobel leant forward. 'It is the way of the world everywhere.'

Shacklock snorted and threw down his napkin. At the head of the table, Josiah sat back in his seat and locked his hands behind his head.

Shacklock shook his head. 'It is the way of the world because we allow it. Those children up in the hills, at Kikrani, will probably go to bed hungry tonight while we sit here with food we cannot eat. Just twenty miles away there are families who could exist for a month on what has been served here, at this table.'

'What would you have us do, Your Grace?' Southwell's mouth turned up. 'Shall we package up the remains of our table and put them on a mule? Send it up there?'

'Why not? But perhaps a donation, of money or grain, would be put to better use.'

'An honourable suggestion, but you would be mistaken, my friend,' said Frederick.

'Why so?'

'Where would it end? Of course there are poor in this city. At the docks, in the streets. The cost of goods has risen tremendously and not all can cope. We have suffered, too.' Frederick jabbed a finger at Southwell. 'This gentleman will confirm what I say. Our profit margins have shrunk greatly in recent years.'

'Quite correct.' Southwell tapped his teeth.

'But you have enough to give to groups protecting the temples from ruin?' Shacklock made a noise deep in his throat. Allegra watched as he spread his palms out flat on the table. 'Let me tell you something I saw this week. I was down at the docks, trying to find a ship that would take a letter to my sister. There was a woman, a beggar, sitting on the quay-side, surrounded by her children. Maybe five infants in total, the oldest no more than ten, the youngest a baby at her breast. I must have walked up and down that quayside a dozen times, looking for a ship that would not charge an extortionate rate. I gave her some coins. I might have given her more, had the captain of a ship not emptied my pockets in exchange for my mail. As I was leaving, the woman stopped me. With the baby still feeding, she offered herself to me, right there. For the cost of a bag of grain, I could have taken her behind one of the many shacks on the harbour-side and seen about getting her in the family way again.'

Adelphe gasped. Richard Southwell blustered in his seat. 'Really, this isn't the time or place ...'

Shacklock held up his hand. 'It is a glaring demonstration of the poverty experienced by some, not one mile from the front door. Surely you know I'm right? Children running around barefoot, bitten by lice, hungry. When my ship docked all those weeks ago, and my trunk was unloaded from the boat, I saw dozens of children running around the passengers, their hands open. All eager for a coin, anything, in exchange for carrying a trunk. I cannot be telling you something you don't already know.'

The table was still. Allegra breathed quickly, words crowding into her mouth. *I have, I have seen those children!* But she could not say it and instead looked down at her plate.

'Adelphe, as someone who has grown and been brought up in this town, surely you must know what I mean?' Shacklock asked her directly, but Adelphe sat, mute, fixing him with a cold stare. A jewelled flower, pinned in her hair, flashed in the fading light.

Josiah broke in. 'Anthony, what you describe is tragic, but perhaps it is only a tiny fraction of life here.'

'Is it?' Shacklock stared at his old friend, squinting as though he were trying to spot him at the end of a long tunnel. 'Some of the villagers I met today were talking about giving up their life here and scraping the money together for passage to America. Imagine being so desperate, so empty of choices, that there is only the prospect of leaving for a new land.'

'I can imagine it,' Josiah said quietly.

Shacklock fell silent and Allegra saw a little of his fire diminish. A connection fizzled between him and Josiah, which drained some of the force from Shacklock. He ran his hand through his hair wearily. He was not quite finished yet. 'Let me tell you something else, to go back to our earlier conversation about the precious temple. My church—my actual, physical church in Jedthorpe—it is a humble affair. Services take place in a cold hall, with a roof that lets in water and pews that have long since been burned for firewood. We sit on the floor most days and stand to sing. Yet every family who comes on a Sunday is fed and helped to wash their clothes. We do not spare a penny on the building. What is a building, anyway? Something constructed for the use of man only.'

'I cannot agree with you.' Richard's eyes glittered in the fading light.

'I would not expect you to.'

'I consider, Bishop, that you are an exception,' Edward said. His voice was high and strained. 'I've never been to England, though I hope to visit my grandfather one day in Woking. I can't imagine the way you order your church is typical. Other bishops have visited Greece before. Please do not take offence if I tell you they do not act in your manner.'

Shacklock laughed. 'Oh, I can quite believe it.'

Josiah tapped his fingers on his lips, brow creased. Allegra noticed beads of sweat gather at his temples and she leant forward to pour him a glass of water.

Shacklock spoke again. 'I'm quite sure there are men amongst my superiors in the church who regret my being elevated to such a position of power. There are those who would sit in their draughty, beautiful churches; never go out amongst their people, but claim to know them. "O, it is excellent to have a giant's strength, but it is tyrannous to use it like a giant."'

The words were out before Allegra could stop them. '"Could great men thunder, as Jove himself does, Jove would ne'er be quiet."' She trembled, aware of Edward's glare, but she could not help it; she knew *Measure for Measure* well. Across the table, Shacklock caught her eye and smiled.

Josiah drained his glass of water and sat forward, elbows thudding softly on the table. He looked around at the dinner guests. 'I think, friends, we should agree that there are things we would like to change, but cannot. And that we should all find our own, Godly way, and live like good Christians. Be that to protect our cultural heritage, which is no small feat,' and here Richard Southwell tilted his head in acknowledgement, 'or, as the bishop does, bring comfort to the poor.' Josiah stared directly at Shacklock as he said this, who looked back, steely.

Constance murmured something and brushed Josiah's arm. He dipped down to hear her and pressed his hand over hers. 'Please, would you excuse my wife? The hour draws on and Constance is tired. Allegra ...?'

Allegra immediately stood up, glad of the distraction. She slipped round to Constance's chair, aware of her husband's continued frown. The men around the table rose as Constance stumbled slowly to her feet. Allegra wound an arm around her and, with a small nod of her head as a farewell to the group, helped her mother-in-law from the room. As they reached the bottom of the stairs, up towards Constance's room, Allegra heard Josiah speak again, inviting the dinner guests to finish their cheese course in the sitting room. She imagined this was a suggestion again at odds with the English way of doing things; part of her hoped the Southwells would be most offended at the suggestion, but too constrained by their ideas of decorum to complain.

As Constance placed her foot on the bottom stair, Allegra pressed her hand into the small of the woman's back and looked around. The guests were slowly making their way to the sitting room, the Southwells walking together, muttering. They were followed by the Greens, and then Josiah and Edward. Shacklock came last. His eyes skirted the hallway, fixing on a fixture or a lampshade and then flitting away. Finally, Allegra saw his gaze come to rest on the back of Josiah's head as his old friend moved away from him.

~ 17 ~

July 1899

Constance kept to her room for the next few days. She slept heavily and very often would not wake when Allegra arrived in the mornings to dress her. Allegra had left her in peace the first morning after the dinner party, but when Constance slept in the following day, she sat on the edge of her mother-in-law's bed and watched her closely. She could not imagine how a simple dinner party had caused such strain. Allegra had helped Constance to dress and prepare, and Constance had sat at the table for no more than two hours before being assisted back up the stairs to bed.

But it was clear that Constance's weariness was not feigned or embellished. When she was awake, half-moons darkened the flesh beneath her eyes. Her shoulders sagged as she bowed over a mug of hot water and lemon. Allegra made sure the pillowcases and bed sheets were fresh, sensing that something about Josiah's dinner party and the company had taken its toll on the older woman.

Three days after the dinner, Allegra helped Constance into the bath. She had not been soaked for a few days, Allegra preferring to sponge Constance down while she was so tired. However, as the heat grew and the house baked, the need to bathe became stronger. After waking Constance one morning, Allegra ran the bath water and prepared some towels.

When she returned to the bedroom, Constance had swung herself round the side of the bed and her feet were dangling over the top of her slippers.

'Wait a minute, I'll help you.' Allegra hurried over.

'I can do it. I want to do it.' Constance stood up, grimacing. Her voice was clearer than it had been for days. 'There.' She stood up straight. 'I *can* do it, after all.'

'Good, that's good. You must be feeling better. Can you walk to the bathroom?'

'I think so.' Constance waved Allegra's hand away and stepped forward, one hand outstretched, as though she were feeling for some hook in the air to help her along. 'There. Oh.'

She looked down. The effort of standing up—or perhaps just the timing—nudged a gush of water from her body. Pink fluid slipped down her legs, over her slippers, and onto the carpet.

Allegra moved quickly. 'Don't worry, I can manage this.'

Constance stared down, unable to stop the water dripping. A low moan escaped. Her knees sagged and she sat down on the carpet. Her nightdress dropped into the urine but she made no attempt to move it. 'Oh, I hate my body.'

Allegra crouched down opposite, tears near, sadness clenching in her ribs like a fist. 'Come on, Constance. Let me get you clean.'

'I couldn't even sit up for dinner with that man. After all this time, I can't stand properly and look him in the eye.' Constance's voice was bitter.

'What man, Constance?'

'When I met him, I was younger than you. My body wasn't collapsing about me then.'

'Who do you mean, Constance?' Allegra gingerly moved the edge of her mother-in-law's nightdress from the puddle. 'Richard Southwell?'

'Not that pious fool!' Constance spat. 'The bishop. Anthony.'

'You knew him a long time ago?'

'I've known him longer than I've known Josiah.' And Constance took on a distant look, remembering.

'How did you meet?'

But Constance had finished. The effort of rising from the bed had exhausted her, and she held out a hand for Allegra to help her up. Allegra did so carefully, and led her to the bathroom. Constance said nothing while she lay in the cool water, closing her eyes as Allegra washed her.

After Constance had bathed and been settled back in bed, wearing a clean nightdress, Allegra gathered the soiled clothes and bed sheets. She waited until Constance began to breathe steadily and, sure her mother-in-law was comfortable, headed for the laundry room.

Just outside the bedroom door, Allegra stopped. Shacklock was standing on the landing, peering at the old photograph of his time at the theology college that had so fascinated him and Josiah a couple of weeks earlier. His eyes were screwed up into tiny points, creases at his temples. His face cleared when he saw Allegra.

'Good morning. How is Constance?'

He spoke lightly, but there was an undercurrent to his tone. Allegra's father spoke in the same way when he asked Allegra about Edward. Allegra hung back, sheets bundled in her arms. She hoped Shacklock wouldn't look too closely.

'She's sleeping.'

'Ah.' Shacklock moved away. 'Best not to disturb her. Has she been ill for long?'

Allegra hesitated. Anthony Shacklock was direct, that much she had learned. The truth was that Constance had been deteriorating from the moment of Allegra's marriage; now, with Constance's incontinence, her decline seemed to have sped up. Allegra doubted if Josiah or Edward even suspected how ill Constance had become.

She looked down at the sheets. For the last two weeks she had taken Constance's bed sheets and nightdresses to the laundry when the maids were elsewhere and washed them herself. She had seen to it that the padding she placed in Constance's underwear was also laundered out of sight. If Josiah and Edward didn't realise how unwell Constance was, she was partly responsible.

Allegra nodded mutely. Tears and regret filled her throat and she could not speak. They spilled over, washing down her cheeks and neck. Shacklock, watching quietly, drew her away from the bedroom door, firm fingers on her wrist. He led Allegra to a small sofa tucked away at the other side of the landing.

They sat together until Allegra stopped crying and then she spoke. Whispering, so not to wake Constance, she told Shacklock about Constance's condition, indicating at the sheets. 'She doesn't want Josiah or Edward to know. I've been washing these sheets when no one is around. I dry them on the rooftop. No one goes up there in the middle of the day and the heat dries them quickly.' She sniffed and looked at Shacklock, who had said nothing. 'Have I been very foolish?'

'No.' Shacklock smiled. 'You have been a good friend to Constance. It must be a pressure, keeping all this secret. But it was not fair of Constance to ask you to keep it to yourself.'

'She's been very kind to me. My mother—you know I grew up without a mother.'

'Yes.'

'Constance saw to it that I could come to her as a daughter might do a parent. That was in the early days, when Edward and I were courting. Before she became ill.'

'And now she is very ill,' said Shacklock gently. 'I think you have kept this secret long enough. It is time to tell Josiah. He is a doctor, after all. There might be a simple remedy to Constance's trouble.'

'I doubt it.' Allegra sniffed. 'I think Constance fears the news that Josiah might have to give her. That's why she wants to keep this private. She can be very closed off, you know.'

'Yes, I do,' Shacklock said quietly and looked away. Outside a herd of goats meandered down a nearby hill, the clunk of their bells echoing across the landing.

'Anthony, I think Constance is dying.'

There, the words were out, and they could not be undone. Allegra sat, mute, shocked at herself. Not once had she even formed the thought, regardless of saying it out loud. Sitting here with Shacklock gave her strength. She heard herself speaking again.

'She has been weakening for so long. I'm worried it is a cancer, or her kidneys failing.'

'If that is the case, the urgency to tell Josiah is greater.'

'I know.' Allegra looked down at the bed sheets. 'You're right, of course. Edward will be angry with me for keeping it a secret. He'll sulk for days, but I'm used to that.'

Shacklock raised an eyebrow but said nothing.

Allegra gripped the sheets. 'I have to take care of these things first. I need to wash them out. Besides, I think Josiah is out on a call. I'll tell him when he gets back.'

Shacklock was suddenly energised. He stood up, slapping his thigh. 'You shall not do this alone. I'll help.'

'Oh, you couldn't!' Allegra's eyes widened. 'It would not be right. The sheets are … well, they're soiled.'

'Allegra, I'll let you in on a secret, since you seem to be so good at keeping them. I have visited many houses in my parish, where the mother is in labour and the father is completely bewildered. Three or four children crawling around on the floor, not a clean bowl or a means of heating water in the house. These situations have warranted my help, and I have helped.' Shacklock rocked on his heels, pride glittering across his face. 'Last year I delivered three babies.'

'Three!'

'Yes. One died a week later but the other two lived. There is nothing to fear in women's bodies. Other times I have arrived after the baby has been born and there is only the cleaning to do. So be it. Hand me those sheets. I will help you and be glad of it.'

Allegra passed them over mutely and followed Shacklock down the stairs towards the washroom. There was no one else about—the maids were tending the garden. Josiah had started seeing patients again and was out on a home visit. Edward was at his club. He had left before Allegra rose, closing the door to their bedroom with a subdued click. Her eyes had opened at the sound, knowing she was alone again.

The washroom was a small annexe, built onto the side of the house, next to the kitchen. A deep stone sink stood under the window, a mangle to one side. Bars of soap and hand-held metal grinders lined the sink. Shacklock, obviously used to the set-up of a washroom, turned to the stove at the other side of the room and began to boil water.

They stood side by side, leaning against the sink. Allegra rolled her sleeves up and Shacklock removed his jacket. Together they scrubbed and washed, pounding the soiled sheets, each noting the discolouration of the water but saying nothing. The water was allowed to drain away and was replaced, Shacklock straining to heave a bucket of hot water into the sink. At one point he slipped on the wet floor, soaking his shirt through. Allegra grabbed him, hauling him back on his feet, fighting back the laugh that surprised her with its suddenness.

After an hour of sloshing and rinsing, the sheets were ready to be put through the mangle. Both took up their positions silently. Allegra fed the sheets through while Shacklock wound the handle. Finally, they took the sheets up to the roof, taking care not to be seen by the maids.

As the last peg was gripped in place and the sheets were on the line, Allegra sighed and looked out at the port of Piraeus. The white sails of ships reaching the harbour broke the blue horizon, the thrum of industry down at the docks wafting on a hot breeze towards the house. Allegra strained to see the small farmhouses dotting the hills down towards the sea front. Some were little more than shacks, others more robust, with smoke drifting from chimneys and animals grazing the brown grass nearby. How many children will be born on these hills tonight? she wondered as the sheets flapped behind her.

'Did you really deliver three babies, or were you saying that to make me feel better? About you helping me wash Constance's sheets?'

Shacklock was picking at his still-damp shirt, pulling the wet cloth from his skin. 'I did deliver three babies, yes. Or rather, I helped at their delivery. One of our church wardens—a married woman—is very accomplished in these matters. I followed her lead.'

'Oh.' Allegra turned away, oddly unsatisfied.

A noise, a shout came from the garden below and she ducked down. The maids were still outside, watering and weeding the vegetables. Aubergines and courgettes ripened in the intense heat. The rooftop was ringed by a wall, about waist height; Allegra knew if one of them were to look up, they would see her, the sheets. The bishop.

He had realised, too. A wry smile upon his face, Shacklock sat down on the terracotta tiles, back against the whitewashed wall. Allegra edged over from her crouched position and joined him.

'You know, they might see the sheets if they look up,' Shacklock whispered.

'I hoped that they would think the other had washed them and put them up here,' Allegra hissed back. 'That they wouldn't check with each other, you know?'

Shacklock nodded and smiled. A young girl's laugh floated up. 'If we go down now, they'll see us.'

'I know.'

'So we're stuck?'

Allegra shrugged. 'They won't be long. It's getting too hot to be outside, anyway.'

'Indeed.' Shacklock flapped a hand in front of his face.

Allegra laughed. 'How ridiculous, us hiding up here like children.'

'Are you hot?'

'Not particularly.'

'I would happily swap a dinner party with the Southwells for a glass of water.' Shacklock caught Allegra's eye, and they both snickered. 'Do you know them well?'

'Not really. They may have been to the house before, but I can't remember. I don't think Adelphe Southwell liked me much.'

Shacklock relaxed against the wall and closed his eyes. 'She struck me as a woman keen to forget her past. Now she is married to a rich man.'

'Maybe.'

'She'll learn the past is the one thing you can never escape.'

Allegra said nothing, but Shacklock's comments set a train of thoughts in motion. She had often wondered what had happened between Josiah and his own father, what had driven Josiah to leave England and settle in Greece, never to return. Allegra's father had known Josiah for a long time, often sending old friends from his regiment to the doctor when an injury flared up. Josiah was particularly good at caring for soldiers with muscle tears or joint problems. When Edward and Allegra became engaged, the major told his daughter he was relieved—Edward was not likely to take her home to England. Major Lucan hinted at a family argument between Josiah and his father a long time ago, but knew no more. Allegra had not asked Edward yet, never seeming to find the right moment. She could glean little from Josiah himself, or Constance, the pair never mentioning the Underwood family.

Now, sitting on the roof, she wondered if Shacklock knew. The odd exchange between him and Josiah last night at dinner—where Josiah had made a pointed comment about being driven from home—left Allegra with the impression that Shacklock knew something else of Josiah's family situation. After all, if anyone else did, it would not be unusual for an old friend to be aware.

'Bishop, can I ask you something?'

Shacklock raised an eyebrow. 'You can, but only if you call me Anthony.'

'Anthony, sorry,' said Allegra, faltering. But she was not put off her line of questioning. 'There's something I've been curious about, since I married Edward.'

'What is it?'

'Do you know … do you know what happened between Josiah and his father? Why Josiah left England and has never been back? My father says there was a family argument. I know Josiah writes to his brother: sometimes I take his letters to the port. But do you know what happened?'

Shacklock was sitting upright, back rigid. He did not look at Allegra.

'Do you know something, Anthony?' Allegra persisted. 'Whatever it is, I can keep it a secret. You've seen I can do that.'

He smiled a little and then sighed. 'Yes, I know what happened. It was a difficult time, and I was not as good a friend to him as I could have been.'

Allegra let him continue.

'Josiah met a girl. He wanted to marry her but his father didn't approve. He—he came to me for advice and I told him to listen to William Underwood. Josiah didn't listen and dropped out of his training.'

'Training?'

'At the theology college. Where we studied. Josiah would have made an excellent man of the church, especially with his interest in medicine. Imagine the good a dean or a curate with some medical experience could do.' Shacklock gazed down at his fingers and, to Allegra, he appeared sad, almost grief-stricken. 'But his heart was taken, his mind was made up. William Underwood never forgave him for what he did, and I'm afraid I rejected him as well.'

'But I don't understand,' Allegra said, shaking her head. 'Forgive me, but I thought men of the church could marry. Couldn't Josiah have stayed at the college and also taken a wife?'

'It was more complicated than that.' Shacklock laced his fingers together, knotting knuckle across knuckle. 'Allegra, I would be betraying a confidence if I told you more. I failed Josiah once, a long time ago; I do not wish to compound that by telling tales that are years old.'

'Oh.' Allegra sat back. She felt deflated and more confused than before. The questions lined up—who was the girl? Did they marry? Was it Constance? But a glance at Shacklock's furrowed brow told her there would be no more answers.

So they sat quietly together. Noises and chatter continued to drift up to them. The maids had moved on to another part of the garden, but were still close by. Allegra realised they had been lucky to make it up to the roof without being seen. She didn't want to risk their luck again by creeping down the stairs.

A low rumble beside her; Shacklock had fallen asleep. He snored gently. Allegra gave him a nudge and his head snapped forwards. 'What?'

'You were asleep!'

'Sorry.' He rubbed his face. 'This is ridiculous.'

'We can't risk going down. We'll be seen.'

'I'm going to take a look. I'm a bishop, for goodness sake. The gossip of some maids shouldn't worry me.' Shacklock stood up and leant over the wall. Allegra stayed still as he lunged forward, her hand on his calf, fearful he would lean too far and topple over. She heard the swish of cloth as he turned from side to side, looking, seeking. And then, suddenly, he was down again, almost on top of her lap.

'They nearly saw me!' Shacklock's face was screwed up, fighting back laughter. 'The plump one, the one who always dusts the sitting room—she looked right up. If a lemon tree hadn't blocked her view, she would have spotted me straight away!'

He edged to the side, freeing Allegra's leg upon which he had fallen. Her face was damp from his shirt, from when he dropped down suddenly. Her hair was pulled from her plait. Allegra put up her hand to brush it down.

'I beg your pardon,' Shacklock said, realising. He pulled back his sleeve to expose a dry piece of cloth and made to wipe her face.

'It's all right, really,' Allegra said, touching his arm.

But Shacklock did not move away. Instead his movements slowed and his hand fell down the side of Allegra's cheek. He touched her gently, his eyes wide, as though he were seeing her for the first time.

The heat seemed to close in and Allegra sucked in air quickly. And then, without warning, but somehow perfectly timed, Shacklock's mouth was on hers, and their lips met, bodies leaning against each other and the whitewashed wall.

~ *18* ~

July 1899

She was not sure, but sometimes Allegra thought that the rest of the family had noticed there had been a change in her. A movement within, a toppling over. She had not written to Emily or read Shakespeare in the drawing room for days. Sometimes, when Josiah spoke to her at breakfast, he had to repeat himself before she heard him. Edward came and went to his club without a murmur from his wife.

She hadn't suddenly decided she loved Anthony Shacklock, of that Allegra was sure. She was young but not foolish. And what had passed between them, on the roof and in the days since—well, she told herself it barely counted as a transgression. In the daytime, Allegra could stomach such reasoning, and rationalise away the kiss, and the prolonged touch on the inside of her elbow when they passed in the hallway later that same day, and the moment they pressed against each other outside Constance's room. These fragments counted for nothing, certainly not an injustice against her husband.

But, at night-time, as Edward lay still and apart in their bed, and Allegra twitched and ached with heat not caused by the sun, reason melted away and was replaced by the memory of Shacklock's damp shirt, the black hair at his throat and the strength of his hands as he helped her wash, wring, and dry Constance's soiled sheets. They had gone no further than a kiss up on that baking rooftop; and yet, these past nights, Allegra felt she had stepped over into a new kind of world, awake to a new kind of sensation.

Apart from a brief, awkward moment with Edward on their wedding night, when he had turned away from her in anger and shame—though she was not sure of the cause—and an unwelcome advance from a friend of her father's many years ago, Allegra's experience with men had been limited. She had not yet been naked in front of one. Yet she had read enough to know, or at least recognise, the awakening of desire within. She wasn't sure what she had expected when marrying Edward, but she had sensed that wildness and the prospect of tangled limbs was not contained in his buttoned-up, narrow frame. Shacklock, though, carried himself differently. His thick arms and legs spoke of power and movement. Of rolling. When she thought of him, pressure came to unexpected parts of her body and made her sigh.

That moment on the roof, after Shacklock had released her from the kiss, they had sat back, looking at each other the way a chick might stare at a hen, newly hatched. The maids still called out to each other in the garden below, and their footsteps came closer to the house. They were going inside. Shortly the path would be clear for Allegra and Shacklock to slip down the stairs. They lingered, however. Shacklock's leg was pressed against her. Allegra looked down at it and then up at him, at the wet hair clinging to his temples, the scrub of his cheeks and the flecks of black hair piercing the skin of his neck. Allegra had a strong urge to pull Shacklock's face down into the crease of her breasts.

She breathed heavily as he slowly got to his feet. The skin on her shoulder blades tingled, and she wondered what his touch would feel like. Then Shacklock extended a hand and helped Allegra up. Almost the same height, their faces were only inches apart; hot, sweet breath on Allegra's flesh. She moved slightly, wanting to push her lips to his again. But he stood back, frowning.

'We should go downstairs. While the maids are out of sight.'

Shacklock turned, but it was a half kind of movement. Allegra did not feel his body was closed off to her, despite the shift away. Instead she read it as punctuation, a pause in the moment. She followed him down the stairs and, as he opened the door into the kitchen and Allegra stepped through, he touched the bottom of her back in a lingering way that made her shiver.

∽

A few days after that moment on the roof, it was festival day. Piraeus had several festivals, which Josiah and his household had learned to bear with good humour; a day to commemorate an event in history, or saints or religious days saw the servants of the house disappear, leaving the Underwood family to fend for themselves. When Edward was young, Josiah and Constance would take him into the kitchen and let him explore the cupboards, safe in the knowledge that the fiery tempered cook was tucked away with her own family for the day. The Underwoods would attempt to cook omelettes, pancakes, or pile jam on top of bread. Josiah and Constance, indulgent for the day, would allow Edward the space to experiment, making sure they washed up after themselves and returned the kitchen to some order, ready for the following day.

Now the house was full of adults, the forays into the kitchen were minimal. Instead, the cook made sure that pies and flans were cooked the day before. Eggs were boiled and left in their shells; trays of spiced, sweet aubergines were prepared and left aside for heating. Allegra would have been happy to cook for the family and even suggested as much to Edward when they first married. He would not hear of it.

The night before this latest festival, Josiah announced at dinner that he had asked the cook to prepare a picnic. 'I thought we could go out for the day, up to the Demeter temple, about ten miles away. There's plenty of shade up there and lots to explore. Anthony, you haven't visited that area yet, have you?'

'I have not.'

'Then it's settled.' Josiah clapped his hands. 'We'll take a couple of mules so we don't have to carry everything but, in deference to my good friend,' here, he nodded to Shacklock, 'we won't ride. If we time it properly we can leave in the early morning when it's still cool, and return in the afternoon when the temperature drops.'

They were sitting around the dinner table, four of them: Josiah, Shacklock, Edward and Allegra. Josiah sat at the head as usual, with Shacklock to his left, his son and daughter-in-law to the right. Constance had taken dinner in her room, though Allegra would have been glad of her company. She spent most of the evening looking down at her plate, knowing her cheeks would burn should she catch Shacklock's eye.

'What about Constance?' Allegra dabbed her mouth on her napkin. She had still not told Josiah about her mother-in-law's condition, though had pressed Constance to tell her husband herself. 'She is still not well, and it is too far for her to walk.'

Shacklock glanced across the table at Allegra but said nothing.

'It is a concern, of course.' Josiah thought for a moment. 'She should not be left alone.'

'I could stay if you wish,' Allegra offered, but Edward shook his head.

'Certainly not. If I'm going to be bored by a temple all day, you can be bored with me.'

Josiah snorted. 'Thank you, Allegra. I don't think it will be necessary for you to stay. The cook said one of the maids would stay here anyway, instead of going home for the festival. Something about an overcrowded house—the entire girl's family is coming to stay. I could ask her to keep checking on Constance and take her up a tray of food.'

Allegra bowed her head, reminding herself to make sure that Constance had a stash of paddings hidden away, and clean nightclothes within easy reach.

As they left the table, Shacklock stayed behind. Edward left to smoke cigars with his father. Shacklock stared across the table.

'You still haven't told Josiah about Constance's condition. You must.'

'I told Constance to tell him. She said she would think about it,' Allegra whispered. 'Whatever happens, I'll tell him tomorrow, when he's away from the house and will have time to take the news calmly, instead of rushing up to Constance's rooms and worrying her.'

Shacklock considered this, head tilted. He was wearing another white shirt, as ever, with an open collar. In the first days of his visit, he had asked permission to walk about the house with his shirt neck undone. Josiah had laughingly flapped him away. 'Wear what you want, man. You will, anyway.' Shacklock had now stopped asking and his tan had deepened—Allegra looked at his brown skin and felt an ache in her fingers to touch it.

'Maybe you are right,' Shacklock was saying. 'It will come as a shock, to hear about Constance's decline, and a few hours away from the house would be good for him. But you must tell him tomorrow.'

'I will.' Allegra stood up straight and stared directly at Shacklock. Her breath came quickly. 'I am a good judge of the right moment.'

She did not wait to hear his response, sensing his reply would be clumsy. She left the room, heading for the stairs and Constance.

∽

It was difficult to check on Constance the following morning as Josiah made sure he spent some time with his wife before the party set off. Allegra rose early, leaving Edward snoring and sweating in their bed, but Josiah was already in Constance's room, sitting beside her and talking quietly. He looked up at Allegra as she slipped round the door.

'You are kind, Allegra, coming to see Constance before we leave.' Josiah motioned for Allegra to sit with them. 'Constance was just telling me she feels much better today.'

'Is that so?' Allegra settled on the opposite side of the bed. 'Do you need help to bathe?'

'Not now, dear.' Constance looked over to the bathroom door, her eyes dreamy. To Allegra she did not appear well at all. Worry gnawed at her.

'I can stay with you, Constance,' she offered again. She had said the same to her mother-in-law the night before, after dinner, even suggesting that Constance insist upon it so that Josiah and Edward would not object. But Constance had refused.

She did so again. 'You should go out and enjoy the day. I will be perfectly fine.' She smiled too widely. 'Just be sure to stay out of the midday sun.'

'I will.' Allegra squeezed Constance's hand. 'I'll leave you both.' As she left, she heard their talk resume, voices low and whispery as paper, and hoped Constance was telling her husband the truth about her failing body.

The group left the house just before eight o'clock. Allegra had retrieved pies and pastries from the kitchen, and Josiah had loaded a mule with two large tin flagons of water. He winked at Allegra as he strapped them onto the animal. 'We can't leave it to fate to decide if there'll be streams up there, like our good bishop.'

Shacklock had not yet appeared, which was unusual. The past few weeks had seen him rise early and set off on a walk, either to the harbour or into the hills. Allegra glanced around her as she fixed a basket of food to the mule. Edward was in the garden, picking lemons and dates to take. He had barely spoken since getting out of bed, face as still as stone. He had muttered about missing the crowd at his club, but said nothing to his father.

Shacklock came out to meet them just as they were ready to leave.

He looked fresh and alert; he had not overslept. A straw hat was perched on atop thick hair and he wore a handkerchief around his neck. He held up his hand in apology.

'I am sorry for my tardiness. I was trying to finish a letter to the parish back in Malta. I'll take it down to the port when we return.' He turned casually to Allegra. 'Mrs Underwood, have you one to post to your cousin?'

Edward's eyes widened, surprised at a question he would never ask. Allegra, though, was pleased. 'I am halfway through one. I should finish it tonight. I would be glad to share the cost of postage.'

'It would be my treat.' Shacklock touched his hat. 'I'll take your letter to port as well.'

'Fine, fine.' Josiah was impatient to be off. He passed Shacklock the reins for one of the mules. 'Here, old friend. As a reward for your late-ness. We can walk together and remember riding Bertie Winthorp's horse at Stephens College.'

Shacklock snorted. 'I had forgotten that. He wasn't pleased when it disappeared from the stable.'

The men walked in front, leading the way up the burnt, scrubbed grass. Edward and Allegra followed, slowly. Edward muttered under his breath, glaring at Shacklock's back, kicking gravel and stones. Allegra watched but said nothing.

They walked solidly for three hours, stopping only occasionally for water. Lizards scuttled across their path, tongues flashing, brown bod-ies twitching into the shadow. Lavender and myrtle was heavy in the air, and the call of a bird, too high up to identify, cut through the muffling heat. It was blazingly, unforgivably hot.

Josiah was eager to carry on, limiting their breaks to only a few min-utes. By the time they arrived at the Demeter temple, however, all were hot and damp. Allegra's hair clung to the back of her neck in sticky swathes, even though she had pinned it up and wore a hat. The men all walked in shirts, boots and trousers dusty. Allegra was glad of her long skirts, heavy as they were. At least her legs were free underneath and, if she moved suddenly from side to side, a pleasing breeze crept under the folds to cool her calves. She had made the decision to go without stock-ings that morning, knowing that Edward would be unlikely to notice. The morning had been bearable because of it.

The temple was built high into a rock face. Chunks of grey, rough boulders marked the path up to it, sections worn away by thousands of feet passing that way. Wheat sheaves and winged serpents, the motifs of the god, Demeter, were carved into the stone façade. High above, a figure of a woman dressed in robes towered forward. She held a pig under one arm and a snake was wound around her ankles.

'Demeter, goddess of health and the harvest,' Josiah said, pointing to the statue.

Shacklock nodded and turned back to the mules, unloading them. He led them to a small stream nearby. With a quick look to see where Edward was, Allegra followed him down to the trickle of water stubbornly continuing to break through the aged rocks. She sat down on a stone and removed her boots. Shacklock gave an approving nod as she dangled her feet in the cool water.

'I'm going to tie up these animals in the shade and will do the same,' he said, and was true to his word. The mules were tethered to a tree some distance from the path, protected from the sun, and then Shacklock sat beside Allegra, pulling off his socks and sighing as bare feet were soothed by the stream's pulse.

There was no need for chatter. Josiah sat a short distance behind them, setting out the picnic rug and unwrapping slices of melon. Edward had disappeared somewhere, and they heard the scramble and clatter of feet making their way up to the temple. The sounds carried down to them in the still buzz of the morning heat. Shacklock's hand was on a rock, next to Allegra's. Their skin touched.

Edward came back to the group after a while. He was whistling nonchalantly, a bored look upon his face. 'I haven't been up here since I was a boy.' He slumped down on the rug next to his father. 'Took me an hour to look around the place.'

'And what did you see?' Josiah looked at his son with amusement. He was used to the brevity of Edward's attention.

Edward shrugged. 'Few crumbling monuments. There's a statue or two that haven't been destroyed, surprisingly. A herb garden.' He sighed and folded his arms behind his head. 'Nothing that exciting.'

'I hoped we could be here all day.'

'Why?'

'This is your history, boy!' Josiah laughed sardonically. 'You grew up here, even though you steadfastly refused to learn the language.'

'Sending me to English schools didn't do anything to encourage me.' Edward's eyes narrowed. 'I do speak some Greek, actually. You just don't hear it.'

'Where?' Josiah sounded surprised. 'Where do you speak Greek?'

Shacklock tilted his head, listening as well.

'At my club.'

It was not an answer that Josiah evidently wanted to hear, for his tone became curt. Allegra's fingers moved closer to Shacklock's, and she shifted her body slightly so to hide their hands from the others.

'The club.' Josiah spoke shortly. 'That place you go to every day.'

'I find it relaxing.'

'What do you do there?'

'This may surprise you, Father, but I don't imagine it's very different from the clubs you hear about in London. We play cards. Read the English newspapers. There's a billiards table.'

'Who do you meet there?'

The question was simple; it only required a simple answer. Allegra sensed this was a question Josiah had wanted to ask for some time.

'Friends,' Edward said eventually.

'Who?'

'No one you know.'

'No one who could offer you a position? A way to earn a living?' This last was said by Josiah, sharply.

Edward stayed tight-lipped.

'You didn't want to train to be a doctor, you didn't want to clerk at the port. What do you want to do?' Josiah pressed.

'I don't know, Father.' Edward picked at a thread on his shirt moodily.

'You have to find something. You cannot be without activity or employment.'

The silence that fell between them was mutinous and sullen. Edward made no comment. Instead, after a while, he got up and moved over to a shaded part of the rocks. He leant against one and pulled his hat down over his eyes.

Josiah looked at his son for a long moment. Glancing carefully behind, Allegra saw his expression sadden, the creases around his eyes softening. He did not look much like Edward, except for their shared high forehead and the way their noses edged slightly off centre. Sometimes Allegra had wondered if Edward would look like Josiah as an old man; in the early days of her marriage, she hoped he would. Recently, though, the thought of staying married long enough to see her husband an old man depressed her.

In the end, Josiah realised his son was not going to come back and talk. Instead, Edward really was falling asleep. His breathing relaxed and deepened and, after a while, his mouth drooped open. Josiah sighed.

'Maybe a sleep after our long walk is a good idea,' he said. He smiled over at Allegra and Shacklock. 'I'm going to rest. We can have lunch later, if you agree. And Allegra?'

'Yes?'

'If you go exploring, please ask the bishop to go with you. I wouldn't want you to have an accident and be all on your own. Some of the rocks are quite sharp and there are a few nasty drops here and there. Anthony, would you mind?'

'Of course.' Shacklock waved a brief hand towards his friend and, as Josiah settled himself on the blanket and closed his eyes, he turned back to Allegra. The atmosphere changed between them. Josiah could not have known what he had done, saying such a thing; he could not have known what permission he was giving. Allegra and Shacklock's hands had lingered close together; now, softness and tenderness was replaced by a sensation all together more urgent. Shacklock took Allegra's whole hand in his, still hidden from the others by the positioning of her skirts. He squeezed it, so tightly she thought she would gasp; instead she did not, but manoeuvred her fingers so she could clench him too, fiercely.

They glared at each other. To a stranger, they would appear to be sharing an angry moment. It was far from that; the skittishness that so often accompanied fury did sit in Allegra's stomach, but it was shadowed by a feeling of rawness, primitiveness. She wanted Shacklock to take her by the hand he held so tightly and lead her into the hills.

They got to their feet quietly. As they passed Josiah on the rug, he opened his eyes and smiled briefly. Allegra forced a smile back, feeling that all her teeth were on display and that her father-in-law would think her expression odd. But she could not arrange her face into its normal shape. Her clenched jaw ached.

Shacklock led the way through the rocks. Allegra followed, content to let him find the path before them. They clasped hands again as soon as they were out of sight of the picnic area.

They did not head for the temple, where others might have stumbled across them. Instead they climbed further up the rocks, travelling almost a mile beyond the herb garden and statues. The scent of jasmine followed them. As they walked, rocks began to be separated by larger areas of scrub and bush; soon they found themselves in a tiny plateau ringed by a jagged half circle of stone, weatherworn and bleached by the sun. They were quite alone.

Shacklock stopped. 'Here,' he said simply. He dropped to his knees within the small stone circle, pulling Allegra down with him, so that they knelt together. He gripped her hands for a moment, holding them in front of her breasts, before releasing.

The kiss on the roof had been unexpected and cautious. Now their lips clashed together, teeth scraping flesh. Shacklock's skin was rough; bristles caught on Allegra's cheek, but she pushed towards him, searching for his mouth with her tongue. She had never kissed Edward like this. She buried her hands in Shacklock's hair, grabbing handfuls, pulling, knowing she might hurt him but not caring. He groaned as she threw back her neck and she felt the scratch of his chin on her flesh.

They lay down together on the burnt grass, Allegra's hands on Shacklock's face, his hands moving to her waistband. She felt him tug at her blouse and the fabric spill from her skirt; his hands were inside, over the top of her slip. Over her breasts, dry palms separated from her skin by smooth, slippery satin. Allegra held her breath; so this was what it felt like, to be touched in this way. As a girl, in the days before her marriage, she sometimes lay in her bed in her father's house, and ran her hands over her chest. She had tried to imagine what it would be like to be with a lover. Her body had responded to the sensation, to her own gentle, timid fingers, but not like this. Now she wanted Shacklock to take her whole breast in his hand, to hold it savagely, to put his mouth upon it.

Then Allegra pulled back and, without taking her eyes from his face, unbuttoned her blouse. She had not completely given herself over yet; the thought of returning to the picnic with a torn shirt troubled her enough to push Shacklock's hands aside for a moment. She pulled her slip down so that it fell about her waist and showed herself to him. He made a soft moaning noise deep in his throat and opened his mouth on her breast.

The feeling of him pulling, taking her in, circling her nipple with his tongue lit an ache within Allegra that pooled at the bottom of her spine and in the private flesh between her legs. She gasped, locking her arms around Shacklock's neck, legs riding up to straddle his. She felt hardness in his groin, unashamed and raw, and an unwelcome, jolting memory of Edward and that failed moment at the start of their marriage zipped across her mind. She shook it away, moving her hips against Shacklock's. Their rocking became stronger and faster until, panting, he eased away and slid his hands under her skirts.

His hands pushed aside her undergarments. Allegra felt pressure build again deep in her abdomen as Shacklock's fingers moved round and round in a tiny circle. She felt she was moving towards something, some giddiness, and clung to him. Then, unable to hold back anymore, Shacklock pulled his trouser buttons open and moved into her.

The sensation of being full, of being filled in a way like never before made Allegra cry out and her eyes flew open. A small pain gathered at the top of where his body moved in hers; not enough to stop, not enough to slow down. That feeling of being close to toppling diminished slightly, but she searched for it. The rhythmic movement back and forth sped up again; pressure and heat again, there, and there. And then, as the sensation almost became unbearable and she wondered if she could stand it, Shacklock's hips buckled and she felt him shudder inside her. He shouted into her shoulder and she felt fuller than ever, the tip of him throbbing out the completion she had so nearly achieved.

They lay still for a while, Allegra's legs still wrapped around Shacklock, his body still part of hers. She felt him ebb and settle, and threads of wetness slipped down her thighs. She did not want to move.

Shacklock panted, his head close to her breast, and he kissed her skin tenderly. His hand reached up to stroke her face and then fell to her waist. He cupped her bottom and pulled her close. 'Allegra,' he said once and closed his eyes.

They may have drifted; Allegra felt the fluid between her legs cool. After a long moment, Shacklock pulled back and arranged his trousers, smiling. They sat up and he slowly buttoned her blouse.

Allegra watched his face as he fumbled with her shirt. His hands

were made for work, not delicate tasks like this, but she let him continue, liking the concentration creasing his brow. She brushed hair from
his damp forehead and trailed her fingers down his face. He caught
them with his own, putting them to his lips. She wondered if he would
speak; this whole time only one word—her name—had passed between
them. What is there to say? she thought. We know what we want from
each other.

She wondered how much time had passed. Maybe an hour, maybe
more. The sun blazed high in the sky; now, only after they were done
did Allegra realise how hot she was. There had been no shade where
they lay. She got to her feet, brushing down the grass and dust, tucking
her blouse back into her skirt. Her underwear felt damp; she paused,
curious. What remained of their time together ran down her inner
thigh. It startled her with its unashamed hurry, tracking a silver path
across her skin.

Shacklock had also stood up and was turned away from her, bent at
the waist, attending to himself. Allegra wondered what he was doing,
but the scoop of his back told her he wanted to be private. She felt
unsure, aware there were matters of which she had no knowledge or
experience, even after being married for a period of months. Allegra
stood quietly, eyes searching the skyline, the blue of Piraeus glittering
like a fish in the distance.

What she failed to see, however, was Edward. He was crouched
behind a large rock a hundred yards or so from where Allegra and
Shacklock had laid down. He had left their picnic area a short while
after they had departed, hoping to catch them up. His sleep had been
thin and uncomfortable; his body burned with indignation at the conversation with Josiah, and sour bubbles broke through his dreams.

He had expected to find his wife and Shacklock at the temple. When
he did not, he turned, surprised, for the herb garden. Ahead he caught
a flash of Allegra's grey skirt; he did call out but they did not hear. By
the time he caught up with them, they were lying down, seeing nothing
but each other.

He had watched the whole act, open-mouthed, hidden by the rock.
Allegra's movements, Shacklock fumbling for her clothes. A horrible
spike of ownership pierced his chest and threatened to stop his breath;
that's *my* wife being made love to. That's *my* wife being touched by

another man. He didn't see Allegra's hunger for Shacklock and the way she undid her clothes for him. Instead, Edward saw a man taking something that was his, the way a thief slipped his fingers inside a gentleman's pocket and removed a watch. The thought that Allegra might have wanted to share her body with Shacklock did not cross his mind. The outrage and injustice was almost too much.

He had closed his ears to the shouts and gasps, but knew what they meant. And then there came the silence, and the sighs, the slow rising to feet. Edward risked a glance, just as Shacklock caught Allegra's hand and led her back down the hill, towards the temple. Edward sat back on his heels, his breath coming a little easier. Anger burned in his throat, and questions. How long had this been going on? When did it start? Was there an intention, a plan for the future? Edward ground his teeth, thin jaw flexing. He had not given in to his father's gentle pressure to marry only for it to be over within a few months. He wondered what his old friends would say, should he and his wife separate, or what his father would make of it. No doubt Josiah would twist it round to being his son's fault.

These were not thoughts that passed through Allegra's mind as she picked her way through the rocks, back towards the temple. As her boots scuffed and crushed the stones on the path, she was aware only of the man holding her hand and the strange sensations their union had left in her body. She felt marked. Her breasts felt tender and burned by Shacklock's kiss and the scrape of his cheeks. The damp point at the top of her thighs ached. She had no idea how Shacklock compared to other men, not even Edward, only that the soreness Shacklock had left was not unpleasant and she was now aware of a thirst that she feared would never be met.

As they neared the picnic area, Shacklock gently untangled his fingers from hers. It was one thing to assist a young lady on a walk—the daughter-in-law of an old friend, no less—and quite another to be caught holding her hand when the path was flat and clear of obstacles. Allegra relinquished Shacklock's hold reluctantly. Shacklock had such large hands; her small curl of fingers folded into his like a flower. She followed him as they neared the others, his shoulders rippling like the side of an ox as he swung on.

Only Josiah remained at the picnic area, just waking as they approached. His hair stood up in tufts and he rubbed his face sheepishly. 'Have I been asleep long? Never get old, Allegra.' He pulled himself up to a sitting position. 'I don't know how our friend does it, all that walking. My bones ache after just a few hours.'

He beamed proudly across at Shacklock, who had moved to the water tureens and was filling some mugs. Allegra offered a half-smile to Josiah and sat down next to him.

'What did you see up there? Make much of the temple?' Josiah accepted a drink from Shacklock and drained it. 'I expect you aren't much interested in our old monuments, if your talk at the dinner table a few nights ago is anything to go by.'

Shacklock said nothing but tipped his head to the side in a non-committal gesture. He joined them on the picnic rug, sitting apart from Allegra, looking away.

'What about the herb gardens?' Josiah turned to his daughter-in-law.

At this Shacklock looked up and a feeling of panic seized Allegra. Of course, they had not stopped at the temple or the gardens on the way up or down the hill. But they could not possibly say that.

Allegra shrugged uneasily. 'They were pretty, as ever. The scent was lovely.' She bent over her mug.

'Ah, here's Edward. Maybe a second visit to the temple has refreshed his opinion of them.' Josiah waved towards his son a little too brightly, and Allegra saw how eager he was to forget about their earlier spat.

Edward threw himself down against a rock, not joining them on the rug although there was room. His face looked tight and contorted and Allegra stared at him. The panic in her stomach bubbled up; had he been far behind them? Had he seen anything?

'The temple is still the temple, Father,' Edward said and pulled at his boots. 'The herb garden is a mess, though. Someone has been up there, digging the plants up.'

'Really?' Josiah looked at his son, confusion across his face. 'Allegra and the bishop have just been up there—did you see any of that?'

'We weren't there for long,' Shacklock interrupted. 'We passed through and went further up the hill. There is an excellent view of the port from here. Can you see any islands, do you know?'

Allegra saw how easily he distracted his old friend and the knot in her stomach eased a little. She listened to Josiah talk enthusiastically about the small outcrops and inhabited islands there were in the area, his voice spilling over her like water in a soothing way. She relaxed and sat back on her elbows, though remained aware of Edward's stiffness and the way his mouth pinched together. But if he had seen anything, he would say, she told herself. She could not imagine her husband sitting quietly if he had known what had just passed between his wife and the friend of his father.

In fact, Edward spoke very little that whole afternoon, and instead tasked himself with setting out the picnic hamper and tending to the mules. Josiah, thinking his son was still angry at him, became quiet himself, saddened into stillness. Shacklock, with an apologetic glance at Allegra, pulled his hat down over his eyes and slept after lunch. Only Allegra continued to try to lift the mood and conversation, until the day cooled and it was time to go back down the hill to the villa.

~ 19 ~

Constance was able to rise and join them for dinner more often in the following days. The day after returning from the temple, Allegra had gone to check on her mother-in-law and found her awake and eager to talk. She was relieved to hear Constance say she had told finally Josiah about her new problem and that her body leaked. Josiah had prescribed a powder, which Constance mixed with water and sipped as she spoke with Allegra.

Allegra's relief, though, at Constance's news was secondary to the gladness she felt at what had happened at the temple. Of course, she told Constance nothing of what had passed between her and Shacklock. Instead she enthused about a temple she hadn't seen since she was a child and a herb garden she hadn't visited, just to talk; just to purge herself of the energy that balled together in her chest.

This must be what desire feels like, she thought, as she scrubbed Constance's bed sheets the following day. Whatever Josiah had prescribed for her mother-in-law had yet to work and the sheets still needed to be cleaned. Allegra, though tired, welcomed the distraction. She had barely slept the night before, thinking of Shacklock's hands, reliving the moment his fingers plunged inside her, followed by that thick, unashamed part of him. She longed to have him back, and such thoughts led to a restless night; she tossed and turned in their bed until Edward grew exasperated and stomped off to a spare bedroom with his pillows.

Allegra grew hungry for a glimpse of Shacklock. She lingered in the sitting room in the afternoons, an unread play open on her lap or a half-written letter, listening out for his footsteps in the hall. Some days Shacklock was able to time his daily walk to end before the house woke from their regular naps, and they sat within touching distance in the sitting room. Later, they became more daring. On a handful of occasions, when Josiah was out on a call and Edward was again at his club, Shacklock pretended to stride into the hills, only for him to sneak back into the house and Allegra to creep along to his room. There, for an hour only, they lay together, exploring each other anew, each time more urgent and thrilling. Hunger and desire made them both unashamed. Allegra moved around Shacklock's room naked, feeling him watch her from the bed, taking pleasure in his rising interest. She relished the way he studied her body and its imperfections; the dimples on her elbows, the crease of her buttocks, her small breasts. She had never known such open interest in her body. Likewise she strove to know every inch of him. She traced her fingers down his chest, covered in black, black hair, thicker as it neared his groin.

The best moments, for her, were the minutes after making love, when both were satisfied and there was time to lie together. Shacklock would slip an arm beneath Allegra's head and hold her close in his narrow bed, her back against his stomach, their legs plaited together. With his other hand he would stroke her side, making her shiver, but not to create desire. More to love, she thought once, but would not allow the thought to come again.

There was only one time when coolness came between them during these moments in his bed. Shacklock had received a letter, forwarded by the church in Malta. He had read it at the breakfast table, eyes narrowed. Later, he spoke little, though his tenderness returned when Allegra appeared in his room.

'The letter. Do you have to go back to Malta?' Allegra asked, after they had finished and were lying together.

Shacklock did not reply. Instead he rolled onto his back, arm thrown across his face. Allegra moved round to look at him.

'I wish you would tell me.' She tucked her head down onto his chest. But still he said nothing and, when the time came to dress, he dropped a sad kiss into Allegra's hair. She paused, angry, knowing something grieved him that he could not share.

When the end came, though, the shock was terrible.

~ 20 ~

It did not end the way it might. They were not caught in an embrace in the sitting room, or laundry room, or anywhere else. Such a discovery would have been unlikely, for Shacklock adopted an air of quiet detachment when they were outside his room. He no longer lingered behind at the dining table to talk to Allegra, or find an excuse to appear beside her at the sink when she washed Constance's sheets. Instead, he saved his need for her until Allegra appeared in his room; then they were quickly shed of their clothes and reserve.

They still read together, however, in the sitting room in the late afternoon. The rest of the house were either out or taking naps. Shacklock and Allegra sat beside each other on the high-backed sofa, a volume of plays between them, taking it in turns to read aloud. *The Winter's Tale. The Tempest.* They started *Othello* but stopped, uncomfortable. Both took on many characters' voices, sometimes writing down the roles they were to play lest they forgot. Little scraps of paper, two lists side by side. Allegra kept these notes, tucking them inside her jewellery box at night. There was power in the columns of names, with hers and Shacklock's at the top. She came to treasure the time they spent together reading almost as much as the unclothed, fierce moments in Shacklock's room.

One afternoon saw them in their usual perch, on the sofa. They had trained their bodies to sit a respectable distance from each other in these public rooms, though they were closer than they might have been, given their need to share the book. Edward was at his club, Josiah was visiting a patient. Allegra and Shacklock had spent a heady hour in his room, their lovemaking now slower and deliberate, though no less intense. There had been little time for talking after. They had dressed and Allegra had pinned her hair back up. Sometimes Shacklock liked her to take it down; other times she left it up, neck exposed. That after-noon he had sat on the edge of the bed, watching her scowl into the mirror, jabbing pins here and there.

'You are more beautiful than any temple I've seen,' he said, and came over, tracing a finger from the start of her hairline down the ridges of her spine, bringing goosebumps to her flesh.

Wisps of auburn hair broke free as Allegra bowed over her Shakespeare in the sitting room. They were nearing the end of *The Winter's Tale* again, Allegra reading the part of Perdita, the lost daugh-ter who came back to the king. She spoke the final scene slowly, letting the words fall, tears coming into the corners of her eyes.

When she stopped, she turned to smile at Shacklock, embarrassed. 'I'm being a child. I'm sorry.'

Shacklock shook his head, his own eyes wide and glassy. He hadn't moved as Allegra read her final piece. 'You performed that so beauti-fully, Allegra.'

She blushed and waved her hand.

'No, you really did. You have a way of taking me into Perdita's mind. I felt like I was feeling all she felt. I wanted to scream at the king, for destroying his family. You did that.'

'I've always loved this play.'

'I know, but this is something more.' Shacklock leant back on the sofa and looked at Allegra. 'Don't rule out acting, Allegra.'

The heat reddening Allegra's cheeks spread, bringing a mottled look to her neck. A shifting mix of embarrassment and pleasure fought for control in her chest. She spoke quietly. 'I've always wanted to act. I used to drive my father mad, pestering him to read Shakespeare and dress up like the characters—which we did, most evenings. But I'm not sure.'

'Why not?'

Allegra hesitated. Shacklock's tales of walking unannounced into the houses of the poor in his parish, the anecdotes about rejecting the spoils from the table of a rich member of his congregation—Allegra knew Shacklock did not see the definitions of class or social propriety. He skated over them, like a bear on ice, punching through to the people he wanted to speak to, when he wanted to speak to them. He would therefore not understand or recognise the validity of Allegra's wariness about taking to the stage.

But their raw, unpolished desire for each other had also shaped Allegra. Just as she had stood naked in front of Shacklock in his bedroom, Allegra was now prepared to shed her inhibitions when it came to honesty about her emotions. It was something to marvel at, this readiness. She had never felt like that with Edward, not even in their early days of courtship. She felt as though she could talk to Shacklock about anything.

So she continued. 'Actresses have a reputation. Unfair, surely, but there, nonetheless. I know that some people frown at the idea of women on the stage.'

Shacklock shrugged. 'So what?'

'I wouldn't want to hurt my father.'

'But why would you? Who would sneer at you? Look down their nose at you?' Shacklock opened his hands expressively. 'Only people who know no better and live their lives as a series of judgements. Those kind of people don't matter. If you can stand up on a stage and move an audience as you've moved me just now—well, that's a gift. But if you decide against it, make those *your* decisions. Be true to what you want to do. Don't be constrained by the perceptions of other people.'

'If only everyone could live the way you do, dear Bishop!' A high-pitched voice from the doorway.

Allegra and Shacklock snapped their heads round to see—Edward stood in the doorway, his eyes bright, face pale. His hair was slightly damp; he had just returned from his club and was hot from the walk. He stepped fully into the room. Shacklock rose to meet him, Allegra just behind.

'Edward, I didn't know you were there.' Allegra dropped the Shakespeare onto the sofa, almost as though she were trying to throw the book away.

'Evidently. *You*, sir,' Edward pointed a trembling finger at Shacklock, 'what right do you have to give another man's wife career advice?'

Shacklock took a step closer to the furious young man. 'I meant no offence. Allegra and I often read together; she clearly has a talent and a deep love of the stage.'

'It's *Mrs Underwood*,' Edward bit. 'This is the first I have heard of my wife's theatre interests. Of course, I would not allow her on the stage. But that is something between us, as husband and wife. I'd thank you to keep your opinions to yourself.'

'Mrs Underwood asked my advice,' Shacklock said, nodding his head in deference to his use of Allegra's married name.

'And you should not have given it. I forbid any more of these meetings. Allegra, you are not to read with the bishop again, do you understand? And you will drop this nonsense about becoming an actress.'

'Edward, it was only talk …'

'I don't wish to hear any more!' Edward flicked a hand in Allegra's direction. He was close enough for her to smell sweet oil on his skin. 'As for you,' Edward turned back to the bishop, 'I will remind you that this is my father's house and you are here as his guest. A guest should remember his manners and not trespass where he is not welcome.'

Allegra caught her breath.

'I don't know what you mean.' Shacklock looked steadily up at Edward, the way a bird might look at a mouse from a great distance. He seemed quite calm.

'I think you do. I will not be a cuckold.' Edward's voice was barely audible; his eyes bulged.

Allegra gasped. 'Edward.' She touched his arm. He immediately swung round, hand raised; Shacklock stepped forward. He cuffed Edward's arm away, so the blow fell on Allegra's shoulder rather than her face. Allegra stumbled backwards, banging into a small table.

There was a tussle; Shacklock still clung to Edward's arm, preventing him from turning to strike. But, although the bishop's frame was strong and firm, from long walks and countless hours undertaking the physical care of his parishioners, he did not have the rage of a man believing himself to be cheated. Edward slid from Shacklock's grasp and, before Shacklock could right himself, Edward punched him, knocking him to the floor. Shacklock gave a shout, landing heavily, and then Edward was upon him again, grabbing his scalp and pulling his head up to punch again. Two quick jabs to the face and something cracked. Shacklock yelled again and Edward stood back, shocked, as Shacklock's broken nose began to bleed.

'Anthony!' Allegra was down on her knees, pressing the fabric of her skirts to Shacklock's face. His face appeared oddly twisted, red shiny flesh stretched over splintered bone. He sat up, tipping his head forward, pulling the shirt from his waistband. Blood spilled down his neck and onto the white cotton.

Edward sat down abruptly on the sofa. He stared at his fists, still clenched. Allegra, covering Shacklock's hands with her own and pressing down to stop the flow of blood, thought how young he suddenly looked; like a destructive child, realising the damage he had caused after a moment of temper. But then Edward looked at her and she could still see anger marking his face, thinning his lips.

'I saw what happened that day at the temple,' he said. He glared harder at Allegra, who looked away. 'And *him*—a man of the Church.'

Shacklock coughed and spat slowly into Allegra's handkerchief, hastily produced. He rose shakily to his feet and sat in a chair opposite Edward. He pulled his shirt up to his nose, exposing his stomach. He didn't seem to care, however. Through snorts and gulps as the blood continued to flow, he spoke. 'That day at the temple. It was the first time. The start of it.'

'The start of it?' Edward stared incredulously. 'Where do you think it will end? Only in your disgrace, and hers!'

Allegra remained on the floor, where she had crouched beside Shacklock. She couldn't move.

Shacklock lowered his shirt, red and shiny. Blood was smeared over his lips and chin, but the gush appeared to be slowing. 'I care very much for Allegra.'

'Enough to ruin your reputation? Your ministry?' Edward jabbed a finger in Shacklock's direction. 'I married Allegra because my father wished it. If you make a fool of me, I will see to it that every newspaper, every Synod member receives a letter stating what you have done. Seducing my wife in the house of your friend!'

'Edward!' Allegra gasped.

'I shall not consider anything else, other than ways to destroy this man of yours.' Edward sneered. 'How much older than you is he? Twenty-five, thirty years? He's old enough to be *your* father.'

'Edward, this will do no good.' Shacklock spoke in a gargled voice. Allegra watched him, frightened. Her insides were a puddle of hot oil. She took Edward's threats seriously and was frightened; if her father heard what she had done, the shock would bring him to the brink of collapse. The sweet, army major, who had taken such tender care of her since the death of her mother; if he were to find out what had happened between his daughter and Shacklock, the kindly old man would take to his bed for a week. But, then, a new, strong voice inside Allegra screamed out; let Edward try to shame them! Let him write his letters!

Except Shacklock's demeanour worried her. He seemed to have folded within himself. The strength carried in his muscles and across his broad back had evaporated. Instead he looked like a starving man at the end of a long race. Allegra didn't think Edward's fist to be the cause of this change, even though the well-placed hits had done their damage.

Shacklock wiped his nose again. 'You wouldn't do that, Edward. If you won't consider your father—and your mother—or Allegra's father in all of this, then think of the harm you would be doing to people you've never met. The families I work with, in my parish in Jedthorpe. If I am embarrassed in the press and stripped of my ministry, who will help those men and women then?'

Edward sneered. 'It's the risk you take when you play the fool with a married woman.'

Shacklock fell silent. He did not look at Allegra, or Edward. Instead he gazed into the distance, eyes peering over the top of his bundled shirt.

'What are your intentions?' Edward suddenly asked.

'Edward …' Allegra began.

'Be quiet. I do not want to hear you speak. Shacklock?'

Shacklock slowly shook his head. Still, he stayed mute and avoided eye contact with all in the room. Watching him, Allegra felt the panic rise more and more. Edward's question was one she had only just begun to ask herself, since Shacklock received the letter from Malta. He had not yet divulged its contents, but she was sure he had been summoned back to the island. He had been at Piraeus for over two months, probably too long for the mission in Malta. If he were to leave, what then?

'Do you intend on taking my wife back to Malta with you?' Edward persisted. 'I would have a say in this, as you would expect.'

'I had not thought that far ahead,' Shacklock muttered eventually. 'This thing of ours,' he nodded over to Allegra but still would not look at her, 'it began so suddenly.'

Allegra got up. She sat down on the chair nearest to Shacklock. His tone, the way he held himself was like nothing she had seen in him before. She wanted him to look at her but he seemed as far away now as the mother she had never known. His distance hurt her physically.

Edward, though, seemed galvanised by Shacklock's hesitance. Allegra could see now that her husband had wanted to subdue Shacklock for the whole time he had been in his father's house. Edward's snide remarks and raised eyebrows made in private, when Shacklock could not see; the disdainful way Edward would turn his shoulder slightly at the dinner table and bar Shacklock from the conversation: now these small acts of social pettiness were bricked on top of each and Edward was emboldened. His anger and fury had driven away all insecurity and anxiety he felt in Shacklock's presence. He had a half-smile on his face.

'Here's what you will do. When my father returns from his house call, you will sit him down and tell him you must leave immediately for Malta. This very night. You will pack your bags and go down to the harbour, where you will find a boat—any boat—making a journey across the Ionian Sea.' Edward leant forward. 'I do not care if the ship's captain rinses the coins from your pockets—whatever the cost, you will leave this house tonight. You will not attempt to contact my wife again, you will never come and visit. Unless my father returns to England and travels to York, you will never see him again. In return, I will say nothing about what has passed here today. I will accept my wife back, as though she is unsullied. I will say nothing to your superiors back in Jedthorpe or the press, and you can go back to your ministry.'

Shacklock's head hung low. All air seemed to be extinguished from him and, to Allegra, he appeared to be a large, unwieldy cake, not baked for long enough.

Edward stood up. His posture was taut, back erect. He nodded curtly. 'I will leave you now. I do not wish to speak to you again and, when I come down for dinner this evening, you will be gone.' With that he turned and stalked from the room. He did not look around, he did not hesitate. It was as though he knew perfectly well what Shacklock's decision would be.

Allegra and Shacklock were left alone in the room. Shacklock's nose had started to bleed again, dropping onto the carpet.

Automatically, Allegra bent down, looking for something to dab it away. Shacklock leant back with a groan and handed her the soiled handkerchief. With the other hand he pulled up his shirt again to stem the blood.

'We should have been more careful,' Allegra said, her voice barely above a whisper.

'Allegra.'

'What are we going to do?' Tears stung and Allegra blinked them back. 'I cannot leave, just like that. There's Constance to think of. My father. He would be heartbroken if I disappeared without saying goodbye.'

'Allegra.'

'I have some money. Not much. It's maybe enough for a month or so but I'd have to find work.' Allegra's voice sped up, words falling from her, stinging her lips. She talked so Shacklock would not, filling the silence so it did not matter that he said nothing.

Except, of course, he did speak. He reached forward and, with a bloodied hand, caught Allegra's shoulder. He touched her on the mark Edward had left with his misdirected blow, making her ache. 'Allegra, there is nothing we can do.'

'So we'll just have to leave, won't we? I don't want to, but yes, perhaps we should. My father would take us in for a day or so, maybe, if we don't tell him ...'

'No, Allegra.' And Shacklock finally looked at her. His eyes were tired and creased but he did not avert his gaze. Allegra gave a small moan and slithered sideways, sitting on the floor again.

'No?'

'We have no choice.'

'But we *do* have a choice, we could ...'

'Allegra, if we do as you suggest, if we leave here together and go to your father's house, or Malta, or wherever—what then? What will that mean for my ministry? Edward will keep to his word. He will write to the Jedthorpe Synod and the newspapers. The papers—I wouldn't care what they say about me—but the *Synod*. If word gets to them that I am here, when I am supposed to be in Malta, and if word gets to them about us—it would be all over.' Shacklock held out his hands. 'I would be stripped of my rank, I would be forced to leave the church in Jedthorpe, which I have done so much to build up. What would happen to all those men and women whom we help? Who would feed them when they are starving, or fight for them?'

Allegra blinked. 'But who will fight for me? If you leave and you don't take me with you?'

To which Shacklock said nothing.

'I am married to Edward in name, only. Our marriage is empty; he doesn't love me. You saw that today. What did he say—he married me because Josiah wished it? He doesn't want *me*. He wants to punish *you.*'

'I know that.'

'But you would allow it anyway?'

Shacklock sighed. 'Allegra, I have to go. You have to stay. What we've had, these last few weeks ... I'll never forget them. But I have to go.'

'Is that all there is, then? A promise that you'll remember me?' Tears gathered but Allegra would not let them fall. 'Remember this, then. Edward couldn't consummate our marriage. I didn't tell you that. He couldn't do it. You did.'

Shacklock closed his eyes.

'I thought you cared about me. But you care for your ministry more. Any threat to your role as bishop, and you bend, as easy as a bed sheet.' Allegra got to her feet. Her body trembled, and she wondered if she would throw up. She swallowed forcefully and tried to still her voice. 'I hope I provided you with enough entertainment.'

There was more, but she could not say it. Instead, hand to her mouth, bloodied skirts swinging, Allegra walked from the room. Like Edward, she did not look back, but it took every effort of self-will to keep her eyes on the doorway. She ached to run back to Shacklock and throw her arms around him, plead with him. Instead she thought of Hermione, the broken but unbowed queen in *The Winter's Tale*; Allegra forced her body to become taut and still. Regal.

~ 21 ~

October 1899

Allegra was at her father's house, where she had been for the last six weeks. She sat in her usual place, the easy chair in the parlour, and listened as her father spoke quietly to the cook in the next room. She heard the rough rise and fall of his voice and loved him for it; normally such a guttural man, more used to barking commands on the parade ground, he now spoke barely above a whisper. He was worried sick and didn't know what to do. He had never known Allegra to be like this and he talked to anyone, everyone, on his quest to make her better.

The truth was, that despite Major Lucan's various postings and travel, he had barely known a life outside the army, save for the brief, tender year with Allegra's mother. He still washed his socks in the kitchen sink every night and dried them on the fire guard, much to the servants' exasperation. He would be content with tinned beef and bread every day, if the cook chose to serve it. His life was one of order and explanation—with one obvious exception. From the moment his bloodied, screaming daughter was placed in his hands, he had bent his strong, regimental form into a new shape. He became a father first, soldier second. Maps on the desk on his study were replaced with scrawled drawings. Medals and battlefield souvenirs struggled for space in display cabinets alongside corn dollies, misshapen attempts at pottery, an arm from a treasured doll. This last was all that was left after the major's dog got hold of Allegra's dear Rosebud, and shook the porcelain form to pieces. The major would have taken the dog and had him shot but, again, he listened to the pleas of his sobbing child and installed a wire gate across Allegra's room, preventing the dog from entering.

Allegra was the major's most treasured prize. As a young man he had fought at Balaclava in the Crimea; in later years he commanded troops during the Zulu Wars, for which he received a commendation. But the clank of bayonets and the whistle of rifles paled next to the tinkle of his daughter's laugh or the sound of her feet scampering up the hallway. Before her marriage, Allegra joined him at every regimental dinner he was invited to among the old soldiers who had made their home in Greece. As a child, she sat at his right hand on the odd occasions when he hosted dinner parties, often falling asleep as coffee and cigars were served, barely waking when he carried her to bed. Allegra grew to know the major's friends, who took her into their hearts as well. Some bought her tin soldiers at Christmas, mainly to amuse her father; all loved her when she pretended to play with them, assigning new roles to the uniformed tin men. 'This one is Papa, this one is Emily.'

Today though, like yesterday, and the day before that, the major was troubled. His daughter was here, in his house, and not with her husband, and she was not eating. When she did taste something, be it bread or fruit, she would bring it back up again. Allegra sat in the easy chair in the parlour or lay on her bed, all day, every day, barely moving, not even reading her books. Her skin was pale and waxy, and she complained of a pain in her chest. She had not explained why she had returned to her home without Edward, or what had happened, or how long she would stay. She would only write, pages of letters to Emily, her cousin, but showed no interest in going out for a walk, or sitting with her father in the evening. The poor major was losing sleep with worry.

The major consulted with the cook, the one servant who had known Allegra from childhood. Might it be the heat? It had never affected Allegra before in this way, but stranger things had happened. If not the heat, what about the water? Might the well, from which the house drew its supply, be—Lord forbid—diseased? The cook, a wide, Greek woman with a smattering of English, shook her head and kept silent. She had her own opinion as to Allegra's ails and suspected Allegra knew as well. Indigestion, fatigue, sickness; these were signs this hardy Greek mother of six recognised.

The major, however, did not. Instead he urgently tried to find more tempting foodstuffs for his daughter to try. Rice puddings, pale custards, thin soups. The cook pursed her lips and made them all, having the maid take them to Allegra on a tray. Today she had made a cheese pastry, a delicate wrap flavoured with herbs. The maid brought it to

Allegra, who was sitting in her chair, eyes closed, lips damp. The girl set it down on a small table and backed away, reluctant to wake her. She retreated back to the pantry to report the mistress was asleep.

Except that Allegra was not asleep. She was wide awake, though her eyes were tightly shut. She had found it useful to sit like this, setting up her eyelids as thin, warm barriers to the intruding world, a world that insisted on talking to her. Her throat was sore from retching and vomiting, and she tried not to breathe in the scent of the pastry.

Two weeks after Shacklock had left, when she was sure what was happening to her body, Allegra had risen in the middle of the night, taken a mule and walked to her father's house. It had taken her all day to reach the major's home and her progress slowed in the height of the sun, but she did not stop. Edward had not awoken when she slipped from their bed. He had barely spoken to her since that day in Josiah's sitting room, except at dinner, when it was unavoidable. Josiah, puzzled and hurt by his friend's sudden absence, occasionally still asked Edward if he knew anything, any reason why Shacklock would pack up and leave so quickly. Edward would squeeze his lips together and glare down at his plate.

The major had been astonished to see his daughter. He had answered the door himself, holding a book in one hand and a paintbrush in the other. He had been making a model of Sevastopol in the Crimea, he explained sheepishly as he showed Allegra in. Why was she here? Where was Edward?

He had yet to receive an answer to such questions and, by now, had stopped asking. Major Lucan had decided that Allegra had left Edward and had given up on the marriage. A shame, a scandal, near enough— but she was his daughter. He would protect her. But if only she would eat!

The sickness had taken her by surprise. She knew it was coming, of course, and that she would likely suffer for a few weeks. In one of the bags she had tied around the mule, Allegra had packed a book stolen from Josiah's study, about maternity and the pregnant body. Sickness, heartburn—she waited calmly for these, but when they arrived she was frightened and shocked by their ferocity.

She had accepted her pregnancy without fear. It was a likely occurrence, given her youth, and the regularity that she and Shacklock met.

She accepted that the little seed rolling around in her stomach was real. She had longed for a baby, after all, when marrying Edward.

What Allegra could not allow herself to do, now, was to think back to how the pregnancy had occurred. In the first days when she waited for her monthly, and began to take note of the number of days she was late, she found herself going back over the occasions when the change might have occurred. When a new life burst inside her. The times her insides felt on fire, in a deeply pleasurable way—was it then? Or was it during those moments when her body folded Shacklock's wetness into her own, pressing together a life?

Such thoughts brought only resentment and an aching frustration. Allegra hated him for leaving. She hated him for showing her what love could be.

She did not consider writing to him and telling him what she knew. Instead she wrote to Emily, divulging all. It was a risk, Allegra knew, to put such detail down and she wrote that her cousin should burn her letters. But she was desperate. She told Emily to write back to her at her father's house.

A letter from Emily had arrived that morning and Allegra had read it quickly. She scanned the contents and had set it aside, weary. Emily's advice, that she should go back to Edward, was not welcome. Allegra told herself that Emily knew little having never been married. A maid had arrived with breakfast. Allegra waved the girl away and closed her eyes.

∽

The major did not take afternoon naps as Josiah had done, so the house thrummed along as usual throughout the day. Allegra could hear her father in his study, humming as he added the finishing touches to his Sevastopol battlefield. He had spread the work out over a billiards table and used wet paper to create hills and mounds. Some old friends from the now-disbanded regiment were due tomorrow to inspect it. Allegra knew the pattern of their visits from being a child. The friends would arrive with their bags of soldiers, all hand-carved and painted, and they would set to work. For hours they would enact the battle, knocking over swathes of tin men, whooping and hollering as the battle became more frenzied. Allegra used to love watching them and would bounce on a chair behind her father's desk, swept along with their excitement. The major had invited her to join tomorrow, for old time's sake, but she had declined. She was no longer that girl watching grown men pound groups of toy men into splinters and dust.

The major stopped humming abruptly; there was a rap at the door. A maid bustled down the hallway, closely followed by Allegra's father. Uninvited visitors were infrequent and the old man was curious.

Allegra was drifting towards sleep when a sound cut through— her father gasping. She heard the low rumble of voices, and the major cough, which she knew to be the sound of him considering. Then droning again as a discussion started up. Then footsteps, down the hall to the parlour. A man opened the door wide and stepped into the room. It was Edward.

Allegra sat up, her mouth suddenly empty of saliva. 'What are you doing here?'

Edward edged into the room. He held his hat in front of him, turning it round and round. 'I rode.'

'In this heat?'

'I set off last night. I stayed at an inn along the way. I've covered a few miles today, that's all. I needed to see you.'

'Why?'

Edward motioned to an empty chair. 'May I?'

Allegra shrugged and watched, shocked, as her husband sat down gingerly. She did not know this cautious Edward. The Edward she knew was bold. *That* Edward would not ask if he could sit—he would simply settle himself wherever he chose. She watched as her husband fidgeted with his coat, inching his way towards a conversation.

'How are you?' he asked eventually.

'Just as you see. But you did not travel all these miles, to ask about my health.'

'No. It has been a long time.'

'Six weeks.'

'Really six weeks? My mother misses you.'

'I miss her.' Allegra kept her voice still, aware of the tightrope she was walking. There was so much to be wary of; Edward was the cheated husband, after all. He could walk out of there and broadcast the news, if he hadn't already. But she hated him also, for what he had done to drive

Shacklock away. The intensity of feeling surprised her, at first, that she could hate so cleanly, and hate so many.

'It's my mother that brings me here.' Edward frowned. 'I will not say his name, but since *he* left my father has become difficult. He cannot manage my mother.'

'Difficult?' Allegra could not imagine Josiah being anything but pleasant and kindly.

'Mother has taken a turn for the worse. My father doesn't know what to do. He avoids her. He spends most of his time in his study, or out seeing patients.'

Allegra stiffened. 'Constance is ill again?'

'She's losing blood. I cannot say how, it is embarrassing.' Edward looked away. 'You most likely know. She is getting weaker and soils her sheets often. No one can cope with it.'

'You have a house full of servants, Edward.'

'But they are not you! The maids hate to clean up after her and I am afraid they won't do it for much longer. She needs to be bathed, and it is humiliating for a young maid—they are only girls and they don't like to do it. They make sure my mother knows it.'

'I cared for your mother every day,' Allegra said. 'In that way.'

'I know.' A tired look passed Edward's face. 'Mother told me. She said what you did for her.' He faltered. 'I am grateful and I want you to know I don't blame you for keeping it a secret. Mother told me she asked you to.'

'How generous of you. Are you asking me to return to your house?'

'Yes.' Edward held up his hand. 'It may be that my mother does not have long. I hope she reaches Christmas, but maybe not. I do not say this to make you feel guilty, or obliged.'

'I feel neither,' Allegra said quietly.

'I say it because it is true and I would have her final days comfortable, surrounded by those she loves.'

Allegra felt the shock of his words. Edward had never talked to her in such terms—love, being needed. She placed her hands under her legs, lest he could see her tremble.

'We would not have to share a room,' Edward continued. His colour was up. 'Neither of us would like that. Maybe, in time … But I must ask this favour of you, for my mother. I have kept my silence, even though my father is frantic with worry about why you left, and a little angry. I can protect you from that, but I must have you return to the house. For Constance, not me, you understand?'

Allegra said nothing. She wondered if her father could hear them, but he had never been one for eavesdropping in hallways. After several weeks, Major Lucan had accepted that his daughter did not want to discuss her reasons for returning home, and had allowed the house to adapt back to what it was before Allegra had left. A place was set for her at the dinner table, next to her father. The cook baked sliced peppers in sweet sauce, her favourite from childhood. It was almost as though Allegra had never married.

The major would be content to let her live with him for the rest of his days, until they were eternally parted. Allegra was as sure of this as she was of the baby growing in her womb. Her father would swell to the size of a lion in the doorway if anyone dared to call and judge his child; bellows usually only heard by his men on the parade ground would rattle the dirty, stained windows of his home should anyone refer to Allegra's honour and damaged reputation. In the early days after leaving Edward, Allegra had huddled beneath that blanket of protection.

But, as the sickness grew, and the cook began to cast long glances in her direction, Allegra knew the days she lived under the major's unquestioning protection were numbered. Her father might stand in front of visitors and speak for his daughter but, once a child appeared, his devotion might falter. A small part of Allegra trembled to think he would be disappointed.

Her hand fell absently to her stomach and she stoked her dress gently, stopping before Edward noticed. 'How ill is Constance?'

'Terribly. You would not recognise her. The weight has fallen from her and her skin hangs loose.' Edward pinched his fingers around his wrist. 'Her arms are as wide as this. And there is a smell about her, constantly.' He bowed his head. 'It hurts to say this about my own mother. I cannot see her living long past Christmas.'

'As bad as that?'

Edward nodded. 'My father has not said, but I think he acknowledges it, too. He walks in the garden, weeping. Once, after wine, he said the best he could do for her was to give her a good death. I know he has drugs he can use to keep her free of pain.'

Allegra felt tears. 'Has he used them?'

'Not yet. But soon.'

A small silence into which Edward sniffed and Allegra stared at the carpet. Such twisted emotions, fighting inside! Hatred towards the man in front of her, who had driven away the one person who had given Allegra a taste of love and fulfilment; hatred towards Shacklock for allowing himself to be forced to leave and refusing to fight for her; and guilt, worry, for the woman who had been the closest to a mother Allegra had ever known. She knew she had abandoned Constance too, walking away from her as well as from her marriage. And what about the baby?

Once, when she was a child, Allegra had fallen from a horse. She had been riding on a flat piece of land, owned by one of her father's friends. He had lent her the horse and she had joined the friend's daughters as they took a riding lesson. They were more advanced than Allegra and able to control their steeds, whereas Allegra struggled to turn her horse and control the canter and trot. But she was young and proud and determined to keep up. She tried to match the other girls' pace, even as they attempted to clear some small jumps. The major's friend, aware of his duty of care towards Allegra and that she was the object closest to the major's heart, warned her to wait out the jumps. But Allegra would not and, as her horse galloped full pelt towards the small wooden blocks, she felt herself slip from the saddle. For what felt like an age, Allegra slid slowly off the leather seat; the ground blurred past, the drum of the horse's hooves roared in her ears. But she could not stop the inevitable fall. She knew it would be hard and painful, and she might break a bone, or receive a blow to the head as the horse continued. The world seemed to grind to a halt and Allegra felt herself tipping towards the edge, unable to stop, torturously aware of what was about to happen.

She did fall, of course, and she was injured, though not as seriously as she might. A hoof caught her right arm, bruising it badly, and Allegra's knees were sore from her landing. Her father's friend scooped her up quickly and ran back towards the house, seeing to it that the wounds were cooled and cleaned. But, what lingered with Allegra more than the black marks upon her flesh and the embarrassment at falling so spectacularly in front of her friends, was the sense of inevitability;

the feeling of leaning over the edge, knowing she was about to topple, but being unable to do anything about it. For weeks after the accident, she had a recurring dream that she stood on top of the Demeter temple, the stone crumbling before her, pitching her body down the mountainside towards the sea. Her father put the night terrors down to delayed shock and, after he had tended to Allegra and wiped away her tears in the middle of the night, would admonish her again for taking such risks on a horse.

As she sat on her father's sofa in his sitting room, listening to her husband talk about the approaching death of her mother-in-law, Allegra felt the sensation again, of skidding towards a fall and being unable to stop it. She swallowed, forcing down the heartburn bubbling up inside.

'Before I decide whether to return to you,' she said, a sad laugh echoing in her mind—that she had a choice!—'there is something you should know. I am having a child.' She paused. 'I am not sure of the dates, but I think it will arrive in April, or thereabouts.'

Edward sat rigidly, his eyes staring hard at a point above Allegra's head. 'That would mean …'

'Two months ago, yes,' Allegra said.

'Two months?'

'Don't make me say what we both know.'

Edward stood up abruptly and, for a second Allegra thought he was about to leave. His face was pink and sweat gleamed on his forehead. He walked towards the window, which faced out towards the blue of the sea. For a long moment he was silent, rocking on his heels, hands clasped tightly together behind his back.

'Have you written to tell him?' he asked finally, without turning round.

'No. I do not intend to.'

Edward came back to the sofa slowly. 'A child.'

'Yes.' Allegra leant back against the back of the chair, throat squeezed against rising nausea.

'Despite what you think of me—of our marriage—I have always wanted a son.' Edward sat down again and Allegra stared at him, startled.

'We didn't talk about it, Edward, but I assumed …'

He reared a little in his seat, brushing away any reference to the lack of physicality in their marriage. 'A son would be something to be proud of. I imagined taking my boy with me—grown, of course—to receptions at the Town Hall. The Harbour Master's Christmas Gala.'

Allegra waited.

'You have no choice, then, Allegra, but to come back with me. You cannot live here with your father, bringing up a child alone.'

'I would not be alone.'

'But without your husband.'

'But you are not the ...'

'To our friends and neighbours I am. And if you were to tell the truth, what then? You would never be accepted into polite company again and what would that mean for the child? His—or her—prospects would be severely limited. You know what it is like here, how tight this community is.'

Edward rubbed his chin, a smile appearing, and Allegra saw the Edward she knew creep back. 'You know what this means, don't you?'

'Perhaps you might explain.' But Allegra could not avoid a note of sullenness, and she hated herself a little for it. Sulking was the preserve of the powerless child and showed Edward the impossibility of her position.

'You will have to return with me. We could explain away your sudden departure as early-pregnancy hysteria. A loosening of sanity—I'm sure it happens all the time.' Edward slapped his thigh, grin becoming wider. 'In return for allowing you back into my father's house and caring for my mother, I will keep your secret. The world will think that the child is mine.'

'But ...'

'There is nothing you can counter with!' Edward laughed. 'What alternatives do you have? Your bishop is not going to ride in here and rescue you—he put up little fight when I sent him on his way at the end of the summer. I doubt he would be any more willing to return for you if he knew the truth.'

And she knew he was right. 'But the child, Edward. I want to know what you mean by the child?'

'What I mean by ... oh, I will treat the boy as if he is my own, do not worry about that. Or, yes, even if the baby is a girl. I will be a good father. We will put this episode behind us.'

Edward stood up again and smoothed down his trousers. Fullness had come to his bottom lip, and he stuck out his chin, man-about-town again. 'I'll leave you to tell your father you are returning with me. How long to pack your things? An hour? You can't have brought much, sneaking off as you did.'

He dipped down and dropped a kiss on Allegra's head. And, with a bounce in his step, so different to the cautious way with which he stepped into the room, Edward left. She heard him talking loudly in the hallway and then being shown out.

Then, as the major appeared, bewildered, shirtsleeves pushed up and paint on his arms, Allegra bent forward and put her head in her hands. Tears and nausea rose together and the drumming sound of a horse's hooves filled her ears.

~ *21* ~

Earls Court ~ May 1917

From her position in the carriage, Violet could just make out the front page of the passenger's newspaper. He was a wiry, sallow man and held it up close to his face. Leaning carefully to the side, Violet read the headline, about a surprise air raid on an unnamed coastal town. Her mother had mentioned it that morning. They had been sitting around their small kitchen table, finishing up the last of yesterday's bread before Allegra went out to queue for more. Violet had listened to her mother's shocked voice read the report out loud; Germans had attacked a town near Dover and, without warning, dropped bombs on unsuspecting crowds as they lined up outside a greengrocer's.

'Which town?' Violet had asked and Allegra had shaken her head.

'The piece doesn't say. The War Office wants to keep it quiet, no doubt. But imagine the worry for people with family in that area! No names are reported, no clues as to who has been hurt!' Allegra had folded the newspaper abruptly.

Now, as the underground train rattled its way to Waterloo, Violet listened to other passengers discuss the raid in whispered tones. A damp air of worry hung around the compartment; Londoners had lived through fear brought by the Zeppelins, floating over the Channel, and were confident that searchlights and a wireless alarm system would protect them from airborne enemies. Now this attack and deaths of so many at an unspecified, unnamed coastal town, ghostly in its anonymity, had punctured their confidence, as completely as hot air escaping from an open oven door.

The train pulled into Waterloo and Violet found the connecting line for Woking. The weather had warmed up and she walked without a jacket, knowing she would attract stares as she passed through the station. A group of women queuing beside a tea trolley turned, tutting, as she strode by, and Violet tossed her head. *The Germans can drop a bomb on our people in broad daylight and these women are frowning because I don't wear a coat? As if it matters now!* Violet lengthened her stride but did not hurry away, part of her wanting someone in the group to speak up.

The arrival of the Woking train saved her from confrontation and Violet found a seat away from a group of soldiers, home on leave. Some of the girls at the theatre had shared tales of men returning from France. They spoke of soldiers wild with anger after many months in tight, narrow trenches, of others shaking and silent. Only recently, one of Violet's friends had been trapped on her own in a carriage by a soldier clearly suffering from shock; he had sat by the sliding door so she could not leave and, in a monotone voice, had recalled every death he had witness or caused. By the time Violet's friend had reached the theatre, she was nauseous and shivering.

A carriage towards the rear of the train was empty and Violet settled in for the short journey out to Threadstone Hall, to see her father. It had been some time since their last meeting and Edward had written to her, asking for her to visit. Violet had read the letter aloud to her mother.

'He wants me to go out to see him. This week,' Violet had said. It was a few days before the coastal bombing raid reported in the paper and they were sharing a kipper at the table. Allegra, hungry for the food of her childhood, had bought lamb cutlets from the butcher and peppers from an expensive grocer on Kensington High Street. The splurge had emptied most of her purse. For the rest of the week, she and Violet would live frugally. Fish was plentiful, however; one of their actresses was married to a vendor at Smithfield market.

'When was the last time you were out there?' Allegra asked.

'To Woking? Probably a year or so. Don't raise your eyebrows. We've been busy, with the theatre.'

'You should still take time to see your father, Violet.'

'I'll go in a couple of days. I promise.' And Violet had bent her bead over the kipper, avoiding her mother's eye.

Although Allegra rarely chided her daughter and was mild in her admonishments in comparison to the mothers of Violet's friends, she did persist in reminding Violet she should maintain a relationship with

Edward. Allegra and Edward had lived separately for a long time, from Violet being only a few years old. When she tried very hard, Violet could draw out some cloudy childhood memories of the time they were all together; evenings in the parlour at Threadstone Hall, playing with the cat in front of the fire. Josiah, in poor health himself by then, had crouched down on cracking knees and taught the infant Violet how to tease the cat onto its back, by scratching and rubbing its fur. Edward chuckled in the background and Violet remembered how he'd swung her up onto his knee when the cat became bored and inevitably lashed out. She thought he had dabbed the bright red scratch on her pudgy arm with his handkerchief, but maybe she imagined that part. Maybe it was from a play she had seen at her mother's theatre.

But then came her parents' separation and the move to rooms in Earls Court. Josiah had seen to it that Allegra and Violet had furniture, and Allegra's father, the major, living in chaotic and splendid isolation in Greece, sent over an allowance. But evenings beside the fire were gone; coal or firewood was expensive and now saved for Sundays in their small flat. Violet couldn't even take her cat with her, a fact that distressed her more than the absence of her father.

And then the looks began. Odd, lingering looks from Edward when she visited him. Allegra would take Violet when she was young, dropping her off at the front door of the Threadstone Hall and then disappearing round the corner to a bookshop where she would browse and read, but never buy. Once, when Allegra collected Violet, the girl talked about how her father glared at her when he thought she wasn't looking.

'It's as though he doesn't like the way I look,' Violet said to her mother, holding her hand tightly as they crossed the High Street and walked towards the train station. 'Do we look so poor? I'm wearing my best coat and, after all, if we are poor it's because he won't give you any money.'

Allegra had said nothing but, glancing from the corner of her eye, Violet saw her chew her lip. Later, back at their rooms in Earls Court, she tried to pass it off. 'It's probably nothing, Violet. Your father can be peculiar at times, that's all.'

As an adult, the visits to her father had dwindled even more. Violet went out to Woking once a month, then every couple of months. Now she visited twice a year. Sometimes, when he was feeling well, Edward came into town and met her, taking her for tea at his club in Piccadilly or bought her gloves at Covent Garden. But even that stopped some time ago. As the train pulled into Woking and Violet set off on the walk to Threadstone Hall, she wondered—for the first time—how ill her father had become.

A maid answered the door and took Violet's hat, saying nothing but obviously noting the shabby fabric and fading flowers decorating the brim. 'Mr Underwood is sleeping but asked that he be woken when you arrive,' the girl said, and showed Violet into a small anteroom off the hall. The walls were lined with books and, even in the summer sun, the room was cold. Violet lingered in the doorway for a few moments, looking up at the goblins carved around the skylight. They had frightened and fascinated her as a child, and she remembered tales from her Great Uncle Charles, about how he'd had the carvings installed just to annoy the ghost of Violet's great-grandfather.

She didn't have to wait long before the maid came back. The maid led her up the stairs, past a sitting room and other bedrooms. Edward's bedroom door was closed. The maid knocked and Violet's eyes widened as a husky, old voice croaked out a welcome.

Edward was sitting up in an armchair, wrapped in a purple and green striped dressing gown. He had evidently been deep in slumber for the grey, saggy flesh of his face was marked with lines from where he had hugged his pillow. He had hurriedly passed a comb through his thinning hair, bringing it to order. Wisps stood up around his ears.

'Violet.' They embraced briefly. Edward motioned to an empty chair opposite. 'Was the journey long? It must have been. Are you thirsty? I'm sure we could stretch to tea and some ginger biscuits.' He flicked a finger at the maid, and Violet smiled, in spite of her shock at his appearance. Her father hadn't lost the ability to infuriate the domestic help.

But, as she sat down to face him, Violet's dismay at Edward's decline grew. Always slim, his frame had narrowed painfully. She could make out bones in his wrist as he reached out to take her hand. The gesture was unexpected and she held his fingers gently, afraid she might snap the fragile bones as easily as breaking a bird's leg. The flesh had fallen away from his neck, leaving only sinew and tendons. Even his skin colour had changed; the area around his eyes was yellow and dry.

Edward smiled. 'I know.'

'Are you very ill?' Violet asked in a rush.

Edward patted her fingers and sat back. 'I'm afraid I am. It is a cancer of some sort, probably of the liver. It would explain my stomach. Look how blown up it is.'

Edward opened his robe slowly, letting Violet see the distended stomach under his pyjamas. She gaped.

The maid came back then and Edward tucked himself away, leaving the girl to pour tea and serve biscuits. After she had left, he spoke again.

'I'm sorry for the tone of my letter, Violet. It was wrong of me to plead that you come and I certainly didn't want to make you feel guilty. It hasn't been easy between us for quite some time. But, you see …'

'I'm glad I came,' Violet trembled over her cup and saucer. She drank too quickly, the scalding liquid burning her tongue. 'Is there anything the doctors can do? Some kind of treatment?'

'Only rest,' Edward said. 'I'm afraid I was a coward and, when the time came when I eventually saw my physician, it was too late.'

'I can understand your fear, but surely …' Violet returned her tea to the little table beside them. 'If there's bad news to face …' She stopped, sensitive to how she might hurt Edward's feelings. More and more, in the last year or so, she had become aware of the weight of words, and how they might hurt.

Edward had closed his eyes and was rocking his head from side to side. 'You are so like him,' he muttered.

'What? Like who?'

Edward opened his eyes. Violet sat stiffly, wondering at his sudden change of mood.

'Father, are you feeling unwell? Do you need me to fetch someone?'

'There is another reason why I asked you to visit.' The tendons on Edward's neck stood out as he strained to put strength into his voice. 'I do not have very long. I must use the time we have honestly and tell you what you deserve to know.'

'What do you mean?'

'First, I want you to understand that, really, it did not matter to me. There were moments when I let my feelings get the better of me and I regret that. But I always felt like your father, even if I didn't always show it.'

'I don't understand.'

'Violet.' Edward shook, the effort of the moment rattling his body. 'When you grew up, you looked so much like him. It was unavoidable—

every time I looked at you, I saw his face. I'm sorry, for it was then that we grew apart. I should have been stronger and not allowed who you looked like to shape how I felt about you.'

'Who do I look like? I don't know what you are saying.'

'Your father. Your real father.' And then Edward slumped back, the air wheezing from his lungs. 'I knew your mother would never tell you, so I asked you here today so I could. It was a brief affair, when your mother and I were first married. Before we came to London, even. A friend of my father's. He seduced her—or maybe he didn't, maybe it was the other way round—but it doesn't matter now. Now, wait a moment ...'

Violet had stood up, her hip banging into the little table beside them, rocking it from side to side. Tea sloshed over the edge and onto the carpet. She watched it puddle and felt a pain, deep inside her chest. The urge to run was upon her.

Edward caught her hand, his grip surprisingly firm. 'Violet, please. Sit down.'

'A friend of your father's? Who was he?'

'I'll tell you everything, if you sit down again. Please.'

Against the wishes of every sinew in her body, Violet sat down again slowly. Her legs trembled with the desire to take off and she plaited them together. She reached out, trembling, for her tea and took another, deep drink.

'Better?' Edward studied her. 'It's the shock that makes you want to run. I've thought about telling you, over the years, but I always came back to the question—what good would it do? The man had little interest in your mother once I'd discovered the affair, and I didn't want to expose you to rejection.'

'Why are you telling me now?'

'This.' Edward cast a hand over his body. 'I'm failing. I don't have long, no matter what I say to myself every day in the mirror.' He shook his head sadly. 'Too many secrets. I couldn't leave you without telling you the truth.'

Violet said nothing but raised her cup again, the china chattering against her teeth. She had not felt shock like this before, in such a physical way. She had once disturbed an actress and her lover, at Allegra's theatre, and had been mortified by the sight of pale, bucking flesh, but the shock she felt then was mixed with a peculiar desire to laugh. She had giggled her way home and told Allegra about it at tea, hiccupping her way through the story, recalling how her cheeks had burned for the man's pitiful white buttocks. But a shock like this—felt so strongly along the line of her chest, enough to squeeze out the breath? No, she had not experienced this before.

'I shall tell you who he was, even if you decide to do nothing with the information,' Edward continued.

'Go on,' Violet said after a pause.

'His name was Anthony Shacklock. He was a friend of my father's who came to visit us in Greece. My father had not seen him for a long time—I think there had been a falling out—but Shacklock came to stay for a couple of months. Your mother and I had not long been married. Things were—well, troubled, is perhaps the best way to describe how it was between us. Whether Shacklock took advantage of that, I don't know. But they started an affair a month after he arrived and it continued for a number of weeks.'

'You discovered it?'

'I saw them together.' A look of distaste and Edward continued. 'I was appalled but said nothing at the time. Then, later, I heard Shacklock encourage your mother to take up a career in the theatre and I confronted them. Oh, I know, look at Allegra now, with her own theatre! She ploughed every penny of her inheritance from the major into that venture. But at the time, nearly twenty years ago, a woman setting foot on the stage was quite scandalous—it may have changed now, I don't know. I told Shacklock he had to leave, straightaway.'

'And he did?'

'He did. I know it hurt your mother, that he didn't stay and fight for her, but he left. There's something else, though.'

'What?' Violet wondered what could be more revelatory than the tale her father was relating right now.

'The reason Shacklock left so quickly, the reason he didn't stay or take your mother with him—he was a man of the church.' Edward's mouth twisted. 'A bishop, no less. He had a ministry near York and the prospect of a scandal was too much for him.'

'He was a bishop?' Violet whispered. She felt as though she was wearing one of her mother's corsets and a team of maids were pulling the cords about it, crushing her ribs.

'He may still be a bishop, for all I know. We didn't make contact with him when we came back to England, and he certainly never visited Josiah, your grandfather. Where he is now, I have no idea.'

The urge to run was upon Violet again before she could stop up and she jumped to her feet. This time the cup and saucer spilled to the floor and Edward moved his feet delicately out of the way. 'I have to go outside.'

'All right.' Edward looked exhausted. 'I'll wait for you. You will come back, Violet?'

'I will.' And Violet spun out of the room, leaving the door open. Edward heard her trip down the stairs and let herself out, the front door slamming with a boom, bringing the startled maid out into the hallway. After a few moments the girl came up the stairs.

'Is everything all right, sir?' she asked, eyes widening at the spilled tea and broken crockery on the carpet.

'My daughter has had a shock.' Edward pointed to a writing desk to the right of his bed. 'She will be back later. Pass me some paper and a pen, will you, and clear up this mess?'

The maid nodded, dumbly, but obviously burning with questions. She took out the paper and lingered for a few moments, taking her time with clearing up. Then, as it became apparent that Edward would say nothing more on the matter, she left, sighing as she walked down the stairs.

∽

Allegra's theatre was on Colbert Mews, a small street off Earls Court Road. The theatre was an unobtrusive, redbrick building with a pale blue awning. She had purchased the building fifteen years before from an old Jewish family in the area, who had used the building as a warehouse, and who were planning to move back to Poland. The patriarch of the family, a short, tidy man called Glass, had been greatly interested in the idea of a woman going into business for herself and, before contracts were signed and money exchanged, he took Allegra out for tea. Sitting in a hot, throbbing café, falafel on the table and the eternal hiss of a boiling kettle behind her, Allegra struggled to find the right words to say. But there was something about the bearded, long-haired Jew, tucked neatly into his brown suit, which told Allegra the truth would be more interesting to him than the lie she conjured for others. A lie she repeated to various Underwood relatives, for example. She told them— even Josiah—that her venture was an act of memorialising her father, who shared her love of theatre.

But, sitting around a table with Solomon Glass, Allegra had the strong feeling that the old man would not accept such a story and, with the casualness of a stranger, would press her for the truth. And the truth was that Allegra relished being part of a profession where women could command the same fee as men; she saw the celebrated actress, Ellen Terry, perform at the Lyceum, and was left with a profound conviction that actresses, at the top of their profession, deserved to be paid well. Money, she told Solomon Glass, meant independence.

She named the theatre 'Lucan's Playhouse', in honour of her father. It staged productions put on by touring companies and in-house plays starring a stable of actors Allegra employed. The theatre could seat around a hundred people but, as the war dragged on, most performances only attracted thirty or so. At the matinee the day before the bombs fell on the south coast, twenty tickets were sold. Allegra collected the accounts from the box office when she arrived that afternoon and took up her usual seat on the front row to frown over the figures. On stage, a small group from the theatre's band of actors were rehearsing *Macbeth*, about to be performed for the first time that following week. Occasionally, Allegra looked up from her books, murmuring the lines with them. The director sat only feet away and was up and down, shouting out instructions.

'Where's Hector?' the director was asking now. An actress had walked onto the stage, clutching a bundle of papers, and was about to start reading aloud from them. The director, a dumpy woman with a large chest, pointed at the script. 'Why isn't Hector here for his cue? Is he late?'

'He isn't here at all,' the woman holding the papers said. Allegra looked up. She knew the actress on the stage well; Miriam wasn't one to sound nervous. She had raised three girls of her own and the grandchildren of her only son after he and his wife had died of scarlet fever. And yet her voice quavered a little.

'Why isn't he?' the director pressed.

'Michael isn't here either,' came a voice from the back of the stage. Another woman stepped forward, moving from light into shadow. She also held a script. 'I was going to step in as Duncan.'

'The first performance is next week!' the director exploded. 'This won't do!'

'Hector turned eighteen at the weekend,' Miriam said quietly, by way of explanation. A murmur rippled around the rest of the cast. Allegra heard the shuffle of feet.

'Ah.' The director seemed to deflate. 'I see. And Michael?'

'His mother had a telegram this morning,' someone said.

Allegra set down her accounts, finances forgotten. She hadn't known Hector was so close to being conscripted; he would have gone, of course, first chance he had. As for Michael's mother ... Allegra closed her eyes to the news that a black-rimmed note had arrived, knowing that Michael had an older brother.

A choked silence descended on the actors on the stage. They stood like statues, still figures in an orb of yellow light. Allegra liked to keep costs down as much as possible during rehearsals, so only the stage lights were on. The actresses hovered inside a pale oval. Occasionally one would step out or step in but, at that moment, all those on stage lingered, immobile, accepting the news. It had been heard before and would be heard again, but had lost none of its capacity to shock.

'Well, we'll just have to manage,' the director finally said, and a hum returned to the stage. Women started to move again, continuing their work, making do. Allegra heard some hurry through their lines, knowing they wanted to be home to see to remaining children or touch their men-folk. News like that reaching Michael's mother always had such an effect.

Allegra was about to squint down at the accounts again when she thought of Violet and looked around. She strained her eyes to see beyond the stage, into the shadows, but could see no one. No Violet. She had not yet returned from Woking. Allegra looked behind, to see if her daughter had come in quietly and was sitting on one of the chairs on the back row, like she sometimes did, to give herself a few extra minutes to go over her lines. Violet had always struggled with scripts; Allegra remembered long nights just before a performance, when Violet would pace the kitchen floor, chanting phrases, scenes, in an effort to consign them to memory. She did not prepare in advance—that was her trouble.

It was a fact Allegra reminded her of many times. But Violet was simply not one to sit and learn. Instead, she was eager to be outside. As soon as she was old enough, Violet walked everywhere by herself; up and down Kensington High Street, through Holland Park. Restlessness seemed to fill her bones and heat her blood, and the worst kind of days for her were when the weather or some other constraint kept her at home. Once, when she was twelve and they had argued, Violet walked across the city to Waterloo, where she caught a train to her grandfather's house in Woking. Josiah had sent Allegra a telegram, his astonished amusement at his granddaughter's unexpected arrival contained in the few short lines, and he then made arrangements to return Violet home the following day. She didn't tell her mother what had compelled her to walk five miles to Waterloo station, only that she had felt the need to move. To *stride*. After a few weeks of quiet reflection following the incident, Violet started to swim in the pools at Hampstead Heath, even though Allegra expressly forbade it. But she knew the girl continued, her wet hair giving her away.

For an idle moment, Allegra wondered if Violet had decided to walk back to Earls Court today, after visiting Edward out at Threadstone Hall. It was not impossible, she acknowledged, though a trek of thirty miles might have been beyond even Violet.

Then, a door at the back of the theatre swung open, letting in the final rays of the day's light, and Violet appeared. Allegra turned round to look at her fully. Her daughter looked different. Violet's eyes were red, her cheeks blotchy. She walked with her hands clasped in front of her, held low.

'Violet, here!' Allegra waved to her. But Violet did not appear to have heard her. Instead she looked in the opposite direction, past the director, who had turned round to see what had caused the disturbance, tutting out her irritation. Violet lifted an apologetic hand in the direction of the stage and then found a seat, some rows back and away from her mother.

Allegra stared at her curiously. Had she really not heard her? She had shouted quite loudly, relief at her daughter's arrival adding force to her voice. Certainly, it had been enough to disrupt the actors on stage. But Violet did acknowledge Allegra was in the same room and looked studiously elsewhere, anywhere but in her mother's direction.

❦

As the days passed, Allegra grew more and more certain that her daughter was troubled. They had always talked, she and Violet, having lived so closely for so many years. After Allegra separated from Edward, there was little money. Almost all of Allegra's inheritance from her father had been ploughed into the theatre. Edward made sure Violet had a new wardrobe every year and put money into an account for her; occasionally, Josiah would send a parcel of books. But, for the main part, Allegra and Violet had to manage. There was not much money to be made in the theatre, no matter what those in the West End said. Allegra could only pay her actors a small amount; she made sure they were paid equally though, men and women, which is why so many continued to perform on her stage. After the bills were settled each month, very little was left over.

Despite this, and despite the evenings where there was nothing to eat except yesterday's bread, Allegra thought she and Violet were content. They would sit around the kitchen table for hours, setting out performance schedules for the coming months, working through director's notes so they could inform the two ancient stage hands what they needed to do for a certain play. They wrote advertisements for the free local papers and devised ways of promoting the theatre and selling more tickets. Violet was fully involved from being a child and, after school, would sit in the ticket booth while Allegra stood at the front of house. Then, once an evening performance was over, they would take a steady walk back to their tiny flat in Earls Court, stopping off at a fish stall on the way. As they strode they would talk endlessly, walking arm in arm, Allegra feeling the pressure of her daughter's fingers on the inside of her elbow.

Now, since her trip out to Woking, Violet had spent more time away from the flat than ever before, excusing herself from the planning sessions around the kitchen table with mumbled words about meeting a friend in Holland Park; words so obviously untrue that Allegra had not the heart to challenge her.

One evening, though, two weeks after Violet had returned from seeing Edward, she stayed at home with Allegra. The theatre had closed for the evening and they sat in the kitchen, balls of wool scattered across the table, needles gently moving back and forth. An advertisement had been put in the national papers for women to knit socks for men at the front; balls of wool could be collected from a local church and completed garments were to be returned there. Allegra and Violet had made only a few pairs so far. Tonight, with the accounts done and the theatre closed, they sat together.

Violet sighed and twitched her way through the first row of stitches, pursing her lips as she neared the end and turned the needle. Allegra glanced at her, knowing how much her daughter hated these tasks. She felt the scuff of Violet's boot as the girl twirled her foot, her body always moving, always in motion. But still Violet carried on with her knitting, wanting to do her bit. She would have rather have been down at the church hall, packing the socks into parcels and seeing to it that they were conveyed to the train station ready to be shipped out, but there were no positions like that available—she had asked. So Violet tried to marshal her body into this small task, fidgeting on her chair. Her stitches were tight and the wool became hot in her hands. She gritted her teeth and tried not to hear the squeak of wool moving over metal needles.

'Miriam was at the theatre earlier,' Allegra said, breaking the silence. She paused with her own knitting and took a sip of tea. 'She told me she'd been walking on Hampstead Heath at the weekend with her grandchildren. Some men were swimming. Soldiers, probably, on leave. Do you remember when we were there, last summer?'

There was no reply from Violet.

'We took a picnic, didn't we? Ham and pickles. And then we heard that sound. Like a series of thuds. Booms. In the distance, nowhere near the Heath.'

'It was the bombs at the Somme,' Violet said, not looking up. 'I saw a piece about it in the paper soon after.'

'Did you?' Allegra tried to imagine how big an explosion would have to be for the sound to carry across the Channel. 'We heard that noise the whole time we were there. In the end, I stopped noticing.'

'I didn't. I'll never forget it.'

'That's perhaps as it should be.' Allegra picked up her knitting again. 'A sound like that should never be forgotten. That's why doing something like this, this knitting—we're reminded what other people are giving up, right now.'

They continued for a while, a clock on the mantelpiece above the small coal fire ticking out their distance from each other. Allegra again peeped at her daughter, watching the way Violet frowned as her knitting became more unyielding and damp from her wet palms. Violet gnawed the inside of her cheek. She stopped suddenly and glared up at Allegra.

'What is it?'

'Nothing. Sorry, I was thinking,' Allegra said hurriedly, her daughter's hostility putting her on edge. 'Just what it would be like in France right now. Hellish at the Front, no doubt. Maybe just as difficult towards the coast.'

'There is someone you could ask,' Violet murmured.

'What did you say?'

Slowly, 'I said there is someone you could ask.'

'Don't be silly. I don't know anyone at the Front, not now Michael's brother has been killed. His mother received a telegram the day you visited your father.'

At that, Violet lay down her knitting on the table and got up. She moved to her bag, thrown down beside the couch that doubled as her mother's bed and took a sheet of paper from it. Then, without speaking, handed it to her mother.

'What's this?'

'Read it,' Violet said eventually. 'There *is* someone you know at the Front. Or not far from it.'

Allegra looked at the letter, typed on clean white paper with an embossed corner. The Diocese of Jedthorpe, she read, and her heart thudded in her ribcage. The letter was brief, just a few lines. When she had finished, she looked up at her daughter, eyes wet.

'He's in France, then,' she said eventually, her voice like a broken reed.

'Has been for a year. Since the Somme. He ministers at a hospital in a place called Villers-des-Champs.' Violet drew up her chair again. She had been startled by her mother's reaction, having expected initial denial or bluster. She had not expected Allegra to acknowledge Shacklock so openly, so readily. She looked into Allegra's tired, worn face, lines gathered around her eyes like creases in a map and, for the first time in a fortnight, felt sorry for the way she had distanced herself.

'When did this arrive?' said Allegra, meaning the letter.

'Yesterday. I wrote to his ministry to find out where he is. The Jedthorpe address took some tracking down, but the library helped. I even asked Emily, but whatever she knew, she was keeping to herself.'

'No doubt. Emily has been a good and loyal cousin for many years. Is Edward behind this?' Allegra thought of her husband, still bound to her after all these years. They had not divorced. She had asked, once, in the early days of their separation, but Edward had refused. She had not asked again, accepting that he hated her too much to give her her freedom.

'He told me the last time I went to Threadstone. Father—*Edward*—is dying.'

'Is he?' Allegra's eyes widened, but she did not feel sorry. Instead, she felt like she might had she read about the death of a distant king in the newspaper.

'That's why he told me.' Violet turned the letter around so she could see Shacklock's name printed on the paper. She traced a finger over the black typescript. 'I think he felt he owed it to me to tell me the truth.'

'I see.' But Allegra did not—she did not see Edward divulging a secret as incendiary as this out of a feeling of moral responsibility. She imagined him glowering in his rooms at Threadstone, casting out grenades full of malice, and then sitting back as they blasted her family apart.

'Why didn't you ever tell me?'

There, Allegra thought. The question that she knew was coming, from the moment her daughter was born and she saw thick, black eyebrows upon the infant's face. That and Violet's hair; dark, like the pelt of night when gaslights were shut off. If she had looked a little less like Shacklock—maybe more like Allegra even—Edward could have loved her as a father should. Instead, Shacklock's girl grew up to be an inverted mirror of him; short and strong, determined in her own mind. She wore skirts where Shacklock wore trousers, but Violet carried her true father's spirit inside her skin and Edward turned away when she was a few years old.

Allegra realised that Violet was looking at her, properly, for the first time in two weeks. She sighed, climbing another rung up an invisible ladder to the point where the truth would have to come out.

'It was a very brief affair, Violet,' she began. 'A few weeks, that's all. Shacklock was much older than me, a friend of Josiah's. But it could not last. Shacklock was not even supposed to be in Greece. He'd come over to see his old friend. He and Josiah had argued, many years ago, though I never knew why. Shacklock had left his posting in Malta and visited him.'

'Father said you hadn't been married long.'

'That's true. But the marriage was failing already. It wouldn't be fair to say why, but Shacklock appeared at a time when the problems between Edward and I became unavoidable.'

Violet laid her hands on the table, her left hand forming a fist agitatedly. She forced it still, staring at Shacklock's name on the letter, trying to peel back the details of his character from the formation of the letters. 'Why didn't you leave with him when Edward forced him to go?'

'Edward told you that much, then.' Allegra grimaced, the scene in Josiah's sitting room playing out in her mind, when Shacklock bled into her skirt and stained his own shirt, and the moment she walked away, knowing he would not follow her.

'He said he saw you. Together.' Violet blushed. It was impossible for her to think of her mother in such a way. 'He also said that Shacklock didn't fight for you.'

'He didn't,' Allegra said simply. 'His church was more important to him than I. I thought that what we'd had for those precious few weeks was something worth going into battle for—he made me so happy during those weeks, you see. But what could I do? I was married. Imagine if I had tried to divorce Edward. I would have lost everything—I would have been cast out. A divorced woman is frowned upon even today. You know this. How many of your school friends were not allowed to invite you to tea because you live with your mother and not your father?'

Violet caught her lip between her teeth, remembering. Allegra was not the only mother living alone amongst her school friends; many of Violet's classmates had lost a father in France. But Allegra was the only woman bringing up her child alone without being a widow. The parents of certain friends made it plain they did not approve of their daughters socialising with Violet.

'But you and Father are not divorced,' Violet said stubbornly.

'Oh, Violet.'

'What happened when you told him? When you told Shacklock about me? Surely he must have wanted to see me. Edward said he left you easily enough, but what about *me*?'

At that, Allegra stood up. She pushed back her chair and dropped her knitting back onto the table. That was a question she could not answer. She moved to the sink.

'Mother?'

Allegra reached for a dishcloth and began to absently wipe down plates, already washed. She moved them on the dish-rack noisily, blocking out Violet's questions.

Except, of course, Violet repeated them. She reached out for her mother's elbow and turned her around, gently but with force.

There was nothing for it but to tell the truth. 'I didn't tell him.'

'Ever?'

'Ever. He doesn't know, even now. There seemed to be no point—it would not change his mind. He would not risk his church to be with me.'

'I cannot believe this.' Violet's face was white and shocked. 'You didn't tell him?'

'Violet ...'

'No.' Violet took a step back, now close to the flat's front door, which opened directly into the kitchen. 'All my life I've felt Edward's absence, as though he is not really interested in me. He takes a passing regard from time to time, as though I am a pet to be attended to.'

'Edward didn't want me to tell Anthony! He would not have taken me back if I'd told Shacklock about you.'

'But what about after you left him? You owed Edward nothing then—you could have written to Shacklock at any time.' Violet grabbed her bag and reached for her coat hanging on the back of the front door. 'You made a decision for all of us, and I'm the one now living with it.'

'Where are you going?' Allegra held out her hand for her daughter, still gripping the dishcloth.

'I don't know.'

'Violet, please!'

'There's nothing more to say to each other.'

And, with that, Violet turned and walked out of the flat. She left the letter from the Diocese of Jedthorpe on the table and, as the door slammed behind her, the paper flapped in the gust of air. Allegra caught it, the pain crushing her stomach almost overwhelming, and she read again the brief few lines, lines that had jammed into the breach between her and her daughter.

✐

Two days later, Violet stood on the platform at Victoria. Trains steamed and spluttered, blasts of mist enveloped those lingering beside her. Men in khaki uniforms, some of them drunk, swayed together in tight knots. There was talk of 'One more, while we still can,' and Violet saw the flash of silver hip flasks being passed around. Someone offered it to her and she shrank back, frightened.

Sweethearts lingered together. A dried flower was pressed into a palm here and there; women wiped their faces and then tucked soiled handkerchiefs into their man's chest pocket. Some men stood with their mothers, the strain of an unavoidable parting lining the cheeks of care-worn women, who looked upon their sons with piercing hunger. Violet glanced all around her, taking it in.

She held her bag by her side and swung it nervously. Inside were a brown skirt and a white pinafore, upon which Violet had painted a red cross. The day before, the recruitment officer at the Voluntary Aid Detachment office at Whitehall—a puckered-mouthed old woman wearing a high-necked dress—had listened patiently to Violet's rehearsed attempt to sign up, and just as kindly rejected her.

'You don't really have nursing experience, my dear,' the woman had said. 'Why don't you see about registering with a munitions factory? Or the Land Army?'

'I need to get to France,' Violet had said quietly.

The woman looked at her with sympathy. 'Part badly, did you? Write to him. They always make sure the men get their letters, even at the Front.'

Violet shook her head and walked away. Behind her another girl, around the same age and clutching a handkerchief, approached the registration desk. Violet heard the same story repeated and stood on the pavement for a while, breathing in the traffic fumes and thinking hard.

As she waited, a group of women gathered close by. One held out a sheet of paper and the three huddled round, heads touching. One spoke: 'Victoria, then. Ten o'clock tomorrow morning. The train takes us down to Dover, and then a boat over to Calais. We'll be sent on from there.'

'Can we take much with us?' asked another.

Violet leant to the side, listening, trying not to be noticed.

'One small bag, it says. Pack plenty of knickers, girls. We won't get much chance to wash our clothes.'

The women sighed collectively, one mumbling it would be like working in the East End all over again. They moved into the building behind, where the woman with the puckered face and stout frame waited for them.

Violet lingered outside. Trams and a high-topped bus rattled past, soldiers on leave staring down at the chaotic London streets with vacant eyes. Most wore officer's flat caps, and some sat next to a girl. She wondered if they were holding hands, up on the bus, away from prying eyes. Maybe hands were inside blouses, men desperate for the press of flesh after so long in a stinking, rain-soaked trench. And Violet thought again about what the bishop, *her father*, was doing out in France.

Resolution. An idea that had formed at the edges of her mind stood up and announced itself. She had keys to the theatre; she knew where the costumes were kept, having washed them many times.

That was how yesterday went—the soft, maternal rejection at the Whitehall Detachment office, the discovery that nurses were leaving from Victoria. And now Violet stood on the platform while a train belched steam, a homemade nurse's outfit in her bag. No papers.

~ 22 ~

Present Day

Jess sat opposite Billy, reading through the letters written by Allegra Underwood to her cousin Emily. Brown with age, the manuscripts sat in a pile on the table, edges frayed, silent paper grenades. Jess finished reading a letter from Allegra to Emily, sent in the summer of 1917. The panic conveyed in the terse lines made Jess wince.

'Still cannot find her. Someone at the theatre said she raided the costume box—she must have had the clothes with her when she left from Victoria. Miriam saw her there and said she was carrying a small bag. She's gone to France, I know she has.'

Jess laid the letter slowly down on the table. Billy sat quietly, waiting. He was biting the flesh around his thumb; occasionally his teeth cracked into his nail, the hard, studded sound carrying far in the emptying Hampstead library. He had passed over a bundle of letters to Jess when she arrived, ordered chronologically. He had extracted letters that dealt with Shacklock's arrival in Greece and the affair with Allegra, and their discovery by Edward, and skipped through letters sent to Emily soon after the Underwoods arrived back in London. The last letters in the bundle were those describing Violet's discovery about the true identity of her father; Edward had written to Allegra to tell her what he had divulged, and Allegra had paraphrased it in a later letter to Emily. Then Allegra's letters stopped abruptly in 1917, eventually beginning again when Allegra tried to reach the battlefields in her frantic search for her daughter.

'Lucky for us that Emily ignored Allegra and didn't burn the letters. Did Allegra ever find out what had happened to Violet?' Jess asked. 'Did you get that far with the letters to find out?'

Billy shook his head. 'I don't think so. She died in 1919, before

Shacklock's body was taken back to Jedthorpe. If you remember, my old university friend says in her thesis that Allegra closed down her theatre very suddenly in 1917. I think she lost heart after Violet disappeared and then sold it when the war was over so she could fund a search for her daughter. Wouldn't you do the sameif it was your child?'

Jess turned her head. It was too awful an idea to contemplate. She thought of Megan, sweet and innocent at twelve, only five years or so younger than Violet had been in 1917. She felt a rush of sympathy for Allegra. 'The genealogical website said that no further records were available for Violet, didn't they? At the Shacklock library this week when we checked. No marriage record, no death record. Nothing to suggest she had a child.'

'Meaning she may have met up with the bishop in France and they both died soon after.'

'What date did Shacklock die?'

Billy pulled out his copy of *The Life of Bishop Shacklock* from a rucksack on the floor. He flicked through the first few pages. '17 September 1917.'

'What else does it say about him?'

Billy cleared his throat and started to read out loud. ' "By 1916, following the Somme offensive, reports had started to filter back through church channels about the appalling effects of the war upon young soldiers. In private correspondence, army chaplains writing to members of the church hierarchy described terrible wounds, lingering deaths and the shocking effects of gas. It was not long before Shacklock heard of these reports and was galvanised into action. Although well into his sixties by that point, he persuaded the Synod in York to allow him to travel to France where, away from the fighting, he tended to injured soldiers in a hospital at Villers-des-Champs." '

Billy stopped reading and looked up. 'He went to administer to the sick. Fits with what we know of him—man of action, and all that.'

'I'd say after reading Allegra's letters to her cousin, we know very little about Shacklock,' Jess said. 'Or, whatever we think we know about him, we should reassess.'

'Well, whatever we think we know, we're no closer to finding out how Violet came to be buried with Shacklock. What happened to her? Shacklock was said to have died of a heart attack, wasn't he?' Billy bent over the *Life* again. 'Something he picked up in the hospital. But what happened to Violet?'

'There's only one sure way of finding out,' Jess said, the whirlwind of the past week exhausting her. She thought of Hayden, waiting back at his flat for her. And of Alec, who hadn't called.

'We'll have to go to France.' Billy beamed. The prospect obviously delighted him. 'Do you know anything about French archives? How they are organised?'

'Not a sausage. I can't speak French, either, apart from to ask where the swimming pool is, or order a coffee.'

'Me neither.' Billy tapped the table, the prospect of a French research trip making him fidget. 'But we have a name now, don't we? Violet Underwood. No one's had a name before, certainly no one who looked at the French side of the mystery.'

'She probably didn't travel under her real name. Allegra didn't find her, remember.'

'We need to start somewhere.'

Jess sat back, thinking. Billy was right, of course. It was an obvious step; in fact, for the first time, it seemed that the path was laid clearly for them. Up to this week, Jess had stumbled across clues and wasted months pursuing dead ends. Now, France loomed as a place where the complete story might unfold.

'What about Professor Waller?' she asked. 'How can we get him to fund a trip to France?'

Butterfield started to gnaw on his thumb again. Jess could see the flesh around his nail was pink and sore. 'We'd have to make it sound so boring he wouldn't want to come along, but important enough to cough up the expenses.'

'Or we fund it ourselves and don't tell him,' Jess said quietly.

Billy's thumb fell from his lips. 'We would be going behind his back again.'

'Like we are now. Today.'

'This would be different, Jessica.'

'You were the one who said you wanted to stick it to him!' Jess laughed. She felt suddenly flooded by recklessness and embraced the sensation gratefully. The weekend would be easier if she could convince herself she didn't care—about anything. 'What could we get away with?

A week away from the library?'

'It depends what we say to Waller. Family crises or something? And what about your kids? Can you manage to be away from them for a week?'

Jess thought of James and Megan and her resolve slipped a little. If she were to disappear for a week, even James would notice. Megan would find it very difficult; Jess remembered school residentials when she had to pre-arrange phone calls in order to talk to her tearful daughter before lights out.

But, after Alec's revelation, a week away might be just what was needed. Jess gritted her teeth against the memory of his words.

And there was another thought, unspoken as yet but defined, lingering in the background. *Hayden.* Jess reached for the letters and started to put them back in order.

'Whatever we decide to do, we need to think about Waller,' she said. 'Look, I'm going to stay over in London tonight, after all. I might come back and read more in the morning. Why don't you head home and start planning how we can make this thing work?'

Billy nodded, already ahead of her. He began to pack away his laptop and notepad, his eyes distant and dreamy.

They parted outside the library, hugging awkwardly. Suddenly feeling a rush of gratitude towards him, Jess hugged harder than necessary, so that when they released each other, Billy was smiling, embarrassed and pleased.

'This might work, Jess,' he said. 'We might be almost there.'

Jess held up her hand. 'Waller's said that before. Let's see.' But Butterfield was right. She felt closer than ever to identifying the woman buried with Bishop Shacklock and finding out how she got there.

Then Billy was away, walking back to the tube station. Jess watched him leave, part of her going with him, part of her spinning around on the Hampstead street, pinging from thought to thought. Hayden. Alec. Shacklock. Her kids. Waller. Hayden.

And now, France. She shook her head, marvelling again at the way the week had turned out, wondering what she would say to the professor, what she would to Alec. As she smoked a cigarette and then started to make her own way back to the tube, she thought of what she would say to Hayden.

Part 3

France

~ 23 ~

Present Day

The townsfolk of Villers-des-Champs had an understated way of celebrating Christmas. Unlike Abbeville, the nearest city, there were only a few festive lights hung around Villers and, on the bridge crossing the river that cut the town in two, a solitary green wreath had been propped against the stonework. An afterthought of ivy and twine. Leaning against the window, screwing his eyes up against the condensation, Billy tried to read the red sash around the wreath as their car pulled up alongside it, waiting for the lights to change.

'Joyeux Noël' he said from the back seat. 'Noel—do you think people still call their children Noel these days?'

Hands whitening around the steering wheel, Hayden glanced at Jess sitting beside him. His irritation at Billy had manifest on the ferry when the researcher had grilled him over coffee while Jess was looking around the onboard shop. Jess had warned Billy in advance, of course, that Hayden would be joining them on their trip to France and would be staying with her in whatever accommodation they decided to book. Billy had asked nothing about Hayden and who he was, sensing Jess was reluctant to divulge more than she had to. But this had been the first Billy had heard about Jess's plans for their stay; he had hoped they would share a place together on their trip—not for any romantic reason or because he harboured secret feelings towards her, but simply because of the cost. A week-long excursion to France just before Christmas had made a serious dent in his finances and displeased his wife. Now, with Hayden joining them, it seemed that the expense would only increase: separate cottages or hotel rooms would have to be booked.

Hayden was made fully aware of Billy's annoyance during the brief interlude on the ferry when Jess was not around. 'Do you know I had to tell Waller that my father had had a heart attack, and that's why I needed this time off?' Billy had said, rolling a sachet of sugar between his fingers. 'What did you have to tell your boss, to get time off so quickly?'

'I am the boss,' Hayden had replied, which did little to appease Billy's temper.

'I suppose it's nothing to you, then, to book a cottage for a week.' Billy's voice was little more than a sneer.

Hayden studied the plump man sitting opposite him, with his straining rugby shirt and red acne. He knew a little of Billy's reaction to the news that Hayden would be coming to France, though Jess had been more preoccupied with the arrangements for her children than her colleague's feelings.

The day Jess returned from London, after working in Hampstead with Billy, Alec moved out of their home and back to his parents'. Neither asked if the separation was permanent and, in a painful conversation with James and Megan, said they needed some time apart. Megan had been bewildered and tearful, James silent and angry. So far, though, they seemed to have fallen into a tentative pattern. Jess lived with the children during the week and, at the weekend, when James and Marie spent time with their father at their grandparents' house, Jess travelled down to Hayden's Fulham flat.

She would arrive at Saturday lunchtime and, after a nap, would almost be the Jess Hayden knew and waited for. Almost, but not quite; she often felt that the centre of her had drained away, or that she had been hollowed out. Her stomach hurt. It was impossible to be distracted from the thoughts of her children. In their moments together on Saturday afternoons, and again on Sunday mornings when Hayden scampered down the stairs of his flat to switch on the heating and then return, hands cold, to lay on her body, Jess was there for him but it was not how she had been before.

She had told Hayden a little of what happened about Alec's affair, though she did not linger long over this detail, aware of her own hypocrisy. As ever, the children were her focus. 'Megan isn't sleeping well,' she divulged over lunch at a noodle place on Fulham Road. 'She comes in with me most nights. James seems to have decided he can't be bothered with it all and barely speaks to Alec or I. I can't blame him. We've shattered everything they knew.'

Hayden had listened but said nothing. Instead he ordered them both a beer. When it came, he drank his own quickly. 'They won't know what to expect. They'll be wondering if you'll get back together or what will happen if you don't.'

'Did you think those things?' Jess thought of Marie. 'You must have been a similar age when your parents split up.'

Hayden shrugged. 'I guess so. I was probably like James and tried not to show that it had affected me. But yeah, I hoped there would be a way back. I thought about daft things, too.'

'Such as?'

'Such as if I could keep my name—my surname, that is—given that Dad was no longer living with us. Crazy, I know. But I worried if I'd have to stop being Hayden Llewellyn and become something else. Take on my mother's maiden name, for instance. Hayden Price—can you imagine?'

Jess felt a pain deep within her chest and she thought of Megan, tossing and turning beside her in bed at night, the way she ground her teeth together. The way James retreated to his bedroom from the moment he returned home from school and how he refused to join his mother and sister at mealtimes. They had known nothing else but to return to a house where Mum and Dad would both be there. She wanted to phone them, right at that moment, at the noodle bar, the urge almost taking her breath.

But then Hayden had stood up and pulled her to her feet, slipping a note down onto the table to pay for their meal. He steered her out onto the street, hands easing her coat over her shoulders and he pressed against her, the freshness of his aftershave staining her skin as he bent forward to hold her close. Jess breathed him in, grateful, drowning.

They had driven through snow to get down to Dover. Jess and Billy had come down on the train, meeting Hayden at Kings Cross. They'd hired a car from a Hertz nearby, splitting the cost between them. Sensing the researcher's resentment from the moment they met, Hayden had offered to drive, an offer he repeated once the boat reached Calais.

As they entered the town of Villers-des-Champs, the ill feeling between the two men was tangible and had made for an uncomfortable journey. Jess sat alongside Hayden while Billy fumed in the back, passing inane comments on the countryside as they drove through the Pas-des-Calais region. Jess had never heard Billy talk that way before; at the Shacklock Library she had barely spoken to him before he became involved in the hunt for the woman buried with the bishop. She had never known him to feel it necessary to fill the silences with foolish chatter. But the Billy sitting in the back of the hired car couldn't keep quiet. Metal statues painted white punctuated the road south from Calais, shapes bent into athletic poses; Billy had something to say about each of them, his voice filling the car. Occasionally Jess spoke, but Hayden remained quiet. As they drove on and the silence deepened, Billy's voice took on a vitriolic tone, as though he had won something.

'The cottage owner said to follow the road behind the back of the town hall and then take a sharp right up the hill,' Jess said as they crossed over the bridge into Villers-des-Champs and neared the town hall. They passed a couple of restaurants and bakeries, and a convenience store with fruit and vegetables perched uninvitingly in boxes on the street. Hayden drove past the town hall, a white building lit up by brilliant spotlights, and then swung the car up a steep, narrow road, lined on one side with a row of houses, a high wall running along the other. The car juddered on the cobbles and Jess held the car door tightly.

'There, number five.' She pointed to a thin house, painted brown. A window on the ground floor and a pale, green door; above, another window. A one-bedroomed cottage with a sofa bed in the living room. A small kitchen at the back, with a downstairs toilet and shower. Jess had found it online, as well as a similar cottage a few doors up.

'This is ours, then,' she said as Hayden pulled the car up to the thin curb and switched off the engine. He slowly unfolded himself from the car. Billy strained to look up the dark street and leant across the seat.

'Is number eight up there?'

'Should be.' Jess opened the boot and took out a bag. She passed one to Billy, who had got out and was now shaking his legs on the pavement beside her. 'Can you find it? The owner said she'd leave them both unlocked with the keys in the kitchen.'

'I'll take a look.' Billy started to say something else when a church bell started to toll just above them. The rounded peal rang up and down the street, filling their ears. They looked and realised the wall opposite the row of cottages marked the edge of the churchyard. The church itself was built into a hill and loomed over the street.

Hayden, lighting a cigarette, came to join them. He waited until the bells rang seven times and spoke. 'That will be why this place is only a hundred and fifty euros a week. We've got to put up with that for the whole time we're here.'

'That's their church,' Jess said softly, turning back to Billy.

'Where Shacklock was found?'

'And the woman. Violet.'

They paused and for a moment a bubble formed between them. It excluded Hayden, who looked at them both quizzically.

'Right, tomorrow,' Billy said after a pause. 'I'll call down for you after breakfast and we'll make a start?'

'Sure.' Jess smiled, properly this time. Excitement lit like a small flame inside and warmed her stomach.

She transferred her bag to the other hand and, watching Billy walk up the street to find his cottage, turned back to Hayden. He had finished his cigarette and was taking out a bag from the boot, wrestling a box of food under his arm. Somehow he managed to slam the boot closed and then the two of them stepped into the little cottage.

The landlady had thought to leave the heating on and warm air pillowed around them. Hayden shut the door slowly and looked for somewhere to put down the box. The doorway opened straight into the living area, a fairly long room with a dining table at the far end.

Jess looked into the next room. 'Kitchen's quite big. The bathroom is just through here as well.'

'It will do for a week.'

Jess removed her coat slowly. She threw her scarf on the pale green sofa and sat down. 'You'll stay that long, then?' Her voice was hesitant.

Hayden placed the box of supplies on the tiled floor and dropped down next to her. 'Is that all right with you?'

'Yes, of course. But we hadn't talked about it, so ...' Jess trailed off. She felt exhausted: the lurch of the ferry in choppy, winter seas had prompted nausea, embarrassing her. She had thought she was too old for travel sickness. Only constant movement kept it at bay and she walked around the onboard shop and café endlessly. For the last hour she had longed for bed, whatever the cottage was like.

Hayden rubbed his hand gently on her knee. 'When you asked if I'd like to come with you, I said I would. I meant for the whole trip, not just a few days.'

The touch of his fingers was soothing and Jess reached out with her own to take Hayden's hand. The urgency of being together had eased over the past week or so, perhaps because they were becoming more comfortable with each other. Where once their bodies met quickly, now they lingered and held back from the moment. Where once the thought of being together had hastened their step to the tube or the flat in Fulham, they strolled and took their time as they wandered down Fulham Road, talking, feeling their way towards each other with words.

Jess edged against Hayden and closed her eyes. 'I am so tired.'

'How were James and Megan this morning?'

Jess had taken the children to Alec's parents' house before heading to the train station. James had been disinterested in his mother's cautious attempts to explain her absence and arrange phone calls, whereas Megan had been upset. The parting had been difficult. Jess opened her eyes again, the image of Megan's stricken face painted on her eyelids.

'I'm going to phone them tonight. After a shower.'

'I'll nip out while you do. They don't need to hear me in the background.' Hayden dropped a kiss on Jess's head and stood up. 'We passed a shop on the drive here. I'll walk down there. Of all the things we didn't bring—wine.'

Jess nodded wearily and, rubbing the tired muscles in her neck, stood up from the sofa and stumbled towards the bathroom.

~ 24 ~

June 1917

A few well-timed tears and frantic scrabbling through her bag had fooled the ticket inspector at Victoria Station, who took pity on Violet and allowed her to board the train for Dover. It had been easier than she'd thought, the harried inspector in a rush to empty the platform of soldiers and volunteers. Already crammed, Violet squeezed into a carriage with a dozen or so other women, some sitting on the floor, others on bags. Elbows and knees clashed, good-natured remarks were swapped, and hands were thrown out to steady themselves as the train pulled away, steaming out of Victoria. Managing to edge into a space near the window, Violet watched as wives and mothers ran alongside on the platform, feet pounding the concourse, faces lined with fear. Many wept openly and called out to their men, last words for the soldiers to hear before their voices became a memory or words on a page.

Some of the women in Violet's carriage sniffed. One woman clutched a locket, others rose and settled as the train throbbed south to the coast. Sensing these women were robust and talkative, Violet made herself as small as possible and closed her eyes, leaning against the wall of the carriage so that the others might think her asleep. The ticket inspector might have been convinced she was a nurse, but the women of the Voluntary Aid Detachment in her carriage would not be as gullible.

After a while, Violet actually did sleep. The night before had been long and broken by dreams. She had left the volunteers office at Whitehall and returned to Earls Court, taking care not to be seen by a neighbour or friend. She had let herself into the theatre and removed what she needed from the costume box, stuffing everything into her bag. She had slept for an hour or so in the seats before apparitions of a woman holding a pen over a register and shaking her head forced her to rise early and make her way to her bank. Edward had seen to it that a small amount of money had been deposited in her name, every year on her birthday. Violet had never touched it. The money was now wrapped in a sock in her bag, a fact Violet checked regularly.

At Dover, a small boat, dwarfed by the ships carrying men, took the women from the coast to France. An older woman, helping the younger ones into the vessel paused as she took Violet's arm and looked closely into the girl's face. 'I don't know you,' she said. 'Where did you work before this?'

'The East End,' Violet muttered quickly, remembering the conversation between the nurses outside the office at Whitehall. She pulled her arm away and tried to step into the boat.

The older nurse held her tight. 'Who did you work with? You barely look old enough.' Then a shout as the boat lurched and a nurse nearly fell, and Violet shook the woman away. She swung herself into the boat and pressed herself against the wood, keeping out of sight, feeling the older woman's eyes upon her.

The crossing was rough and soon all were suffering, Violet included. Paper bags were passed around and, when these were filled, women leant over the side, into the wind, letting go of their stomachs. Violet was sick until her knees gave way and she slipped down, purple bruises behind her eyes, the rise and fall of the boat acting like a shutter; images snapped through her mind, of her mother, Edward, the soldiers at Victoria station. Eventually she gratefully tumbled into a thin sleep.

Then they landed on the shores of France. Violet was pulled to her feet by someone and, wiping her mouth, stumbled into a lorry. The engine roared and they were off, sunshine beating down on the canvas roof. Violet held onto her bag with one hand and the tarpaulin with the other. She was in France, she had made it. Now they were on their way to Calais and, from there, she had to make her way to Villers-des-Champs without being found out.

~ 25 ~

Present Day

Despite her weariness, Jess slept fitfully, shuffling in the bed beside Hayden. The church bells pealed out the unforgiving hours between sunset and daybreak, though with the window shut and thick curtains closed, the sound was muffled. Jess stared at the ceiling, listening to the bells echo down the street and then to the softer, rhythmical rise and fall of Hayden's sleep. He had slipped under quickly, moments after they made love. His long, naked body curled behind Jess, the arm thrown across her waist becoming heavier as sleep settled in.

Finally, around three o'clock in the morning, Jess fell asleep. She woke with a start sometime later, to a room still dark, but with the fuzzy glow of daylight breaking through a gap in the curtains. Downstairs she could hear the low drone of voices and the scrape of chairs around the dining table. She groaned and rolled over to look at her watch. It was gone nine. She blinked up at the ceiling, the contours of the rough paintwork now clearly visible. She would have to walk past the dining table to get to the bathroom and she was sure Billy was downstairs with Hayden. Jess groaned again, resenting the fact her work colleague would see her like this. At least Hayden had brought their suitcases upstairs, and she was able to pull on some pyjamas.

Billy, though, was polite enough to nod a brief hello when Jess came down the stairs and then turn back to his coffee. Hayden appeared to have been up for a while as there was bread on the kitchen counter, butter, and a pot of coffee boiling on the stove. He followed Jess through the kitchen and touched her back as she reached over to turn on the shower.

'You were so deep in sleep I thought I'd leave you,' he said. 'Billy's been here about half an hour.'

'Are you and Billy getting on any better?' Jess yawned and pulled her top over her head. She stepped into the shower cubicle, gasping as hot water hit her skin.

'Let's say we've reached an understanding. He told me all about your professor. Wallow, Waller, whatever his name is.' Hayden grinned. 'About finding out who this woman is and sticking it to him. Sounds as though the dear Prof has been a bit of an arse—I can sympathise with Billy wanting to hit him where it hurts. We have a shared appreciation for karma.'

He was wearing a new blue shirt, one they'd bought together a week ago. There was a logo on it, some white Cyrillic script that he'd liked. His tall frame stretched up through the doorway. Jess closed her eyes and let water wash over her face. When she opened them again, Hayden had gone.

She dressed quickly, having scurried back up the stairs wrapped in a towel. Again, irrationally she knew, she resented Billy for being there and seeing her like this.

He was deep in conversation with Hayden when Jess finally sat down with them at the dining table. Hayden stood up to pour them all another coffee when Jess arrived. 'Billy was telling me your plans for today.'

'Plans?' Jess raised an eyebrow and took a sip. 'We haven't made any, as far as I was aware.'

Billy started to speak and then paused, the bells cutting him off again. After the tenth ring, he started again. 'I was saying to Hayden that we should start at the museum here in Villers.'

'Museum?'

'It's the town museum. They have a section about the soldiers hospital.'

Jess said nothing but again felt a wave of hostility towards her fellow researcher. She knew about the museum, of course, but felt irritated that Billy had had to remind her. He'd obviously done some research before their trip. Jess, frantic with worry about the effect the separation with Alec would have on her children, had done nothing except glance over the notes taken a month ago at the British Library, Threadstone Hall and West Hampstead Library.

'Billy said this woman—Violet—may have travelled to France disguised as a nurse,' Hayden said.

Jess nodded. 'Yes, possibly. It's what Allegra suggested in her letters to her cousin, Emily. Violet took some clothes from the theatre.'

'The museum has records about the nurses who worked in the hospital,' Billy said.

'Yes.' Jess noted the sound of concession in her voice, though she was not sure to what she was conceding. 'But remember, Allegra looked for her daughter. She's bound to have checked the VAD records. She didn't find her.'

'VAD?' Hayden asked.

'Voluntary Aid Detachment. Nurses and other auxiliaries. Many of them were middle-class and had nursing experience. If Violet did pretend to be a nurse, she might have travelled under an assumed name, otherwise Allegra would have found a trace of what happened to her. And the VAD records have also been checked by other researchers: all of those who volunteered at the hospital returned to England. No one working for them was left behind.' Jess drank her coffee again.

'So the records say, but we know archives can be fickle.' Billy grinned. 'We should look again and keep in mind any names Violet may have used instead of her own.'

'Such as?'

'Let's just see. You know, better than anyone, Jessica, how manuscripts can send you on a twisted path, only to straighten out again when you least expect it.'

Hayden snorted and took a piece of bread while Jess narrowed her eyes at Billy, wondering what transformation had occurred overnight. He seemed completely unflappable and his enthusiasm shone out. Jess thought of Megan and the girl's boundless energy, the way she treated each homework project with undisguised glee.

She stood up abruptly. 'I need to phone home. Give me twenty minutes and I'll join you.' With that, Jess picked up her mug and walked back up the stairs to her phone, blinking back sudden tears.

~ *26* ~

June 1917

After a drive of only ten minutes or so from the port, the truck carrying Violet rattled to a halt. The women jerked abruptly, some crashing into others, some landing on the floor.

A few cursed. 'You might have given a lady warning before throwing her on the floor!' one bellowed, a stout Cockney woman, and she turned, grinning at Violet. 'Like being back with my old man, that is.'

Around her, women laughed and helped each other down from the truck. Violet took the Cockney woman's hand and was tugged down onto the road. They were in a town centre, which she presumed must be Calais, but she was not sure; the street thrummed with busy uniforms, men in a variety of dirty grey khaki disappearing into buildings and offices. Lorries and cars scooted past, tables were set up on the street and men queued up beside them. Violet followed the women from the truck slowly, watching men being given slips of paper and then scurrying away to bars and cafes.

It had been raining. The street was wet, steam rising from the gutters as midday sun beat down. There was a strange metallic smell in the air. It can't be gunfire, Violet thought, knowing they were some miles from the front. But then a line of lorries roared past and she saw into the open spaces inside: men on stretchers, sheets bright red. She moved unevenly on the cobbled ground, realising she could smell their blood.

'In here.' The Cockney woman gave Violet a gentle shove. They were outside a three-storey building from which someone had draped a drab sheet with the word 'Volunteers' painted on. 'This is where we register.'

Violet swallowed and stepped inside, taking one last look at the lorries, and the heave and rush of life in the street.

'There,' the Cockney insisted and pointed inside the hall where dozens of women in brown coats lined up. The ceiling was high and ornate: this had obviously been a building used for ceremonial purposes before the conflict had given it a different purpose. Violet looked around at the hundreds of women volunteering as nurses and auxiliaries. A throng of lives put on hold or, in some cases, ignited. Many wore an ornament of their past. A brooch here, an expensive scarf there. A broken nose on one and a mangled lobe from which an earring had been torn on another. Violet held onto her bag and her collection of clothes stolen from her mother's theatre, knuckles whitening around the straps.

Then she heard the voice of a fat woman wearing a uniform that strained at the bosom, standing beside an urn of tea and a trolley of sandwiches. She was shouting that the new arrivals should eat.

Realising she had not eaten properly for two days, Violet suddenly felt famished and walked over. She was handed a cup of weak tea and two small sandwiches made with potted meat. She ate quickly, the sticky paste gummed to the roof of her mouth.

A small group stood beside her, also eating and looking ruefully at the sandwiches. One of them laughed.

'It won't get any better, wherever we're posted.'

'If there's even time to eat,' said another woman, protruding teeth sitting on her bottom lip. Violet tried not to stare and shifted slightly to better hear.

'They need people at the hospitals near Abbeville, so my brother told me. He was there for a while before coming home.'

'I heard that, too,' said the third in the group, an impossibly tall girl with red hair. She looked down at her companions. 'At least we'll be of some use if we go there.'

'Maybe. My brother was at the hospital at Villers. He said they were short of everything—no bandages, no iodine. All they could do was chop off a leg and hope for the best.'

The group fell silent and they all bent over their tea. At the mention of Villers, Violet listened closely.

'Maybe we'll be posted somewhere else,' the rabbit-toothed one said.

'I don't care much.' The girl with red hair sniffed. 'I signed up as a VAD as soon as I turned twenty-three. Want to do my bit wherever.'

'I heard that some hospitals are so desperate for help they'll take anyone, whether you are a VAD or not.'

Then a call from the other end of the room, back near the door. All those not already registered were to make themselves known at the desk immediately, ready for assignment. Trucks had arrived and were ready to take them on.

At that, the room began to empty and Violet watched with alarm as women flocked to the door, swinging themselves into the backs of trucks. A dozen or so women were left, and they all dropped their tea-cups onto the trolley and hurried to the desk at the far end of the room.

Violet followed them. She heard the women in the queue in front give details of their recent postings: some in Ireland, some in towns around England. One or two had served in Mesopotamia. She swallowed, tasting the stale sandwiches again, realising she had no idea what she was going to say or how to persuade those in charge of the detachment to allow her to go to Villers-des-Champs.

But the woman behind the desk was in a hurry. Her eyes were too lined and creased for her age, and her blonde hair had greyed at the temples. She rubbed her eyes and glanced up at Violet.

'Name?'

'Pardon?'

'Your name.'

'Violet. Shacklock.' The name was alien in her mouth. Violet glanced away, looking around at the carved flowers and cherubs on the walls, some cracked and damaged. A few had been painted over with cheap whitewash that looked hurried and slapdash.

'Age?'

'Twenty-three.' Violet remembered the women beside the tea trolley, and how one had signed up as soon as she reached that age.

'Where have you served?'

'The East End.' The answer came a little too quickly. The woman behind the desk finally looked up.

'Are you a VAD or something else? You look too young to have done much more than hold a nurse's bag.'

'I'm blessed with a youthful face,' Violet said, keeping her voice calm. She thought back to the evenings spent in her mother's kitchen, pacing back and forth, reciting lines. She tried to remember her mother's advice; that she control her breathing when taking to the stage and pause between words. She also remembered the girls who had said that some hospitals were desperate for help. Violet spoke slowly. 'I can't claim to have delivered babies, but I cleaned up. Helped the mothers.'

'This is nothing like the East End.' The woman laid down her pen. 'Can you clean a wound?'

'Yes.'

'Hold a man while his stomach is stitched up? Hold another while a leg is removed, and he calls you a whore for not taking away his pain?' The woman's tired eyes glittered. She wore a thin silver wedding ring, which she touched and twisted.

Violet swallowed and counted silently to ten. She had the strong sense that her answer would determine whether she would go any further on this journey, to find Bishop Shacklock, or whether she would be sent back to the boat with a kind but firm rejection ringing in her ears.

'I don't know,' she said finally, letting her breath go in a rush. 'I've never seen those kinds of wounds. I've never seen a dead body or been with someone as they die. So the honest answer is that I just don't know if I can do those things you ask of me. But I'm here. I'm ready to try.'

The woman watched Violet carefully, fingers tapping her wedding ring. 'You will be asked to do things that you might not understand or see the reasons behind. But you are to do them, and with your whole heart. There will be sacrifices and discomforts and, undoubtedly, moments of intense sadness. You will be expected to smile through them and be strong for the men who live. We need our volunteers to give courage and comfort.'

Violet nodded, feeling tears at the corners of her eyes.

The woman seemed satisfied, and she signed a card in front of her. 'Here. Take this. There's a truck outside that can take you to the British Red Cross hospital at Rouen.'

Violet took the card slowly. 'I had hoped to go to Villers-des-Champs.'

The woman sighed and sat back in her chair. 'Why is that? I cannot post everyone to the place of their choice. Only to the place where they are needed.'

'I understand that the hospital at Villers has its challenges. Maybe I can do some good there.' Violet held out the card again, pleading inside. *Please, please. Send me to Villers.*

The woman closed her eyes and for a moment Violet thought she would say no, and that she would have to find her own way. But then the woman nodded and took the card back. 'Agreed. You may think you are lucky today, to get a posting of your choosing. But, when you get there, you will see you are not.' She crossed out something and wrote again before handing the card back. 'Here. Take this to the truck furthest down the road. He is going to Villers.'

'Thank you.' Violet felt close to tears again. She turned away, ready to walk out into the sunshine and noisy street, but then stopped and turned back. '*Thank you.*'

And then she did leave, squinting in the light, peering down the road for the vehicle that would take her to Villers-des-Champs.

~ 27 ~

After speaking to Megan for half an hour and wrangling no more than a few words from James, Jess finally felt ready to join Billy. She sat on the edge of the bed she shared with Hayden, the morning sun streaming in through the window. Pigeons from the church across the cobbled street rose and flapped as one body, the beat of their wings audible even over the noise of the town just a few hundred yards away. Someone called outside; a reply, and a laugh. Life shuttled back and forth, the normal pulse of routine and daily business in a small French town. Jess thought of Megan and her timid excitement at a day out planned by Alec's mother. *It's all right to feel happy*, and Jess had gripped her phone tightly, trying to send that message to her daughter. It was a thought she had tried to impress upon herself on their trip out to France.

Billy was waiting by the door when she came down the stairs, impatient. He was ready for the off and a small rucksack dangled from a hand. Hayden had set up a laptop on the table and was sitting, frowning at the screen.

'What will you do while I'm out?' Jess asked, dropping a hand gently onto Hayden's shoulder, holding her body at an angle so Billy wouldn't see. Ridiculous, she thought. *He knows Hayden is staying here with me.*

'I've got some reports to go through and, if I can wrangle it, I'll hop onto the neighbour's internet and send everything through to the office.' Hayden looked up. 'You okay?'

Jess shrugged. Church bells rang again, and an idea came to mind. 'Billy, before we go to the museum, we should visit the church.'

Billy opened his mouth, as though he were about to say something, but closed it again. 'Fine. Let's go there first.'

He stepped out onto the street. Jess followed, pausing to kiss Hayden.

He was distracted by his work and had turned back to the screen by the time Jess left.

She stood outside, the cold December air seeping through her coat. The church towered heavily above them. A neo-Gothic building with square, sharp, jutting angles and a black-slated roof. Steps led up to it, steep enough to make Jess's thighs sing as they made their way to the graveyard. As they approached the building, they stepped into the church's shadow and Jess felt the temperature drop further. She was hot from the climb but still pulled gloves out of her pocket. She put them on and watched her breath spiral away in white clouds. She waited for Billy to join her.

They stood silently for a few moments, steadying their breath, before moving off. 'Have you been here before?' Billy asked, his voice sounding hoarse from the effort of climbing the stairs.

'No. But I have a rough idea where the woman is buried. The reports from other researchers say she is in the west part of the churchyard.'

'Does she have a headstone?'

'There's supposed to be something. The Americans, the men who brought the bishop back to Jedthorpe—they were in a hurry. They reburied her in Shacklock's empty grave and left. The priest of the church was incandescent, apparently, when he discovered what they had done. Gossip got back to him about the woman and he arranged for a headstone to be erected. Of course, he didn't have a name to put on it. Look.'

They had found it. Jess pointed to a rounded piece of stone, about two feet in height. It rested near the church wall, tucked behind other, bigger monuments. It stood in the sunshine and, although weatherworn, had been carefully maintained, as had all the graves in the churchyard. A fleur de lis had been carved near the top of the stone, above a simple inscription.

'"*Lieu de repos de l'âme inconnue. En paix,*"' Billy attempted.

'Translated as "Resting place of an unknown soul. At peace,"' Jess said. She swallowed thickly. The pale stone was incidental amongst the other, elaborate monoliths. Although well tended, the grave seemed forgotten and separate, a fact that troubled Jess. She brushed away a leaf from the stone. 'Such a little monument.'

When she looked up, she saw that Billy had tucked in his bottom lip. 'And yet she has cast a long shadow,' he said.

'Yes.' That was what troubled her; that the unnamed woman had been folded into a bigger narrative—who she was in relation to the bishop—and even here, in her final resting place, her identity seemed suppressed or overshadowed. Jess flexed her fingers, *quick quick*, to keep warm but also out of a sense of frustration. She felt the woman—maybe Violet, maybe someone else—deserved better.

'We have to do this, Billy,' she said, but she didn't look at her colleague. 'We have to give this woman a name. Make her a person again.'

'We will.' Billy shuffled his feet, impatient again, but this time Jess shared his sense of purpose. She stepped back.

'What time is it? Just after eleven? We could get an hour or so of work done at the museum before they close for lunch.' She clapped her padded hands together, the snapping sound startling a pigeon nearby. 'Let's get to it.'

So they both turned to leave and walk down the stone steps again, relieved that the hardest part of the climb was over. Jess turned, just as they descended, squinting her eyes into the sun, picking out the silent grave by the wall. It gleamed in the sunlight, a little pale nub of stubbornness.

~ 28 ~

June 1917

Wet, grey fog lay on the ground as the truck finally rattled into Villers-des-Champs. Fields lined the road; there were no hedgerows here as in England and crops grew inches from the wheels of the trucks. In the distance, farmhouses and animal shelters were blocks of blurred black. Violet and the few other women who had made the transfer from Calais squinted out into the gloom. The weather had changed since they left the coastal town and the mist prompted an odd sensation. Violet had the sense she had transgressed, had stepped over into another world.

They crossed a bridge, and a river swelled beneath. The driver and his companion in the front seats muttered a few words, which were translated by one of the women crammed beside Violet. 'He says the fields have been sodden for weeks. They can't grow turnips or potatoes.'

'Imagine what it must be like for our boys at the Front, fighting in this,' another said quietly. There were grimaces all round, and they turned to look at the town.

A couple of shops were open, and a bar, but none were busy. A barber's shop had a sign touting for business and an old man was bent over a customer, scissors in hand. Men and women hurried on their way, sticks of bread under their arms, looking quickly about them. The baker's wall had been damaged and bullet marks dotted the stonework, reminding Violet of the air bubbles caused by cockles on the sands at Brighton as a child. And then the truck roared past the town hall and up a narrow, cobbled street. Peering round the truck's canopy, Violet saw a large shape, indefinable at first, and then a church loomed fully into view. It was huge and imposing and seemed to threaten the small houses dotted around it with its vastness.

They sped past, lurching up the hill until the land flattened out again, and then the truck took a sharp right turn about half a mile down the road. They stopped. The truck had pulled up outside an isolated, grey building, partially swallowed by dark green ivy lying wetly on its walls. The driver turned off the engine and shouted.

'What did he say?' someone asked. 'Are we here?'

In answer, the driver appeared at the back of the truck and motioned for the women to disembark. 'Hospital, hospital,' he repeated.

They all jumped down, holding bags, unsteady in the mud. The air was a moist, fine drizzle. Violet's teeth chattered. She couldn't remember the last time she had felt dry.

'Hospital,' the driver said again and pointed to a small door to the left of the building. The women walked towards it uncertainly, opened it, and stepped inside.

Many hours later, lying on a bench that would become her bed for the next few weeks, Violet recalled that first moment, and the cautious step into the building. The door led into a wide, open space; interior walls not essential to the building's construction had been knocked down, and the space was filled with row upon row of camp beds. Men lay upon them, white sheets pulled up to their chins. The sheets of some were stained red. Women in nurse's uniforms moved among them, holding bedpans or flannels. They did not notice the new arrivals. Instead there was only noise. A wave of sound, whirlpools of moans and whispers, a brutal, unexpected scream from somewhere. Violet reached out, her hands searching for something to hold, to support her, the way a drowning woman reached for a boat.

But there was nothing to hold onto, no walls, only empty space. She swayed, and another woman steadied her. Violet forced herself to stand up straight, worried her inexperience was now glaringly apparent. But the women around her were pale and shocked, the sight too much for them all.

Then they were spotted. A large woman wearing an apron that must have once been white but was now a sad, telling pink, marched over. 'Reinforcements?' she snapped, hair pinned back savagely under a cloth hat. She didn't wait for anyone to reply. 'Put your bags in that room behind you'—she pointed to a door—'and get to work. The men are brought in every day, those who don't die on their way here. Do what you can.'

And she was away, turning hurriedly on a thick heel. The women stood silently for a second and a couple of the younger girls began to cry. But then they all moved swiftly, Violet carried along with them. They took out aprons from their bags and tied back their hair. Someone helped Violet secure her hair under a white piece of cloth, bundled up at the nape of her neck. Then, as a body, they moved into the crowd of wounded, seeping men, shouting and calling to each other for water or flannels, as though they had never worked anywhere else. Violet found herself doing the same, hands reaching for rags to stem a wound or wipe a brow.

~ *29* ~

Present Day

'The chateau that was converted into the hospital has fallen into disrepair,' Billy explained. They were seated around a wooden table in the reading room of the museum and he was setting out a notepad and a collection of gnawed pencils. 'This museum was established in the 1980s. There's a model of the hospital somewhere in here. The chateau was commandeered. It's about a mile past the church.'

Jess had been impressed. Billy had obviously prepared for their museum visit and phoned ahead. A curator was there to meet them when they made it across town from the church, and the curator could speak English. When they arrived, the slightly built man with a purple birthmark across half his face welcomed them and showed them to the reading area. There was no one else around and Jess wondered if the museum had opened for them especially.

'You said you wanted to read through the records for the hospital staff?' the curator had asked in a high, accented voice. He had put a box on the table and, opening it, Jess found a bundle of small, white cards, names written on each. There were dozens of them.

'We did.' Billy looked at the box on the table. 'Is this everything?'

'Oh no.' The curator smiled knowingly. 'Many more boxes. But this is where to start—these are the registration forms. For all the chaos of that time, the matron kept detailed records of who worked for her. You look through and tell me which nurse you are interested in and I will see what else we have. There were many women working here—VADs, local volunteers. Women who had no experience but wanted to help. We have copies of the Voluntary Aid Detachment records—at least, the names of the nurses. The rest of the papers were sent back to the Red Cross many years ago. But you may find something in what is left.'

He left them and Billy and Jess settled in, taking handfuls of the small cards, each bundle wrapped with a tired, grey piece of string. It was apparent that the cards had not been looked at for many years.

'Do you think Allegra did this?' Billy asked. 'Looked through these cards, searching for her daughter?'

'She was bound to. Wouldn't any mother?' Jess squinted at a gathering of cards, teasing the tight knot holding it together. 'The hospital was here for the entire war, wasn't it? Some hospitals had to move, to keep away from the fighting. But not this one. So many women must have passed through its doors.'

'But maybe not many British women. We might find something.' Billy rubbed his eyes and glared down at the cramped, inky script.

They worked through the cards mainly in silence, picking out the names: Marie, Celeste, Aveline, names flooding over them. Occasionally they stopped to say something: 'Listen, Winifred Bailey from Farnborough registered the same day as her sister, Julia. And their mother, too, by the looks of it. Family enterprise, then.'

But for the most part, Jess and Billy worked on quietly. Around mid-1917 the matron's handwriting changed, and they surmised she had been replaced. They read on, looking for one particular name, hoping to see Violet appear somewhere.

She did not and, after half an hour when the cards were all read, they both sat back in their chairs, disappointed.

Jess rubbed her face. 'We knew there wouldn't be anything glaringly obvious,' she said. 'Allegra or even a later researcher would have a reference to Violet, if there was one in here.'

Billy nodded, but the disappointment was clear on his face. 'Now what?'

Jess thought for a moment. At the other side of the large room making up the museum, the curator polished a glass box containing what appeared to be surgical instruments. Jess knew enough about battlefield injuries to shudder at the thought of what was contained in that box.

'Let's see what other records the museum holds,' Jess said. 'The curator said there was more. There might be treatment record books. We know Violet arrived here sometime in May or June, 1917. Let's say she died that same year and was buried with the bishop. If there are any records of the work undertaken here during this period, we could read through and see if something relates to Violet.'

'It's a long shot,' Billy said glumly, and Jess recognised the disappointment settling like a stone in his stomach. It was something she had felt many times at the start of her research into the mysterious woman buried in the French graveyard.

'Don't despair,' she said encouragingly. 'Think how far we've come in the last few weeks. It took me six years to get to this point, no thanks to Waller. And you said yourself, you never know what the archive might throw up.'

Billy sighed, not exactly reassured. He stood up. 'I'll go and talk to the curator and see what else he has.'

He left the table and walked across the single room comprising the museum. Jess heard his low voice and saw the curator nod slowly. Billy returned.

'He's got some treatment record books. He'll bring them up.'

'Fine. I'll nip outside for a smoke while he does.' Jess stood up, reaching for her coat and bag, and saw Billy's wide-eyed stare. 'What?'

'In all the time I've known you, I didn't know you smoked.'

Jess shrugged, but felt sadness squeeze her chest. She wondered just what kind of Jess Billy thought he knew; hard working, frustrated, unadventurous, grounded. And here was a different kind of Jess; smoking, trailing a younger man after her, separated from her family. Jess took out her cigarettes, not sure herself what kind of Jess she was now.

'Call me when he comes back,' she said, and walked out into the cold morning air.

~ 30 ~

At the end of the first day, Violet lay on the hard bench with a thin blanket as her only cover, her bag as a pillow. Around her women snored, their bodies aching, their bones weary from hours bent over torn, mangled forms of men; some men more complete than others, some misshapen and missing a foot, a leg, an arm. One of the women who had arrived that day with Violet had tended to a young man whose shoulder and half his chest had been torn away. 'I don't know how he still breathes,' she had said in the early hours of the morning, when the women had lain down to sleep.

Violet was exhausted but was afraid to sleep. Red filled the space between her eyes and eyelids, a memory of blood, pouring or oozing, and exposed, raw flesh. She held her eyes open, focusing on a beam or a crack of light in the room. The door to the women's private area was closed and the night shift were out, moving among the men whose pain knew no light or shade. Sounds filtered through. A cry, a curse, followed by a swift apology. Violet had seen nurses pack tiny bags of white power into open wounds, two or three of them holding the man down while he thrashed and shouted. Foolishly, after observing this procedure more than once, she had asked what was in the bags. 'Salt,' was the brisk reply. 'Purifies the wound.' Violet had hung back, appalled, face draining of colour. No wonder the men screamed so. 'It's all we have,' said an experienced nurse, moving on to the next patient.

She had emptied bedpans and boiled water, copying a friendly French woman, Cecilia, who took charge of that business. She pushed sticks of wet wood into the stove that belched dirty smoke onto the ward. Then, when a nurse called out to her, Violet sat beside men nearing death. She did not know what to do so watched women around her as they held men's hands and talked to them softly. When the first boy died, probably not much older than she, Violet disappeared for a few moments into the nurses' sleeping area. Her stomach felt weak and loose, and she bowed over the sink, waiting to be sick. But she was not and instead splashed water on her face. She was hurried out quickly when another consignment of injured men came in.

After a few hours, the reason for her being there at the hospital at Villers faded away. She did not think of the bishop for many hours. In fact, when she saw a man in a black suit, moving through the beds and pausing to talk to a soldier here and there, Violet felt no curiosity, other than a moment of wonder that a man would be here without a uniform or an injury. It was only later that she realised the man must have been Shacklock, the man who had drawn her to the hospital and plunged her into such hell.

There had been no time to talk to him though. Instead, the day quickened its pace. More men died, more men screamed. Violet wiped faces and changed sheets where she could; she touched a wound only when she had to. Suddenly it was midnight and the night shift was up. A woman scribbled notes down in a book, walking through the beds, checking with the women. She then passed the book to another nurse on the night shift and, with a huge yawn, jerked her head to the sleeping quarters. Violet followed her, eyes glazed, limbs heavy.

But she could not sleep.

~ *31* ~

A solitary crow edged closer to Jess as she finished her cigarette outside the museum. No doubt the black bird was in search of food. It became daring, jumping almost onto Jess's feet. She kicked out at it, still loathing birds as much as she had done as a child. The crow hopped away, casting a sullen look in her direction, and then flapped after the butt of her cigarette.

Billy was thumbing through a manuscript book, a hurried, bold script covering the pages. Jess sat down next to him.

'A treatment record?' she asked.

Billy nodded. 'Somewhat. Not everything, of course—there were hundreds of men at the Villers hospital at any one time. But the Matron made notes about who died each day, which men had a limb amputated, as far as I can make out. It's pretty grim reading. Did you know they used to pack salt into open wounds to clean them? Imagine that.'

Jess said nothing. Another two books lay on the table but Billy had extracted the one covering the period between May and September 1917. Billy was wearing white gloves, obviously at the request of the curator. He trailed a finger down the page.

They read together for about ten minutes and then both spotted it at the same time. 'There!' Billy almost shouted. 'Read that!'

Jess had seen it too, and read out loud. '"East End girl comforts men. Sat and recited poetry to Private Burden until he died. No nursing skill but works hard. Obvious training in theatre—helps to entertain the men."'

Billy read the text again, lips moving, and then turned to look at Jess. 'It's got to be Violet!'

Jess held up her hand. *Caution.* 'It's possible. Whoever she was, she must have made an impression to be included in a treatment book. I wonder if Allegra ever read this.'

'It depends if the books were open to the public back then.'

They turned the pages, quicker now, eyes scanning the paper. Another mention of the theatre girl gave them both a jolt. *Private Denham died at six o'clock this morning. Asked for theatre girl before expiring and she rose from her bed to be with him. She promised to pass on his possessions to his mother.*

'Whoever recorded this obviously didn't know Violet's name,' Billy muttered. 'Pity. We still need something concrete.'

'Listen to this,' Jess interrupted. She had read further down the page. '"Bishop and theatre girl worked together, tending to patients. They read to over fifty today. In order to avoid future confusion in this record, will refer to 'Bishop' for the man and 'Shacklock' for the girl."' Jess sat back. 'What does that last sentence mean?'

Billy's eyes were wide. 'Whoever wrote this wanted to make it clear the two were different people. Was Violet known as Shacklock when she worked at the hospital? Did she assume his name?'

Jess was bewildered. 'Can't be. Can't be—why has no one noticed this before?'

'Did Waller look at these treatment records?'

'Who knows? He might have sent a researcher and not looked through them himself.' Jess pointed to the box of white cards they'd flicked through earlier. 'But there was no Violet Shacklock amongst the cards. No Shacklock at all, as I recall.'

'You're right.' Billy smoothed his gloved hand over the treatment record, thinking. 'You must be right—if there *had* been, someone would have identified a nurse called Shacklock years ago. But this book here,' and he tapped the pages, 'this book seems to suggest a girl called Shacklock—who had experience in the theatre—worked at the hospital and formed a bond with the bishop. It can't be a coincidence.'

Jess got up and reached into the box of index cards. 'Do you think the registration is incomplete? That maybe Violet's card isn't in here?'

Billy shrugged. 'It's possible. Maybe cards were lost. It was a chaotic time, after all. And what's more, even if a researcher had come across this reference in the record book, what would they have? Nothing more but a red herring, a mention of a nurse called Shacklock who had worked in the East End. They wouldn't have made a connection, as they didn't know what we've found about—about Allegra, and Violet, and the bishop.'

'Do you think—is it possible the registration cards relating to Violet have been removed?'

Billy held out his hands. 'If so, by whom? The plot thickens.'

Jess imagined a rose bush, tall and dense, with a single red rose at its centre. She sighed and returned to sit beside Billy. 'What's the date here? July 1917. What else does the book say?'

~32~

A young man lay awake the night Private Denham died. His bed was a foot away from the dying soldier and, after Denham had been taken away and Violet stared down at the stained mattress, the man spoke up.

'You are very kind. To read to him like that.'

Violet, unable to tear her eyes from the red, sticky remainder of Denham's broken body, could only shake her head. She felt exhausted but unlikely to sleep ever again. Denham had seemed well only a few hours ago, his wounds apparently on the mend. No one had foreseen that something would burst inside his body and spill out onto the sheets.

'You *are* kind,' the soldier pressed. He spoke with a clipped, rich voice and, although he wore only a bed-shirt, Violet had been at Villers long enough to recognise the tone of an officer. She finally looked up.

'I have no idea what I'm doing,' she said, tears falling freely. 'It's not kindness. It's desperation.'

'None of us know what we're doing.' The soldier spread his hands. 'Not here, not on the Front. Certainly, it seems, not back at headquarters, though such heresy will no doubt see me shot.' He smiled and Violet saw he had all his teeth, unlike many of the men at the hospital.

'How were you … what …' Violet's voice trailed away. Two weeks at the hospital had taught her many things, but she was still unable to ask the men able to answer how they had been wounded.

'Sniper. Through the ankle. My foot was amputated.' The man lifted his leg and then she saw the stump. The soldier's hands twisted the bed sheets. 'When I'm strong enough, they are going to move me to a convalescent hospital back in Blighty. I've been learning to walk again.'

'Oh.' Violet didn't know what to say next but then a woman arrived with fresh sheets and a basin of warm water.

'The man here, he is gone?' It was Cecilia, the local woman who volunteered as auxiliary support. She was the help who boiled water and cleaned out bedpans, taking to her task as robustly as the most experienced nurse. Short and stout, with feathery hair, she had helped Violet soak bandages and scrub down soiled beds. She positioned her compact frame in the space between Denham's and the officer's bed.

'They've taken Private Denham away,' Violet said, looking at the bowl of water. 'What's that for?'

'We need the bed.' Cecilia motioned for Violet to stand. She shuffled to the side, blocking the officer's view. 'Help, please.' She flicked an odd look over her shoulder at the man and then handed Violet a rag. Then she set about scrubbing Denham's blood from the thin mattress.

Violet paused, tears drying on her cheeks. Around her men coughed and moaned. Over Cecilia's bowed back, she saw the officer lying on his pillow, eyes closed. Violet stared, longing to return to the nurse's quarters and lie on her bench to do the same. Then, at a noise from Cecilia, she plunged her hand into the warm soapy water and began to scrub.

~ 33 ~

Present Day

At the end of the treatment record book, almost at the last page, Jess and Billy found another reference. For much of July and August, the record book only spoke of deaths and amputations; the damp, misty weather had given way to fierce summer, weakening many of the already damaged men. Some succumbed to dehydration or died from 'excessive stomach cramps'. It had troubled Jess and Billy to read such words: that a soldier could make it to the relative safety of the hospital after suffering a wound on the battlefield or in a trench, only to expire in pain because of the heat. Jess thought of James, a year or so younger than boys who signed up to fight a hundred years before. She imagined him in uniform and the thought brought a tightening to her throat.

'Here's something,' Billy said, snapping Jess's attention back to the manuscript. Someone new had taken up the record keeping, and another script filled the page. The writing was difficult to discern. Jess read the passage carefully.

Cecilia and Violet saw to the beds. Had them stripped and washed, ready for the night shift. Mopped the floor. Tomorrow they will assist the bishop to take some of the stronger men out into the garden.

'There she is. Our Violet. It's got to be her. But who is this Cecilia?' Jess asked, looking up.

'No idea. Look, there's more for the following day.' Billy pointed to a sentence further down the page. ' "Cecilia reported that Captain Hendry has become increasingly agitated and refuses to be treated by anyone other than Violet. It is known he was exposed to gas at the time of his injury." ' Billy wrote on his notepad. 'We need to know who Cecilia and Captain Hendry were.'

Jess opened her mouth to speak, an idea forming, when the curator appeared at the end of their desk. He held a bunch of keys in one hand, shaking them conspicuously.

'It is time to close,' he said firmly, his tone indicating little room for argument. 'The museum does not normally open on Mondays. I've given you long enough; you can come back tomorrow.'

Billy gaped, taken aback at the abruptness of the Frenchman's words, but a nudge from Jess dissuaded him from speaking out. Instead he nodded and began to gather his notes.

'Thank you,' Jess said quickly as the curator made to move from the table. He was tight-lipped and flushed, adding an ugly depth to the purple birthmark covering much of the left side of his face.

They stepped outside onto the pavement, the museum door banging loudly behind them. Jess laughed. 'It was good of him to open up especially for us,' she said to Billy. 'Don't look so furious.'

'I'm not. Anyway, it's past lunchtime.' Billy looked up and down the street. 'See anything open?'

Jess could not. The shops and bakers nearby were closed, though the bell above a bar's glass-fronted door jangled as patrons passed through. Billy scowled down the street, trying to decide.

'Right, I'm going for a beer,' he said at last. 'And something to eat, if the bar has anything. Want to join me?'

Jess thought of Hayden and the supplies he had bought last night. 'I'm going back to our place,' she said. 'But thanks. Listen, if you want to call it a day, we can. Why don't you come down to the cottage for dinner later?'

Billy looked pleased, though he worked hard to hide it. 'Sure. Not much we can do until tomorrow anyway. We'll have a look to see if there's anything in the nurses' inventory about a Cecilia, and see what we can find out about this Hendry chap.'

'Great. Seven o'clock okay?'

Billy waved a hand over his shoulder and set off, marching purposefully towards the bar. Watching his arms swing regimentally by his sides, his rucksack bouncing haphazardly on his back, Jess wondered if today had been difficult for him. If being with her was not easy and he needed a drink. Or he could be missing his wife, she told herself, marvelling again that she hadn't guessed he was married.

When she got back to the cottage, Hayden had already opened a bottle of wine. His laptop was packed away, and he had found a radio from somewhere. It was tuned into a station that seemed to play only music, save for the occasional advert. Jess listened as she took off her coat and unwound her scarf.

Hayden was in the kitchen. Over the radio, she heard the sound of drawers being opened and a knife hitting the chopping board.

'I'm back. Have a productive morning?' Jess asked, leaning around the kitchen door. Hayden had his back to her and didn't turn around.

'Suppose so. Dull but productive, yes.' He threw his knife down onto the kitchen surface with a noisy clatter and then reached for a bowl.

Jess watched, curious. He still hadn't looked at her. *Is he angry at me?* The hair at the back of his neck stood up as though he had been grabbing it with wet hands.

'I'm starving,' she said after a pause.

'I waited for you. There's bread and cheese, and I'm making a salad. That's about the extent of my skills in the kitchen.' Still, his back to her.

Did he expect me to come back and make us something? Jess thought of their meals together at Hayden's flat: coffee and toast. If they wanted anything else they ate out. Looking at his back bent over the kitchen counter, she didn't know what else to do other than to walk over to him and clasp her hands around his waist. She held him tightly and pressed her face against Hayden's back. 'That sounds perfect,' she said quietly, hoping it would be enough.

Then Hayden did turn around. As he bent over to kiss her, she saw that his face was white and a heavy crease had slashed the skin above his nose, between his eyebrows. Jess had known him long enough to know his skin became marked in such a way when he had been frowning. She caught his head in her hands, fingers pressed on either temple.

'What is it?' she asked. 'What's wrong?' He looked a little like James had done during his exams. She resisted the impulse to smooth Hayden's hair back from his face.

But Hayden shook his head. 'It's nearly ready. Are you done for the day, then?'

'Yes. The curator kicked us out of the museum.' Jess smiled, remembering the man's angry purple face.

'Good. I won't be drinking alone.' Hayden gently untangled himself and poured wine into two stubby glasses. He handed one over to Jess, who sipped slowly.

'Speaking of which, I invited Billy over for dinner tonight,' she said. 'Otherwise he'll be eating alone.'

Hayden shrugged. 'No problem.' But he seemed distracted again, and he looked around the kitchen as though he was seeking a reminder of what he was about to do next.

Jess watched. 'Are you really all right?'

Hayden did not answer. Instead he drained his glass, set it down on the kitchen counter, and then pulled Jess to him again. His hands were inside her jumper, the touch cold on her bare back, and she did not resist as he led her up the narrow wooden staircase to their room.

c√∞

After, they slept. Jess had left the window slightly open before leaving for the museum that morning and the cold lay bitterly on their skin. They had climbed beneath the duvet and the toll of the church bells woke them, ringing out five times. Jess rolled onto her back, Hayden's hand slipping from her thigh. Her head ached. The radio played downstairs.

'It was lucky I hadn't left anything in the oven,' Hayden mumbled from deep in the bed. He pulled the duvet up to his chin. 'Lord, it's freezing.'

'The window's open.' Jess slipped out to close it, hiding behind the curtains so no one in the street below could see her. A streetlight at the bottom of the cobbled row cast a pale yellow glow up the narrow road.

She hurried back under the covers, Hayden moaning as she pressed her cold flesh to him.

'You bugger,' he said, and she laughed. He seemed back to normal. Whatever darkness that settled upon him earlier had left.

They held each other for a while, listening to the odd thrum of a car as it rattled up the cobbles. A chatter of voices from somewhere, a child singing.

'Mum phoned while you were out,' Hayden said abruptly. His mouth was pressed to Jess's forehead, and she felt the grind of his teeth. She said nothing, but waited.

Hayden sighed and then eased away. He pulled himself up in the bed and switched on the bedside lamp. 'Has she mentioned Terry to you?'

Jess moved to a position to see Hayden clearly. 'No. But we don't talk so much now ...'

'He's the latest. The supper club? That's him.'

'She went away with him last month? Yes, I remember now. She didn't tell me his name.'

'Terry, Kenny, Gordon, Martin—it's easy to lose track.' Hayden's voice was flat. 'Terry has been around for a few weeks. She phoned to say she's moving in with him.'

Jess sat up, leaning back against the headboard. She tried to remember her last meeting with Marie, in the coffee shop. There had been nothing said about a Terry, she was sure. All she could remember was their conversation about Hayden; his purpose in relationships, how he came and went when a woman disappointed him. Jess could remember that part of the conversation clearly.

'Moving in is a big step,' she said cautiously.

'Exactly. I asked what she would do about her house—if she would keep it for a while and see how things worked out. But she said no, she was going to sell.' Hayden plucked the duvet cover. 'It took her so long to buy that house. Did you know that? After the divorce she had enough for a deposit but the mortgage was tough.'

Jess thought of Marie's holidays. The new clothes and shoes that appeared every time they met. Marie did not appear to be a woman with money worries. 'I didn't know. I thought she had money after leaving your dad.'

'She has money now. But not back then. Whatever Dad gave her she used to pay the deposit on the house. She worked a bit as well when I was growing up. Supermarket work. But money was tight. When I started work, I paid off a chunk of the mortgage.' Hayden twisted the sheets into damp peaks. 'It wasn't difficult, I'm good at my job. Cost of a few bonuses, that's all. I wanted to help her out. And then she was left some money by my granddad and didn't need to worry about money anymore.'

'It was generous of you to help,' Jess said softly. So that was why Marie was able to afford the holidays and clothes—her son had paid off her mortgage. 'What happens with the sale, if it goes ahead?'

Hayden sighed. 'She said she'll split the profit with me. But it's not that.' He rubbed his face. 'You know how she is, around men. There's a man here, a man there. I hoped when I paid the mortgage off that she would feel secure again, you know? Maybe she had been looking for someone to replace Dad all along and I thought if she had a house of her own, she could—ease off a bit, I suppose.'

'Except she wasn't looking for anyone to replace your dad,' Jess said, the need to defend her friend suddenly very powerful. An indefinable ball of anger gathered in her stomach. She thought of Marie, larger than life, dominating the Student Union bar, targeting a fresh-faced undergraduate, who was egged on by his mates. Or flirting with a mechanic or a lecturer. Marie had her reasons for seeking out a certain type of company, but money wasn't at the heart of it. And whatever Marie did, she did with laughter and ease. There was no air of desperation to Marie out on the town. Jess wondered at Hayden's perception of his mother. 'Who are we to judge, anyway? She didn't hurt anyone.' *Not like I have*, the thought sliding into her body like a knife.

'She's known this man for six weeks. How the hell can she be thinking of throwing away her security just like that?' Hayden clicked his fingers savagely.

Jess looked out of the window. The curtains were still open but the netting and the dimness of the room gave them privacy. She expected that it would be dark at home as well, back in York. Though home, of course, was no longer the compact space it had been before the problems between her and Alec. Now Alec lived with his parents, sleeping in the bedroom he had used as a teenager, and James and Megan lived in a house without their father. Alec had said he would move back for a couple of weeks while Jess was away, after the kids had had a weekend with their grandparents, and he'd dropped some things off before Jess left for France. She had been surprised to find herself close to tears when he arrived, rucksack in hand. He looked as though he was going camping, only in his own house. Jess had moved nothing since they separated and the furniture was in the same place, but Alec had shuffled around the living room like a man stepping onto a ship.

'Perhaps your mum thought the time was right for a change,' she said. 'From what I remember of your old house, it was pretty big. Maybe *too* big, especially when you live on your own. Sometimes a house is just a reminder of how lonely you are.'

'Don't be ridiculous.' A line of steel through Hayden's voice. 'You have rose-tinted view of my mother, Jess.'

Jess threw back the duvet and stood up. The ice of the room stung her skin, but she didn't care. 'Don't talk to me like that.'

'It's true. You think because you meet up with her once a month and she shares details of her sex life, you know her.' Hayden also pushed the duvet away. He reached for his jeans. 'You don't. You had no idea I'd paid off her mortgage, did you? She doesn't tell you everything.'

'And you have no idea what we talk about!' Jess shivered but did not want to put her clothes on. At that moment, it felt important to be naked.

Hayden snorted and his head disappeared inside his jumper. 'That house is her independence. If she throws her lot in with some random bloke, she'll end up hurt. Or worse, at my door.'

'Jesus.' And then Jess did start to dress. 'Who has a warped perspective now? Marie is a grown woman and can make her own choices. She doesn't have to explain them to you. Not anymore—you aren't a kid.'

They looked at each other, Jess struggling to fasten her trousers. Then Hayden walked off, feet thumping down the stairs to the kitchen. Jess heard the radio snap off and the remains of their uneaten lunch being thrown into the bin.

She finished dressing slowly. She hadn't known that Hayden had paid off Marie's mortgage; in fact, Marie had let Jess believe she had been given a settlement by her ex-husband. And yet, Jess reasoned as she pulled on her socks, it was none of her business and up to Marie how much she revealed about her finances. Jess had certainly not told Marie about the time Alec's job had been under threat and they'd considered re-mortgaging their house.

We only know our friends as well as they allow us. Jess thought of Billy and how shocked she had been to discover he had a wife. And she thought of Waller, realising she knew absolutely nothing about the professor either, other than his research and what he was like in the library. She had heard once he had a wife, but he never mentioned her and Jess didn't know if there were children.

She paused. Billy might have kids, for all she knew. *There might be a squat little Billy running around a Jedthorpe garden.* And then Jess laughed, the image refreshingly absurd. The clatter of plates from downstairs stopped, and she knew Hayden was listening. She felt comforted.

~ 34 ~

July 1917

Captain Hendry had asked for her again. Cecilia delivered the news as she returned from stoking the stoves that heated water in a side room. Black and foul, the stoves belched smoke and took an age to boil kettles, but they were the only means the auxiliaries had. Cecilia and some of the local women took it in turns to chop the firewood and stoke the furnaces. They were strong and used to this kind of labour. Some of the British girls helped but were unused to swinging an axe.

'Violet, he is asking for you.' Cecilia pointed back to Captain Hendry.

Violet, winding a fresh bandage around a soldier's arm, looked over at the officer. He was sitting up, his legs swung over the side of his bed. There was a space between the end of his stump and the floor. He had been moving around more and Violet had helped him a few times, hands ready in case the captain stumbled with his crutches.

'My father employs a blacksmith,' he had confided on one of their tours around the hospital. 'I'll have a new foot in no time. A mechanical one.'

Now Captain Hendry held up a small book though, sitting some distance away, Violet could not make out what it was.

'He wants to read with you again,' Cecilia said. She pursed her lips and wiped her cheek. Dirt from the stoves smeared her skin. 'Other men are sick. You don't need to go.'

'I'll go.' Violet sighed. She had read with Hendry three times that week from the small book of poetry his mother had sent him. Mostly Keats, some Coleridge. Hendry liked to lie back on his bed with his eyes closed as Violet read out loud. Sometimes the men around her settled down to listen as well.

As Violet approached Hendry's bed she saw he held a new book.

'Just arrived,' he said. 'Another package from my mother.' He handed it to her.

'*Macbeth*?' Violet turned the slim volume over in her hands. Her breath felt too hot for her throat, as though it were a swollen balloon about to burst. She thought of her mother's theatre, women rehearsing on a darkened stage and absent, missing men. A longing for Allegra pressed on Violet's chest. She wondered what attempts her mother had made to find her.

'Shall we read it?' Hendry asked. His eyes were bright and cheeks were flushed. His scalp shone pink and raw through pale blonde hair.

'I have very little time, Captain Hendry,' Violet said. Her voice was quiet, little more than a whisper, but a man, walking among the rows of soldiers, turned around. He was thickset and short, and wore black trousers with a grey shirt. He rounded the end of Hendry's bed and sat down.

Hendry bristled and Violet saw the captain's jaw clench. 'Bishop,' he said. 'Did you want something?'

Violet had moved to pull up a chair next to Hendry's bed. She paused, hand gripping the wooden frame. She had seen Shacklock several times in the last month but had not yet spoken to him. The truth was she had no idea what to say. The man had acted upon her like a magnet over the summer, drawing her across the water, severing the link she had with her mother. The urge to find Shacklock had been so embracing it had squeezed the past and future from her, closeting her in a vacuum of discovery. And here he was, right in front of her, at ease and not, for once, pinning a man down so a doctor could amputate a limb or praying over a dying soldier. The bishop's strength was well known in the hospital and he made himself useful to those tending to the sick.

Now, though, Shacklock was smiling and looking at Captain Hendry. 'Did I hear you had been sent *Macbeth*? Forgive me, it's a play I've always loved.'

Hendry's jaw still twitched. His stump swung awkwardly. 'It was a present from my mother.'

'Not all of our patients receive parcels. You are a lucky man.'

'Do you think so?' Hendry asked pointedly, the leg with a missing foot moving faster.

'Luckier than most.' The bishop turned to face Violet. Blue eyes glittered; his eyebrows were dark though the hair at his temples was peppered with white. Violet sweated into her makeshift uniform.

'I don't think we've spoken yet,' the bishop said. He held out his hand. 'Anthony Shacklock.'

Violet allowed her hand to be encased in the man's strong grip. She looked down, sure that he could hear the voice shrieking inside her: *I'm holding my father's hand, for the first time. I'm holding his hand!*

But, of course, he heard nothing and Violet only nodded. 'I'm Violet,' she said.

'Do you have a surname?'

'Shacklock.' Violet said this quietly, wishing she had chosen a different name when she registered as an auxiliary at Calais.

The bishop paused, and a puzzled look passed his face. 'The same as me?'

'No relation,' Violet said quickly. The conversation had happened so unexpectedly, she couldn't think her way through the next few moments.

'Well, there's a coincidence. Where are you from?'

'London.'

'Forgive me, but you seem very young to be a nurse.'

Captain Hendry interrupted. 'Probably no younger than the men she cares for, Bishop.' He shuffled on the bed, hands plucking at the sheets. His moustache twitched.

'True.' Shacklock held up his hand. 'I meant no offence.'

'I'm twenty-three,' Violet said, remembering the conversation amongst the girls at the registration office. 'I've worked in the East End, helping deliver babies.'

'Ah.' The bishop closed his eyes. 'I did that too, as a younger man. But it was a long time ago.'

'You delivered babies?' Hendry glared at the bishop, hostility now unmasked.

'Back in my diocese. A small town called Jedthorpe, not far from York.' Shacklock tapped the book in Violet's hands. 'I've seen you read to our friend before. It's good of you. Not all the nurses have the time.'

'I don't mind.'

'Well, it is kind of you.'

'I suppose you are too busy to listen, Bishop,' said Hendry. 'With all the men you need to see.'

'I can take a minute. Would you mind?'

Violet hesitated. Behind, she heard Cecilia soothing a soldier who had awoken from a nightmare, a soft wash of French chatter drifting across the room. Cecilia had become a friend, working closely with Violet, showing her how to manage the dragon-like stove and handle huge kettles of boiling water. The woman had quickly deduced Violet had no nursing experience but did not betray her secret to the matron who stalked the rows of beds. Instead, Cecilia seemed to have assumed that Violet was looking for someone—a sweetheart, maybe, who might pass through the hospital's doors. During the snatched moments given over to lunch or tea, the women sat together in the nurses' room, and Cecilia talked about her family. No children or husband of her own. A brother who had been killed in the early years of the war, and a much younger sister. Elderly parents. Her father still worked at his barber's shop in town. It wasn't something Cecilia wanted to do. Working at the hospital had given her … she couldn't find the right word and instead made a punching motion with her fist. Violet had nodded, understanding.

She caught Cecilia's eye as the Frenchwoman helped the distressed soldier sit up. They smiled at each other, sharing another unspoken understanding.

'I'll read a little,' Violet said, turning back to the book lying in her hands. She opened the first pages and began.

As she read, she sensed the bishop start to nod his head, slowly, rhythmically. It was encouraging and Violet read through the first act, more than she'd planned. Sitting on the bed, Captain Hendry also relaxed, though he did not close his eyes as normal and his stump still twitched agitatedly.

The bishop sighed when Violet drew to a close. 'Beautiful,' he said. 'You have experience on the stage. That much is clear.'

'A little.' Violet hesitated, unsure of how much she should say. She imagined Allegra standing in their kitchen back in Earls Court, shaking her head frantically, eyes pleading that Violet say no more. 'My mother owns a theatre. I have acted a little. But mostly I watch.'

'Is that so?' Shacklock looked at Violet closely. 'I was once very interested in the theatre.'

'Oh?'

The bishop fell silent, and he seemed to drift away. He stared blankly at a wall. Someone at the other end of the large room starting shouting and sobbing. A flurry of uniforms surrounded the man's bed and someone called for a doctor. Another woman raced over with a bottle and a pile of bandages. Shacklock raised his chin to look over, but his eyes were glazed.

'You were involved in the theatre?' Violet pressed, needing to make a connection with the man but still imagining Allegra imploring her to stop.

'No, not involved.' The bishop finally looked away from the commotion around the distant soldier. 'Someone I once knew wanted to become an actress. She would have been very good, too. We read together.'

'Well, I think you read very well,' Captain Hendry broke in redundantly. His face was oddly arranged, mouth twisted at one corner as though he were biting the inside of his cheek.

'Thank you,' Violet said. A nurse at the end of the room shouted for assistance; the wounded soldier making the noise had managed to throw off those tending to him and was trying to stand up. The group around Hendry's bed could see the man's legs finished at his knees.

'Poor soul.' Bishop Shacklock was up on his feet. 'Come, Violet. We should assist.'

'Of course.' Violet stood up as well. She handed the book to Captain Hendry. She felt as though she should apologise to the soldier, for breaking up their reading session. But the bishop was already hurrying over to the other end of the room. Violet took strength from the purposeful swing of the man's back and, with a brief glance at Hendry, swiftly followed.

Hendry watched, eyes narrowed, openly chewing the inside of his mouth. He dropped the book on the floor.

~ 35 ~

Present Day

Billy wore his determination to get one over on Professor Waller like a badge but Jess had come to learn that, despite his professional frustration, Billy could be extremely discreet. The tension between Jess and Hayden must have been obvious at dinner; the conversation between them was stilted and uncomfortable. Hayden listened to Billy's account of their discoveries in the museum that day with impatience and then offered a forcible opinion of his own as to where their investigations should take them next. He advised they should turn their attention to the war records and check out the local military cemeteries—of which there were many—to find out more about Captain Hendry. When Jess pointed out that most war records were kept in London and, even if Hendry was buried in France, his soldier's grave would not reveal anything about the man himself, Hayden had sat back at the dinner table, his frustration apparent. Billy had dipped his head over his wine glass and said nothing.

'I mean, this is the obstacle we're facing in trying to identify the woman,' Jess had said, trying to explain, though Hayden appeared to have lost interest. 'Those graves up in the churchyard don't tell us anything about a person, save for the bare minimum.'

'There isn't even a headstone here for the bishop now,' Billy pointed out, taking a piece of bread. 'Not now he's buried back in Jedthorpe.'

'That's right. The priest had the headstone removed soon after he discovered Shacklock's body had been taken. There isn't a record of what was said on it.'

'You do see some graves with information about how a person died,' Billy said, dipping his bread in a smear of dressing left on his plate. 'Modern ones, I mean. Sometimes a family will record how their relative died, especially if they died young or in unusual circumstances. A murder, for example.'

'But, like you say, that's a modern practice. I think we should do what you suggested earlier,' Jess said. 'We should try to identify this Cecilia and see if we can find something about her. Maybe there will be a reference to her work as an auxiliary during the First World War. Maybe we'll find something about who she worked with.'

'It's tenuous, though, isn't it?' Billy said, and he sounded gloomy. 'We don't have much concrete to go on. All the signs suggest that the woman buried with Shacklock is Violet Underwood, but we've nothing definite. Even the reference to a Violet Shacklock in the treatment record at the museum is open to interpretation. And there's no Violet in the nurse's or auxiliary's registry. We need something more than this to make it worthwhile.'

Billy didn't go on but Jess knew what he was thinking. They needed to find some hard evidence to validate their trip to France. They'd both risked their jobs, possibly even their careers, by deceiving Professor Waller and making the trip in secret. Without finding unequivocal, unambiguous evidence that the woman in Shacklock's grave was his daughter, Violet Underwood, the excursion could jeopardise their careers.

At that Hayden got up from the table and started taking dishes into the kitchen. He did not clatter them into the sink or slam cupboard doors noisily as before, but his exasperation was clear. Billy and Jess, still seated, shared a glance. Jess sighed. She had grown accustomed to Hayden's impatience and inability to understand that sometimes archival work could be painstaking and thankless. Once, back in his flat at Fulham, when they were planning the trip to France, Jess had tried to explain. 'Working in an archive can be arduous,' she'd said. 'Sometimes I think it's like trying to prune a rose bush. You have a goal in mind— finding something, a gem, a flower to work with and shape—but along the way there are snares and traps. You can find yourself being led down all kinds of branches, each of which have their own snags. Look at Waller—he's spent his entire career trying to find out who this woman is, and he's constantly getting tangled up.'

Hayden had shrugged, not understanding or caring. 'It's not worth it,' he'd said. 'I'd just cut the damn rose bush down.'

After Billy left, Jess thought about helping Hayden in the kitchen but instead went upstairs to their bedroom, to where her phone was on charge. Without pausing to consider the cost of using her mobile again, she rang Alec's parents' house, praying that Alec would recognise her number and have Megan or James answer, if they were still awake. He did; Megan answered and Jess had curled up on the bed, pressing the phone tightly to her ear, listening to her daughter's voice.

She woke early the following morning. Hayden was lying beside her, still and silent, and the room was in darkness. After speaking to her children the night before, Jess had fallen asleep; now her bones ached, suggesting a deep, deep slumber, and she had slept in her clothes. And yet she still felt exhausted, the events of the past week still tattooed on her body. Jess padded down to the shower, careful not to wake Hayden and stood under the hot water for a long time.

It was barely eight o'clock when Billy knocked on the door. Jess was not surprised to see him; their talk last night about finding something to make their furtive trip worth the risk had troubled them both. Billy held out a bag of croissants and smiled.

'You raring to go as well?' he said.

'I am. Come in. Quick coffee?'

They ate together around the table they'd shared not twelve hours earlier. Upstairs Hayden slept on though, as they finished and rinsed their plates and cups in the sink, they heard the creak of the mattress as he rolled awake.

'I'll leave a note,' Jess said and motioned Billy towards the door. She had a strong desire to be away before Hayden came down. She scribbled on a piece of paper torn from her notepad and left it next to the bag of croissants. They closed the front door quietly behind them and then stood in the cold street, realising they still had half an hour before the museum opened.

'Do you want to visit the grave again?' Billy asked. He pointed up to the church toppling over them. Hundreds of pigeons gathered in the bell tower and on the ledges of the square spire.

'I don't think so.' Jess thought of the woman's sad little plot with its half-moon stone. The visit to the churchyard had affected her more than she had revealed to Billy. In recent weeks, as she came closer to putting a name to the skeleton, Jess had become ashamed of how she had viewed the woman in the past. The nickname of 'the Cuckoo' made her uncomfortable now and was never said out loud. After reading Allegra Underwood's desperate letters at the library in Hampstead, Jess no longer thought of the search for the woman's identity as an academic undertaking. Instead the letters, sent to Allegra's cousin, spoke of a frantic search for a lost child. The treatment record in the museum had also been difficult reading. Jess had thought of James constantly as her finger traced the manuscript; he was only a couple of years younger than the men wounded so severely on the battlefields, after all. Violet's death so soon after her arrival at Villers was, Jess thought, no less a tragedy. She could only hope Violet was not alone and that Shacklock, or Cecilia, or someone Violet thought of as a friend was with her at the end.

So instead of climbing the steep steps up to the church again, Jess and Billy took a slow walk through town towards the museum. School children hurried past, lunch bags bouncing on their backs, scarves streaming as they scurried towards the school gates. Mothers dragged stragglers by their hands. They passed a barber's shop, old men waiting patiently for their turn. Jess stopped at a grocer's to buy cigarettes and they finally arrived at the museum a few minutes before the curator opened up.

He didn't seem surprised to see them. Instead, he opened the heavy panelled entrance doors and welcomed them through. They went back to the table they'd occupied yesterday, and the curator fetched the boxes of documents and manuscripts.

'We won't be too long,' Billy told the curator when he placed the registry cards and treatment record books on the table. 'We need to check something and will be out of your way.'

The curator shrugged and wandered off to the front desk where a small group of teenage school children had gathered. Whatever interest he had in Billy and Jess's work had waned.

Jess picked up the bundle of white registration cards that recorded the women who had worked at the hospital. 'Cecilia. Bet there is a dozen Cecilia's in here.'

Billy watched over her shoulder as she shuffled through, both murmuring the names of the nurses and auxiliaries who had volunteered to help wounded soldiers almost a hundred years ago. As before, they did not come across a Violet Shacklock or a Violet with any other surname.

But they did find a Cecilia, just the one. 'There.' Billy jabbed at the card Jess held, though there was no danger she might miss it. He read out loud. ' "Cecilia Deniel. Auxiliary. 1916-1918. Villers-des-Champs." '

'The dates will be when she worked at the hospital. And she's from the town.' Jess turned the card over to see if anything had been written on the back. 'Well, we know who she is. She keeps appearing in the treatment record with Violet so must have worked closely with her. We need to find out if there are any papers relating to her.'

'How do we do that?' Billy screwed up his face, thinking. Behind him, the school children clattered around a table, talking loudly as they pulled textbooks from their bags. One of them produced a phone and started to play music.

Billy tutted but before he could speak up, the curator stalked over to the teenagers' table. He spoke rapidly, pointing at all of them, referring to them all by name. The group quietened down immediately and a chastened young boy handed over his phone.

Billy turned back to Jess, eyebrow arched. She nodded, thinking the same thing.

As the curator passed their table on the way back to his desk, Billy caught his attention. 'Excuse me. Can we ask you something?'

The curator joined them, frowning at the registration cards now scattered on the table. Feeling rather like a teenager herself, Jess started to gather the documents together.

Billy was undaunted. 'We need to find out more about an auxiliary who worked at the hospital. Cecilia Deniel. She was from Villers.'

The curator waited in silence.

'Do you know of a Deniel family still in the area?' Billy motioned over to the teenagers now working quietly. 'You're from Villers, yes? If you could help us, we'd be grateful.'

The curator cleared his throat. 'Deniel, yes. One family of that name. Though the woman—Cecilia? She won't be alive now.'

'Of course,' Jess broke in, returning the registry cards to their box. 'But if we could contact the family, it might help. We think Cecilia worked with a woman we're researching. Maybe there are papers, documents …'

Her voice trailed away as the curator shook his head, a physical representation of the doubt she felt. She remembered Billy's words from the night before—how tenuous this kind of research was. But then she remembered stumbling across the reference in the Synod papers back at the Shacklock library in Jedthorpe. It seemed so long ago now; and yet that one document had revealed the bishop was not where he was supposed to be and led them to this point, to the museum in a little French town.

'We know it's a long shot,' Billy said. 'But we've little to go on. If you wanted to make contact with the family first on our behalf, go ahead.'

The curator sighed. 'The barber's shop. A few streets away—do you know it?'

Billy and Jess shared a glance. They'd passed a barber's shop that morning.

'We know where it is,' Jess said.

'It's been there since before the war,' the curator went on. 'Owned by the Deniel family. They might be able to help.'

'Thank you.' Billy's face broke into a wide grin, his excitement clear. Jess smiled, feeling it too. She imagined them as acrobats, swinging from one trapeze to another, from one discovery to the next.

They stood outside the museum for a few moments, deciding on tactics. Jess smoked, considering whether she or Billy had the best French. Neither was accomplished and their language skills were limited.

'How can we explain what we're looking for?' Billy asked. He watched as Jess drew on her cigarette. 'It's not easy to say what we're doing.'

'No, it's not.' Jess exhaled. She wondered if Hayden was up and about yet, and if he'd seen her note. She'd been brief, mentioning only that she and Billy were going to the museum again and would be back around lunchtime. She flicked her cigarette stub away. 'We should keep it simple. No need to go into details. We can say we're researching the hospital and discovered that a Deniel worked there. We'd like to learn more about what it was like—they were an established family in the town and so on. Ask if they know anything, if there are any papers.'

'Do you think the family will have papers?'

'No idea. But we didn't know about the letters Allegra sent to Emily, did we? We didn't know those papers existed. And we didn't know that the bishop went to Greece when he should have been in Malta.' Jess gave a short laugh. 'We're not even supposed to be here, are we? We've both lied to Waller. Keep the faith, Billy.'

~ 36 ~

August 1917

It was not difficult to see the value of Bishop Shacklock's presence in the hospital. After their first meeting around Captain Hendry's bed, Violet paid more attention to Shacklock's movements and his activities with the men. Their brief meeting, when she had read from Hendry's book, had jolted Violet back into a sense of normality, or as close to it as she could be in an environment where men died easily and in great pain. She had come to France to find her father, after all. Without telling Cecilia why, she made excuses to work alongside the bishop and observe how he interacted with the men.

He prayed with many, unsurprisingly, but Violet also saw him play cards, write letters home for the severely wounded, change beds and dressings and, when the weather was fine, help those able to stand to hobble to the garden outside. On other occasions, Shacklock held men down for stitching or the packing of salt sachets in open wounds. Violet saw, though, how he looked away, grimacing as men screamed, his face white.

By August, the hospital had become unbearably hot during the day and not much better at night. The windows were thrown open, women walked the rows of beds with jugs of water, encouraging men to drink. When Violet lay down in the evening, her uniform was wet with perspiration and her hair stuck to her cloth cap. A stale odour crept throughout the hospital; raw, unabashed sweat. The river running through Villers flowed nearby and during snatched moments, the women washed in the water. No one dared to undress and wade in; the current was too fast and the men too close by. But the moments when she was free to sit with her bare feet in the cool flow, away from the groan of the injured and Captain Hendry with his requests for her attention, were brief interludes that Violet clung to.

One afternoon, when most of the men slept or read, Violet stared at the blue strip of water from a hospital window and slipped outside. The matron had adapted one end of the room for men who were able to sit and had found a selection of battered old armchairs from other rooms in the chateau. The chairs were all occupied by soldiers, reading, writing letters, or looking outside. Hendry was amongst them. He had begun asking for Violet every day and, although Cecilia did her best to refuse him, he could be persistent. Now, with Hendry occupied with a book, Violet saw her opportunity to take a moment for herself. She hurried up the bank behind the chateau to the river's edge.

As she rounded a crop of rocks, she saw she was not alone. Bishop Shacklock sat with his back to her, his feet and socks off, legs in the stream. He turned as Violet stumbled by.

'Hello,' he said.

Violet paused. She had not anticipated meeting him. Shacklock's white feet, with black hair sprouting around his ankles, embarrassed her. He had rolled his trouser legs up to his knees and his calves were thick and strong. She edged back, knowing she would not remove her own shoes and stockings in front of him, even if he said he didn't mind.

'Please, there is room enough.' Shacklock pointed to a smooth rock nearby. 'I often come here when the heat is unbearable.'

Sensing she could not refuse without appearing rude, Violet accepted the bishop's invitation and sat down. 'So do I. But I've never seen you here.'

'It would be nice for the men as well, don't you think?' Shacklock raised his feet up and down, splashing gently in the water. 'Let them come and feel the soothing flow of water. I've always thought that fresh air and being outdoors helps heal the body.'

'I don't think Matron would allow it,' Violet said. 'Infections.'

They sat silently for a while as the water churned on. Broken branches were borne past; a bird flapped down to the river's edge and dipped down between the reeds. The sun rose high in the sky and Violet stared at the water, yearning to jump in.

'How long have you been at the hospital?' Shacklock asked, breaking the quiet between them.

'A couple of months, I think. I can't really remember.'

'Yes, time does become rather stretched in this place. Or squashed, depending on your perspective. I've been here for a year or so.'

'As long as that?'

The bishop sighed. 'I wouldn't like to think how many men have passed through these doors. Terrible injuries. Well, you've seen for yourself.'

Violet had. But sitting here, on the river's edge, surrounded by the thrum of insects and feeling the heat of the sun on her back, she did not want to think about the mangled, sobbing men who had arrived on the backs of lorries. Instead she preferred to stare at the little brown bird on the bank opposite, fragile amongst the dense undergrowth yet gamely hopping from root to branch, pecking at the wet earth. Its determination was fascinating. Water lapped threateningly close, but the bird pushed on in search of food, single-minded in the way that only delicate creatures constantly on the alert can be. Violet felt sleepy and ineffective just watching it. Sunlight lilted across the water's surface, the river smoothing over rocks in its midst, throbbing on relentlessly towards town. Violet felt her body relax but she could not tear her eyes from the bird.

'I see you've been reading to Hendry again.' Shacklock's voice sounded unusually shrill and Violet realised she had been close to dozing.

She leant forward and trailed her hand in the water. 'A little. When I have the time.'

'He had another parcel, I believe. More books.'

'From his mother. She writes regularly.'

'Well, *she* has the time.'

Violet frowned. 'Why do you say that?'

The bishop pointed back to the hospital where Hendry sat with others near the open windows. 'Captain Hendry's father owns an estate in Norfolk. Apparently Hendry Senior works in the War Office.'

'How do you know this?'

'Matron was contacted soon after Hendry arrived here.'

'Oh.' Violet felt the bishop was implying more than he was saying but she couldn't unpick the layered thread of his meaning. 'Well, he seems to be coping with his injuries.'

'The ones we can see, anyway,' Shacklock said quietly. He threw a dried piece of grass down into the river and they watched it ride hurriedly away.

They sat together for a while longer but the rattle of a lorry pulling into a courtyard reminded them both that the river offered only a brief respite. Shacklock got to his feet first and held out his hand to help Violet up. Again, she felt the strength in his wide hands. She smiled, brushing down her skirt.

'Thank you.'

And then they started the walk back down the hill towards the hospital, to the area where recovering soldiers sat and read, and where the windows and doors were thrown open. To where Captain Hendry watched their progress closely, a new book shading his eyes.

~ 37 ~

Present Day

As they neared the barber's shop, Jess grew increasingly nervous. She had never approached a descendant before about accessing privately held manuscripts: her research led her into the rarefied world of the archives, where documents had reference numbers and had to be ordered from a reception desk in advance. She was used to working in large reading rooms or freezing museums, warmed only by an ineffective heater or a begged cup of tea. The material Jess normally worked with had already been handed over for future generations to study, the individual to whom they belonged recognising their academic importance. She was completely unused to explaining the relevance of a manuscript that might—or might not—be in the possession of someone with a family connection. The kind of historical research with which she was accustomed did not equip her for this. Jess glanced at Billy, wondering if he felt the same, but he was straining to see inside the shop, looking to see how many customers were left.

'He must work fast, Monsieur Christophe Deniel,' he said, reading the proprietor's name from the shop sign. 'Look, no one waiting now and the shop was crowded when we came by, not half an hour ago.'

Billy was right. The old men who had lingered in the shop window earlier had disappeared and the barber was finishing up with his last customer. Deniel was tall, and he stooped over a man in a chair in front of a large mirror. The barber had thick grey hair flowing almost to his shoulders.

'Why is it that hairdressers can't look after their own mops?' Billy muttered as they stepped inside. A bell announced their arrival with a tinny rattle.

They waited until Deniel had finished and the customer had paid and left the shop. The barber then began talking in French, indicating to the vacant seat in front of the mirror. Billy held up his hand.

After a few false starts and several hurried glances at Bill's phrase book, they confirmed that the barber was indeed Christophe Deniel. The man listened to Billy's broken attempt to enquire about his family and then gestured to the empty seats by the window.

'My mother—Felicity Deniel,' the man said. His nose had been broken at some point in the distant past and his bare arms were covered in blue tattoos. As he spoke, the unmistakable waft of cognac drifted towards Jess and Billy. 'Cecilia is my mother's—aunt, you say?'

Jess and Billy shared a glance. So the curator had been right—this was Cecilia Deniel's family.

Jess shifted her feet. 'We're trying to find out more about Cecilia's work in the hospital. The hospital at the chateau—she worked there during the war. Do you know anything about it?'

Christophe Deniel shook his head. 'I was very young when Cecilia died. Old lady then, understand? But my mère knew her.'

Jess nodded, signalling she understood. 'Thank you. Could we speak to your mother?'

Then the door jangled open, and a customer stepped inside. Like the others before, it was an old man, twirling a hat in his hands. He saw Christophe and started to talk immediately.

Christophe stood up. 'I have customers. Leave me a number. I will call you.'

Billy jotted down his mobile number on the back of a newspaper and passed it over. He seemed on the verge of saying something but Jess, seeing Christophe's attention had switched to his customer, tapped his arm. *Patience.*

So they left, stepping back outside into the damp air. They stared at each other, the barber's shop glass reflecting the morning sun.

'We'll wait, then,' Billy said.

'We have to. How old do you think he is? Christophe?' Jess glanced in at the window, to where the barber was throwing a robe around his customer and reaching for a comb. 'Nearing sixty?'

'Meaning his mother is probably in her eighties. Maybe we'll get a call soon, then. What do old ladies do all day?'

'It depends.' Jess imagined Marie at eighty, zooming around a care home on a motorised scooter. 'We don't know what her health is like.'

'Now what?' Billy swung his arms impatiently. He looked up and down the street. A traffic warden was strolling casually amongst the parked cars outside the town hall, thumbs hooked into his jacket. 'I hate all this hanging around.'

Jess laughed. 'You should be used to it. You must have spent hours waiting for papers to be brought up from the depths of some archive. I have. Never fails to irritate me.'

Billy said nothing but kicked out at a stone.

Jess checked her watch and saw it was coming up for ten o'clock. Hayden would be up, probably working. He would have seen her note. Suddenly Jess felt weary. She did not want to fight with him anymore.

'Look, I'm going to go back and see what Hayden is up to.'

'Fine.'

'Shall we meet later? Will you let me know if you hear anything from this Felicity lady?'

'Sure.' But Billy was moody and non-committal, and Jess thought of James. He had barely spoken to her on the phone last night. Megan—Jess was both pleased and saddened to discover—was her usual, chatty self.

'All right. Well, I'm walking back to the cottage, if you're heading that way.'

Billy sighed. 'Don't suppose the bar is open yet. Go on then.'

With one final glance at Christophe Deniel at work and both feeling deflated, they started to walk back across town, towards the church and the cobbled street.

~ 38 ~

As August slipped into September, the summer deepened and the sunlight seemed to thicken. The windows in the hospital were left open through the night, though it made little difference: bed sheets became sticky with sweat. The men with open wounds suffered more than others. Their bedclothes became smeared repositories of their leaking flesh, and not even repeated washing in boiling water could whiten them again.

Occasionally, if the wind blew in the right direction, bombs and explosions away at the Front could be heard. The soldiers tended to stop whatever they were doing at that time and listen. Those reading looked up; those playing cards paused, a suit or flush in hand. Some closed their eyes or threw an arm across their face, no doubt remembering the explosion that had shattered their legs or blasted them off their feet.

The nurses and auxiliaries paused when the explosions started, though not for long. To the drumbeat of war, they changed dressings and stitched flesh. Violet, sweltering in the stove room over a stone basin of dirty linen, held the sheets tightly in her fists, remembering a walk on Hampstead Heath a year ago, when the noise of the Somme floated across the water and into the heart of the city.

The sound affected all of those in the hospital, though the soldiers who had been exposed to gas or suffering a nervous complaint struggled with the noise more than others. Some men, who appeared to be healing well, would stop writing letters home, sit bolt upright in the beds, and scream. One man who had severe lacerations to his lower legs tried to run from the room; Matron and a couple other nurses caught him as his legs gave way and carried him back to bed.

Then one day, when there must have been a particularly determined offensive at the front, the sound of bombs crept even closer. Some in the hospital were sure they could hear gunfire, though that was unlikely. Still, the booms of the shells were loud enough. Violet had been changing sheets near to Captain Hendry's bed when the orchestra of war began. She had gasped, as had others in the room, and had stood up quickly to listen. Somebody whistled, somebody else muttered about the poor boys they would see later. But Captain Hendry stayed quiet, lying in his bed, a sheet pulled up to his chin. Glancing over, Violet saw his mouth moving rapidly.

She moved towards him and bent down. 'Captain? Hendry, are you all right?'

The man's eyes were glazed and fixed. For a moment, Violet wondered if he had fainted with his eyes open, if such a thing were possible. A pulse ticked hurriedly at his throat. She made to touch his forehead and see if he was hot but then, with her fingers curled over his skin, Hendry's hand shot out and grabbed her wrist.

Violet gasped; the captain's grip was fierce. 'Hendry, you're hurting me. Let me go. Please.'

But Hendry did not let go. Instead he turned to face her, his eyes were still unfocused and smeary, as though he was looking at her under water. His fingers dug into her flesh.

Violet made a small noise of pain and tried to pull away. 'Captain, please. It's Violet.'

Hendry gave no indication that he understood her, or that he had even heard her words. Instead his hand hooked into Violet's flesh, fingernails digging in. Through the pain, Violet became aware that he had cut her and that blood was running down her arm.

She looked around frantically. There was no one close by, apart from men lying in beds. Cecilia was at the opposite side of the room tending to a man with a nasty eye wound. Violet knew she would have to shout to attract help.

'Hendry, let go.' She tried to pull away with all her strength. Her calves banged into the bed next to the captain's and knocked a tin bowl to the floor with a clatter. The soldier asleep in the cot gave a jerk but did not wake up.

Still, Hendry would not let go. He continued to stare at Violet with the same glassy look. His face was white and taut, lips pulled back into a thin line. As his hand squeezed even tighter and Violet thought for the first time that he might break her arm, she became aware of something else: that Hendry looked frightened.

Suddenly another hand appeared and Bishop Shacklock was by her side. He gripped Hendry quickly and, with a forceful motion, pulled the man away. Hendry released her and, sobbing, Violet pulled her arm close to her body, flesh singing. Shacklock was breathing heavily, and he stood over Hendry, his frame filling the space between Violet and the soldier's bed.

Hendry's eyes had cleared, and he sat up, blinking. 'Bishop?' It was obvious he had no idea what had just happened.

Shacklock stood for a few moments, glaring down at the man. His hands were balled into fists and Violet wondered if he would hit the soldier. She touched Shacklock on the shoulder.

'Please, I'm all right.'

Still Shacklock said nothing but his hands relaxed. After a long moment he turned away from the bed and took Violet by the elbow. He led her away to the nurse's quarters, pausing once to look back at Hendry who was watching them, bewilderment and a little anger crossing the captain's face.

'You will need something on that,' Shacklock said quietly when they stepped into the nurses' room. There was no one inside. It was the afternoon, so the night shift had rested and were now at the river. The day shift were all busy seeing to the men. Shacklock went to the supplies cabinet and took out a cloth, wetting it in a sink at the far end of the room. 'Here.' He pressed it on Violet's bloodied wrist.

'Thank you.' She sat down on a bench, her legs suddenly shaky. Despite the heat of the day, she felt terribly cold and gritted her teeth in an attempt to stop them chattering.

The bishop watched and then sat down beside her. He took her wrist gently and wiped away the blood. Small half-moons appeared on Violet's skin from where Hendry's nails had dug in. 'You could so with some iodine on that.'

'There isn't any. It ran out last week. Matron's been trying to find some, hectoring every convoy that comes in.'

'Well, then. Let's clean it as best we can.'

'He's never done anything like this before,' Violet said, feeling she had to say something, though her teeth rattled as she spoke.

'Not to you.'

'I can't understand it. It's like he wasn't really there. I don't think he could even see me.'

Shacklock reached for a towel and patted Violet's arm dry. 'You'll be bruised, I'm afraid. It's lucky he didn't break your arm.'

Violet pulled her arm back, body trembling. She pressed her wrist between her breasts, the way she might have held a broken bird, fragile bones damaged in flight. The bishop's hint that Hendry may have hurt others had not passed her by, though she could not believe it. The captain could be agitated and demanding, but she had not seen violence in him.

'Some men have been damaged in ways we can't see,' Shacklock went on, watching Violet closely. 'You weren't to know this—I doubt if even Matron and the more experienced nurses could have foreseen it. But there's never been a war like this before. The weapons used now are not like any we've seen. Is it any wonder that men carry wounds that we can't heal with a bandage, or that barbaric practice of cleaning a cut with salt?'

'Has Captain Hendry been damaged? Beyond the physical injuries, I mean?'

'I believe so, yes. I think you should be careful around him.'

Violet could not help herself: she smiled.

The bishop sighed. 'I know I might appear overly cautious, but I would give the same advice to any woman here.'

'Yes, I think you would,' Violet said, the pain in her wrist subsiding. She looked into the bishop's wide, expressive face. He had thick eyebrows and her hand strayed to touch her own, also dark and heavy. 'It seems a … fatherly thing to say, I suppose.'

Shacklock looked at Violet oddly. 'Maybe it is. But please take care with Hendry.'

'Do you have children, Bishop Shacklock?' The question was out before Violet could stop it, spilling over like water. She held her breath, wondering what his reply would be. Allegra had said she had never told Shacklock about *her*, about Violet, but Violet waited for his response anyway, in case there were other children she didn't know about. Brothers and sisters, she thought, with a jolt.

But Shacklock shook his head. 'I never married. So no, no family.'

'There's never been anyone?' Violet ploughed on, knowing she was becoming impertinent but feeling reckless.

'No, no one who would have me.' Shacklock looked around. 'Are you sure there's no iodine anywhere?'

'I'm sure. There's really never been anyone?'

Shacklock turned back to look at Violet, his brow creased and troubled. 'Why the interrogation? Are you looking for evidence of a link between us, simply because we share a surname?' His voice was curt and sharp, belying the annoyance he was starting to feel.

Inwardly, Violet cursed her decision to assume his surname upon her arrival in France. It was too obvious, too much of a coincidence. She looked down at her arm where Captain Hendry had left his mark. The indentations left by his nails throbbed brightly. They were like little half-promises, Violet thought; hints of circles only, suggestions of a wound.

She looked up again, and saw the bishop moving awkwardly, twitching and uncurling his left hand. It seemed to prompt something within her; the words tumbled out unbidden. 'My name isn't really Violet Shacklock. I said that because I've travelled here without my mother knowing and she is bound to try to trace me. My real name is Violet Underwood. And you knew my mother, didn't you? Her name is Allegra.'

~ 39 ~

Hayden was sitting at the dining table in the small living room when Jess arrived back at the cottage. His laptop was on and he was working. Numbers scrolled down the screen and he was in the middle of jotting something down on a notepad when Jess opened the door. He looked up.

'I didn't expect you back so soon.'

Jess removed her coat slowly. The cottage was warm and filled with the scent of coffee. She rubbed her hands together, easing heat back into her fingertips. Hayden's voice was calm and steady, giving no hint of anger still lingering from the night before.

'We've got to wait. Billy and I found a descendant of someone who might have worked at the old hospital. But she's elderly and we can't talk to her until she's ready.'

Hayden nodded and pushed back his chair. He held out his hand and drew Jess to him. 'I'm glad you're back.'

And Jess felt better; the ache in her stomach eased and she let herself be held. The fight had sapped more strength from her bones than she had realised. She felt close to tears. Outside a lorry roared past, the spin of tyres over the cobbles sounding like rifle cracks. Jess jumped and held onto Hayden's arm tightly.

There passed a few moments of quiet, Hayden pushing his face into Jess's stomach as she stood against him. Then he reached up and smoothed back the hair from her face. 'Did you eat? We could go for a late breakfast somewhere.'

Jess nodded, not mentioning that she had eaten with Billy earlier that morning. 'That would be nice. There's bound to be a café open somewhere.'

Hayden pressed a few keys on the laptop, saving his work, and then took his coat from a peg behind the door. Pulling her own coat back on and scrabbling for a pair of gloves, Jess followed him out onto the narrow street.

They walked, hand in hand, down the hill into town. It was busier than it had been earlier that morning when Jess walked with Billy. Now, shoppers hurried about, some carrying rolls of Christmas wrapping paper, others bags of groceries. Cars circled the town hall at the bottom of the hill where there were a few parking spaces. As they approached the building, Jess saw a war memorial. She paused, pointing it out to Hayden.

'I can't believe I've never noticed that before,' Jess said and walked over to it. The memorial was angled at the centre of the parking area and appeared to have become a feature around which cars manoeuvred when looking for a space. Jess had to wait for a car to go by before stepping close to the stone tower. The memorial was a white column with sharp corners. Names and inscriptions were chiselled into each side, the sun making them difficult to see. Jess walked around it.

Two sides of the memorial were given over to a list of names from the First and Second World Wars. Jess could not translate the valediction prefacing the names but assumed it confirmed that those listed below had perished in the fighting. She scanned the side listing those who died in the First World War quickly, but saw no sign of a Deniel or a name she recognised from the museum records.

The other two sides of the cubed column memorialised resistance fighters shot near the town hall in the early 1940s. Someone had left a bouquet of flowers at the base of the tower and the stone was clean and well preserved.

Jess was leaning in to read the names listed at the bottom of the memorial when Hayden spoke. 'Are you nearly done? I can see a place open and I'm starving.'

Jess stood up and backed away to where Hayden was standing. She felt irritated: why could he not see the value of such a monument and at least look at it? Years ago, a group of people had toiled over the carved column, probably for months, and then struggled to set it upright. Someone might have driven over from Abbeville with a mechanical crane; Jess could imagine them, men dressed in dirty overalls with dirty necks, shouting encouragement to a timid driver as he eased the memorial into place. And the names, carved on the four sides—perhaps the stonemason knew the people whose names he was recording. Perhaps he went to school with some of them or ran beside a resistance fighter, away from steel-capped boots, scooting around a corner quicker than his friend who was shot down. Jess had felt ashamed that she had not seen the memorial earlier; now that she had, she wanted to give it the honour of reading all the names engraved upon it. But Hayden was tutting at the side, his readiness to leave as bright and clear as the day. Biting down on her annoyance, Jess cast one last look over her shoulder and joined him. They crossed the road to where a café was just opening up.

They ordered and ate, although Jess did not finish her croissant. Instead she drank coffee and tried to quell the quiet anger she still carried. She looked out of the window at the ceaseless motion of the town. They were the café's only patrons so chose the best seat, beside the window but tucked away from the draught creeping in under the front door. Hayden ate and ordered more coffee; they talked, but their conversation was light and cautious. Jess did not elaborate about the work she and Billy had done that morning and Hayden did not ask. He did not mention Marie, either. Their talk was as substantial as the foam on Jess's coffee. Jess listened, stirred her drink and nodded in the places she was supposed to nod, as Hayden did, too. By the time they had both finished and Hayden signalled for the bill, Jess felt deeply unsatisfied and longed for Billy to call her mobile.

'Let's take the long walk back, over the bridge,' Hayden suggested when they left the café and walked back into the cold again. 'The road does a loop back towards the church and our street.' He pulled up his collar and extended his arm for Jess to hook hers through.

They walked along the main street, past a shoe shop and a printer. Like the war memorial, Jess had not noticed them before. It seemed as though the town was opening up to her, the shops announcing themselves. She slowed her pace and Hayden slowed with her. They both looked in at the windows as they passed.

'You know, this town is a slow place compared to Jedthorpe, but I'm beginning to like it,' Jess said.

Hayden squeezed her fingers. 'Perhaps we can take a drive to

Abbeville one day. There'll be more to do there. Maybe even a nightclub or a late night bar.'

On the road a van door slammed shut. A man, whistling, appeared on the pavement holding a bouquet of flowers. He disappeared into an office nearby where women sat at desks near the sheet glass window. Jess watched him hand them over to a girl, whose hands flew to her mouth. Jess smiled, remembering a similar moment, many years ago.

They strolled on, nearing the river that cut the town in two. As they approached the stone bridge, the Christmas wreath they saw a couple of days before still tied to it, Jess's phone rang. She pulled away from Hayden and fumbled in her bag for it.

She expected to see Billy's number flash up, but it did not. Instead, Megan's number appeared. Jess answered quickly, panic rising in her chest.

'Megan?'

'Mum?'

Jess sighed and mouthed her daughter's name to Hayden. He nodded silently and walked a short distance away.

'Hi, babe. What's up?'

'Where are you?' Megan's voice was uncharacteristically sharp. 'You sound like you're outside. I can hear water.'

Jess had leant over the wall running alongside the bridge and the river rushed beneath. 'I'm walking through town. There's a river here. That's what you can hear. What's wrong? You don't sound like my Meg.'

Megan paused and then started speaking, the words tumbling out. 'I was talking to James last night. We were supposed to be in bed but neither of us could sleep. He said he didn't think you and Dad would get back together, and that Dad would move out for good. I know you said he was staying with Grandma for only a little bit, but James said he might always live there and that you two would ...' Her voice trailed away.

Jess squeezed her eyes shut. 'We would what, Meg?'

'You two would get a divorce. That's what James said.' Megan sounded close to tears. In the background a school bell rang and high-pitched voices chattered past. Jess realised her daughter was phoning on her mobile, burning through her pre-paid minutes.

Not for the first time that week, Jess wished she could reach through the phone and touch her child. She imagined Megan standing in a classroom, padding from one foot to another as she realised she would be late for her next lesson, but unable to disconnect the call.

'Is James right?' Megan's voice again. It cut through the swell and throb of the river below. 'Will you and Dad get a divorce?'

'No.' She didn't know where the certainty came from but suddenly it was there, like a line of granite. Hayden had stopped about halfway across the bridge and had lit a cigarette. He was leaning against the stone wall. He wore a long brown coat that he'd bought for the trip over and the damp of the morning clung to him, adding a silver border to his frame.

'Really, Mum?' Megan was speaking again.

'Really.'

Megan exhaled noisily into the phone, the girl's relief buffeting her mother in static waves. When she spoke again her voice had changed and become more relaxed. 'When are you coming home?'

'At the end of the week.'

'That long? Why can't you come back sooner? If you and Dad are going to be all right …'

'I still have work to do, Megan. But as soon as it's done, I'll be back.'

'Like Arnie?' Megan giggled.

Jess laughed. 'You haven't even seen that film. But yes, like Arnie. You'd better go, Meg. You'll be late for your next class.'

'Okay. Talk later?'

'Yep. Love you.' Jess ended the call and returned her phone to her bag. She stared down at the river, water rushing under the bridge. A branch had caught on a rock some time earlier and debris funnelled around it. A couple of ducks swam gamely against the current, necks straining with effort. Jess watched them, understanding what made them act in such a way, to give themselves completely to a task that seemed futile.

'Megan all right?' Hayden had finished his cigarette. He tossed the stub out into the water and the ducks strained towards it, thinking it food.

'She's worried.' Jess took an offered cigarette and drew deeply. 'James, too, probably. Not that he'd tell me.'

'About what?'

Jess paused. The ducks had reached Hayden's cigarette stub. The female, the stronger of the two, took it in her beak and quickly discarded it. It was not what she expected it to be. Her companion, a colourful mallard, trailed after her as she struggled further upstream in search of bread.

The silence lengthened between Jess and Hayden, but he waited for her to speak. 'This has been very hard for the kids,' she said eventually.

'Bound to be,' Hayden said. He peered over the wall again, looping his hands together.

'And she misses me.' Jess sniffed. 'This bloody research. I should be at home.'

'Is that what you think?' Hayden spoke quietly and looked down into the water. 'Well, perhaps you should.'

Jess looked at him. Hayden's body was curved over the stone wall and his lips were pursed, the bottom lip pushed into the top. He hadn't shaved. 'You know I can't. Billy and I—we've got to come up with something. Our careers are on the line. And, well, I'm here with you.'

'Yes you are. But do you want to be?'

The breath caught painfully in Jess's throat. 'Of course I do.'

'Then make a decision. About where you want to be. And don't torture yourself with it.' He finally turned round to face her. The coat was open at his throat and he dug his hands into his pocket. 'It's that simple.'

'But it's not, Hayden. Not for me. I have children—my life is more complicated than yours.'

Hayden spun away, the tails of his coat flapping. He walked towards the far end of the bridge and for a second Jess thought he was leaving, that he wouldn't turn back. The river surged beneath them, branches snapping, waves sloshing up the banks. It thundered through the town, dissecting Villers-des-Champs like a scalpel.

And then Hayden turned around and walked back to her. His face was creased and contorted, and his shoulders were tight. He moved like a man unwilling to head in that particular direction, as though his body throbbed under his skin.

'Jess, you make a decision and you stick to it. That's what you do.'

'I can't.'

'You can.'

'These are my kids, Hayden. My *children*. They are suffering because of what has happened between Alec and I.' Jess forced her feet to stay still, mirroring Hayden's control. 'When you have a family, your life is no longer black and white.'

'It was for my mother.'

Jess had nothing to say to that. Instead, a shutter slammed on the flower delivery van delivering to the office behind them and she jumped. The driver shouted into the street at a car parked too close and then roared his engine into life. He swung the van away from the curb and was off. As he drove over the bridge, the driver peered at Jess and Hayden, standing feet apart but not together.

Hayden's face had changed again and the anger that had shaped it earlier was replaced with weariness. He looked exhausted, more tired than Jess had ever seen him before, even in the mornings after their first few nights together. That had been a different kind of tiredness, one that drew them together in a giggling, conspiratorial embrace. Now, Hayden was pale. Jess could tell the words about his mother had broken from him unexpectedly and left only emptiness, as though they were the cap on a bottle of air, which had dissipated and drifted away on the breeze.

An urge to wrap her arms around him took her, but Jess kept her arms by her side. Just as she kept her friend's name—Hayden's mother's name—at bay.

~ 40 ~

The bishop's shock at Violet's words seemed to crush his chest. He buckled in on himself, folding into his shirt abruptly, pulling himself together like the wounded men they had seen, shot through the stomach. Violet watched, alarmed. She had not expected a reaction such as this; to her, Shacklock was a bull, a strong animal who moved with purpose.

'Bishop?'

He held up his hand, asking for a moment, and then took several deep breaths. He inhaled noisily and then spoke. 'Allegra Underwood. She is your mother?'

'She is. You knew her, back in Greece.' It was a statement. Violet had been confident in what she had discovered back in London, and the physicality of Shacklock's response confirmed it. 'She was married to Edward Underwood.'

'Yes.' The bishop's breathing eased and colour came back into his cheeks. 'I remember.'

Violet waited. There was more the bishop would say, she was sure. After a moment, he spoke again.

'How old are you, really?'

And she knew why he asked. She slowly pulled her cap from her hair, feeling the damp on the back of her neck and at her temples. Her hair was like Shacklock's; thick and dark, and he stared at her.

'I'm seventeen.'

Shacklock raised his chin, eyes closed. Violet watched, wondering if she was observing a man suddenly being confronted with his past, or if his past had been a constant shadow. She wondered if he thought of Allegra often, if her memory walked with him through his days, or if he never thought of her. She had seen soldiers dragged back from the front and conveyed to the hospital, their past tattooed over broken chests, or a memory that pierced their sleep with screams. But not all men carried their near-history in such a way. Some men slept easily, lying as still as stone and gave no hint as to their experiences on the Front. Sometimes Violet wondered if the violence of their past disappeared along with an amputated limb, cut away from their body.

'You were born in …'

'1900,' Violet finished. 'In May.'

She watched him work it out and then saw the past take on a brutal physicality; Shacklock's eyes flew open and a hand went to his mouth. Violet wondered if he might be sick.

'Bishop?'

'I … I didn't know.'

'My mother didn't tell you. I was raised as Edward's daughter.'

'But Edward—he knew. He *saw* us.'

'I don't know about that.' Violet did not want to think of the man she had considered her father stumbling across her mother and her lover. 'It was Edward who told me about you.'

'When?'

'This summer.' Someone out on the main ward cried out, and a bed-pan overturned. The sound of guns and bombs at the front continued to drift through the open windows.

'That's why you're here, then.' The bishop looked at Violet's arm, still oozing blood from Hendry's fingernails. 'It isn't to nurse—we can all see you have no nursing experience.'

'No. But I've helped, I think. A little. I'm here because I wanted to find you.'

Shacklock stood up abruptly and started to pace the nurses' quarters. There wasn't much room; narrow cots and benches were pushed closely together, so the bishop's legs scuffed the bed clothes and pulled sheets onto the floor. He turned back to face Violet and then turned away. Then back.

'I don't see how this can be true,' he said, coming close to her again. 'Your mother and I … it was such a long time ago, and we parted badly. But she would have told me.'

Violet said nothing, recognising the man before her was speaking more to himself than to her.

'She would have told me,' Shacklock insisted. 'I *knew* her. No, there must be some mistake.'

'You can't have known her as well as you thought. And Edward—he wasn't interested in her either.' Violet sighed. She thought of her father—the man she called Father—sitting in his rooms at Threadstone Hall. He preferred his own company and sometimes disappeared for periods of time. Days, weeks, without a word. He never said where he went, though when he came back, he seemed lighter, as though a rock had been rolled off his chest. And then, watching Shacklock roam the room, Violet understood about Edward. 'I don't think Edward cared for women at all.'

The bishop had stopped pacing. His eyes took on a faraway look, and he stood, motionless. Violet watched shadows cross his face. The act of remembering caused Shacklock pain. He sat down on a camp bed opposite Violet, a closed fist rubbing his chest in a circular motion. 'Did Allegra come back to England?' he asked. 'Did she become an actress, like she'd hoped?'

'She came back, yes. We live in London. But she didn't become an actress. Instead she set up a theatre, in Earls Court. It doesn't make much money, but we get by. My mother is devoted to it.' Violet thought of Allegra bent over account books into the small hours, a single light bulb burning above her.

'She established a theatre?'

'She was left money by my grandfather. The major, not Josiah.'

At the mention of Josiah, his old friend, Shacklock's shoulders drooped further and he bowed his head. A tremor passed through his body like a wave, a tide of memory. When he looked up, his eyes were bright. 'What of Josiah?'

'He died, too. Years ago.'

Shacklock closed his eyes. 'And Constance?'

Violet shook her head. 'My grandmother died before I was born. I never knew her.'

Shacklock passed a hand over his face. A pained expression slipped into the lines about his eyes, packing out the creases of his skin. He took a few moments, and had opened his mouth to speak again when the door clattered open and Cecilia stood in the sunlight.

'Bishop, you are needed,' she said loudly. She looked quickly back over her shoulder; there was a crash and a shout, and the sound of running feet. 'The noise, bombs from the Front—some of the men ...'

Her voice faded away, but she did not need to say more. Shacklock was up and scurrying from the room. He moved, Violet thought, like a man running away rather than running toward, and she knew he had found relief in Cecilia's summons. Violet stayed where she was, holding her bruised wrist.

Cecilia stood to one side to allow Shacklock to barrel past. She watched him for a moment and the way he charged towards those creating a disturbance and then her attention switched back to Violet. She came over to the bench where the girl sat. 'Violet?'

Violet held out her arm, smiling ruefully. Cecilia took it gently.

'Who did this?' the Frenchwoman asked.

'Hendry, though I don't think he meant it. The bishop stopped him.'

'And? What else?' Cecilia moved to the side and sat down next to her. She waited, expectedly, her round head leaning to the side. Outside the commotion had quietened, and the nurses seemed to be wrestling back control. They heard the sound of a soldier being restrained and sedated. 'What else?'

Violet shook her head, but Cecilia did not move. She waited. And Violet, tongue loosened, so desperately wanted to tell her. Sighing, Violet turned to face her friend. 'Can you keep a secret?'

~ 41 ~

Present Day

They did not finish their walk together. Instead, Hayden stayed on the bridge, taking another cigarette from the packet in his pocket, blowing plumes of smoke over the water. Jess watched for a few moments but it was clear he wanted to be left alone. He inhaled deeply on the cigarette, and the clouds around him were thick. She turned around and walked back towards the café, to the war memorial and towards the cottage.

She was not far from the cottage when her phone rang again. This time it was Billy. He spoke hurriedly, launching straight into the conversation, his urgency burning through the phone.

'Christophe Deniel contacted me. He says we can meet his mother this afternoon.'

'This afternoon? That's great.' Jess stopped walking. 'Felicity, wasn't it?'

'Yes. Turns out she didn't marry Christophe's father, and she and Christophe lived with Cecilia for a while when he was young. Felicity's mother was Cecilia's sister and disowned her daughter when she became pregnant.'

'Did Christophe tell you this?'

'He did. He was about four when Cecilia died and can't really remember her. He says his mother is still in good health and might be able to help us.'

'Where do we meet her?' Jess stepped to the side to allow a woman pushing a pram to pass.

'At the barber's, after Christophe closes up at five.' Billy sounded amused. 'He seems to want to be there.'

'He probably wants to protect his mother.' Jess watched the woman with the pram gamely swing the heavy front end through the grocer's narrow doorway. 'We're strangers, after all. He'll want to make sure Felicity is safe.'

'Or he wants to hear things he's never heard before, but always wondered about. It happens in families all the time—all these secrets.'

Jess looked at her watch. It wasn't yet noon. The thought of going back to the cottage and waiting for Hayden to return was not appealing and Jess had the strong sense they had nothing more to talk about. She imagined him frowning down at the water, hunch-shouldered, waiting until his cigarette had burned down to the stub so he could throw it at the ducks again and watch their confusion.

'Billy, I know what we could do in the meantime.' An idea took hold and Jess thought about her suitcase, back at the cottage. 'Do you have walking boots with you? Meet me outside your place in twenty minutes.'

∽

Billy had guessed where they were heading from the moment Jess met him outside his cottage and pointed up the hill, past the church. He was wearing well-worn walking boots and waterproof trousers, and a bottle of water poked out the top of his rucksack.

'It's only a mile or so, isn't it?' Jess said, eyeing Billy's supplies.

He shrugged. 'You don't know what we might find up there. We have all afternoon, unless you're meeting …'

His voice trailed away as Jess shook her head, probably more firmly than necessary. Billy looked at her with momentary curiosity and then shrugged, heading up the cobbled street.

They were going to the place where the hospital had once stood. Billy led the way, boots scuffing. 'The chateau fell into disrepair in the 1960s, apparently, after the last of the owner's family died. There's not much of the original building left.'

'Still.' Jess didn't need to elaborate. They both wanted to see where the building had been, where Violet and Cecilia had worked together in 1917. They wanted to see the last place the bishop had ministered and tended to the sick, and where Violet had spent her last days. They panted their way up the steep gradient, rounding the churchyard and eventually reaching the top of the hill above the town, where the land flattened out into wet, green fields.

'Quite a view.' Jess shaded her eyes, looking back down over Villers-des-Champs. She could make out the town hall and, in front of that, a small white column that was the war memorial. Several streets snaked away from the main road, cottages and houses crowding for space.

They turned and carried along a rough road cut into the fields. Turnips were piled in huge heaps every hundred metres or so, and Jess wondered who they were for: whether they were to feed animals over winter or the townsfolk.

Billy held his nose as they passed by one such mountain. 'From what I remember reading about the hospital, the men would have been fed on this.'

'Turnips?'

'And potatoes, if they were lucky. Maybe bread from the town. Rations as well—tinned meat. Jam. Some still received parcels from home.'

'And the nurses?'

Billy pulled a face. 'The same, I expect. Some might have received parcels, others not. Not Violet. No one knew she was here, remember? Her diet can't have been great.'

They fell silent after that and walked further up the road. Then they saw the ruins of the chateau. What had once been a large and impos-ing building was now a roofless shell, save for a small section where wooden, lichen-covered beams were exposed. Stone slabs lay piled and cracked in the grass, ivy growing through the crevasses. As Billy and Jess approached, they saw the remnants of sculpted eaves, an indica-tion of the building's historical grandeur. A bell tower had toppled over years before and become a nest for pigeons; they rose in a cooing, grey cloud and swooped away, over the fields.

'Did you say the building was commandeered during the war?' Jess asked, gingerly picking her way through the bricks and stones towards the only part of the chateau still standing.

'Yes. The owners were given a lump sum of money after the war ended, supposedly to cover repair work.' Billy looked around. 'They probably thought they'd hit the jackpot. From what I understand, the building was already falling apart when it was taken over as a hospital. The owner lived in a small wing in the years after the war and let the place fall to pieces.'

Jess thought of the treatment record books back in the museum and the suffering endured by so many within the building's walls. 'So many men, here. Such pain.'

They reached the shell of the building. Water dripped from exposed, rotten beams and it looked to be on the edge of collapse. Moss grew up the walls, breaking through the crumbling paintwork and there were rusty drink cans piled in a corner. Jess leant down, squinting at writing daubed on the walls in blue paint.

'Graffiti,' Billy said. 'We won't find anything from the time the hospital stood here.' He kicked at a loose can.

Jess stood up, disappointed. On the walk up to the chateau she had daydreamed about what they might find—a bed frame, maybe. A signature on a wall penned by a soldier years ago. But there was nothing like that. The history of the place had been stripped away or allowed to fall in on itself. What was left was the humdrum reality of decay, interrupted only by modern vandalism.

'I don't know why, but I had hope for so much more,' Jess said. 'I knew the place was a ruin, but still … I somehow thought the place would feel more tangible. More *connected*, if you know what I mean, to its past.'

'I do know what you mean,' Billy said. 'You want it to feel more real than a bunch of papers in an archive.'

'Exactly.'

'The building has been exposed for too long. To the elements and to people. Whereas archives are protected, aren't they? You don't get vandals ripping up manuscripts or books—well, not unless they are academic nutters.' Billy grinned. 'I've felt like screwing up a letter by Waller's precious bishop now and then.'

'Me too.' Jess thought back to a time, only a few weeks ago but somehow very distant, when she could have cheerfully set fire to a box of Shacklock's papers.

'One thing that won't have changed over the years is the weather.' Billy zipped up his coat. Rain fell softly, thudding on the grass and brambles. The river pounded close by. There was no shelter and dark clouds lingered on the horizon, threatening heavy weather.

Reluctantly, Jess and Billy turned back, heading towards the town again, shoulders hunched against the cold. Jess looked behind as they walked, glancing back at the mounds of decay, a line of sadness wrapping heavily around her chest.

~ 42 ~

A few days later the storm broke. The heat had steadily increased until Violet thought she could bear it no longer and would have to go against all decorum and swim in the river in her underwear. Some of the auxiliaries whispered about a secret visit to the river in the middle of the night, when Matron was asleep, when they could strip off and cool themselves out of sight of the hospital and the men. But so far no one had dared to do so, and the women suffered on, fanning the men whenever possible and making even the unwilling drink plenty of water.

Then, a matter of days after Violet had confronted the bishop with her story, the clouds turned black and ugly, and the rain came. Men were sitting outside when the first crack of lightning rendered the sky and they had to be helped inside, clothes unexpectedly soaked to the skin. Violet came out to assist, wrapping an arm around the waist of any soldier nearby. The third person she helped back to bed was Hendry; he had paused before allowing her to take his weight, but there was no time for reticence. The storm was too violent. Violet hurried him back to his cot and then ran to close the windows.

It was a difficult evening. The storm was not like other storms Violet had known. This one seemed to squat malevolently over the hospital, refusing to move. Violet was used to storms that filled the London streets with hot, crackling energy for only a few moments, buffeting her mother's theatre before heading north to the suburbs. Storms at home were thrilling. Only once in England had she been frightened by the weather. It was during a trip to the Brighton coast, when she and Allegra had watched the clouds gather out at sea, wincing as white jagged lines pierced the sky. Allegra had insisted that they linger on the pier long after the other tourists had made their way into the hotels or cafes, despite Violet's growing anxiety. Violet remembered how her mother stared at the water with a look upon her face not unlike the stray, starving dogs they occasionally saw around Earls Court. By the time they eventually returned to their boarding house, Violet was drenched and shaking. Allegra had barely noticed and strode around their room, charging to the window, to the bed, to the window again.

At the hospital, the rip and shout of thunder and lightning was worse than the thud of bombs, many miles away. Men who had been unaffected by the distant drone of war now curled up under their bed-clothes as the storm raged above. Others wound their blankets around their fists, eyes glazed open, drooling. Hendry sat on his bed with his legs swung round, shaking softly. Violet watched cautiously from a dis-tance, fearful of the way his frown creased and the tick in his jawline. A hush fell over the hospital and everyone turned to look out the win-dows, to see white lines blaze the horizon and rain to lash down.

'This is hard on the men,' said a voice at Violet's ear and she flinched, turning around. It was Bishop Shacklock. He, too, was wet; he had been outside with the men and had been caught in the sudden downpour. He wiped a hand across his damp forehead and smiled ruefully. 'I had to carry one fellow back in here. He turned to stone the second the light-ning struck. I can only imagine where his mind has taken him.'

He spoke quietly but Violet could see Cecilia watching intently from across the room. The Frenchwoman was changing a dressing on a soldier and had paused, bandage in her hand. They had not talked about Violet's revelation about Shacklock being her father since the day Hendry had acted so oddly, but Violet sensed Cecilia had thought of bringing the subject up many times in the days that passed. Now, as the bishop muttered in Violet's ear, the Frenchwoman tipped her head to one side, as if she were straining to hear.

'Someone who once ministered in Jedthorpe with me now works at a convalescent hospital back home,' Shacklock said. 'He wrote and told me that men were returning with injuries no one could see.' He balled up his fist and tapped the knuckles against his temple.

'What do you mean?'

'Injuries in the mind. Memories of what they have seen disturbing their sleep—when they can get to sleep. Some men are even incapable of talk. The war has stolen their tongues.'

Violet turned to look back at the still figures lying in the beds. Row upon row of silent, white statues, faces turned towards the ceiling or the windows beyond which the storm raged. The sky, blue and brilliant only hours before, was now ugly and grey, distorted by the lines powering across it. Violet was reminded of the sight, observed as a child, of a young woman who had thrown herself on the electrified tracks at the recently opened Piccadilly station. A suicide, at the time the station was busiest. Allegra had suggested they take the new underground train home as a treat. She had held Violet's hand on the platform as men in high collars hurried past and women, rebelliously travelling alone, had swept the platform surface with long skirts. The train came into the station just as the woman jumped. Violet remembered how the husky shouts of shocked men bounced along the rounded walls. And she remembered the woman's face. Allegra had tried to protect Violet from the scene, throwing her arms around her child and pulling Violet up onto her hip where the girl buried herself into her mother's neck. But curiosity was brutal, and Violet edged around to see, pressing her face against her mother's flesh in such a way so that her eyes could make out the remains on the track. The woman may have been beautiful, but what was left of her face was now transformed and pulled into something hideous, partly hidden by the blue of her torn dress.

A thrust of lightning flashed across the sky, brightening the room for a moment. Then, almost instantaneously, the crash of thunder. Someone—a soldier—screamed. Violet jumped and flung out her hands. *Mother*, she thought—but Allegra wasn't there. Instead another hand caught hers and gripped tightly. Warm and damp, folding her fingers into his like a giant bear, Shacklock held on. He pulled her towards him. She let him, remembering how Allegra had held her that evening on the train platform. Allegra's skin had smelled of smoke, of the rush of the train and, underneath that, of sweat. Violet didn't mind: sweat meant work and Allegra was always happiest when she was working. They'd spent the day trying to source theatre seats, Allegra finally settling up with a man at Borough Market near London Bridge. She had helped to load the chairs into the back of a cart with directions to the theatre and, when she bent down to speak to Violet, her face had been flushed and cheerful. 'It's really happening, Violet,' Allegra had said. 'Just you watch—we'll be putting on our first play by Christmas.'

The proximity of Shacklock's strong, sturdy body was welcome. Violet's arm pushed against his and he smiled encouragingly at her. 'It will be all right,' he said. 'The storm will pass.'

Violet turned back to the windows to watch. She did not see Hendry glaring across the room at them, staring openly, the stump of his wounded leg swinging quickly back and forth over the edge of the bed.

~ 43 ~

Present Day

Billy had sensed something had changed between Jess and Hayden, acknowledging the shift without actually referring to it; he suggested they both walk back to his cottage from the chateau and work there for a while before heading back to the barber's at closing time.

'We need to have a clear idea of what we want to ask Felicity when we meet her,' he said as he and Jess walked back down the hill towards Villers-des-Champs.

Matching his stride, Jess didn't answer. They both knew there wasn't much preparation they could do, other than be ready to make notes. But she gave silent thanks to her colleague, grateful for his offer of a hideaway for a few hours.

'I hope this lady can speak English,' she said quietly. 'We'll be stuffed if she's relying upon us to translate.'

'Ah. I hadn't thought of that.'

'Nothing we can do about it now. We should meet her and, if we need to, arrange for a translator to come with us on a later date.'

They neared Billy's cottage and, glancing down the street, Jess saw that the lights in her own house were off. Hayden must still be out, she thought. She reached inside her rucksack.

'I'm just leaving a note,' she said to Billy. 'I'll be back up in a second.'

She wrote as she walked, slowly making her way down the cobbled street. A brief note, matter-of-fact. She would be back later after meeting Felicity Deniel. No mention of their argument earlier. No mention of the change that had occurred over the past few hours, a change that now seemed as permanent as the war memorial just out of sight. She paused for a brief second outside the cottage door, and then pushed the note through the letterbox, not waiting to see if Hayden was actually inside, sitting in the dark. She hurried back towards Billy's cottage without looking over her shoulder.

The layout of Billy's cottage was almost a mirror image of Jess's, although the furniture was different and in different places. The table was in the kitchen instead of the living room, and they sat with their backs to the oven to drink coffee. Billy wrote a few things down on a sheet of paper, questions for Felicity, but both knew the exercise was pointless.

'We should let Felicity to speak, just as she likes,' he said.

'Freely.'

'Yes. Because we want to know everything.'

'Everything she can tell us about Violet and the bishop.'

'Nothing held back. No hesitation, no desire to protect someone's memory. I just hope Cecilia talked to her about the war, and that Felicity can remember.'

'Me too.' Jess stirred her coffee cup. 'She might want to protect someone, though.'

'But it was so long ago. What harm can it do?'

Jess shrugged. 'Who's to say? We don't know what story Felicity has. We're talking about two people dying here. Unexpectedly.'

'Do you think Violet and Shacklock could have been murdered?'

Jess blinked. 'Wow.'

Billy nodded. 'Imagine Waller's face if we write a paper revealing *that.*'

'I don't see it, though,' Jess said. 'A murder, I mean. How could it be covered up? There would have been a scandal—news would have slipped out somehow. And what about motive?'

'I don't think it's impossible.' Billy refilled his coffee cup. 'Remember, we're talking about a unique time. Men in close proximity, many wounded. Some possibly suffering from shell shock. Do you know much about that?'

'Only what I've seen in documentaries.' Jess thought back to an evening, a few years ago, when she and Alec had caught a programme about the last of the Tommies, the British soldiers who were now weary, shaky old men. Interviews with them were interspersed with archival footage, painful to watch even after a distance of ninety-odd years. Jess remembered how her tongue became stuck to the roof of her mouth as she stared at the images of jerking, black-and-white men, rolling around on a hospital floor, their faces contorted by fear that had not left them. 'Poor buggers,' Alec had muttered.

'Shell shock made men act oddly,' Billy said.

'That's putting it mildly.'

'You never know what might have happened. Those men, so far from home and in pain. No family around to support them. I'd expect that some of the wounded were shipped back to England, but not all. If they recovered, they'd have been sent back to the Front. Others would have stayed in the hospital longer, possibly to stabilise before being transferred.'

'It must have been a frightening time for so many.' Jess thought of the old men on the television programme and how their voices, wobbling with age, still carried an undertone of bewilderment and sadness. 'I can't begin to think how scared they must have been back then. Especially the youngsters.'

'Hopefully Felicity Deniel can shed some light on what happened,' Billy said. 'Then we can get this wrapped up and go home.'

'Are you missing your wife?'

Billy shrugged. 'It's Christmas. Of course.' He peered over his mug and coughed. 'What about you?'

Jess glanced at him, though Billy kept his eyes trained on the table. He'd asked nothing about Hayden, even when Jess broke the news that Hayden would be joining them on the trip to France. Despite the tension between the two men at the start of the journey and the uncomfortable atmosphere on the way to Villers, Billy had acted as though Hayden was another researcher coming along for the ride. Jess recalled how Billy and Hayden had even discussed the hunt for the skeleton's identity the morning before. She sighed and took a sip from her own mug.

'You've been extremely tactful about the situation,' she said eventually. 'Alec and I separated a few weeks ago.'

'I'm sorry to hear that.'

'It wasn't because of Hayden. Or maybe it was. I don't know.' Jess placed her hands, palms down, on the table. 'Alec told me he'd been having an affair. It had been going on for a few months.'

'Ah. So you left him and started seeing Hayden?'

'Not exactly,' Jess said slowly. Just as with the suspicion that the bishop and his daughter had been murdered, Billy was laying bare the stark truth of what had happened. Jess's mouth moved awkwardly as she spoke again. 'Hayden had actually been on the scene for a week or so before Alec told me about his affair.'

'So you both had affairs?'

'Yes.' Jess's voice was small.

'But you haven't told Alec about yours?'

Jess sighed. Guilt sat in her stomach like an undigested meal. She had let Alec move out of their home and go back to his mother without saying a word about her own actions. He had packed a small bag in the early days and returned to their house when she was out one day to collect more things. His deodorant had disappeared from the bathroom. His watch and cufflinks were no longer on the bedside cabinet. And still Jess said nothing; instead, at weekends, she packed a hold-all of her own and boarded a train for London, crossing the city to Fulham and to Hayden's flat. Her bag was light, but the handles cut into her fingers and rubbed on her shoulder blades, lingering long after she'd unpacked in Hayden's bedroom.

'I haven't told him,' she said finally. 'I know. I should have.'

Billy shrugged. 'It's not my place to judge. But the fact that you *haven't* implies something.'

'It does?'

'That you were looking for a way to get out. Of the marriage. If you weren't, you would have owned up like Alec did. Maybe see if you could make things right again.'

Jess looked at her nails. She knew it was wrong of her not to tell Alec about Hayden, but Billy's explanation didn't sit easily. It didn't quite feel right. 'I don't know, Billy. I don't know what I want, really. I felt so *sure* when we got married and when the kids came along. I thought I knew what I wanted and who I wanted to be, and whom I wanted to be with. That feeling didn't go away, even in the early years, when James didn't sleep—he was a bugger for that, you know. I didn't get a full night's sleep until he was three. But even then I felt content. I felt like I had purpose.'

'You don't feel like that anymore?'

'I don't.' Jess blinked away tears. The words startled her with their nakedness. 'But I didn't really contemplate leaving. Until Alec dropped his bombshell, I had no thought that we would separate, even with all the problems.'

'What were the problems?'

Such as the fact we became strangers, Jess thought. Such as there were too many evenings where we'd sit together on the sofa, but not really together, the friendship we once shared draining away into the flat screen TV, the thick carpet, the shelves of DVDs that we worked hard to buy but had no energy to enjoy. Such as the fact I had almost forgotten what it felt like to be wanted or have someone interested in what I had to say. Or what it felt like to have an arm curl around my waist in the middle of the night.

But these were things that Jess could not say. Instead, she said, 'We didn't talk like we used to do and things weren't right elsewhere. I'm sure you can guess, I won't embarrass you. But leave him? No, I hadn't planned on doing that.'

'So you were prepared to keep on with your affair behind his back then?'

'Billy ...' Jess exhaled noisily. 'You have a way ...'

'What?'

'You can be so diplomatic at times—you've not asked once about Hayden, and there were all those times in the library when you bit your lip and said nothing when Waller acted like an arse. But then—'

'Then other times I'm horrendously blunt?' Billy smiled. 'My wife tells me that all the time.'

Jess dipped her head. 'I've worked alongside you for years and I didn't even know you were married. I feel bad about that.'

'You mean for not asking? Waller always kept you on a tight leash. Or maybe you are guilty of being a bit like him—unable to see past the end of your nose.' Billy reached down into his jeans pocket and produced his wallet. He took out a crumpled photograph and passed it over.

Jess looked down. A dark-haired woman laughed up into the camera, mouth open, creases around her eyes. She looked about the same age as Billy. She was in a wheelchair and as Jess looked closely, she saw the woman's arms and hands were twisted upwards.

'Gemma,' Billy said, taking the photograph back. He smoothed it out with his thumbs, slowly. 'There was a car accident when we were both at school. Seventeen. Her mind is fine and she can speak—well, enough so I can understand her and we don't care about anybody else.'

'You've been together since school?'

'I was driving.' Billy stared clear-eyed at Jess. He said the words plainly, no hint of emotion in his voice.

Jess looked back, nodding carefully. She was not sure of what to say. She suspected Billy had heard all kinds of reactions to the news over the years and that there wasn't a set script.

'We'd been going out for about six months when it happened. I'd just passed my test. And don't say it.'

'Say what?'

Billy held up his hand. 'I would have asked Gemma to marry me anyway. We make each other happy.'

'That's great, Billy. Really great.'

'She's still Gemma, you know. Not a disabled person or paraplegic, or whatever name you want to give her. Just Gemma.'

'Of course.'

'There are days, after putting up with Waller's crap at the library, when I can't wait to get home. Gemma makes all the bad stuff go away.' Billy folded the photograph up and put it back in his wallet. 'I'm sorry if that isn't the case for you.'

'With Alec?' Jess looked down and thought back to the early years, before the kids and then when they were little. It *had* been like that, once upon a time. She used to finish work at an office in town and hurry home to her husband, so they could eat pasta in front of the television after James and Megan had gone to bed, and look through the prospectuses Jess had picked up from local colleges. Alec had always been encouraging. 'I suppose we started taking each other for granted. Work, the kids, the house.'

'The boring stuff, but the *safe* stuff. You might not think it now but James and Megan will thank you for a boring kind of life when they're older. We've been trying to have kids for the last ten years.'

'Is it harder because of Gemma's injury?'

'Actually it's me.' Billy gave a short laugh, though it did not reach his eyes. 'Gemma's fine. She's stronger than many women her age. Waist up that is.'

'I'm sorry, Billy.' And suddenly Jess longed to speak to her children, and to hear Alec's voice in the background. The kitchen in Villers was too quiet; Billy had not put on the radio or switched on the television.

Even the sound of a programme they couldn't understand would have better than the silence. At home, Jess would have walked through the door to find James on the PlayStation or bent over his Nintendo. Megan would be thumping out dance steps in her room, pop music blaring down the stairs. Alec would be chopping food in the kitchen and crashing around with the saucepans in a way that never failed to infuriate Jess. She wanted to hear the tinny sound again, the jarring clang that cut across the background drone and fizz.

She felt tears and pressed her fingers to her eyes quickly, hoping Billy would not see. But of course he did. Silently he got up and fetched a roll of toilet paper from the downstairs bathroom. He handed it to her and then turned back to the counter, flicking the kettle on again.

~ 44 ~

September 1917

There had been a delay in the shipping out of wounded soldiers, though the nurses were never told why. They only knew more and more men were brought to the hospital and fewer left. The hospital became unbearably cramped; Violet felt her calves press into the mattress of the cot behind when tending to a man. Some men complained of the breath of other soldiers on their faces as they tried to sleep. The nurses' quarters was commandeered and turned into a treatment room. A doctor came down from Belgium and started to operate on the men who had been hit in the face, patching them up and keeping them in the nurses' room away from the others before they could be transferred.

Violet and Cecilia found an old storeroom on the second floor, not much bigger than a cupboard, and started to sleep in there. It was witheringly hot. There were no windows and no ventilation so, after a brief discussion about the appropriateness of leaving their door open, they jammed the door ajar before they took to their beds.

'Close it when you need to change out of your uniform,' Cecilia had commanded.

'Of course.' Violet crammed their bags under the cot beds. 'But no one prowls around at night, only the women. We'll be safe with the door open.'

For the next week they were incredibly busy and Violet had no time to talk with the bishop again. She overheard the Matron telling another nurse that there had been a fight-back by the enemy some way up the lines and they started to see bayonet injuries. Men arrived with their stomachs falling through their clothes, faces white and pinched, many suffering for hours before finally succumbing. A few casualties were very young; one lad arrived on the back of a cart with his side ripped open and, as Violet helped take him down and carry him into the hospital, he asked for his mother in an unbroken, reedy voice that made her weep. She fell asleep on a stool beside his cot and, in the morning, when he still hadn't died, wrote a letter home for him.

The bombardments sounded closer, too. In a few snatched hours of sleep, Violet dreamed of flares being sent high into the night sky, white light picking out twisted and wretched forms lying in the mud. Her skin was drenched and wet when she woke.

On Sundays, the bishop held bible readings for the men able to sit up. Chairs were taken outside again and set in a circle, with Shacklock on a stool at the centre. Violet and Cecilia helped to settle the men in place as he started to read a passage out loud. Some days Shacklock read from Exodus, emphasising the healing of the sick. Other times he read from Psalms, about hope. He avoided passages about the love of family, divulging to Violet one Sunday morning that it would unsettle the men to think too much about those back home.

Captain Hendry was one of those who sat with Shacklock on Sunday mornings. Since the day he had grabbed Violet's arm and been wrestled away by the bishop, he had said nothing to either. Even Cecilia had noticed his silence; whereas Hendry had asked Violet to read with him in the past, he now turned his head away when she approached his bed, pretending to be asleep when she stopped by his cot.

'He's troubled,' Violet said to Cecilia after Hendry had once more ignored her when she walked by.

'He should think himself lucky,' Cecilia had said. Her apron was stained with blood; she had assisted in the amputation of a young man's legs, just below the hip. 'Some of these men won't make it out of here. His father is coming next week to collect him.'

'Hendry's?'

'He's a lord, or something. I heard Matron say he wanted to take his boy to see someone who could make him a new foot. He'll be gone next week and will be someone else's problem.'

Until then, Violet thought as she joined Shacklock and the men for the Sunday prayer group, *I can make the last part of his stay pleasant.* Her arm no longer ached from where Hendry had held her. The cuts from his fingernails had healed, and she had almost forgotten what it had felt like to be hurt by him. She looked at the soldier sitting quietly in an armchair, one trouser leg folded up at the ankle. When he caught her eye, she offered him a smile.

The bishop was nearing the end of a Psalm and some of the younger men were looking tired. One tucked his chin down into his pyjama top and closed his eyes. Another leant against the arm of Violet's chair. Shacklock noticed but read on, smiling. When he finished, he closed his bible softly.

'I am glad that some of our friends here find the readings so restful,' he said.

'It's the heat,' Cecilia offered apologetically.

Shacklock held up his hand. 'It is comforting. Let the boys sleep. I hope in their rest they know that their Lord is caring for them.'

'Read us something else.' A voice, suddenly, louder than necessary. One of the sleeping men grunted and shifted.

Violet turned. It was Hendry. He was staring, wide-eyed at the bishop. 'Read,' he repeated more forcefully.

Shacklock rubbed his hands over the bible slowly. He glanced at Violet. 'Of course. What would you like to hear?'

'Find something in there about an old fool.' Hendry's hair stood up in greasy clumps. Violet saw creases cutting savagely across his forehead. 'There must be something about making a spectacle of yourself.'

Shacklock laid the bible down in his lap. The other men sat rigidly. The sound of the river throbbing down the hill was the only sound.

After a moment, Shacklock spoke up. 'Something is troubling you, captain.'

'Find it!' Hendry roared. The sleeping men jerked awake at the sound, turning quickly in their chairs, faces panicked. They moved like fragile, fearful birds in their seats. Hendry spoke again, dropping his voice only slightly. 'You know where to look. I want to hear about an old man making a fool of himself over a woman.'

Violet leant forward in her chair, alert and confused. Cecilia was up, too, moving to stand beside Hendry. The Frenchwoman had her hand on the back of his seat, as though she were about to touch him, but had thought better of it.

'Captain, you have something eating at your heart,' Shacklock said, his voice still low and steady. 'If it gives you peace to hear a reading about a foolish man, of course I will find one. But I don't think it will.'

'*A fool's mouth is his ruin, and his lips are a snare to his soul,*' Hendry said loudly. 'Proverbs.'

Cecilia dropped a hand onto his shoulder. 'Come, you need to rest.'

The man brushed her away, slapping Cecilia as he might slap a fly. He glared at Violet, who was watching the scene unfold, wide-eyed.

'You. And an old man like him.' The captain's chin wobbled, a pointy little dagger.

'Captain, you are mistaken.' The bishop smiled benignly. He opened out his hands. *I am no threat, I am no threat.*

'I've seen you!' The dagger went up and down rapidly. 'During the thunderstorm. Holding her like that. You thought I didn't notice, but I did. My father will be here in a few days. He'll see to it that you are sent home.'

'Captain, you are tired and making no sense.' Cecilia reached for him again. She glanced at Violet, shaking her head slightly. Violet understood what she meant. *Do not tell this man the truth about you and Shacklock.*

Violet stood up slowly and came to the other side of Hendry's chair. The bishop stayed where he was while men—those still awake, at least—watched on in silence. Violet held Cecilia's gaze above Hendry's head, blinking out her agreement. *I will say nothing.*

'Captain, let me take you back to your bed,' Violet said. She kept her voice level and smooth. It was the first time she had spoken to him in days and he shifted to face her, bewilderment now crowding his face. Then his brow cleared and Violet saw a much younger man appear, one with a light heart and easy manner. She wondered if this was the man he had been before the war, and felt a great sorrow towards him. 'Hendry. You are tired, that's all. You need to rest.'

Hendry shook his head, but the anger had evaporated. He searched the faces of the men around him but didn't seem to find answers. Then he sat back in his chair and allowed Cecilia to touch his shoulder again.

After a moment, the two women coaxed him out of his seat. He came gradually, like a man being pulled apart, and then followed them without a word back into the hospital. Shacklock remained motionless, watching from afar as Violet and Cecilia eased the young captain back into his bed. The women also said nothing as they pulled back the sheet and settled Hendry down, only sharing a look as they moved away from his bed.

~ 45 ~

Present Day

Jess and Billy waited at his cottage until just before five o'clock and then started the walk back down the hill towards the barber's shop. The street lamps came on, creating a line of white light that threaded past the church, the bakers, the tabac. As they walked together, Jess and Billy noticed a few more shops had put up Christmas decorations; tinsel and fairy lights now crowded the window displays.

Jess paused as they passed the cottage she shared with Hayden. A light was on inside, though the curtains were drawn. Hayden had obviously returned from town. He had not called her mobile or knocked on Billy's door. She sighed, knowing what it meant. More significantly, however, Jess recognised the detachment she felt. She wondered if they would have their last conversation after her return from meeting Felicity Deniel.

They approached the barber's, standing to the side to allow a last customer to leave. An old man with a fresh haircut brushed passed them and shouted over his shoulder to Christophe Deniel, who was sweeping up hair clippings inside. He saw Jess and Billy waiting by the door and signalled them in.

'Close the door,' he said as they stepped into the barber's shop. 'I'm done.'

Billy dutifully closed the door and, as an afterthought, turned the little 'ouvert' sign around to show 'fermé'.

'It's good of you to arrange this,' Jess said. She scanned the room— there were two seats pushed up against mirrors on the left side, a sink on the right, and a desk with a till and bottles of shampoo. At the back of the room was a curtain, which had been pulled to the side to reveal a set of stairs. Jess wondered if that led to the upstairs flat, and if that was where they were to meet Felicity.

It was. Christophe Deniel finished his sweeping and pressed a button on the till, a roll of paper spewing forth with a tinny rattle. He was totting up the day's takings. Leaving the till to its noisy business he flicked his head over his shoulder. 'This way. My mother, upstairs.'

Billy and Jess followed him up the set of narrow steps, which led, sure enough, to a small, one-room flat. A single bed with a checked quilt was pushed against the wall on the left; to the rear was a sofa and a television. Christophe Deniel obviously lived solitarily and simply— there were no pictures on the walls and no ornaments. To the right of the room was a small kitchenette and a table. Around it were four wooden chairs of differing sizes and, on one of them, sat a petite, grey-haired lady.

Christophe approached, speaking quickly in French and the pair embraced. Christophe towered above his mother and, as she reached up to touch his face, Jess saw a pair of twisted, arthritic hands, knuckles bent out of shape. Then Felicity Deniel picked up her coffee cup, holding it in her palms, nesting it the way Jess had seen a burn victim once do on a television documentary. She felt a rush of affection towards the old woman, stranger that she was, and came towards her.

'Miss Deniel? My name is Jess. I am a researcher from England. This is my colleague, Billy. We are very grateful that you have agreed to see us.'

Felicity Deniel stared up at Jess blankly and for a moment, Jess had a sinking feeling that their fears had been realised—that the old lady couldn't speak English and they would learn nothing tonight. But then the lady smiled, baring brilliantly white dentures.

'I am grateful, too. I have waited a long time to tell Cecilia's story.' The voice was as gnarled as her hands, but Felicity's smile was wide. She indicated to the chairs opposite and, with her son taking a seat to her left, the group gathered around the table.

Christophe poured coffee for them all. Then he took out a tin of brown cigarillos from his pocket, lit one, and sat back. His detachment was clear—he was there to look after his mother, but would play no part in the conversation.

'We're not sure where to start,' Billy said after adding cream and sugar to his coffee. 'Perhaps if we tell you a little about us and what we're researching?'

Felicity nodded encouragingly.

'We—that is, Jessica and I—we work at a library not far from York. The Shacklock Library, named after a bishop whom we believed worked at a hospital during the First World War, alongside your aunt, Cecilia Deniel.' Billy paused. 'The bishop died in 1917 and was buried here, in Villers-des-Champs. You may know this already, but when a group of the bishop's supporters exhumed his body so they could take him back to England, they found the skeleton of a young woman buried with him. We're trying to find out the identity of that young woman.'

Felicity said nothing but continued to listen.

Jess picked up the story. 'We discovered from archives in the British Library and at Threadstone Hall, a house in Woking, that Shacklock may have travelled to Greece in 1899 to visit friends. Other letters that we found in Hampstead, London, suggest that Shacklock may have had an affair while in Greece and become a father.'

'It took quite some digging to discover this,' Billy said, his pride unmistakable. He took a large gulp of coffee.

'We don't know if Shacklock knew he'd had a child,' Jess went on. 'It was a girl. But we think she travelled to France to meet him when he worked at the hospital just up past the Villers' church. We don't know what happened, but we think somehow the bishop and this girl died— possibly around the same time—and were buried together.'

'We think the woman discovered with the bishop was his daughter,' Billy finished.

They waited. For long time, Felicity Deniel looked at them silently. The air was filled with the musky scent of her son's cigarillos. Christophe sat, impassive. Jess became concerned they had said too much, that their story was too complicated and the old lady, for all her proficiency with English, had not understood them.

But then Felicity spoke. 'Yes. It *was* his daughter. Cecilia told me all about it. The girl was called Violet Underwood.'

~ 46 ~

Later that evening, after Hendry's outburst at the bible reading, and after the men had settled down to sleep and the room had fallen into some kind of stillness, Violet and Cecilia took their mugs of tea out into the garden. It was still unbearably warm and, with no one around, they removed their stockings and loosened the buttons at their throats. Violet was exhausted. Two lorries had arrived unexpectedly to take those able to travel back to the coast and home to England. Violet and other VADs had spent the afternoon carrying men on stretchers and sliding them onto the lorry floor, or helping those able to walk to find their seats. Then the vacant beds needed to be stripped, sheets boiled and put through the wringer, and set out to dry. The floors were mopped; fluid had seeped unnoticed under some cots and required scrubbing. Violet did so without thinking about what she might be touching. She had grown used to the smell of blood. It was only when she had finished and changed her apron that she stared down at the soiled garment, her soiled hands.

Captain Hendry had stayed in his bed for the rest of the day. He hadn't eaten, leaving his turnip soup untouched. Knowing he'd recently had a parcel from home, Violet had offered to open the brown wrapping and take out some cake to supplement his meal, but Hendry had not opened his eyes and ignored her. She was sure he was not asleep.

She could see his shape from the garden, rigid under a white sheet. 'What do you make of what happened today?' she asked quietly.

Cecilia tapped her mug. 'I think Hendry gets worse.'

'His mind has been damaged.'

'Yes.' Cecilia sighed and sat back in her chair.

'Why did you tell me not to say anything about Shacklock being my father?'

Cecilia shrugged simply. 'Not wise to tell a secret like that to someone who is angry with you.'

Violet thought. 'But he thinks we're lovers, the bishop and I. It's so absurd!' Laughter. 'If only he knew.'

'Cecilia is right, though.' A voice cut through the growing dark. Bishop Shacklock appeared between their chairs, wearing his usual black trousers and a clean grey shirt. His clothes had become soiled during the day—the work had been heavy going and he had lifted many men onto the lorries. Even now, a few hours later, he was flushed and pushed his shoulders back and forth, stretching out his back. 'So you told your friend about us.'

His voice was level but firm and Violet looked at him. She couldn't be sure if he was angry or not.

'I did,' she said eventually. 'Cecilia won't tell anyone.'

Cecilia nodded, the mug of tea pressed against her lips. 'Do you want to sit?'

Shacklock looked at the Frenchwoman for a long moment, as though he were sizing her up. Cecilia kept her face set and still, and eventually the bishop shook his head. 'No, thank you. Do you know anything of Hendry's father?'

'Nothing,' Violet said. 'Only what you told me—that he's some rich fellow who is well connected.'

'Exactly.' Shacklock's agitation seemed to overwhelm him. He rubbed his unshaven chin and came around the front of their chairs to face Violet and Cecilia. 'That's what worries me.'

'What can he do?' Violet said. 'Clearly Hendry is unwell. Anyone can see that it's ridiculous to think there's anything between us. Like that, I mean. Hendry must have seen you put your arm around me during the storm, that's all. Look, even if he does go running to his daddy, it can be explained away.'

'I hope so.' The bishop exhaled nosily. 'But I'm not convinced. Do you know when he's arriving?'

'Soon, perhaps tomorrow,' said Cecilia. 'The matron has asked that we find somewhere for him to stay in town. Somewhere suitable for a man of his wealth.' She snorted. 'I was going to ask a friend of my father's if he'll put him up. I can't imagine he'd want to sleep above a barber's shop.'

'We don't have long, then.' Shacklock started to pace the grass. His boots left heavy prints. 'Violet, you'll have to talk to Hendry. He won't listen to me.'

Violet stared at him. 'Are you serious? What good would it do? Hendry's not in his right mind—nothing I say would get through.'

'But you have to try. Tell him there's nothing between us, not the way he thinks.'

'Why? It won't do any good.'

'You have to try!' Shacklock spun to face the women in the chairs, shocking them with the strength of his shout. He rubbed his chin again and crouched down so he was at their eye level. 'I'm sorry. But it is important. Hendry must understand there is nothing improper between us and he mustn't find out that you are my daughter.'

Violet watched the man rocking on his heels before her, taking in the scuff of his hair, the flush on his skin that she saw now was not down to the heat. 'Why does it have to be such a secret, anyway?' she asked quietly. 'Why can't I tell anyone about us? It's not like you aren't allowed to get married and have children.'

'I didn't imagine you would be so foolish.' Shacklock stood up again, his knees creaking. Cecilia tucked her feet under her chair as he began to walk up and down again. 'If word was to get back to my ministry about you, I would be asked where your mother is. Why we weren't married. I'd be told to leave. I'd have to give everything up.'

'Except for me, though. You wouldn't have to give me up.' Violet kept her gaze on his face. 'We could start to get to know each other, after all this time. Doesn't that count for anything?'

'Of course, but … you don't understand.'

'No, I think I do.' Violet looked over her shoulder at the sleeping men. Some were snoring lightly, others moaning. 'I wonder if the families who wait for these men would give up their child for anything. Or anyone.'

'That's not fair.' Shacklock came to stand in front of Violet again. 'You have no idea of how difficult it was to leave your mother. You have no idea of the pain of leaving a child behind.'

'No, I don't.' Violet put down her mug and stood up, waving away Cecilia's concerned look. She felt on the verge of tears. Then she turned around slowly. 'What do you mean?'

'What?' Shacklock was agitated again.

'How do you know what it's like to abandon a child? You didn't even know about me until I arrived here. You didn't know my mother was pregnant when you left—she never told you. So what did you mean?'

'I don't follow.'

'You said I had no idea how painful it is to leave a child. You obviously do—how is that?' Violet cocked her head, as though listening to a distant drum. '*How is that*? Were there others?'

'I don't know what you are talking about.'

'Do you have other children? Did you leave them as well, just as you left my mother?'

Shacklock's body seemed to tremble, as though a current was being passed through it. He swallowed and looked between the two women, between the young girl white with shock and the older Frenchwoman, who was leaning forward in her chair, her soft mouth falling open.

~ 47 ~

Present Day

'Yes, she was called Violet. My aunt was her friend.' Felicity said Violet Underwood's name so simply and easily. The old lady smiled as she spoke, nodding almost to herself, and took a sip of coffee. She replaced the mug on the table, eyes shining brightly, and looked from Jess to Billy, and back to Jess again.

It came in a rush—Jess burst into tears. They came too quickly for her to stop them; she touched her face shakily, as though she could not believe what was happening to her body, but the tears continued to fall. They slid down past her lips and down onto her T-shirt. She fumbled in her pockets for a tissue and found nothing. Christophe Deniel reached behind him to the kitchen counter and handed her a roll of paper towels. He continued to smoke as Jess wiped her face.

Billy stared at his friend. His own face was pink. He patted Jess's hand awkwardly. 'She's been searching for a name for a long time,' he said to Felicity apologetically.

'Six years,' Jess said and blew her nose. She tried to control herself. But memories of days spent alone in the Shacklock archives and stacks, rummaging through boxes of dry, boring papers overwhelmed her and she cried again. She thought of her own research, long since abandoned, and saw the names of forgotten church women stretching back into history in a sad, unimportant line. Waller, with his demands and blue trousers, and the way he would phone at weekends when she and Alec were out with the kids. She thought of how she had come to hate the nameless skeleton, even though she was angered at the way the woman's body had been desecrated and a bone removed, simply so a man could order tests and make a name for himself. And Jess felt fresh shame at her own sneering, dismissive reaction to the skeleton. *The*

Cuckoo. Waller's bit on the side. All the snide comments she had made in the past to Marie and Alec—they were laid bare in front of a little old lady from Villers-des-Champs, and Jess felt humiliated.

Felicity looked on, the smile never leaving her face. A buckled claw reached out and touched Jess's arm. She said nothing but Jess took her hand gently and let the comfort warm her through. After a while the crying stopped. Billy touched her back cautiously, and Jess knew the effort that must have taken. So she sat up, swallowed hard, and took a notepad from her bag.

'I'm sorry. Tell us what you know. Please,' she said. 'It's a story we've waited to hear for so long.'

'Let me tell you about Cecilia first,' Felicity said. Her cheeks were as rosy as apples. She had a small dimple that appeared on the side of her mouth when she spoke and Jess could see the old woman had once been attractive; she imagined a man longing to touch that dimple, to press his thumb down onto it.

'I'd like to hear about her,' Jess said.

'Cecilia was my aunt,' Felicity went on. 'My mother's sister. My mother was several years younger than Cecilia. I think my mother was not—*planned*, is that what you say? She was an unexpected child, so I think my grandparents spoiled my mother. And spoiled people are never understanding. She never met *him*,' and she pointed to her son, 'because I was not married to his father. When she discovered I was pregnant, she made me leave home. Cecilia took me in. She seemed an old lady, even then.'

Jess nodded, encouraging her to go on.

'Cecilia had never married either.' Felicity's dimpled mouth rolled up into a scowl of sorts. 'She lived with a woman when I was young.' She glared at Jess and Billy, as though daring them to speak up, to offer some kind of judgement or challenge. Jess wondered if the old lady had been forced to defend her aunt before; her readiness to do so again was apparent in the tick at her jaw. But Jess and Billy said nothing and Felicity, seemingly mollified, went on. 'She worked. Always working. After the war she became a translator, helping the recovery. She did some work for your British government when the time came to build the cemeteries. So many of them! Have you seen them?'

'Some,' Billy said. 'On school trips.'

'You should go.' Felicity poked at him. 'They surround this place.'

'We will.' Billy cleared his throat and glanced surreptitiously at Jess. 'Ah, Cecilia?'

'She taught me English,' Felicity began again. 'A great gift, you understand? After Christophe was born, I was able to work in Abbeville in insurance. I tried to teach him the language, but he was too lazy!'

It was obviously an old joke and Christophe shrugged easily. He took another pull on his cigarette.

'Cecilia had a brother who died early on in the war.' Felicity reached down and produced a small bag. She pulled out a bundle of old photographs and laid them out on the table. She pointed at an image of a slim, uniformed man, staring vacantly into the camera. 'That's him. My mother's brother. My mother was too young to be involved in the war. But Cecilia volunteered at the hospital.'

'We found her registration card in the town archives,' Billy said. 'It said Cecilia worked at the hospital from 1916 to 1918.'

'That sounds right,' Felicity agreed. 'She wasn't a nurse but did other work, like many of the other local women. Washing, cleaning, at first. Changing dressings. Then she picked up some skills and assisted the doctors and nurses. Cecilia said she used to hold the men down when they packed salt into their wounds—can you imagine?'

'It was a different time,' Jess said quietly.

'It was, but such treatment … pain doesn't change, does it?' Felicity sniffed and then kicked out a purple court shoe, catching her son's ankle. 'Manners, eh? I'll have one of those things. Maybe our guests will, too.'

Christophe Deniel raised his eyebrows but reached for the pack of cigarillos in his shirt pocket. His mother took one. Billy shook his head and Jess, hesitating for a second, accepted one. Christophe then leant around the table, lighter flicking on and off.

Felicity filled her lungs with smoke, her chest crackling, and blew blue clouds up to the ceiling. 'Cecilia said there were hundreds of men who came through the hospital. They were passed back from the front lines as Villers was supposed to be safe. It was, mostly. Not many shells fell here. The men who could be healed were stitched back together and sent to the Front again. When there was an offensive, almost too many men would arrive for the nurses to cope.'

'When did Cecilia meet Violet?' Billy asked, unable to wait any longer.

Felicity glared at him and again Jess could see the type of woman she had once been. The little old lady hunched her shoulders in, making her shape narrow like a dart. Smaller, but no less determined. She took another deliberate puff on the cigarette.

'Before I go on,' she said, staring at Billy, 'I want you to understand that Cecilia was a good woman. She had courage. It is important you know that.'

'Of course,' Billy nodded.

'No.' Felicity scowled across the table. Her bent fingers made some kind of fist in his direction. 'You must not judge her. Remember, as she said,' and Felicity's hand swivelled to jab towards Jess, 'it was a very different time.'

Billy glanced at Jess and back to Felicity, his confusion apparent. Jess, too, had been taken aback by Felicity's sudden change of mood and sternness.

'Felicity, we're here to listen,' she said softly, hoping her sincerity sounded through. 'Please, just tell us what you know.'

~ 48 ~

September 1917

'There *was* another child.' Bishop Shacklock's voice came with a great rendering, as though it was being torn from his throat.

'Another?' Violet found her seat again, hands shaking. Cecilia reached over and took her friend's fingers in her own.

The bishop had now sat down on the grass. His body was curled upon itself, shoulders slumped, knees up. He was not a tall man; he took up only a small space. With his head bowed almost to his chest, he spoke, the words sounding as though they had been pulled from the earth.

'Constance. Josiah's wife. Your grandmother. We knew each other before she married your grandfather.'

'I never met her,' Violet said.

'No, you told me that.' Shacklock had not lifted his head, but the sounds he made, and the muffled, halting noises that seemed to come from deep within, told the women he was crying. 'Until those months when I saw her again in Greece, we hadn't spoken for over twenty years.'

'You met my mother in Greece.'

'Yes.' And then, 'Twenty years before meeting Allegra, Constance and I had a child.'

The shock was great and Violet felt Cecilia's hands automatically squeeze down on hers. Violet blinked, lights dancing at the edge of her sight, and for a second she wondered if this was what it felt like for the soldiers as they prepared to go over the top: the alertness, the sense of being on the edge of a terrible moment.

~ 49 ~

'Shacklock had another child?' Jess touched her forehead. She looked at Billy, seeing her shock mirrored on his face. Billy had gasped and was shaking his head. The light emitted by the single bulb above their heads glinted off the top of his ears.

'Yes. Violet was not the only one.' Felicity tapped her cigarillo on the ashtray. Her movements were dainty yet deliberate. For a brief second, Jess had an image of the old woman, young again, sitting in a street café in a bombed out town, daring to wear bright colours against a grey choke of dust. 'She had come out to France to find her father, to find she was not the only child he had abandoned.'

'Cecilia heard all this? The bishop's confession?' Billy was now making notes on his pad, his hand moving rapidly across the page.

'Confession? Yes, it was, rather.' Felicity showed the glitter of white dentures. 'He probably thought that secret would never come out.'

'You don't have a high opinion of him,' Billy said.

'Cecilia didn't. I didn't know him.'

'Wait a minute.' Jess pulled her notes from her bag. She produced her dog-eared notebook and flicked through the pages, looking past the first notes she made about her discovery in the Synod papers at the Shacklock Library and the bishop's letter to his sister she had located at the British Library. Then the jottings she had made from her time at Threadstone Hall. She found the place and pointed down at the writing. 'Yes, Constance had a baby before she married Josiah.'

'And the baby died. Cecilia told me the bishop was crouched down on the ground when he told Violet all of this. Rolled up into a little ball.' Felicity sniffed, her disdain clear. 'Such an important man, reduced to curling up like a child.'

'Did Shacklock ever tell Josiah about his being the father?' Jess asked, the question posed of Billy. 'Did Constance?'

Billy stopped scribbling. 'Remember, there was the split between Shacklock and Josiah. It was after Josiah left the seminary to marry Constance. We couldn't understand why such good friends would stop speaking to each other.'

'Yes, it seemed at odds with what we knew about Shacklock. He seemed so progressive—all those efforts he made on behalf of the unmarried mothers in his parish. Why would he reject his friend simply because Josiah chose to marry?' Jess patted her hand on the notepad. 'But we know why now—Josiah was taking on the child and marrying the woman Shacklock had had a relationship with. Probably without knowing the bishop was the baby's father.'

Billy whistled through his teeth. 'What everyone thought they knew about Shacklock—all those Americans who revered him and brought his body back to Jedthorpe—it's not true, is it?'

'Oh, I think it is.' Jess thought of her hunt through the volumes of the bishop's letters, how he petitioned for assistance for the poor, how he fought for funds for the orphans in his parish. The unassailable way Shacklock pitched into a debate with politicians about the closure of a school or the reduction of wages in the town's mills. His way with words and the calm yet brutal way he dismantled the pompous and overblown. *A piddling baptismal cup. The egg-snatcher.* The reluctant fondness Jess felt for the bishop clung to her heart with spikey fingers. 'Shacklock did many fine things. But there's another layer to him.'

'Yes.' Felicity finished her cigarillo and, for a second, seemed far away. 'We are all complicated, are we not?'

'So there was another child, before Violet.' Jess nodded encouragingly, ready to hear more. 'And what else?'

~ 50 ~

September 1917

A shout from inside the hospital; a soldier disturbed by a dream. His yelp carried far into the warm night and the small knot of people sitting in the garden heard hurried footsteps and soothing sounds. A moment passed, and the man settled down again, having been hushed back towards sleep.

Silence, too, among those on the grass. Violet gazed down at the brown scrub, burnt by the unrelenting sun until the garden was now not much more than rough carpet, sharp to the touch. Even the recent rain had failed to replenish and bring forth new shoots. The bishop stayed cross-legged on the ground.

Eventually Cecilia spoke, to ask about the baby. What had happened to it?

'She died,' Shacklock said quietly. 'Before Constance and Josiah left for Greece. She was only a few months old.'

'Did my father know? She would be—what, his half-sister?' Violet felt a tug of longing for Edward, and then, strongly, for her mother. She thought of how frantic Allegra must be, how worried she must be for her absent daughter.

'No one knew I was the father. Only Constance and I. I asked her not to tell anyone when she first told me a child was coming. It would have spelled the end of my career in the church. I think she was reluctant to keep the secret at first. Maybe she had other hopes for us. But when she met Josiah, she asked me to keep it a secret, too.' Shacklock raised his head, a sad smile on his lips. 'We both had our reasons to hide what had happened.'

There was another sound in the hospital behind them and the group paused, looking again. A scrape, a dragging noise. Someone pulling a bed across the floor, possibly.

Violet shivered suddenly. A chill came from nowhere and she felt a great weariness. So many secrets, so many versions of history. Her mother had lied to her about her real father, as had the man she had called 'father' for all of her short life. Her grandmother, whom she had never met and barely thought of until now, had carried the secret of a child without breathing a word. And there was the bishop, weighted down by another life he kept from view.

She was trembling, she could not stop. Cecilia rose and wrapped an arm around her. The Frenchwoman leant into her, concern apparent. 'I will fetch you a blanket.' Cecilia slipped across the grass towards the hospital.

Her absence left a gap that Violet felt keenly. She looked after her friend, trying to make out her shape in the dark, but Cecilia was gone. Violet's mouth became flooded with hot, wet worry. She felt on the edge of a precipice; Shacklock's admission had swept the fragile footing from beneath her. Again, what little she thought she knew of him was upended and shown to be false.

Yet, when she turned back to him, she saw how his face had stilled and his body had uncurled a little, opening out to her. She resented him for it, sensing that by talking about his lost child he had felt a stone loosen about his neck and slip away from his body. Now that stone had rolled to her and sat in her lap.

Another noise and this time Violet craned to see into the dark. They were far enough away from the chateau to be outside the rim of light that fell from the windows, though sounds continued to carry in the soft night air. Violet thought she heard a cough and a moan. Then nothing.

'Have you heard from your mother?' Shacklock asked quietly. He was now sitting back on the grass, leaning on hands thrown behind him.

'She wouldn't know where to find me.'

'Ah. Of course. Is it so important she doesn't know where you are?'

Violet looked at the man on the ground before her; his frayed, grey shirt untucked, his black hair still damp from the day's work, his thick arms roped with veins—and felt hatred for him, strong enough to catch the breath in her throat. She saw that he had no idea what it felt like to have someone to belong to him, to be responsible for a child's comfort, safety, its life. Violet's contempt for him sloshed inside and she felt giddy because of it.

Since Allegra had revealed her terrible secret all that time ago, Violet had been buffeted by a crash and surge of emotion. At first she had loathed her mother for keeping such a revelation from her, and had made sure she covered her tracks on her journey out to France—she did not want the woman who had fostered such lies to follow her. When she left England her thoughts about her mother were sure—she did not want to see Allegra's face again. And with that certainty came the inward rage that she had not realised the truth for herself—Violet looked nothing like Edward, after all. And then came the emptying, when anger faded away and was replaced with only numbness, to the extent that there were times, in recent weeks, when Violet had moved through the beds in the hospital silently, like a ghost.

Yet Violet did not know how to say any of these things. Instead she stared at the bishop, hoping a spark of the feelings slopping about inside her would somehow burst out and pierce his eye, prompting tears, forcing its way into his body. But Shacklock stared right back, bewildered and, if Violet was not mistaken, a little angry.

And then there was a movement to the side, just by Violet's chair and her head snapped round. It was not Cecilia, as she expected. It was not Cecilia with a brown blanket in her hands, ready to tuck it around the shoulders of her friend. Instead it was Captain Hendry, leaning heavily on a crutch. In his free hand he held a large knife, the sort used by the doctor when amputating a poor, unfortunate man's limb.

~ 51 ~

Present Day

Jess's hand paused in mid-air, just as she was about to accept another cigarillo from Christophe Deniel. She looked at Felicity, eyes wide. 'Hendry? Hendry had a knife?'

Felicity nodded. She had talked without pause for some time, not hurriedly, but with the air of someone determined to get to the end of her tale. Now, with Jess's interruption, she took a smoke from the packet offered to her by her son and leant back in her chair. Jess noted again how the old woman smoked, savouring each mouthful as though it would be her last.

'You know this name,' Felicity said, offering a statement of fact. 'You do not ask who Hendry is. You knew about him already.'

'We found a reference in the Villers town archives that said Violet looked after a Captain Hendry,' Billy explained, though his face appeared as shocked as Jess's. 'There was nothing else in the records about Violet, but the matron's treatment book said Violet spent time with him.'

'It also said that Hendry had become rather attached to her,' Jess said, remembering.

'Yes.' Felicity turned to her son. 'Do you have cognac? Now would be a good time, I think.'

Christophe turned his mouth upside down in a kind of nonchalant acquiescence and got up, walking across the room to a small cabinet. He returned with four tumblers, each of different sizes, and a bottle of Courvoisier. He half-filled each one, passing the largest glass to his mother and indicating to Jess and Billy they should help themselves.

Felicity took a deep sip from hers and sighed before beginning again. 'Captain Hendry had been at the chateau for some time before Violet arrived. He'd lost a foot to shrapnel and Cecilia said he'd nearly died from a secondary infection. There was also some exposure to gas.'

'Mustard gas?' Jess asked, thinking back to the documentaries she had watched with Alec, and the way survivors had described the scrabble for their masks at the first sight of a yellow cloud drifting across the mud towards them.

Felicity shrugged. 'Who knows? But he behaved oddly. Maybe there was something else—what do you call it, when the mind is affected?'

'Shell shock,' Billy said quietly.

'Yes. Violet read to him many times—Cecilia said she used to do that for the men and write their letters home. Lots of the women did, so Violet wasn't unusual. But Hendry became obsessed with her. He grabbed her once. Cecilia saw the marks on her arm after—he'd cut her skin with his fingernails.'

'Do you know anything about him? Who Hendry was before the war?' Jess asked.

'Cecilia was told he was from a wealthy family. His father was something to do with the War Office. He had influence. I don't know anything more.' Felicity took another long drag on her cigarillo again and then swilled the smoke around her mouth with a gulp of cognac. 'Other than this: the matron told Cecilia that Hendry's family didn't want him to come home until they had made arrangements for him. They paid for someone to fix him a new foot. Cecilia got the impression they were embarrassed at the thought of a crippled son.'

Jess thought of the documentaries again and of the old black and white images of lines of men, hobbling on sticks, an empty trouser leg pinned up. A procession of invalids. They had paid for the war with their body and some were thanked with stares and shock. And she remembered the documentaries speak of marriages failing after the men returned home; violence in the home where before there had been love.

'What did Hendry do to Violet?' she asked, wanting and not wanting to hear the answer.

~ 52 ~

In the fading light, Shacklock had not noticed the knife in Hendry's hand. Instead he offered a tentative smile to the soldier and slowly got to his feet. 'Captain. Could you not sleep?'

Violet, staring at the knife, pressed herself back in her seat, pushing her thin shoulders against the armchair's high back. She breathed in quickly, small gulps of air. Hendry moved closer to Shacklock and Violet saw the knife swing a little, a fat silver strip with a black handle.

Hendry did not respond to the bishop's question. Instead he raised his arm and Shacklock then saw what he held. The bishop took a step back.

'What do you have that for?' he said quietly, hands held out in front. Supplicating.

Hendry remained silent and, nearer to him than Shacklock, Violet smelled the dank odour from the man's body. It reminded her of washing that had been left wet for too long, or boiled cabbage—a fetid smell that, when her mother had been too busy to rewash the sheets, seemed to cling to the cloth and Violet's skin. She wondered how long Hendry had gone without a wipe with a sponge. She imagined staleness creeping into his pores until it became an immutable part of his skin.

He had yet to look at her. Instead his eyes bored into the bishop's face, so Violet was free at that moment to take him in, to see every aspect. The night seemed to draw around them, pulling the three into a bubble, distinct and separate from the rest of the world. Time slowed; the smallest details bloomed large. Violet saw that Hendry's hands were long and smooth, that his knuckles were overlarge pebbles on the splinters of his fingers. She saw his blue pyjamas and the thickness of his dressing gown. She felt and heard the heat of the evening, her ears becoming funnels for noise and sound. More than anything, though, what she could not hear was the footsteps of others. She could not hear Cecilia, Matron, the other women, pattering over the grass to where she sat. She could not hear, but wanted to hear, their shouts and calls to Hendry, and the doctor running with a needle.

Hendry raised the knife higher, so that it was levelled at Shacklock's chest. And then, almost sleepily, Hendry began to speak.

'I know men like you. How long did you wait for your chance with her? While we lay in beds around you, damaged by a war in which you are too old to fight?' Hendry turned the knife, rotating his wrist so that Violet, making herself small on the armchair, saw pink scars criss-crossing the smooth flesh of his inner arm.

'*Captain.*' Shacklock took another step back while emphasising the soldier's rank. 'You have misunderstood us. That's my fault, I know. I am to blame for that. Please, put the knife down and we will talk.'

Hendry did not put the knife down. Instead, he smiled and pushed the knife closer to the bishop, his arm stretching into the gap between them. A thin stream of liquid stained his trousers and Violet watched it pool at his feet. Steam rose from the grass. Hendry did not seem to notice that he had soiled himself.

'Captain, please.' Shacklock spread his fingers, pushing his palms outwards. But he took no further step back. 'Put the knife down.'

'Have you noticed how they arrange the beds in there?' Hendry did not point but Violet knew he was talking about the hospital. 'Nice, orderly lines. No space between the men. Regimented.'

'It has to be that way. There are so many of you.'

'Aren't there? But at least we're alive. Lucky, isn't it?'

Shacklock said nothing. He did not look at the knife and avoided Violet's gaze. She wondered if he hoped Hendry had forgotten about her.

'Our bodies might be broken but not one of us would push aside a fellow soldier. Not like you. Bishop. You are not one of us.'

'The girl is not a trophy,' Shacklock muttered. He edged closer, back towards Hendry.

Violet, watching with wide eyes, shook her head frantically. *What are you doing?*

'*The girl is not a trophy,*' Hendry repeated mockingly. 'What have you promised her? What can you give her that I can't?'

'Captain, it isn't like that between us. Violet and I are not involved.'

It was a mistake to say Violet's name, and the bishop realised this almost immediately. Hendry's face tightened, his lips almost disappeared and his fingers flexed around the blade. A ripple seemed to pass through his body. 'Why should I believe you?'

'Sir, it is the truth. Please, put the knife down.'

Hendry shook his head. Instead he turned his wrist slightly, angling the tip of the blade at the area around the bishop's heart. From the burrows of her chair, Violet heard him sigh and then take in a deep mouthful of air.

Then she saw a hand reach out, thin and white and dotted with pink burn marks from the aggressive hospital stove; fingers moved slowly and Violet watched, entranced, as they made their tremulous way through the night air, fingertips twitching and fumbling. They were reaching for something—the only thing could be Hendry. Violet, heart rising in her throat, screamed silently to take care, to be careful, to go carefully. But the hand continued on its timid path and then, finally, delicately, connected with its target. The hand wrapped around Hendry's wrist, the one twisting the knife. The strange white fingers did not squeeze or hold tightly but the touch was firm and real. And Violet knew this because she was standing and, to her amazement, realised that the hand was hers, that she had reached out and touched Hendry. That she was trying to take the knife from him.

It was as much a surprise to her as it was to the captain—she saw the shock in his eyes when he swung round and the blade caught her across the throat.

~ 53 ~

After Felicity told them about the knife and Violet trying to take it from Hendry, the group sat in silence. There was not a sound in Christophe Deniel's kitchen; Jess, trembling, felt as though they had all dived underwater. The room closed in so that the world outside seemed far away. She wondered if Violet had experienced such a feeling when her throat was cut by Hendry; if she felt her life slip away, if the light faded away gradually or in a rush. And she wondered if Hendry himself felt disconnected during the act, or if he'd been lost to the world of reality a long time before. The effects of gas were so misunderstood at that time, and so unknown.

'Cecilia was in the hospital when it happened,' Felicity said eventually. She smoothed down her already perfect hair. 'Violet had been trembling, she'd said. Probably from the news about Shacklock's other, secret daughter, but Cecilia went to fetch her a blanket. She was lucky. She might have been killed as well.'

'What happened to Violet?' Billy asked.

'Why, she died, of course.' Felicity's eyes were wide, and she appeared incredulous. 'Cecilia was coming across the lawn when she saw Hendry stab the bishop in the back. He was leaning over Violet, trying to stop the blood.'

Jess closed her eyes momentarily, imagining the scene. She hoped, fervently, that Violet's life bled out gently, and that she sleepily made her way towards death.

'Hendry killed them both?' she said.

'He did. And Cecilia ran for Matron and the doctors, and they came out. There was nothing they could do. Violet was gone already and the bishop's wounds were too deep. The knife had entered his neck.'

'What happened to Hendry?'

'Cecilia said she was worried they would have to disarm him and that someone else might have been hurt, but Hendry just sat down on the grass, handed over the knife and started to sing.'

'Sing?' Billy was shocked.

'That's what she said. She couldn't make out what he was singing, but it was something she'd heard the soldiers sing in the hospital from time to time. A song from the trenches.'

'Hendry killed them both,' Jess said softly. 'What a complete tragedy.'

'Very much so.' This was from Christophe Deniel, his only words so far.

Felicity looked hard at her son and Jess wondered how often they had discussed this topic before. An old, worn tension seemed to creep between the two French people, the air turning on the cogs of a familiar disagreement. Sensitive to these emotions, Jess wondered what the disagreement had been about.

Felicity gave her an indication with her next words. 'Cecilia did not want to be part of what happened afterwards.'

'What *did* happen afterwards?' Billy asked.

There was a pause before Felicity spoke again and a look passed between mother and son. Jess became more certain a disagreement had occurred between them. Her curiosity grew, but she waited, hoping the thread would be picked up again, unaided and unforced.

'Hendry's father was a powerful man, remember,' Felicity said, sighing. 'Those in charge of the hospital had little option but to follow his instructions.'

'Which were?'

'To cover it up,' Christophe Deniel broke in. His heavy, smoky frame shifted on his seat. 'What is it called—whitewash?'

'Whitewash,' Billy echoed, nodding. 'Is that what happened?'

'Hendry's father arrived at the hospital the next day,' Felicity said. 'His son had been sedated and moved to a side room where a doctor stayed with him the whole time. Shacklock and Violet were moved to an outhouse.'

'An outhouse?' Jess said faintly.

'It was thought the men would become too distressed if they knew what happened,' Felicity said. 'The bishop was popular, he'd counselled many of them. Violet, too, I understand. She was sweet and kind.'

Christophe sniffed and muttered something in French. Felicity looked at him sharply and then shrugged. 'He thinks the doctor's desire to protect the men and hide what happened played into the hands of Hendry's father. He's probably right.'

'I cannot bear to think of them left in an outhouse,' Jess said. She blinked several times and swallowed back fresh tears. She had seen no sign of an outhouse on her walk that morning up to the derelict chateau but she could just picture it: an old lean-to, roof beams broken and twisted, offering no protection to the bodies placed underneath. What would they have lain on? The bare earth? Would they have been covered over, given a little privacy and respect? She wiped her nose. 'I can't understand how this was kept a secret. We're talking about murder, at the end of the day. Two people were killed—how can that be covered up?'

'Cecilia,' Billy said suddenly. 'She was involved, wasn't she?'

He looked at Felicity, who held his gaze haughtily for a moment and then, as with her son, averted her eyes. Jess felt sympathy for the woman who obviously adored her aunt, but was faced with the unpalatable truth of what her aunt had done.

'She did, that's true,' Felicity said. 'But she was forced. It was not her choice.'

'How did they make her?' Billy asked.

'They knew about the women. She had a lover in town. It would have been a scandal then.' Felicity shifted in her chair, her discomfort at the turn of the conversation apparent. 'It isn't like now, where all kinds of people strike up friendships. Men and men, women and women. Cecilia thought she had been discreet but someone knew. Someone always knows.'

'What did they have her do?' said Jess.

'She was to tell the nurses that Violet had gone home. She was made to remove all references to Violet from the hospital records. Hendry's father was insistent upon that. He wanted to destroy all evidence that Violet had even been there.'

'So if anyone came looking for her, they wouldn't discover she had been at the hospital and they couldn't link her to Hendry,' Billy said. 'Covers all bases.'

'That's right.' Felicity refilled her glass with cognac and then, shakily, slopped more into the remaining three glasses on the table. 'But they couldn't do so for the bishop, of course. He had too much influence. Too much of a presence. He had been at the hospital for over a year— he'd written letters to his parish and others. So they said he had died unexpectedly. Heart attack.'

'And buried him in the churchyard, Violet with him,' Billy said, his voice twisted by anger. 'Her mother searched for her. She gave up her business, everything, to try to find her daughter. She died without ever knowing what had happened.'

Felicity held out her hands warily. 'My aunt had no choice. If she hadn't done it, someone else would have, and her reputation would have been destroyed anyway. And what was a woman, then, without a reputation?'

'It must have troubled Cecilia, though,' Jess said. 'Enough for her to tell you.'

'Yes.' Felicity offered a slight smile to her son. '*He* thinks the same as your friend: that Cecilia should have done something. That she should have spoken up, even years later. Maybe she would have, but the men came and took the bishop's body away after the war ended. What do you say—the window closed? Cecilia tried to put it behind her. Move on.'

'When did she tell you all this?' Jess asked.

'About six months before she died. She had cancer, of the throat. I think she was afraid she would never get the chance again.'

Christophe Deniel coughed. 'She wrote it down.'

'There's a written record of this?' Billy said, eyes wide with hope. 'Is it dated?'

'Yes, and yes.' Sadness settled into the lines creasing Felicity's face. 'My aunt wrote a letter a few weeks before she died in '59. I think she wanted to leave evidence behind about what had happened. In case someone eventually came looking for Violet.'

'Can we see the letter?' Billy said urgently. Jess nudged him under the table—*patience*—but Billy was too excited to care.

There was a long moment of silence and then Felicity turned back to her son. She nodded, a tight look passing her face, and Christophe Deniel reached inside his shirt. From an inside pocket he pulled out a torn, brown envelope and, through a gap in the covering, Jess could make out a sheet of paper, covered in tiny, neat French handwriting, and a bundle of registration cards, identical to the cards kept in the Villers town archives.

∽

'Is this what shock feels like?' Billy said. They were outside in the small garden at the back of his cottage. It was bitterly cold, and they stood beside a wrought iron stove, the type used to offer heat to those who lingered late outside on a summer evening. Billy had lit a small fire inside the stove, using firewood he'd found in the shed. His hands had been trembling throughout and Jess had to help him strike the matches. In the end she gave up and lit a piece of paper with her cigarette lighter.

They both huddled deep into their coats and clutched a mug of coffee. But, despite the cold, neither felt like sitting in Billy's kitchen or the cramped living area, the revelations they had heard earlier seemed to expand within them. It was news to take them outside, despite the biting weather.

They had left Cecilia's letter on the kitchen table. Neither had mentioned it while the fire was lit and the coffee was made. Then they stood outside, blinking into the freezing air, watching white clouds spiral from their mouths as they spoke.

Billy's eyes were too bright, and he looked as though he might vomit. But he gamely held it in check and sipped his coffee instead. Although she also felt bludgeoned by Felicity's revelations, Billy's reaction had taken Jess by surprise; she had not taken the news as physically. The truth was she felt numb and detached, and thought maybe her earlier tears in Christophe Deniel's flat had emptied her of all emotion.

Felicity Deniel had also seemed to deflate after finishing her story. Soon after handing over Cecilia's letter for the researchers to read, the old lady had sagged forward, alarmingly so, her clawed hands knocking her cognac glass. But she insisted she was well; she waved away Jess's concern, though she did allow her son to assist her to the small couch and protested only slightly when Christophe swung her legs around onto the cushions.

'The weight of secrets,' Felicity had said with forced joviality, though her eyes were closing when Jess and Billy left. Jess lingered as long as she could, unable to stop watching the weary old lady who had protected her aunt's name for the past fifty years.

'The first thing we should do is get Cecilia's letter properly translated,' Jess said as a piece of wood snapped and an orange flame licked around the side of the stove. 'We might be able to find someone in town who will do it for us.'

'And then we tell Waller,' Billy said grimly, though there was a hint of satisfaction in his voice.

Jess had to smile. She imagined Professor Waller's face when they arrived back at the Shacklock Library, their notes written up, a paper proposal finalised. His flaccid grey mouth would gape open; he would rock incredulously on his ridiculously squeaky shoes. She wondered if he would remove his glasses at the nose and rub his face in that exasperated way of his.

Or maybe she would tell him over the phone. Maybe she would make a call from the coast before they boarded the ferry, spelling out their terms should he wish to be involved in their announcement. A permanent research position for both she and Billy, with work of their own choosing. A pay rise. Possibly an office of their own, away from the other researchers and students. Waller's own office would be vacant soon, given his impending retirement. That would be just perfect.

Jess's grin widened and the first tendrils of euphoria at what they had discovered began to creep in. She felt her heart lighten and the queasy sensation that had lingered in her stomach since she left Hayden on the bridge earlier that day eased off. But she stayed cautious. Six years had been a long time to devote to one topic—more for Waller, she acknowledged—and she was wary of soaking herself in happiness.

'We might be able to wrap this up and go home in a couple of days,' Billy said. He stared into the fire. 'Gemma would like that.'

Jess thought of Alec, caring for their children in their shared home while she was away. What would it mean to him if she returned sooner than expected? Would it mean nothing, apart from an earlier trip back to his parents' house, where he would lie down on the narrow, single bed he'd had from boyhood? Would he dress himself in the pyjamas his mother laid out, even though he'd slept naked for the last twenty years, and would he sit at the breakfast table with his parents, avoiding a discussion about what he was going to do about his broken family?

Suddenly, strongly, Jess longed for her husband and to feel his thin, dry fingers curl around her own.

'Yes, it would be good to get back home,' she said and when Billy raised his eyebrows, she knew what he was thinking. *Hayden.*

∽

The downstairs lights in the cottage were off when Jess let herself back in after spending an hour in Billy's back garden. She was shivering, frozen to the core, and the warmth of the radiators felt damp and only made her hands tingle. She held her hands above the heater, squinting to make out the furniture in the dark room. There was a glow around the bottom stair: Hayden was up there.

He was packing. A suitcase was open on the bed and he was frowning into it, a folded shirt in his hand. His back was to Jess; he spun around when he heard her foot in the doorway. Music thrummed from his laptop beside the bed.

'I'm getting a train to Calais,' he said after a pause.

'A train?'

'You and Billy will need the car.'

'Oh.' Jess stepped into the room. She looked redundantly at the empty wardrobe and the pile of clothes on the floor. 'When?'

'Tomorrow morning.'

'Right.' The music stopped and then started up again, a light dance track she had not heard before. A need to say something boiled up in her chest. 'We found out who she was. The woman.'

Hayden dropped the shirt into the suitcase. He looked tired and Jess wondered if he would ask, if he would want to know who she was, who the woman was who had shadowed Jess's life for the last six years. If he would care.

But then Hayden smiled. 'Who was she?'

'Violet, as we thought. That's what we've been doing today, finding out what happened. She was killed by a soldier who suffered from shell shock.'

'And the bishop?'

'He was killed, too.'

'What a terrible story. Well, at least you have an answer now.'

'Yes.' The happy jump of the music jarred with the quiet of the room. 'I'm sorry it's ended this way, Hayden.'

'Me too.' Pushing aside socks and underwear on the bed, Hayden took her hand, and they sat together. He locked his fingers through hers.

'I was wrong to be angry. Earlier on the bridge,' he said.

'That doesn't matter.'

'No, I'm sorry. Jess, I told Mum.'

'What?' Jess sat back, shocked. She untangled her fingers. 'You told Marie about us?'

'She called this afternoon. You were gone, I was alone. I'd walked through town, just for something to do. I kept thinking what a mess it was between us, when it could be so simple. We like being together, what else matters? At least, that's what I was thinking when I was walking. Then Mum phoned and put me right.'

Jess's heart was fluttering in her chest like a trapped bird. Wet panic filled her mouth. If Marie knows, she might tell Alec, she thought.

'Jess, it's all right.' Hayden took her hand again, and she felt the smoothness of his palms. 'She couldn't believe it at first and kept asking if I was joking. But I don't think she was angry. We talked for a long time. Probably longer than we've ever done before.'

'She wasn't angry?' Jess said faintly. 'That's not the Marie I know.'

'No, she wasn't. I told her I was here, with you, but that it was probably over. And that you couldn't choose me over your children.' Hayden gave a soft laugh. 'She told me she could understand that, and I should never have asked you to choose. My mother!'

There were two conversations going on, Jess realised now. In saying he had told his mother Jess couldn't put him before her children, Hayden was releasing her and letting her know he understood. But talking about Jess with Marie was also Hayden's way of talking to his mother about his own childhood. Jess studied the man before him, still young but many years past first adulthood; his hair was thick and unashamed, his body had nicks and scars of a life lived hard and fast. But he was young enough to find his mother bewildering. To find her lacking.

'Will Marie ... will she say anything to Alec?' Jess looked down at their hands, entwined.

'I don't think so.' Hayden gave a rueful grin. 'For everything she is, Mum can keep a secret when she has to. Did you know she slept with your professor once? Walker?'

'Waller!' Jess gasped. 'When?'

'A long time ago, apparently. She told me today. After an evening event at the library where you work. In his office.'

Jess closed her eyes, picturing Waller's fusty, ancient frame bent over the desk, Marie's large thighs shuddering beneath him. And then Jess laughed, incredulous that her friend could still shock her after all this time. 'I'm surprised Waller didn't have a heart attack.'

Hayden smiled too, though his mouth was lopsided. He touched Jess's cheek. 'I'm sorry.'

'Don't be.' Jess caught his fingers. 'I've loved what we've had. Honestly. I'm a different person when I'm with you, and after all these years on the domestic treadmill, that isn't something I take for granted. But ...'

'But your life is more complicated than mine, I know.' Hayden's eyes were shining and Jess felt tears prick at the corner of her own. She blinked them back impatiently.

'It was never just about—you know. But it's gone as far as it can go, hasn't it?' Jess smiled sadly.

'Yes. God, I hate it, but yes.' And then Hayden offered his arms, and they held each other, squeezing tightly as the church chimed behind them.

~ 54 ~

September 1917

Four days after the events in the garden, a small group gathered just after midnight and made its way to the churchyard at Villers. There were five of them: two doctors, strong and silent; Matron, who had a fixed, furious expression on her face; Cecilia; and Hendry's father. Walking behind the cart carrying the body of her friend, Cecilia glared at Hendry's father, hating the cut of the man's coat, the arrogance of his step, and the way he waxed the ends of his moustache. He had arrived in Villers the morning after his son had stabbed two people and had yet to ask the victims' names. Instead he had insisted upon being taken to the side room where his son lay, vacant and sedated, lying on his back with half-open, milky eyes. Hendry's father had cast a long look at his son's form, with the empty space under the sheet where his foot should be, and had turned on his heel. Cecilia had heard him barking instructions at Matron and the sharp intake of breath as he stared at the men lying around him. He was not above being shocked at the numbers of wounded, and their injuries, but that did not improve his standing in Cecilia's eyes.

She had hung back as Violet was loaded onto the cart. The bishop had been buried earlier that day, with a small amount of pomp and ceremony. Men able to walk had made their way down to the church, along with a few nurses and curious villagers. Bishop Shacklock was too important a man to be buried in secret, or in the hospital cemetery, which might—Matron had said grimly—be disturbed by bombardments. A priest had been found to offer up a prayer at his graveside. Cecilia had attended, too. She had wondered if the bishop heard the priest's prayers, and if they were alien to him.

Violet was not to be buried with the same attention. Instead, she lay on the back of the cart, wrapped in a canvas sack. She was to be buried with the bishop; Hendry's father had said no one would notice disturbance to a freshly dug grave. He did not want her buried with the other men in the hospital cemetery. With conflict still ongoing and lines between armies unsteady and changing, cemeteries could be disturbed. He did not want the body of a woman being found.

The canvas sacking was at least clean, Cecilia thought as they turned down the lane and made their way down the hill towards the church. After Violet and Shacklock had been discovered in the garden and it was clear they were gone, one of the doctors had run back into the hospital for bed sheets. Cecilia had fallen to her knees and was crawling towards Violet when the doctor sped back; she was pushed aside as the man rolled the bodies in the cloth and then instructed the others to help him carry them to an outhouse. The doctor was not with them as they took Violet to the cemetery to be buried; he was not there to see the blood-soaked sheets and was not there to hear Matron's insistence that Violet be swathed in something clean and new, something more fitting for her long rest. Cecilia wondered if the doctor would say her friend should be left as she was, so keen was he to hide what had happened. He had been stuck to Hendry's father's side since his arrival, apart from when he ran errands at the other man's bidding.

To those who asked, Cecilia said Violet had gone home to England. She said the words quickly and barely above a mutter, hoping that someone would see she was lying and press her for the truth. But only a couple of women asked. A few more men, but that was all. There had been another push at the front, another wave of attack, and the hospital was flooded with more men than they could handle. VADs worked until they could barely stand, resting for only a few hours before heading back out, to wash, stitch, mop. Cecilia was the busiest among them, plunging herself into the work so that she might not see her friend's image every time she paused, Violet's throat split by a red line. She had not slept at all the last four days and, as they followed the clip of the dray down the hill at midnight, her body felt shaky and weary to the core.

Matron, a sturdy woman with a Scottish accent, had given her assurance that she would reveal nothing of the incident in the garden. It was known that her career was threatened and her silence was bought. No one else at the hospital knew what had happened and no one close to the scene knew what had driven Hendry to do it. Cecilia, cut in half by pain, had not divulged the link between her friend and the bishop. There seemed to be a muttered agreement that Violet had rejected Hendry in favour of Shacklock—a story that garnered validity when Hendry's father made an overheard comment to the doctor, that Hendry had always been one for strong attachments. There had been an incident with a girl before the war, and Hendry had been found with cuts to his arms.

About a mile from the churchyard, the cart was unhooked from the horse and Matron was tasked with waiting at the top of the hill with the beast. Hendry's father did not want to risk the sound of hooves waking anyone in the village. For the rest of the road the group walked two abreast, wheeling the cart along. It was unbearably light and easy to manoeuvre. Cecilia wept silently as they marched.

A shovel was carried and, as the church tower chimed one o'clock, the bishop's grave was opened. The doctors and Hendry's father then placed the canvas bag containing Violet Underwood Shacklock in the ground. Cecilia hung back, her face wet and stinging, her throat raw. The idea that Violet would be lost and hidden away was almost as difficult as her death. Sometimes men came through the hospital with nothing to identify them; in a couple of cases, shell blasts had torn their clothes from them. They had somehow survived long enough to reach Villers and Cecilia had tended to a couple of young boys too wounded to say their names. They died soon after; Shacklock had stood beside their grave in the Villers field, saying a prayer. The wooden cross placed above them simply recorded that an unknown man lay silently in the earth. Cecilia wished she had sneaked a cross with her, to place above Violet.

The earth was put back, and the doctors sweated in the cloying heat. Hendry's father helped and, when the last clod was thrown down, he patted the surface with the shovel. Cecilia imagined she saw the relief flood from him, his shoulders bowed with the effort.

Then they were ready to go. Words were muttered—not prayers, Cecilia was sure of that. Instead they were agreements, warnings and, she was sure, promises of money and positions once the infernal conflict was over. She saw the doctors shake Hendry's father's hand and turned away; he had not bribed her. Instead there had been threats and the fear that a woman's life would be ruined and put on public display. Someone had talked and Hendry's father knew her secret.

He did not look at her as he walked past. Cecilia looked at him though, aware that this might be the only time when she could stare so openly at the powerful man. And then she looked back at the grave, where her friend lay. She stepped towards it, hand in her pocket, feeling the pieces of cardboard she had been told to remove from the records earlier that day.

~ 55 ~

Present Day

The church bells woke Jess first; she opened her eyes, stiff-necked, to find herself lying fully clothed on top of the bed. Her nose was like ice and she could see her breath. At some point through the night, the heating had switched off. She got up and slipped under the duvet.

Beside her, Hayden muttered in his sleep and turned over. He was also fully clothed and Jess remembered how they had talked some more after she had returned from meeting Felicity Deniel, before they both lay down on the bed. There had been no thought of undressing and holding each other again. Instead, the closeness that had been absent for the past week crept in unbidden and they talked easily. About Violet, about her work, about Hayden's job, and, as they did, Jess thought that a thorn had been pulled from him, that he seemed to have found peace. He stroked her cheek, once, as they lay together, but that was all.

At ten o'clock, Hayden left. He had phoned a taxi, which arrived promptly. Jess went with him to the door. They had eaten together and drank coffee, but said little. When the taxi driver beeped its horn, they got up from the table but nothing further was said. As Hayden opened the door, Jess wondered if he would go without a word. But Hayden waved to the taxi driver and turned back in the doorway.

'Make it all worthwhile,' he said. He leant forward and kissed her cheek, a chaste embrace that made Jess smile.

And then he got into the back seat of the taxi and tapped the driver on the shoulder. The car zoomed erratically down the cobbled street towards the town and was gone.

✑

About an hour before Billy was due to walk down to her cottage, Jess pulled on her coat and walked up towards the church. Winter's fingers had tightened around Villers and the air bit down, making Jess's scalp tingle as she locked the front door. She pulled her scarf, which was actually Alec's scarf, around her and dipped her chin into it, breathing in the residue of his aftershave.

The rapidity of the past few days had left a physical mark on Jess and she felt winded. Although she'd woken early that morning, her sleep had been hard and breathless, as though she was racing to drag rest into her body. Her shoulders ached as she climbed the cobbles and then the steps leading up to the church. She leant back to look at the spire, feeling it topple towards her, feeling herself ready to slip beneath it. A flurry of pigeons took off from the spire's sharp corner and Jess forced her body to move again, into the churchyard.

There it was, near the church wall. A little round nub of stone. Overshadowed by other graves, other lives recorded and memorialised in rubbed granite. But the stone was clean and Jess touched it, pulling off her glove to trace her palm along the top, the rough surface scratching and announcing its presence on her skin.

Then she ran her fingers over the fleur de lis, letting them dip into the shaped lines. 'Violet,' she said.

There was no one else around so Jess ducked down, knees popping, until her face was level with the carved words. 'Resting place of an unknown soul. At peace,' she said. She was taken by an overwhelming urge to reach out and hold the stone, to embrace it. So that is what she did, shuffling forward so her hands could lock behind it. She held on for a long, long time.

'I will give you back your name,' Jess said when she let go. 'Violet Underwood Shacklock. I promise. That is the first thing I will do: buy you a headstone with your name carved upon it, bold as brass. And I will tell your story.'

There were feet behind and a murmur in French; others were walking in the churchyard. So Jess stood up and touched the stone for one last time. She patted it goodbye, walking away, blinking the tears away.

Then, as she rounded the steps to walk back towards the cottage and meet Billy, she pulled out her phone. Dialled a number. 'Alec?'

Epilogue

Somehow she managed to scrape the money together and book herself on to a battlefield trip organised by a travel agent. The actors helped, pressing money into Allegra's hand on that grey, rainy day when the theatre closed its doors for the last time. Some were in tears; they wouldn't hear of Allegra's protest that the notes in the envelopes were theirs, was all she could give them after selling up. Mothers of dead sons were the loudest of them all, insisting Allegra should go as soon as it was safe, and go with their blessing.

So, one day in the spring of 1919, Allegra crossed the Channel and sat in the back of a truck rattling its way through Calais. She passed by the town hall now slowly being reclaimed by the townsfolk, and remembered speaking to a nurse, thin and pale and prematurely old, who told her a girl called Violet Shacklock had travelled to the hospital at Villers des Champs. It had hurt Allegra to say her daughter's name, more so to ask if she'd travelled under the name of Shacklock. But she knew she would.

Some of those on the battlefield tour were seeking loved ones of their own; sons, who had last been heard of in the area around the town. A few had received confirmation that their soldier boys had died at the hospital and were buried in the cemetery there. Women clad in black sat bolt-upright in the rickety, rattling truck, faces fixed, grief turning them into statues. Allegra, looking out over the wasted fields and pulverised farmland, prayed she would not find her child's name on a white stone and, as they approached Villers, allowed herself to feel a flutter of hope that she might find Violet alive.

The hospital had disbanded, however, and there were few people in the town who could tell her what had happened to the British nurses who worked there. A barber whom Allegra spoke to mentioned that his daughter had worked there, but she had moved away and did not keep in touch. He looked away as he spoke and the young girl standing beside him, sweeping brush in hand, glanced up, curiously.

The pain in her heart, it was so great. As Allegra wound her way up the hill towards the church, it settled into her body like a wound. It was ever present, had been since that day Violet left their flat, when she, her mother, somehow knew she would not see her again. Every day, Allegra's mouth felt full of water, brimming with unshed tears that could not find their way to her eyes. Her grief was like a sickness, poisoning her from the inside. And now her heart felt tired and weak in her chest, and she wondered if it would hold out until she found her girl.

The thought, though, that Bishop Shacklock might have died, had not occurred to her. The barber, eager to have her leave the premises, threw out the news that the bishop who tended the soldier patients was buried in the churchyard and, as Allegra gasped and brought her hand to her mouth, the barber opened the door to his shop and ushered her back out onto the street. She found herself looking in through the window, seeing but not seeing the young girl sweep up hair cuttings. Shacklock, dead! She could not fathom it. She remembered that time, on the hillside in Greece, how he had touched her. Their shared, furtive moments in his room and on the rooftops. And that last moment, in the drawing room of Josiah's house, when Edward told them he knew and Anthony Shacklock left her.

She found Shacklock's grave, with the white, uneven stone, and saw it had been erected in haste. A thin sprinkling of grass lay over the plot and she was careful not to stand on it, respectful and somehow scared of the resting dead. She saw Shacklock's name, etched clumsily. A simple epitaph, just a name and dates. It said nothing about the man, or of his family. Or his children.

She did not know how long she stood there but, when the time came to leave, Allegra felt cold, despite the summer sun, and the breath wheezed in her throat. Her chest hurt more than it should and she wondered if her lips were blue.

'I'm going to leave you now,' she told the grave, the need to say something overwhelming. 'I'm looking for our daughter. She came to find you—maybe she did. You can't tell me now. I need to find her, Anthony. I cannot leave her the way you left me.'

With that, Allegra turned and wound her way slowly out of the churchyard. The bells in the tower above struck the hour and a scattering of crows flapped on the breeze. Their call, long and keening, followed the woman as she made her fumbling way down the hill.

Acknowledgements

This book is a work of fiction. While some places mentioned are real, others are not. The characters are all made-up, too.

However, I have taken ideas from real-life events and stories. For example, the work undertaken by VAD nurses during the First World War was inspiring and the novel imagines what a young nurse would have seen in a hospital, tending to injured soldiers. Wounds were treated with salt, which must have been excruciating. The VAD nurses were caring and determined, personifying the words of Katharine Furse, their Commandant-in-Chief, that they be 'courteous, unselfish and kind'. Furse's letter of encouragement to VAD nurses in 1914 was the inspiration behind the speech made by the registering officer that Violet met at Calais and can be read at http://spartacus-educational. com/FWWnurses.htm There are lots of other online resources about the work of nurses during the conflict which interested readers can turn to.

I have never been to Pireaus and I hope the reader will forgive my imagining what life was like at the end of the nineteenth century. Jedthorpe is an imagined place, as is the Shacklock Library. If it were real, I think I would enjoy spending time there, surrounded by dusty manuscripts.

About the Author

Rebecca Burns is an award-winning writer of short stories and you can read more of her work at www.rebecca-burns.co.uk. *The Bishop's Girl* is her first novel. She lives with her husband and young family in Leicestershire, UK.

Books by Rebecca Burns

Catching the Barramundi

The Settling Earth